"**M**ind-boggling 'What Ifs' abound in
the thrilling novels by James Rollins."
Sacramento Bee

"**O**ne of the most inventive
storytellers writing today."
Lincoln Child

"**T**his guy doesn't write novels—he builds roller
coasters. . . . A must for pure action fans."
Booklist

"**J**ames Rollins knows adventure."
Chicago Sun-Times

"**H**e just keeps getting better and better."
Barnstable Patriot (MA)

"**I**t's something of an insult to characterize
novelist James Rollins as a cross between
Clive Cussler and Dan Brown as some
have done, since his work has considerably
more depth and range than either of his fellow
thriller writers. . . . Rollins delivers."
Charleston Post and Courier

"**T**he modern master of the action thriller . . .
Nobody does it better."
Providence Journal-Bulletin

By James Rollins

Coming Soon in Hardcover

THE DEVIL COLONY

JAMES ROLLINS

AMAZONIA

HARPER

An Imprint of HarperCollins*Publishers*

This book was originally published in hardcover March 2002 by William Morrow and in mass market July 2003 and March 2007 by Avon Books and Harper, respectively, all Imprints of HarperCollins Publishers.

Plant drawings provided and copyright by Raintree Nutrition, Inc. All rights reserved. http://www.raintree.com used by permission of Leslie Taylor; maps by Jeffrey L. Ward.

HARPER

An Imprint of HarperCollins*Publishers*
195 Broadway,
New York, NY 10007.

33614080499410

Copyright © 2002 by Jim Czajkowski
Excerpt from *Altar of Eden* copyright © 2010 by Jim Czajkowski
ISBN 978-0-06-196583-8

First Harper Premium printing: May 2010
First Harper paperback printing: March 2007
First Avon Books paperback printing: July 2003
First William Morrow hardcover printing: March 2002

Printed in the United States of America

Visit Harper paperbacks on the World Wide Web at www.harpercollins.com

10 9 8

*To John Petty and Rick Hourigan
friends and co-conspirators*

ACKNOWLEDGMENTS

Special thanks to all those who helped in the research of this novel, especially Leslie Taylor of Raintree Nutrition, Inc., for the use of her wonderful plant diagrams in this book and for her valuable knowledge of the medicinal applications of rainforest botanicals. I would also be remiss not to acknowledge two resources of utmost value: Redmond O'Hanlon's *In Trouble Again: A Journey Between the Orinoco and the Amazon* and the book that inspired my own, Dr. Mark Plotkin's *Tales of a Shaman's Apprentice*. For more specific help, I most heartily thank my friends and family who helped shape the manuscript into its present form: Chris Crowe, Michael Gallowglas, Lee Garrett, Dennis Grayson, Susan Tunis, Penny Hill, Debbie Nelson, Dave Meek, Jane O'Riva, Chris "The Little" Smith, Judy and Steve Prey, and Caroline Williams. For help with the French language, my Canadian friend Dianne Daigle; for assistance on the Internet, Steve Winter; and for her arduous moral support, Carolyn McCray. For the maps used here, I must acknowledge their source: *The CIA World Factbook 2000*. Finally, the three folks who remain my best critics and most loyal supporters: my editor, Lyssa Keusch; my agent, Russ Galen; and my publicist, Jim Davis. Last and most important, I must stress that any and all errors of fact or detail fall squarely on my own shoulders.

Prologue

JULY 25, 6:24 P.M.
AN AMERINDIAN MISSIONARY VILLAGE
AMAZONAS, BRAZIL

Padre Garcia Luiz Batista was struggling with his hoe, tilling weeds from the mission's garden, when the stranger stumbled from the jungle. The figure wore a tattered pair of black denim pants and nothing else. Bare-chested and shoeless, the man fell to his knees among rows of sprouting cassava plants. His skin, burnt a deep mocha, was tattooed with blue and crimson dyes.

Mistaking the fellow for one of the local Yanomamo Indians, Padre Batista pushed back his wide-brimmed straw hat and greeted the fellow in the Indians' native tongue. *"Eou, shori,"* he said. "Welcome, friend, to the mission of Wauwai."

The stranger lifted his face, and Garcia instantly knew his mistake. The fellow's eyes were the deepest blue, a color unnatural among the Amazonian tribes. He also bore a scraggled growth of dark beard.

Clearly not an Indian, but a white man.

"*Bemvindo,*" he offered in Portuguese, believing now that the fellow must be one of the ubiquitous peasants from the coastal cities who ventured into the Amazon rain forest to stake a claim and build a better life for themselves. "Be welcome here, my friend."

The poor soul had clearly been in the jungle a long time. His skin was stretched over bone, each rib visible. His black hair was tangled, and his body bore cuts and oozing sores. Flies flocked about him, buzzing and feeding on his wounds.

When the stranger tried to speak, his parched lips cracked and fresh blood dribbled down his chin. He half crawled toward Garcia, an arm raised in supplication. His words, though, were garbled, unintelligible, a beastly sound.

Garcia's first impulse was to retreat from the man, but his calling to God would not let him. The Good Samaritan did not refuse the wayward traveler. He bent and helped the man to his feet. The fellow was so wasted he weighed no more than a child in his arms. Even through his own shirt, the padre could feel the heat of the man's skin as he burned with fever.

"Come, let us get you inside out of the sun." Garcia guided the man toward the mission's church, its whitewashed steeple poking toward the blue sky. Beyond the building, a ragtag mix of palm-thatched huts and wooden homes spread across the cleared jungle floor.

The mission of Wauwai had been established only five years earlier, but already the village had swelled to nearly eighty inhabitants, a mix of various indigenous tribes. Some of the homes were on stilts, as was typical of the Apalai Indians, while others built solely of palm thatch were home to the Waiwai and Tiriós tribes. But the greatest number of the mission's dwellers were Yanomamo, marked by their large communal roundhouse.

Garcia waved his free arm to one of the Yanomamo tribesmen at the garden's edge, a fellow named Henaowe. The short Indian, the padre's assistant, was dressed in pants and a buttoned, long-sleeved shirt. He hurried forward.

"Help me get this man into my house."

Henaowe nodded vigorously and crossed to the man's other side. With the feverish man slung between them, they passed through the garden gate and around the church to the clapboard building jutting from its south face. The missionaries' residence was the only home with a gas generator. It powered the church's lights, a refrigerator, and the village's only air conditioner. Sometimes Garcia wondered if the success of his mission was not based solely on the wonders of the church's cool interior, rather than any heartfelt belief in salvation through Christ.

Once they reached the residence, Henaowe ducked forward and yanked the rear door open. They manhandled the stranger through the dining room to a back room. It was one of the domiciles of the mission's acolytes, but it was now unoccupied. Two days ago, the younger missionaries had all left on an evangelical journey to a neighboring village. The small room was little more than a dark cell, but it was at least cool and sheltered from the sun.

Garcia nodded for Henaowe to light the room's lantern. They had not bothered to run the electricity to the smaller rooms. Cockroaches and spiders skittered from the flame's glow.

Together they hauled the man to the single bed. "Help me get him out of his clothes. I must clean and treat his wounds."

Henaowe nodded and reached for the buttons to the man's pants, then froze. A gasp escaped the Indian. He jumped back as if from a scorpion.

"*Weti kete?*" Garcia asked. "What is it?"

Henaowe's eyes had grown huge with horror. He pointed to the man's bare chest and spoke rapidly in his native tongue.

Garcia's brow wrinkled. "What about the tattoo?" The blue and red dyes were mostly geometric shapes: crimson circles, vibrant squiggles, and jagged triangles. But in the center and radiating out was a serpentine spiral of red, like blood swirling down a drain. A single blue handprint lay at its center, just above the man's navel.

"*Shawara!*" Henaowe exclaimed, backing toward the door.

Evil spirits.

Garcia glanced back to his assistant. He had thought the tribesman had grown past these superstitious beliefs. "Enough," he said harshly. "It's only paint. It's not the devil's work. Now come help me."

Henaowe merely shook in terror and would approach no closer.

Frowning, Garcia returned his attention to his patient as the man groaned. His eyes were glassy with fever and delirium. He thrashed weakly on the sheets. Garcia checked the man's forehead. It burned. He swung back to Henaowe. "At least fetch the first-aid kit for me and the penicillin in the fridge."

With clear relief, the Indian dashed away.

Garcia sighed. Having lived in the Amazonian rain forest for a decade, he had out of necessity learned basic medical skills: setting splints, cleaning and applying salves to wounds, treating fevers. He could even perform simple operations, like suturing wounds and helping with difficult births. As the padre of the mission, he was not only the primary guardian of their souls, but also counselor, chief, and doctor.

Garcia removed the man's soiled clothes and set them aside. As his eyes roved over the man's exposed skin, he could clearly see how sorely the unforgiving jungle had ravaged his body. Maggots crawled in his deep wounds. Scaly fungal infections had eaten away the man's toenails, and a scar on his heel marked an old snakebite.

As he worked, the padre wondered who this man was. What was his story? Did he have family out there somewhere? But all attempts to speak to the man were met only with a garbled, delirious response.

Many of the peasants who tried to eke out a living met hard ends at the hands of hostile Indians, thieves, drug traffickers, or even jungle predators. But the most common demise of these settlers was disease.

In the remote wilds of the rain forest, medical attention could be weeks away. A simple flu could bring death.

The scuff of feet on wood drew Garcia's attention back to the door. Henaowe had returned, burdened with the medical kit and a pail of clean water. But he was not alone. At Henaowe's side stood Kamala, a short, white-haired *shapori*, the tribal shaman. Henaowe must have run off to fetch the ancient medicine man.

"*Haya*," Garcia greeted the fellow. "Grandfather." It was the typical way to acknowledge a Yanomamo elder.

Kamala did not say a word. He simply strode into the room and crossed to the bed. As he stared down at the man, his eyes narrowed. He turned to Henaowe and waved for the Indian to place the bucket and medical kit down. The shaman then lifted his arms over the bedridden stranger and began to chant. Garcia was fluent in many indigenous dialects, but he could not make out a single word.

Once done, Kamala turned to the padre and spoke in fluent Portuguese. "This *nabe* has been touched by the *shawara*, dangerous spirits of the deep forest. He will die this night. His body must be burned before sunrise." With these words, Kamala turned to leave.

"Wait! Tell me what this symbol means."

Turning back with a scowl, Kamala said, "It is the mark of the Ban-ali tribe. Blood Jaguars. He belongs to them. None must give help to a *ban-yi*, the slave of the jaguar. It is death." The shaman made a gesture to ward against evil spirits, blowing across his fingertips, then left with Henaowe in tow.

Alone in the dim room, Garcia felt a chill in the air that didn't come from the air-conditioning. He had heard whispers of the Ban-ali, one of the mythic ghost tribes of the deep forest. A frightening people who mated with jaguars and possessed unspeakable powers.

Garcia kissed his crucifix and cast aside these fanciful superstitions. Turning to the bucket and medicines, he soaked a sponge in the tepid water and brought it to the wasted man's lips.

"Drink," he whispered. In the jungle, dehydration, more than anything, was often the factor between life and death. He squeezed the sponge and dribbled water across the man's cracked lips.

Like a babe suckling at his mother's teat, the stranger responded to the water. He slurped the trickle, gasping and half choking. Garcia helped raise the man's head so he could drink more easily. After a few minutes, the delirium faded somewhat from the man's eyes. He scrabbled for the sponge, responding to the life-giving water, but Garcia pulled it away. It was unhealthy to drink too quickly after such severe dehydration.

"Rest, senhor," he urged the stranger. "Let me clean your wounds and get some antibiotics into you."

The man did not seem to understand. He struggled to sit up, reaching for the sponge, crying out eerily. As Garcia pushed him by the shoulders to the pillow, the man gasped out, and the padre finally understood why the man could not speak.

He had no tongue. It had been cut away.

Grimacing, Garcia prepared a syringe of ampicillin and prayed to God for the souls of the monsters that could do this to another man. The medicine was past its expiration date, but it was the best he could get out here. He injected the antibiotic into the man's left buttock, then began to work on his wounds with sponge and salve.

The stranger lapsed between lucidity and delirium. Whenever he was conscious, the man struggled mindlessly for his piled clothes, as if he intended to dress and continue his jungle trek. But Garcia would always push his arms back down and cover him again with blankets.

As the sun set and night swept over the forests, Garcia sat with the Bible in hand and prayed for the man. But in his heart, the padre knew his prayers would not be answered. Kamala, the shaman, was correct in his assessment. The man would not last the night.

As a precaution, in case the man was a child of Christ, he had performed the sacrament of Last Rites an hour earlier. The fellow had stirred as he marked his forehead with oil, but he did not wake. His brow burned feverishly. The antibiotics had failed to break through the blood infections.

Resolved that the man would die, Garcia maintained his vigil. It was the least he could do for the poor soul. But as midnight neared and the jungle awoke with the whining sounds of locusts and the *cronk*ing of myriad frogs, Garcia slipped to sleep in his chair, the Bible in his lap.

He woke hours later at a strangled cry from the man. Believing his patient was gasping his last breath, Garcia struggled up, knocking his Bible to the floor. As he bent to pick it up, he found the man staring back at him. His eyes were glassy, but the delirium had faded. The stranger lifted a trembling hand. He pointed again to his discarded clothes.

"You can't leave," Garcia said.

The man closed his eyes a moment, shook his head, then with a pleading look, he again pointed to his pants.

Garcia finally relented. How could he refuse this last feverish request? Standing, he crossed to the foot of the bed and retrieved the rumpled pair of pants. He handed them to the dying man.

The stranger grabbed them up and immediately began pawing along the length of one leg of his garment, following the inner seam. Finally, he stopped and fingered a section of the cotton denim.

With shaking arms, he held the pants out to Garcia.

The padre thought the stranger was slipping back into delirium. In fact, the poor man's breathing had become more ragged and coarse. But Garcia humored his nonsensical actions. He took the pants and felt where the man indicated.

To his surprise, he found something stiffer than denim under his fingers, something hidden under the seam. A secret pocket.

Curious, the padre fished out a pair of scissors from the first-aid kit. Off to the side, the man sank down to his pillow with a sigh, clearly content that his message had finally been understood.

Using the scissors, Garcia trimmed through the seam's threads and opened the secret pocket. Reaching inside, he tugged out a small bronze coin and held it up to the lamp. A name was engraved on the coin.

"Gerald Wallace Clark," he read aloud. Was this the stranger? "Is this you, senhor?"

He glanced back to the bed.

"Sweet Jesus in heaven," the padre mumbled.

Atop the cot, the man stared blindly toward the ceiling, mouth lolled open, chest unmoving. He had let go the ghost, a stranger no longer.

"Rest in peace, Senhor Clark."

Padre Batista again raised the bronze coin to the lantern and flipped it over. As he saw the words inscribed on the opposite side, his mouth grew dry with dread.

United States Army Special Forces.

AUGUST 1, 10:45 A.M.
CIA HEADQUARTERS
LANGLEY, VIRGINIA

George Fielding had been surprised by the call. As deputy director of Central Intelligence, he had often been summoned to urgent meetings by various division heads, but to get a priority one call from Marshall O'Brien, the head of the Directorate Environmental Center, was unusual. The DEC had been established back in 1997, a division of the intelligence community dedicated to environmental issues. So far in his tenure, the DEC had never raised a priority call. Such a response was reserved for matters of immediate national security. What could have rattled the Old Bird—as Marshall O'Brien had been nicknamed—to place such an alert?

Fielding strode rapidly down the hall that connected the original headquarters building to the new headquarters. The newer facility had been built in the late eighties. It housed many of the burgeoning divisions of the service, including the DEC.

As he walked, he glanced at the framed paintings lining the long passageway, a gallery of the former directors of the CIA, going back all the way to Major General Donovan, who served as director of the Office of Strategic Services, the World War II–era counterpart of the CIA. Fielding's own boss would be added to this wall one day, and if George played his cards smartly, he himself might assume the directorship.

With this thought in mind, he entered the New Headquarters Building and followed the halls to the DEC's suite of offices. Once through the main door, he was instantly greeted by a secretary.

She stood as he entered. "Deputy Director, Mr. O'Brien is waiting for you in his office." The secretary crossed to a set of mahogany doors, knocked perfunctorily, then pushed open the door, holding it wide for him.

"Thank you."

Inside, a deep, rumbling voice greeted him. "Deputy Director Fielding, I appreciate you coming in person." Marshall O'Brien stood up from his chair. He was a towering man with silver-gray hair. He dwarfed the large executive desk. He waved to a chair. "Please take a seat. I know your time is valuable, and I won't waste it."

Always to the point, Fielding thought. Four years

ago, there had been talk that Marshall O'Brien might assume the directorship of the CIA. In fact, the man had been deputy director before Fielding, but he had bristled too many senators with his no-nonsense attitude and burned even more bridges with his rigid sense of right and wrong. That wasn't how politics were played in Washington. So instead, O'Brien had been demoted to a token figurehead here at the Environmental Center. The old man's urgent call was probably his way of scraping some bit of importance from his position, trying to stay in the game.

"What's this all about?" Fielding asked as he sat down.

O'Brien settled to his own seat and opened a gray folder atop his desk.

Someone's dossier, Fielding noted.

The old man cleared his throat. "Two days ago, an American's body was reported to the Consular Agency in Manaus, Brazil. The deceased was identified by his Special Forces challenge coin from his old unit."

Fielding frowned. Challenge coins were carried by many divisions of the military. They were more a tradition than a true means of identification. A unit member, active or not, caught without his coin was duty-bound to buy a round of drinks for his mates. "What does this have to do with us?"

"The man was not only ex–Special Forces. He was one of my operatives. Agent Gerald Clark."

Fielding blinked in surprise.

O'Brien continued, "Agent Clark had been sent undercover with a research team to investigate complaints of environmental damage from gold-mining operations and to gather data on the transshipment of Bolivian and Colombian cocaine through the Amazon basin."

Fielding straightened in his seat. "And was he murdered? Is that what this is all about?"

"No. Six days ago, Agent Clark appeared at a missionary village deep in the remote jungle, half dead from fever and exposure. The head of the mission attempted to care for him, but he died within a few hours."

"A tragedy indeed, but how is this a matter of national security?"

"Because Agent Clark has been missing for four years." O'Brien passed him a faxed newspaper article.

Confused, Fielding accepted the article. "Four years?"

EXPEDITION VANISHES IN
AMAZONIAN JUNGLE

Associated Press

MANAUS, BRAZIL, MARCH 20—The continuing search for millionaire industrialist Dr. Carl Rand and his international team of 30 researchers and guides has been called off after three months of intense searching. The team, a joint venture between the U.S. National Cancer Institute and the Brazilian Indian Foundation, vanished into the rain forests without leaving a single clue as to their fate.

The expedition's yearlong goal had been to conduct a census on the true number of Indians and tribes living in the Amazon forests. However, three months after leaving the jungle city of Manaus, their daily progress reports, radioed in from the field, ended abruptly. All attempts to contact the team have failed. Rescue helicopters and ground search teams were sent to their last known location, but no one was found. Two weeks later, one last, frantic message was received: "Send help . . . can't last much longer. Oh, God, they're all around us." Then the team was swallowed into the vast jungle.

Now, after a three-month search involving an international team and much publicity, Commander Ferdinand Gonzales, the rescue team's leader, has declared the expedition and its members "lost and likely dead." All searches have been called off.

The current consensus of the investigators is that the team either was overwhelmed by a hostile tribe or had stumbled upon a hidden base of drug traffickers. Either way, any hope for rescue dies today as the search teams are called home. It should be noted that each year scores of researchers, explorers, and missionaries disappear into the Amazon forest, never to be seen again.

"My God."

O'Brien retrieved the article from the stunned man's fingers and continued, "After disappearing, no further contact was ever made by the research team or our operative. Agent Clark was classified as deceased."

"But are we sure this is the same man?"

O'Brien nodded. "Dental records and fingerprints match those on file."

Fielding shook his head, the initial shock ebbing. "As tragic as all this is and as messy as the paperwork will be, I still don't see why it's a matter of national security."

"I would normally agree, except for one additional oddity." O'Brien shuffled through the dossier's ream of papers and pulled out two photographs. He handed over the first one. "This was taken just a few days before he departed on his mission."

Fielding glanced at the grainy photo of a man dressed in Levi's, a Hawaiian shirt, and a safari hat. The man wore a large grin and was hoisting a tropical drink in hand. "Agent Clark?"

"Yes, the photo was taken by one of the researchers during a going-away party." O'Brien passed him the second photograph. "And this was taken at the morgue in Manaus, where the body now resides."

Fielding took the glossy with a twinge of queasiness. He had no desire to look at photographs of dead people, but he had no choice. The corpse in this photograph was naked, laid out on a stainless steel table, an emaciated skeleton wrapped in skin. Strange tattoos marked his flesh. Still, Fielding recognized the man's facial features. It *was* Agent Clark—but with one notable difference. He retrieved the first photograph and compared the two.

O'Brien must have noted the blood draining from his face and spoke up. "Two years prior to his disappearance, Agent Clark took a sniper's bullet to his left arm during a forced recon mission in Iraq. Gangrene set in before he could reach a U.S. camp. The limb had to be amputated at the shoulder, ending his career with the army's Special Forces."

"But the body in the morgue has both arms."

"Exactly. The fingerprints from the corpse's arm

match those on file prior to the shooting. It would seem Agent Clark went into the Amazon with one arm and came back with two."

"But that's impossible. What the hell happened out there?"

Marshall O'Brien studied Fielding with his hawkish eyes, demonstrating why he had earned his nickname, the Old Bird. Fielding felt like a mouse before an eagle. The old man's voice deepened. "That's what I intend to find out."

ACT ONE

The Mission

CURARE
family: *Menispermaceae*
genus: *Chondrodendron*
species: *Tomentosum*
common name: *Curare*
parts used: *Leaf, Root*
properties/actions: *Diuretic, Febrifuge,*
Muscle Relaxant, Tonic, Poison

ONE

Snake Oil

AUGUST 6, 10:11 A.M.
AMAZON JUNGLE, BRAZIL

The anaconda held the small Indian girl wrapped in its heavy coils, dragging her toward the river.

Nathan Rand was on his way back to the Yano-mamo village after an early morning of gathering medicinal plants when he heard her screams. He dropped his specimen bag and ran to her aid. As he sprinted, he shrugged his short-barreled shotgun from his shoulder. When alone in the jungle, one always carried a weapon.

He pushed through a fringe of dense foliage and spotted the snake and girl. The anaconda, one of the largest he had ever seen, at least forty feet in length, lay half in the water and half stretched out on the muddy beach. Its black scales shone wetly. It must have been lurking under the surface when the girl had come to collect water from the river. It was not unusual for the giant snakes to prey upon animals who came to the river to drink: wild peccary, capybara rodents, forest deer. But the great snakes seldom attacked humans.

Still, during the past decade of working as an ethnobotanist in the jungles of the Amazon basin, Nathan had learned one important rule: if a beast were hungry enough, all rules were broken. It was an eat-or-be-eaten world under the endless green bower.

Nathan squinted through his gun's sight. He recognized the girl. "Oh, God, Tama!" She was the chieftain's nine-year-old niece, a smiling, happy child who had given him a bouquet of jungle flowers as a gift upon his arrival in the village a month ago. Afterward she kept pulling at the hairs on his arm, a rarity among the smooth-skinned Yanomamo, and nicknamed him *Jako Basho*, "Brother Monkey."

Biting his lip, he searched through his weapon's sight. He had no clean shot, not with the child wrapped in the muscular coils of the predator.

"Damn it!" He tossed his shotgun aside and reached to the machete at his belt. Unhitching the weapon, Nathan lunged forward—but as he neared, the snake rolled and pulled the girl under the black waters of the river. Her screams ended and bubbles followed her course.

Without thinking, Nathan dove in after her.

Of all the environments of the Amazon, none were more dangerous than its waterways. Under its placid surfaces lay countless hazards. Schools of bone-scouring piranhas hunted its depths, while stingrays lay buried in the mud and electric eels roosted amid roots and sunken logs. But worst of all were the river's true man-killers, the black caimans—giant crocodilian reptiles. With all its dangers, the Indians of the Amazon knew better than to venture into unknown waters.

But Nathan Rand was no Indian.

Holding his breath, he searched through the muddy waters and spotted the surge of coils ahead. A pale limb waved. With a kick of his legs, he reached out to the small hand, snatching it up in his large grip. Small fingers clutched his in desperation.

Tama was still conscious!

He used her arm to pull himself closer to the snake. In his other hand, he drew the machete back, kicking to hold his place, squeezing Tama's hand.

Then the dark waters swirled, and he found himself staring into the red eyes of the giant snake. It had sensed the challenge to its meal. Its black maw opened and struck at him.

Nate ducked aside, fighting to maintain his grip on the girl.

The anaconda's jaws snapped like a vice onto his arm. Though its bite was nonpoisonous, the pressure threatened to crush Nate's wrist. Ignoring the pain and his own mounting panic, he brought his other arm around, aiming for the snake's eyes with his machete.

At the last moment, the giant anaconda rolled in the water, throwing Nate to the silty bottom and pinning him. Nate felt the air squeezed from his lungs as four hundred pounds of scaled muscle trapped him. He struggled and fought, but he found no purchase in the slick river mud.

The girl's fingers were torn from his grip as the coils churned her away from him.

No . . . Tama!

He abandoned his machete and pushed with his hands against the weight of the snake's bulk. His shoulders sank into the soft muck of the riverbed, but still he pushed. For every coil he shoved aside, another would take its place. His arms weakened, and his lungs screamed for air.

Nathan Rand knew in this moment that he was doomed—and he was not particularly surprised. He knew it would happen one day. It was his destiny, the curse of his family. During the past twenty years, both his parents had been consumed by the Amazon forest. When he was eleven, his mother had succumbed to an unknown jungle fever, dying in a small missionary hospital. Then, four years ago, his father had simply vanished into the rain forest, disappearing without witnesses.

As Nate remembered the heartbreak of losing his father, rage flamed through his chest. Cursed or not, he refused to follow in his father's footsteps. He would *not* allow himself simply to be swallowed by the jungle. But more important, he would *not* lose Tama!

Screaming out the last of the trapped air in his chest, Nathan shoved the anaconda's bulk off his legs. Freed for a moment, he swung his feet under him, sinking into the mud up to his ankles, and shoved straight up.

His head burst from the river, and he gulped a breath of fresh air, then was dragged by his arm back under the dark water.

This time, Nathan did not fight the strength of the snake. Holding the clamped wrist to his chest, he twisted into the coils, managing to get a choke hold around the neck of the snake with his other arm. With the beast trapped, Nate dug his left thumb into the snake's nearest eye.

The snake writhed, tossing Nate momentarily out of the water, then slamming him back down. He held tight.

C'mon, you bastard, let up!

He bent his trapped wrist enough to drive his other thumb into the snake's remaining eye. He pushed hard on both sides, praying his basic training in reptile physiology proved true. Pressure on the eyes of a snake should trigger a gag reflex via the optic nerve.

He pressed harder, his heartbeat thudding in his ears.

Suddenly the pressure on his wrist released, and Nathan found himself flung away with such force that he half sailed out of the river and hit the riverbank with his shoulder. He twisted around and saw a pale form float to the surface of the river, facedown in midstream.

Tama!

As he had hoped, the visceral reflex of the snake had released both prisoners. Nathan shoved into the river and grabbed the child by the arm, pulling her slack form to him. He slung her over a shoulder and climbed quickly to the shore.

He spread her soaked body on the bank. She was not breathing. Her lips were purple. He checked her pulse. It was there but weak.

Nathan glanced around futilely for help. With no one around, it would be up to him to revive the girl.

He had been trained in first aid and CPR before venturing into the jungle, but Nathan was no doctor. He knelt, rolled the girl on her stomach, and pumped her back. A small amount of water sloshed from her nose and mouth.

Satisfied, he rolled Tama back around and began mouth-to-mouth.

At this moment, one of the Yanomamo tribesfolk, a middle-aged woman, stepped from the jungle's edge. She was small, as were all the Indians, no more than five feet in height. Her black hair was sheared in the usual bowl cut and her ears were pierced with feathers and bits of bamboo. Her dark eyes grew huge at the sight of the white man bent over the small child.

Nathan knew how it must look. He straightened up from his crouch just as Tama suddenly regained consciousness, coughing out gouts of river water and thrashing and crying in horror and fright. The panicked child beat at him with tiny fists, still in the nightmare of the snake attack.

"Hush, you're safe," he said in the Yanomamo dialect, trying to snare her hands in his grip. He turned to the woman, meaning to explain, but the small Indian dropped her basket and vanished into the thick fringe at the river's edge, whooping with alarm. Nathan knew the call. It was raised whenever a villager was under attack.

"Great, just great." Nathan closed his eyes and sighed.

When he had first come to this particular village four weeks ago, intending to record the medicinal wisdom of the tribe's old shaman, he had been instructed by the chief to stay away from the Indian women. In the past, there had been occasions when strangers had taken advantage of the tribe's women-folk. Nathan had honored this request, even though some of the women had been more than willing to share his hammock. His six-foot-plus frame, blue eyes, and sandy-colored hair were a novelty to the women of this isolated tribe.

In the distance, the fleeing woman's distress call was answered by others, many others. The name *Yanomamo* translated roughly as "the fierce people." The tribes were considered some of the most savage warriors. The *huyas*, or young men of the village, were always contesting some point of honor or claiming some curse had been set upon them, anything to warrant a brawl with a neighboring tribe or another tribesman. They were known to wipe out entire villages for so slight an insult as calling someone a derogatory name.

Nathan stared down into the face of the young girl. And what would these *huyas* make of this? A white man attacking one of their children, the chieftain's niece.

At his side, Tama had slowed her panic, swooning back into a fitful slumber. Her breathing remained regular, but when he checked her forehead, it was warm from a growing fever. He also spotted a darkening bruise on her right side. He fingered the injury—two broken ribs from the crushing embrace of the anaconda. He sat back on his heels, biting his lower lip. If she was to survive, she would need immediate treatment.

Bending, he gently scooped her into his arms.

The closest hospital was ten miles downstream in the small town of São Gabriel. He would have to get her there.

But there was only one problem—the Yanomamo. There was no way he could flee with the girl and expect to get away. This was Indian territory, and though he knew the terrain well, he was no native. There was a proverb spoken throughout the Amazon: *Na boesi, ingi sabe ala sani.* In their jungle, the Indian know everything. The Yanomamo were superb hunters, skilled with bow, blowgun, spear, and club.

There was no way he could escape.

Stepping away from the river, he retrieved his discarded shotgun from the brush and slung it over his shoulder. Lifting the girl higher in his arms, Nathan set off toward the village. He would have to make them listen to him, both for his sake and Tama's.

Ahead, the Indian village that he had called home for the past month had gone deathly quiet. Nathan winced as he walked. Even the constant twitter of birds and hooting call of monkeys had grown silent.

Holding his breath, he turned a corner in the trail and found a wall of Indians blocking his way, arrows nocked and drawn, spears raised. He sensed more than heard movement behind him. He glanced over his shoulder and saw more Indians already in position, faces daubed with crimson.

Nate had only one hope to rescue the girl and himself, an act he was loath to do, but he had no choice.

"Nabrushi yi yi!" he called out forcefully. "I demand trial by combat!"

AUGUST 6, 11:38 A.M.
OUTSIDE SÃO GABRIEL DA COCHOERIA

Manuel Azevedo knew he was being hunted. He heard the jaguar's coughing grunt coming from the forest fringes as he ran along the trail. Exhausted, soaked in sweat, he stumbled down the steep trail from the summit of the Mount of the Sacred Way. Ahead, a break in the foliage opened a view upon São Gabriel. The township lay nestled in the curve of the Rio Negro, the northern tributary of the great Amazon River.

So close . . . perhaps close enough . . .

Manny slid to a stop and faced back up the trail. He strained for any sign of the jaguar's approach: the snap of a twig, the rustle of leaves. But no telltale sign revealed the jungle cat's whereabouts. Even its hunting cough had gone silent. It knew it had run its prey to exhaustion. Now it crept in for the kill.

Manny cocked his head. The buzz of locusts and distant trill of birds were the only sounds. A rivulet of sweat dribbled down his neck. He tensed, ears straining. His fingers instinctively went to the knife on his belt. His other hand settled on the strap of his short whip.

Manny searched the dappled jungle floor around him. Chokes of ropy vines and leafy bushes clogged the path to both sides. Where would it come from?

Shadows shifted.

He spun on a heel, crouching. He tried to see through the dense foliage. *Nothing.*

Farther down the trail, a section of shadow lurched toward him, a sleek mirage of dappled fur, black on orange. It had been standing only ten feet away, lying low to the ground, haunches bunched under it. The cat was a large juvenile male, two years old.

Sensing it had been spotted, it whipped its tail back and forth with savage strokes, rattling the leaves.

Manny crouched, ready for the attack.

With a deep growl, the great cat leaped at him, fangs bared.

Manny grunted as its weight struck him like a crashing boulder. The pair went rolling down the trail. The wind was knocked out of Manny's thin frame as he tumbled. The world dissolved down to flashes of green, splashes of sunlight, and a blur of fur and teeth.

Claws pierced his khakis as the great cat wrapped Manny in its grip. A pocket ripped away. Fangs clamped onto his shoulder. Though the jaguar had the second strongest jaws of any land animal, its teeth did no more than press into his flesh.

The pair finally came to a stop several yards down the trail where it leveled off. Manny found himself pinned under the jaguar. He stared into the fiery eyes of his adversary as it gnawed at his shirt and growled.

"Are you done, Tor-tor?" He gasped. He had named the great cat after the Arawak Indian word for *ghost*. Though presently, with the jaguar's bulk seated on his chest, the name did not seem particularly apt.

At the sound of its master's voice, the jaguar let loose his shirt and stared back at him. Then a hot, coarse tongue swiped the sweat from Manny's forehead.

"I love you, too. Now get your furry butt off me."

Claws retracted, and Manny sat up. He checked the condition of his clothes and sighed. Training the young jaguar to hunt was quickly laying waste his wardrobe.

Standing up, Manny groaned and worked a kink from his back. At thirty-two, he was getting too old to play this game.

The cat rolled to its paws and stretched. Then, with a swish of the tail, it began to sniff at the air.

With a small laugh, Manny cuffed the jaguar on the side of its head. "We're done hunting for today. It's getting late. And I have a stack of reports still waiting for me back at the office."

Tor-tor rumbled grumpily, but followed.

Two years back, Manny had rescued the orphaned jaguar cub when it was only a few days old. Its mother had been killed by poachers for her pelt, a treasure that still brought a tidy sum on the black market. At current estimate, the population of wild jaguars was down to fifteen thousand, spread thin across the vast jungles of the Amazon basin. Conservation efforts did little to dissuade peasants who eked out a subsistence-level existence from hunting them for profit. A hungry belly made one shortsighted to efforts of wildlife preservation.

Manny knew this too well himself. Half Indian, he had been an orphan on the streets of Barcellos, along the banks of the Amazon River. He had lived hand to mouth, begging for coins from passing tourist boats and stealing when his palm came up empty. Eventually he was taken in by a Salesian missionary and worked his way up to a degree in biology at the University of São Paulo, his scholarship sponsored by the Brazilian Indian foundation, FUNAI. As payback for his scholarship, he worked with local Indian tribes: protecting their interests, preserving their ways of life, helping them claim their own lands legally. And at thirty, he found himself posted here in São Gabriel, heading the local FUNAI office.

It was during his investigation of poachers encroaching on Yanomamo lands that Manny discovered Tor-tor, an orphan like himself. The cub's right hind leg had been fractured where he had been kicked by one of the poachers. Manny could not abandon the tiny creature. So he had collected the mewling and hissing cub in a blanket and slowly nursed the foundling back to health.

Manny watched Tor-tor pace ahead of him. He could still see the slight tweak to his gait from his injured leg. In less than a year, Tor-tor would be sexually mature. The cat's feral nature would begin to shine, and it would be time to loose him into the jungle. But before that happened Manny wanted Tor-tor to be able to fend for himself. The jungle was no place for the uninitiated.

Ahead, the trail curved through the last of the jungled slopes of the Mount of the Sacred Way. The city of São Gabriel spread open before him, a mix of hovels and utilitarian cement-block structures bustled up against the Negro River. A few new hotels and buildings dotted the landscape, built within the last half decade to accommodate the growing flood of tourists to the region. And in the distance lay a new commercial airstrip. Its tarmac was a black scar through the surrounding jungle. It seemed even in the remote wilds there was no stopping progress.

Manny wiped his damp forehead, then stumbled into Tor-tor when the cat suddenly stopped. The jaguar growled deep in its throat, a warning.

"What's the matter?" Then he heard it, too.

Echoing across the blanket of jungle, a deep *thump-thump*ing grew in volume. It seemed to be coming from around them. Manny's eyes narrowed. He recognized the sound, though it was seldom heard out here. A helicopter. Most travelers to São Gabriel came by riverboat or by small prop planes. The distances were generally too vast to accommodate helicopters. Even the local Brazilian army base had only a single bird, used for rescue and evacuation missions.

As Manny listened and the noise grew in volume, he realized something else. It was more than just *one* helicopter.

He searched the skies but saw nothing.

Suddenly Tor-tor tensed and dashed into the surrounding brush.

A company of three helicopters flashed overhead, sweeping past the Mount of the Sacred Way and circling toward the small township like a swarm of wasps. *Camouflaged* wasps.

The bulky choppers—UH-1 Hueys—were clearly military.

Craning up, Manny watched a fourth helicopter pass directly above him. But unlike its brethren, this one was sleek and black. It whispered over the jungle. Manny recognized its characteristic shape and enclosed tail rotor from his short stint in the military. It was an RAH-66 Comanche, a reconnaissance and attack helicopter.

The slender craft passed close enough for Manny to discern the tiny American flag on its side. Above him, the jungle canopy rattled with its rotor wash. Monkeys fled, screaming in fright, and a flock of scarlet macaws broke like a streak of fire across the blue sky.

Then this helicopter was gone, too. It descended toward the open fields around the Brazilian army base, circling to join the other three.

Frowning, Manny whistled for Tor-tor. The huge cat slunk from its hiding place, eyes searching all around.

"It's all right," he assured the jaguar.

The *thump-thump*ing noise died away as the helicopters settled to the fields.

He crossed to Tor-tor and rested one hand on the great cat's shoulder, which trembled under his touch. The jaguar's nervousness flowed into him.

Manny headed downhill, settling a palm on the knobbed handle of the bullwhip hitched to his belt. "What the hell is the United States military doing here in São Gabriel?"

Nathan stood, stripped to his boxers, in the middle of the village's central plaza. Around him lay the Yanomamo *shabano*, or roundhouse, a circular structure half a football field wide with the central roof cut away to expose the sky. Women and older men lay sprawled in hammocks under the banana leaf roof, while the younger men, the *huyas*, bore spears and bows, ensuring Nathan did not try to flee.

Earlier, as he had been led at spearpoint back to camp, he had tried to explain about the attack by the anaconda, baring the bite marks on his wrist as proof. But no one would listen. Even the village chieftain, who had taken the child from his arms, had waved his words away as if they offended him.

Nathan knew that his voice would not be heard by those around him until the trial was over. It was the Yanomamo way. He had demanded combat as a way to buy time, and now no one would listen until the battle was over. Only if the gods granted him victory would he be heard.

Nathan stood barefoot in the dirt. Off to the side, a group of *huyas* argued over who would accept his challenge and what weapons would be used in the battle. The traditional duel was usually waged with *nabrushi*, slender, eight-foot-long wooden clubs that the combatants used to beat each other. But in more serious duels, deadly weapons were used, such as machetes or spears.

Across the plaza, the throng parted. A single Indian stepped forth. He was tall for a tribesman, almost as tall as Nathan, and wiry with muscle. It was Tama's father, Takaho, the chieftain's brother. He wore nothing but a braided string around his waist into which was tucked the foreskin of his penis, the typical garb of Yanomamo men. Across his chest were slash lines drawn in ash, while under a monkey-tail headband his face had been painted crimson. His lower lip bulged with a large tuck of tobacco, giving him a belligerent look.

He held out a hand, and one of the *huyas* hurried forward and placed a long ax in his palm. The ax's haft was carved of purple snakewood and ended in a pikelike steel head. It was a wicked-looking tool and one of the most savage dueling weapons.

Nate found a similar ax thrust into his own hands.

Across the way, he watched another *huya* hurry forward and hold out a clay pot full of an oily liquid. Takaho dipped his axhead into the pot.

Nate recognized the mixture. He had assisted the shaman in preparing this batch of *woorari*, in English *curare*, a deadly paralyzing nerve poison prepared from a liana vine of the moonseed family. The drug was used in hunting monkeys, but today it was intended for a more sinister purpose.

Nathan glanced around. No one came forth to offer a similar pot to anoint his blade. It seemed the battle was not to be exactly even.

The village chief raised a bow over his head and sounded the call for the duel to begin.

Takaho strode across the plaza, wielding the ax with practiced skill.

Nathan lifted his own ax. How could he win here? A single scratch meant death. And if he did win, what would be gained? He had come here to save Tama, and to do that, he would have to slay her father.

Bracing himself, he lifted the ax across his chest. He met the angry eyes of his opponent. "I didn't hurt your daughter!" he called out fiercely.

Takaho's eyes narrowed. He had heard Nate's words, but mistrust shone in his eyes. Takaho glanced to where Tama was being ministered to by the village shaman. The lanky elder was bowed over the girl, waving a smoking bundle of dried grass while chanting. Nathan could smell the bitter incense, an acrid form of smelling salts derived from hempweed. But the girl did not move.

Takaho faced Nate. With a roar, the Indian lunged forward, swinging his ax toward Nate's head.

Trained as a wrestler in his youth, Nate knew how to move. He dropped under the ax and rolled to the side, sweeping wide with his own weapon and knocking his opponent's legs out from under him.

Takaho fell hard to the packed dirt, smacking his shoulder and knocking loose his monkey-tail headband. But he was otherwise unharmed. Nate had struck with the blunt side of his ax, refusing to go for a maiming blow.

With the man down, Nate leaped at him, meaning to pin the Indian under his larger frame. *If I could just immobilize him . . .*

But Takaho rolled away with the speed of a cat, then swung again with a savage backstroke of his ax.

Nate reared away from the weapon's deadly arc. The poisoned blade whistled past the tip of his nose and slammed into the dirt between his hands. Relieved at the close call, Nathan was a second too late in dodging the foot kicked at his head. Ears ringing from the blow, he tumbled across the dirt. His own ax bounced out of his stunned hand and skittered into the crowd of onlookers.

Spitting out blood from his split lip, Nathan stood quickly.

Takaho was already on his feet.

As the Indian tugged his embedded ax from the dirt, Nathan noticed the shaman over his shoulder. The elder was now exhaling smoke across Tama's lips, a way of chasing off bad spirits before death.

Around him, the other *huyas* were now chanting for the kill.

Takaho lifted his ax with a grunt and turned to Nate. The Indian's face was a crimson mask of rage. He rushed at Nate, his ax whirling in a blur before him.

Without a weapon, Nate retreated. *So this is how I die . . .*

Nate found himself backed against a wall of spears held by other Indians. There was no escape. Takaho slowed for the kill, the ax high over his head.

Nathan felt the prick of spearheads in his bare back as he instinctively leaned away.

Takaho swung his weapon down with the strength of both shoulders.

"*Yulo!*" The sharp cry burst through the chanting *huyas.* "Stop!"

Nathan cringed from the blow that never came. He glanced up. The ax trembled about an inch from his face. A dribble of poison dripped onto his cheek.

The shaman, the one who had called out, pushed past other tribesmen into the central plaza. "Your daughter wakes!" He pointed to Nate. "She speaks of a giant snake and of her rescue by the white man."

All faces turned to where Tama was sipping weakly at a gourd of water held by a tribeswoman.

Nathan stared up into Takaho's eyes as the Indian faced him again. Takaho's hard expression melted with relief. He pulled away his weapon, then dropped it to the dirt. An empty hand clamped onto Nate's shoulder, and Takaho pulled him to his chest. "*Jako*," he said, hugging him tight. "Brother."

And just like that, it was over.

The chieftain pushed forward, puffing out his chest. "You battled the great *susuri*, the anaconda, and pulled our tribe's daughter from its belly." He removed a long feather from his ear and tucked it into Nate's hair. It was the tail feather of a harpy eagle, a treasured prize. "You are no longer a *nabe*, an outsider. You are now *jako*, brother to my brother. You are now Yanomamo."

A great cheer rose all around the *shabono*.

Nathan knew this was an honor above all honors, but he still had a pressing concern. "My sister," he said, pointing toward Tama. It was taboo to refer to a Yanomamo by his or her given name. Familial designations, real or not, were used instead. Tama moaned softly where she lay. "My sister is still sick. She has suffered injuries that the healers in São Gabriel can help mend. I ask that you allow me to take her to the town's hospital."

The village shaman stepped forward. Nathan feared he would argue that his own medicine could heal the girl. As a whole, shamans were a prideful group. But instead, the Indian elder agreed, placing a hand on Nate's shoulder. "Our little sister was saved from the *susuri* by our new *jako*. We should heed the gods in choosing him as her rescuer. I can do no more for her."

Nathan wiped the poison from his cheek, careful to keep it away from any open cuts, and thanked the elder. The shaman had done more than enough already. His natural medicines had been able to revive the girl in time to save him. Nathan turned next to Takaho. "I would ask to borrow your canoe for the journey."

"All that is mine is yours," Takaho said. "I will go with you to São Gabriel."

Nathan nodded. "We should hurry."

In short order, Tama was loaded on a stretcher of bamboo and palm fronds and placed in the canoe. Takaho, now dressed in a tank top and a pair of Nike shorts, waved Nathan to the bow of the dugout canoe, then shoved away from the shore with his oar and into the main current of the Negro River. The river led all the way to São Gabriel.

They made the ten-mile journey in silence. Nathan checked on Tama frequently and recognized the worry in her father's eyes. The girl had slipped back into a stupor, trembling, moaning softly now and then. Nathan wrapped a blanket around her small form.

Takaho wended the small canoe with skill through small rapids and around tangles of fallen trees. He seemed to have an uncanny skill at finding the swiftest currents.

As the canoe sped downriver, they passed a group of Indians from a neighboring village fishing in the river with spears. He watched a woman sprinkle a dark powder into the waters from an upstream canoe. Nate knew what she was doing. It was crushed *ayaeya* vine. As it flowed downstream, the dissolved powder would stun fish, floating them to the surface where they were speared and collected by the men. It was an ancient fishing method used throughout the Amazon.

But how long would such traditions last? A generation or two? Then this art would be lost forever.

Nathan settled into his seat, knowing there were certain battles he could never win. For good or bad, civilization would continue its march through the jungle.

As they continued along, Nate stared out at the walls of dense foliage that framed both banks. All around him, life buzzed, chirped, squawked, hooted, and grunted.

On either side, packs of red howler monkeys yelled in chorus and bounced aggressively atop their branches. Along the shallows, white-feathered bitterns with long orange beaks speared fish, while the plated snouts of caimans marked nesting grounds of the Amazonian crocodiles. Closer still, in the air around them, clouds of gnats and stinging flies harangued every inch of exposed skin.

Here the jungle ruled in all its forms. It seemed endless, impenetrable, full of mystery. It was one of the last regions of the planet that had yet to be fully explored. There were vast stretches never walked by man. It was this mystery and wonder that had attracted Nathan's parents to spend their lives here, eventually infecting their only son with their love of the great forest.

Nathan watched the jungle pass around him, noting the emerging signs of civilization, and knew that they neared São Gabriel. Small clearings made by peasant farmers began to appear, dotting the banks of the river. From the shore, children waved and called as the canoe whisked past. Even the noises of the jungle grew muted, driven away by the noisome ruckus of the modern world: the grumble of diesel tractors in the fields, the whine of motor boats that sped past the canoe, the tinny music of a radio blaring from a homestead.

Then, from around a bend in the river, the jungle ended abruptly. The small city of São Gabriel appeared like some cancer that had eaten away the belly of the forest. Near the river, the city was a ramshackle mix of rotting wooden shacks and cement government buildings. Away from the water, homes both small and large climbed the nearby hills. Closer at hand, the wharves and jetties were crowded with tourist boats and primer-scarred river barges.

Nathan turned to direct Takaho toward a section of open riverbank. He found the Indian staring in horror at the city, his oar clutched tightly to his chest.

"It fills the world," he mumbled.

Nathan glanced back to the small township. It had been two weeks since his last supply run to São Gabriel, and the noise and bustle were a rude shock to him. What must it be like for someone who had never left the jungle?

Nathan nodded to a spot to beach the canoe. "There is nothing here that a great warrior need fear. We must get your daughter to the hospital."

Takaho nodded, clearly swallowing back his shock. His face again settled into a stoic expression, but his eyes continued to flit around the wonders of this other world. He guided the canoe as directed, then helped Nathan haul out the stretcher on which Tama's limp form lay.

As she was shifted, the girl moaned, and her eyelids fluttered, eyes rolling white. She had paled significantly during the ride here.

"We must hurry."

Together, the two carried the girl through the waterfront region, earning the gawking stares of the townies and a few blinding flashes from camera-wielding tourists. Though Takaho wore "civilized" clothes, his monkey-tail headband, the sprouts of feathers in his ears, and his bowl-shaped haircut marked this fellow as one of the Amazon's indigenous tribespeople.

Luckily, the small single-story hospital was just past the waterfront region. The only way one could tell it was a hospital was the flaking red cross painted above the threshold, but Nathan had been here before, consulting with the doctor on staff, a fellow from Manaus. They were soon off the streets and guiding their stretcher through the door. The hospital reeked of ammonia and bleach, but it was deliciously air-conditioned. The cool air struck Nate like a wet towel to the face.

He crossed to the nurse's station and spoke rapidly. The pudgy woman's brow wrinkled with a lack of understanding until Nathan realized he had been speaking in the Yanomamo dialect. He switched quickly to Portuguese. "The girl has been attacked by an anaconda. She's suffered a few broken ribs, but I think her internal injuries might be more severe."

"Come this way." The nurse waved them toward a set of double doors. She eyed Takaho with clear suspicion.

"He's her father."

The nurse nodded. "Dr. Rodriguez is out on a house call, but I can ring him for an emergency."

"Ring him," Nathan said.

"Maybe I can help," a voice said behind him.

Nathan turned.

A tall, slender woman with long auburn hair rose from the wooden folding chairs in the waiting room. She had been partially hidden behind a pile of wooden crates emblazoned with the red cross. Approaching with calm assurance, she studied them all intently.

Nathan stood straighter.

"My name is Kelly O'Brien," she said in fluent Portuguese, but Nate heard a trace of a Boston accent. She pulled out identification with the familiar medical caduceus stamped on it. "I'm an American doctor."

"Dr. O'Brien," he said, switching to English, "I could certainly use your help. The girl here was attacked—"

Atop the stretcher, Tama's back suddenly arched. Her heels began to beat at the palm fronds, then her thrashing spread through the rest of her body.

"She's seizing!" the woman said. "Get her into the ward!"

The pudgy nurse led the way, holding the door wide for the stretcher.

Kelly O'Brien rushed alongside the girl as the two men swung the stretcher toward one of the four beds in the tiny emergency ward. Snatching a pair of surgical gloves, the tall doctor barked to the nurse, "I need ten milligrams of diazepam!"

The nurse nodded and dashed to a drug cabinet. In seconds, a syringe of amber-colored fluid was slapped into Kelly's gloved hand. The doctor already had a rubber tourniquet in place. "Hold her down," she ordered Nate and Takaho.

By now, a nurse and a large orderly had arrived as the quiet hospital awakened to the emergency.

"Get ready with an IV line and a bag of LRS," Kelly said sharply. Her fingers palpated a decent vein in the girl's thin arm. With obvious competence, Kelly inserted the needle and slowly injected the drug.

"It's Valium," she said as she worked. "It should calm the seizure long enough to find out what's wrong with her."

Her words proved instantly true. Tama's convulsions calmed. Her limbs stopped thrashing and relaxed to the bed. Only her eyelids and the corner of her lips still twitched. Kelly was examining her pupils with a penlight.

The orderly nudged Nate aside as he worked on Tama's other arm, preparing a catheter and IV line.

Nate glanced over the orderly's shoulder and saw the fear and panic in her father's eyes.

"What happened to her?" the doctor asked as she continued examining the girl.

Nathan described the attack. "She's been slipping in and out of consciousness most of the time. The village shaman was able to revive her for a short time."

"She's sustained a pair of cracked ribs and associated hematomas, but I can't account for the seizure or stupor. Did she have any seizures en route here?"

"No."

"Any familial history of epilepsy?"

Nate turned to Takaho and repeated the question in Yanomamo.

Takaho nodded. *"Ah-de-me-nah gunti."*

Nate frowned.

"What did he say?" Kelly asked.

"Ah-de-me-nah means electric eel. *Gunti* is disease or sickness."

"Electric eel disease?"

Nate nodded. "That's what he said. But it makes no sense. A victim of an electric eel attack will often convulse, but it's an immediate reaction. And Tama hasn't been in any water for hours. I don't know . . . maybe 'electric eel disease' is the Yanomamo term for epilepsy."

"Has she been treated for it? On medication?"

Nate got the answer from Takaho. "The village shaman has been treating her once a week with the smoke of the hempweed vine."

Kelly sighed in exasperation. "So in other words, she's been unmedicated. No wonder the stress of the near drowning triggered such a severe attack. Why don't you take her father out to the waiting room? I'll see if I can get these seizures to cease with stronger meds."

Nate glanced to the bed. Tama's form lay quiet. "Do you think she'll have more?"

Kelly glanced into his eyes. "She's still having them." She pointed to the persistent facial twitches.

"She's in status epilepticus, a continual seizure. Most patients who suffer from such prolonged attacks will appear stuporous, moaning, uncoordinated. The full grand mal events like a moment ago will be interspersed. If we can't stop it, she'll die."

Nate stared at the little girl. "You mean she's been seizing this entire time?"

"From what you describe, more or less."

"But the village shaman was able to draw her out of the stupor for a short time."

"I find that hard to believe." Kelly returned her attention to the girl. "He wouldn't have medication strong enough to break this cycle."

Nate remembered the girl sipping at the gourd. "But he did. Don't discount tribal shamans as mere witch doctors. I've worked for years with them. And considering what they have to work with, they're quite sophisticated."

"Well, wise or not, we've stronger medications here. Real medicine." She nodded again to the father. "Why don't you take her father out to the waiting room?" Kelly turned back to the orderly and nurses, dismissing him.

Nate bristled, but obeyed. For centuries, the value of shamanism had been scorned by practitioners of Western medicine. Nate coaxed Takaho out of the ward and into the waiting room. He guided the Indian to a chair and instructed him to stay, then headed for the door.

He slammed his way out into the heat of the Amazon. Whether the American doctor believed him or not, he had seen the shaman revive the girl. If there was one man who might have an answer for

Tama's mysterious illness, he knew where to find him.

Half running, he raced through the afternoon heat toward the southern outskirts of the city. In about ten blocks, he was skirting the edge of the Brazilian army camp. The normally sleepy base buzzed with activity. Nate noted the four helicopters with United States markings in the open field. Locals lined the base's fences, pointing toward the novelty of the foreign military craft and chattering excitedly.

He ignored the oddity and hurried to a cement-block building set amid a row of dilapidated wooden structures. The letters FUNAI were painted on the wall facing the street. It was the local office for the Brazilian Indian Foundation and represented the sole source of aid, education, and legal representation for the local tribes, the Baniwa and Yanomamo. The small building housed both offices and a homeless shelter for Indians who had come in search of the white man's prosperity.

FUNAI also had its own medical counselor, a longtime friend of the family and his own father's mentor here in the jungles of the Amazon.

Nate pushed through the anteroom and hurried down a hall and up a set of stairs. He prayed his friend was in his office. As he neared the open door, he heard the strands of Mozart's Fifth Violin Concerto flowing out.

Thank God!

Knocking on the door's frame, Nate announced himself. "Professor Kouwe?"

Behind a small desk, a mocha-skinned Indian

glanced up from a pile of papers. In his mid-fifties, he had shoulder-length black hair that was graying at the temples, and he now wore wire-rimmed glasses when reading. He took off those glasses and smiled broadly when he recognized Nate.

"Nathan!" Resh Kouwe stood and came around the desk to give him a hug that rivaled the coils of the anaconda he had fought. For his compact frame, the man was as strong as an ox. Formerly a shaman of the Tiriós tribe of southern Venezuela, Kouwe had met Nate's father three decades ago, and the two had become fast friends. Kouwe had eventually left the jungle with his father's help and was schooled at Oxford, earning a dual degree in linguistics and paleoanthropology. He was also one of the preeminent experts in the botanical lore of the region. "My boy, I can't believe you're here! Did Manny contact you?"

Nathan frowned as he was released from the bear hug. "No, what do you mean?"

"He's looking for you. He stopped by about an hour ago to see if I knew which village you were conducting your current research in."

"Why?" Nathan's brow wrinkled.

"He didn't say, but he did have one of those Tellux corporate honchos with him."

Nathan rolled his eyes. Tellux Pharmaceuticals was the multinational corporation that had been financing his investigative research into the practices of the region's tribal shamans.

Kouwe recognized his sour expression. "It was you who made the pact with the devil."

"Like I had any choice after my father died."

Kouwe frowned. "You should not have given up on yourself so quickly. You were always—"

"Listen," Nathan said, cutting him off. He didn't want to be reminded of that black period in his life. He had made his own bed and would have to lie in it. "I've got a different problem than Tellux." He quickly explained about Tama and her illness. "I'm worried about her treatment. I thought you could consult with the doctor."

Kouwe grabbed a fishing tackle box from a shelf. "Foolish, foolish, foolish," he said, and headed for the door.

Nathan followed him down the stairs and out into the street. He had to hurry to keep up with the older man. Soon the two were pushing through the hospital's front doors.

Takaho leaped to his feet at the reappearance of Nathan. "*Jako* . . . Brother."

Nathan waved him back down. "I've brought someone who might be able to help your daughter."

Kouwe did not wait. He was already shoving into the ward beyond the doors. Nathan hurried after him.

What he found in the next room was chaos. The slender American doctor, her face drenched with sweat, was bent over Tama, who was again in a full grand mal seizure. Nurses were scurrying to and fro at her orders.

Kelly glanced over the girl's convulsing body. "We're losing her," she said, her eyes frightened.

"Maybe I can help," Kouwe said. "What medications has she been given?"

Kelly ran down a quick list, wiping strands of hair from her damp forehead.

Nodding, Kouwe opened his tackle box and grabbed a small pouch from one of the many tiny compartments. "I need a straw."

A nurse obeyed him as quickly as she had Dr. O'Brien. Nathan could guess that this was not the first visit Professor Kouwe had made to the hospital here. There was no one wiser on indigenous diseases and their cures.

"What are you doing?" Kelly asked, her face red. Her loose auburn hair had been pulled back in a ponytail.

"You've been working under a false assumption," he said calmly as he packed the plastic straw with his powder. "The convulsive nature of electric eel disease is not a manifestation of a CNS disturbance, like epilepsy. It's due to a hereditary chemical imbalance in the cerebral spinal fluid. The disease is unique to a handful of Yanomamo tribes."

"A hereditary metabolic disorder?"

"Exactly, like favism among certain Mediterranean families or 'cold-fat disease' among the Maroon tribes of Venezuela."

Kouwe crossed to the girl and waved to Nathan. "Hold her still."

Nathan crossed and held Tama's head to the pillow.

The shaman positioned one end of the straw into the girl's nostril, then blew the straw's powdery content up her nose.

Dr. O'Brien hovered behind him. "Are you the hospital's clinician? Dr. Rodriguez?"

"No, my dear," Kouwe said, straightening. "I'm the local witch doctor."

Kelly looked at him with an expression of disbelief

and horror, but before she could object, the girl's thrashing began to calm, first slowly, then more rapidly.

Kouwe checked Tama's eyelids. The sick pallor to her skin was already improving. "I've found the absorption of certain drugs through the sinus membranes is almost as effective as intravenous administration."

Kelly looked on in amazement. "It's working."

Kouwe passed the pouch to one of the nurses. "Is Dr. Rodriguez on his way in?"

"I called him earlier, Professor," a nurse answered, glancing at her wristwatch. "He should be here in ten minutes."

"Make sure the girl gets half a straw of the powder every three hours for the next twenty-four, then once daily. That should stabilize her so her other injuries can be addressed satisfactorily."

"Yes, Professor."

On the bed, Tama slowly blinked open her eyes. She stared at the strangers around her, confusion and fright clear in her face, then her eyes found Nathan's. "*Jako Basho*," she said weakly.

"Yes, Brother Monkey is here," he said in Yanomamo, patting her hand. "You're safe. Your papa is here, too."

One of the nurses fetched Takaho. When he saw his daughter awake and speaking, he fell to his knees. His stoic demeanor shattered, and he wept with relief.

"She'll be fine from here," Nate assured him.

Kouwe collected his fishing tackle box and retreated from the room. Nathan and Dr. O'Brien followed.

"What was in that powder?" the auburn-haired doctor asked.

"Desiccated *ku-nah-ne-mah* vine."

Nate answered the doctor's confused expression. "Climbing hempweed. The same plant the tribal shaman burned to revive the girl back at the village. Just like I told you before."

Kelly blushed. "I guess I owe you an apology. I didn't think . . . I mean I couldn't imagine . . ."

Kouwe patted her on her elbow. "Western ethnocentrism is a common rudeness out here. It's nothing to be embarrassed about." He winked at her. "Just outgrown."

Nate did not feel as courteous. "Next time," he said harshly, "listen with a more open mind."

She bit her lip and turned away.

Nathan instantly felt like a cad. His worry and fear throughout the day had worn his patience thin. The doctor had only been trying her best. Knowing he shouldn't have been so hard on her, he opened his mouth to apologize.

But before he could speak, the front door swung open and a tall redheaded man dressed in khakis and a beat-up Red Sox baseball cap stepped into the lobby. He spotted the doctor. "Kelly, if you've finished delivering the supplies, we need to be under way. We've a boat that's willing to take us upriver."

"Yes," she said. "I'm all done here."

She then glanced at Nathan and Kouwe. "Thank you."

Nathan recognized the similarities between this newcomer and the young doctor: the splash of freckles, the same crinkle around the eyes, even their voices had the same Boston lilt. Her brother, he guessed.

Nathan followed them out of the hospital and into the street. But what he found there caused him to take an involuntary step backward, bumping into Professor Kouwe.

Aligned across the road was a group of ten soldiers in full gear, including M-16s with collapsible butt stocks, holstered pistols, and heavy packs. Nate recognized the shoulder insignia common to them all. Army Rangers. One spoke into a radio and waved the group forward toward the waterfront. The pair of Americans joined the departing group.

"Wait!" someone called from beyond the line of Rangers.

The military wall parted, and a familiar face appeared. It was Manny Azevedo. The stocky black-haired man broke through the ranks. He wore scuffed trousers and the pocket of his shirt had been ripped to a hanging flap. His characteristic bullwhip was wound at his waist.

Nathan returned Manny's smile and crossed to him. They hugged briefly, patting each other on the back. Then Nathan flicked the torn bit of his khaki shirt. "Playing with Tor-tor again, I see."

Manny grinned. "The monster's gained ten kilos since the last time you saw him."

Nathan laughed. "Great. Like he wasn't big enough already." Noting that the Rangers had stopped and were staring at the pair, as were Kelly O'Brien and her brother, Nathan nodded to the military party and leaned closer. "So what's all this about? Where are they heading?"

Manny glanced at the group. By now, a large crowd of onlookers had gathered to gawk at the line of stiff Army Rangers. "It seems the U.S. government is financing a recon team for a deep-jungle expedition."

"Why? Are they after drug traffickers?"

By now, Kelly O'Brien had stepped back toward them.

Manny acknowledged her with a nod, then waved a hand to Nathan. "May I introduce you to Dr. Rand? Dr. Nathan Rand."

"It seems we've already met," Kelly said with an embarrassed smile. "But he never offered his name."

Nathan sensed something unspoken pass between Kelly and Manny. "What's going on?" he asked. "What are you searching for upriver?"

She stared him straight in the eyes. Her eyes were the most striking shade of emerald. "We came to find you, Dr. Rand."

TWO

Debriefing

AUGUST 6, 9:15 P.M.
SÃO GABRIEL DA COCHOERIA

Nate crossed the street from Manny's offices at FUNAI and headed toward the Brazilian army base. He was accompanied by the Brazilian biologist and Professor Kouwe. The professor had just returned from the hospital. Nate was relieved to hear that Tama was recuperating well.

Freshly showered and shaved, his clothes laundered, Nathan Rand felt nothing like the man who had arrived here only hours before with the girl. It was as if he had scraped and scrubbed the jungle from his body along with the dirt and sweat. In a few hours, he went from a newly anointed member of the Yanomamo tribe back to an American citizen. It was amazing the transformational power of Irish Spring deodorant soap. He sniffed at the residual smell.

"After being so long in the jungle, it's nauseating,

isn't it?" Professor Kouwe said, puffing on a pipe. "When I first left my home in the Venezuelan jungle, it was the bombardment upon my senses—the smells, the noises, the furious motion of civilization—that took the longest to acclimatize to."

Nathan dropped his arm. "It's strange how quickly you adapt to the simpler life out in the wilds. But I can tell you one thing that makes all the hassles of modern civilized life worth it."

"What's that?" Manny asked.

"Toilet paper," Nathan said.

Kouwe snorted with laughter. "Why do you think I left the jungle?"

They crossed toward the gate of the illuminated base. The meeting was scheduled to start in another ten minutes. Maybe then he'd have some answers.

As they walked, Nathan glanced over the quiet city and studied this little bastion of civilization. Over the river, a full moon hung, reflected in the sleek surface, blurred by an evening mist spreading into the city. Only at night does the jungle reclaim São Gabriel. After the sun sets, the noises of the city die down, replaced by the echoing song of the nightjar in the surrounding trees, accompanied by the chorus of honking frogs and the vibrato of locusts and crickets. Even in the streets, the flutter of bats and whine of blood-hungry mosquitoes replace the honk of cars and chatter of people. Only as one passes an open cantina, where the tinkling laughter of late-night patrons flows forth, does human life intrude.

Otherwise, at night, the jungle rules.

Nathan kept pace with Manny. "What could the U.S. government possibly need with me?"

Manny shook his head. "I'm not sure. But it somehow involves your financiers."

"Tellux Pharmaceuticals?"

"Right. They arrived with several corporate types. Lawyers, by the look of them."

Nate scowled. "Aren't there always when Tellux is involved?"

Kouwe spoke around the stem of his pipe. "You didn't have to sell Eco-tek to them."

Nate sighed. "Professor . . ."

The shaman raised his hands in submission. "Sorry. I know . . . sore subject."

Sore wasn't the word Nathan would have used. Established twelve years ago, Eco-Tek had been his father's brainchild. It was a niche pharmaceutical firm that had sought to utilize shamanic knowledge as the means to discover new botanical drugs. His father had wanted to preserve the wisdom of the vanishing medicine men of the Amazon basin and to insure that these local tribes profited from their own knowledge through intellectual property rights. Not only had it been his father's dream and purpose in life, but also the culmination of a promise to Nate's mother, Sarah. While working as a medical doctor for the Peace Corps, she had dedicated her life to the indigenous people here, and her passion was contagious. Nate's father had promised to continue on in her footsteps and, years later, Eco-Tek was the result, a fusion of razor-sharp business models and nonprofit advocacy.

But now all that was left of his parents' legacy was gone, dismantled and swallowed by Tellux.

"Looks like we're getting an escort," Manny said, breaking through Nate's thoughts.

At the gate's guard station, two Rangers in tan berets stood stiffly behind a nervous-looking Brazilian soldier.

Nathan eyed their holstered sidearms warily and wondered again at the nature of this meeting.

As they reached the gates, the Brazilian guard checked their identifications. Then one of the two Rangers stepped forward. "We're to take you to the debriefing. If you'll please follow." He turned sharply on his heel and strode away.

Nathan glanced to his friends, then proceeded through the gates. The second Ranger took up a strategic position behind them. Ushered along by their escorts, with a view of the four military helicopters resting on the camp's soccer field, Nathan felt a distinct sense of dread in his belly.

None of this seemed to concern Professor Kouwe. He simply puffed on his pipe and strode casually after their armed escort. Manny also appeared more distracted than alarmed.

They were marched past the corrugated Quonset huts that served as barracks for the Brazilian troops and led to a derelict timber-framed warehouse on the far side with the few windows painted black.

The Ranger in the lead opened the rusted door. Nathan was the first through. Expecting to find a gloomy, spider-infested interior, he was surprised to find the large warehouse brightly lit with halogen poles and overhead fluorescents. The cement floor was crisscrossed with cables, some as thick around as his wrist. From one of the three offices lining the back half of the warehouse, a generator could be heard chugging away.

Nathan gaped at the level of sophisticated hardware positioned throughout the room: computers, radio equipment, televisions, and monitors.

Amid all the organized chaos, a long conference table had been set up, strewn with printouts, maps, graphs, even a pile of newspapers. Men and women in both military garb and civilian clothes were busy throughout the room. Several were poring over reams of paper at the table, including Kelly O'Brien.

What's going on here? Nathan wondered.

"I'm afraid there's no smoking inside," their escort said to Professor Kouwe, indicating the lit pipe.

"Of course." Kouwe tapped out his pipe's bowl onto the threshold's dirt floor. The Ranger used his boot heel to squash the burning tobacco. "Thank you."

From across the way, one of the office doors opened and the tall redheaded man who appeared to be Dr. O'Brien's brother stepped out. At his side was a man Nate knew well enough to dislike immensely. He was dressed in a navy blue suit with the jacket slung over one arm, a coat Nate was sure bore the Tellux logo. As usual, his dark brown hair was oiled and combed into perfect place, as was his smartly trimmed goatee. The smile he wore as he approached Nathan and his two friends was just as oily.

On the other hand, his redheaded companion crossed with an arm extended and a more genuine expression of welcome. "Dr. Rand, thank you for coming. I think you know Dr. Richard Zane."

"We've met," Nathan said coldly, then shook the redhead's hand. The man had a grip that could crush stone.

"I'm Frank O'Brien, the head of operations here.

You've already met my sister." He nodded over to Kelly, who glanced up from the table. She lifted a hand in greeting. "Now that you're all here we can get this meeting under way."

Frank guided Nate, Kouwe, and Manny toward the table, then waved an arm, signaling the others to take their seats.

A hard-faced man with a long pale scar across his throat settled himself across the table from Nathan. At his side sat one of the Rangers, his two silver bars suggesting he was the captain of the military forces here.

At the head of the table, Richard Zane sat between Kelly and Frank, who remained standing. To the left was another Tellux employee, a small Asian woman in a conservative blue pantsuit. Her eyes glinted with intelligence and seemed to soak in everything around her. Nate caught her gaze. She gave him the faintest of smiles and nodded her head.

Once everyone else was settled, Frank cleared his throat. "First, Dr. Rand, let me welcome you to the command center for Operation Amazonia, a joint operation between the CIA's Environmental Center and Special Forces Command." He gave a short nod to the silver-barred captain. "We're also supported by the Brazilian government and are assisted by Tellux Pharmaceutical's research division."

Kelly interrupted her brother, raising a hand. She clearly read the confusion on Nathan's face. "Dr. Rand, I'm sure you've many questions. Foremost being, why you've been sought as a partner in this venture."

Nathan nodded.

Kelly stood. "The main objective of Operation Amazonia is to discover the fate of your father's lost expedition."

Nate's jaw dropped and his vision blackened at the edges. He felt as if he'd just been sucker-punched. He stammered for half a moment until he found his voice. "But . . . but that was over four years ago."

"We understand that, but—"

"No!" He found himself on his feet, his chair skittering across the cement behind him. "They're dead. All dead!"

Professor Kouwe reached to place a restraining hand on his elbow. "Nathan . . ."

He shook his arm free. He remembered that call as if it were yesterday. He had been finishing up his doctoral thesis at Harvard. He had taken the next plane down to Brazil and joined the search for the vanished team. Memories flowed through him as he stood in the warehouse—the blinding fear, the anger, the frustration. After the searches were called off, he had refused to give up. He couldn't! He had pleaded with Tellux Pharmaceuticals to help continue the search privately. Tellux had been a co-sponsor, along with Eco-tek, in this venture. The ten-year goal: to conduct a census of the current populations of indigenous tribes and begin a systematic cataloging of their medicinal knowledge before such information was lost forever. But Tellux had refused Nate's request for assistance. The corporation had supported the conclusion that the team either had been killed by a tribe of hostile Indians or had stumbled upon a camp of drug traffickers.

Nate had not. Over the next year, he spent millions continuing the search, beating the bush for any sign, clue, inkling of what had become of his father. It was a financial black hole into which he poured Eco-tek's assets, further destabilizing his father's company. Eco-tek had already taken a devastating hit on Wall Street, its stock value plummeting after the loss of its CEO in the jungle. Eventually, the well ran dry. Tellux made a run for his father's company in a hostile takeover bid. Nate was too wounded, tired, and heartsore to fight. Eco-tek and its assets, including Nathan himself, became beholden to the multinational corporation.

What followed was an even blacker period of his life, a hazy blur of alcohol, drugs, and disillusionment. It was only with the help of friends like Professor Kouwe and Manny Azevedo that he had ever found himself again. In the jungles, he found the pain was less severe. He discovered he could survive a day, then another. He plodded his way as best he could, continuing his father's work with the Indians, financed on a pittance from Tellux.

Until now. "They're dead!" he repeated, sagging toward the table. "After so long, there's no hope of ever discovering what happened to my father."

Nathan felt Kelly's penetrating emerald eyes on him as she waited for him to compose himself. Finally, she spoke. "Do you know Gerald Wallace Clark?"

Opening his mouth to say no, Nathan suddenly recognized the name. He had been a member of his father's team. Nathan licked his lips. "Yes. He was a former soldier. He headed the expedition's five-man weapons team."

Kelly took a deep breath. "Twelve days ago, Gerald Wallace Clark walked out of the jungle."

Nate's eyes grew wide.

"Damn," Manny said beside him.

Professor Kouwe had retrieved Nate's toppled chair and now helped guide him down to his seat.

Kelly continued, "Unfortunately, Gerald Clark died at a missionary settlement before he could indicate where he had come from. The goal of our operation is to backtrack this latest trail to find out what happened. We were hoping that as the son of Carl Rand, you'd be interested in cooperating with our search."

A silence descended over the table.

Frank cleared his throat, adding, "Dr. Rand, not only are you an expert on the jungle and its indigenous tribes, but you also knew your father and his team better than anyone. Such knowledge could prove an asset during this deep-jungle search."

Nathan was still too stunned to speak or answer. Professor Kouwe was not. He spoke calmly. "I can see why Tellux Pharmaceuticals is invested in this matter." Kouwe nodded to Richard Zane, who smiled back at the professor. "They were never one to pass up a chance to profit from another's tragedy."

Zane's smile soured.

Kouwe continued, now turning his attention to Frank and Kelly. "But why is this matter of interest to the CIA's Environmental Center? And what's the rationale for assigning an Army Ranger unit to the mission?" He turned to the military man, raising a single eyebrow. "Would either of you two or the captain here wish to elaborate?"

Frank's brow wrinkled at the quick and piercing assessment from the professor. Kelly's eyes sparked.

She answered. "Besides being an ex-soldier and a weapons expert, Gerald Clark was also a CIA operative. He was sent along with the expedition to gather intelligence on the cocaine shipment routes through the rain forest basin."

Frank glanced quickly at Kelly, as if this bit of information were given a bit too freely.

She ignored her brother and continued. "But any further elaboration will only be given if Dr. Rand agrees to join our operation. Otherwise, additional details will be restricted."

Kouwe, his eyes bright with warning, glanced to Nathan.

Nate took a deep breath. "If there's any hope of finding out what happened to my father, then I can't pass up this chance." He turned to his two friends. "You both know I can't."

Nathan stood and faced the table. "I'll go."

Manny shoved out of his chair. "Then I'm going with him." He faced the others and continued before anyone could object. "I've already talked to my superiors in Brasilia. As chief representative of FUNAI here, I have the power at my discretion to place any restrictions or qualifications on this mission."

Frank nodded. "So we were informed an hour ago. It's your choice. Either way, you'll have no objection from me. I read your file. Your background as a biologist could prove useful."

Next, Professor Kouwe stood up and placed a hand on Nate's shoulder. "Then perhaps you could use an expert in linguistics also."

"I appreciate your offer." Frank waved to the small Asian woman. "But we do have that covered. Dr. Anna Fong is an anthropologist with a specialty in indigenous tribes. She speaks a dozen different dialects."

Nathan scoffed, "No offense to Dr. Fong, but Professor Kouwe speaks over a hundred and fifty. There is no better expert in the field."

Anna spoke up, her voice soft and sweet. "Dr. Rand is most correct. Professor Kouwe is world renowned for his knowledge of the Amazon's indigenous tribes. It would be a privilege to have his cooperation."

"And it seems," Kelly added with a respectful nod toward the older man, "the good professor is also a distinguished expert on botanical medicines and jungle diseases."

Kouwe bowed his head in her direction.

Kelly turned to her brother. "As the expedition's medical doctor, I wouldn't mind having him along either."

Frank shrugged. "What's one more?" He faced Nathan. "Is this acceptable to you?"

Nathan glanced to his right and left. "Of course."

Frank nodded and raised his voice. "Let's all get back to work then. Discovering Dr. Rand here in the city has accelerated our schedule. We've a lot to accomplish in order to be under way at the crack of dawn tomorrow." As the others began to disperse, Frank turned to Nathan. "Now let's see if we can't get a few more of your questions answered."

He and his sister led the way toward one of the back offices.

Nate and his two friends followed.

Manny glanced over his shoulder to the bustling room. "Just what the hell have we volunteered for?"

"Something amazing," Kelly answered from ahead, holding open the office door. "Step inside and I'll show you."

Nathan clutched the photos of Agent Clark and passed them around to the others. "And you're telling me this man actually grew his arm back?"

Frank stepped around the desk and took a seat. "So it would seem. It's been verified by fingerprints. The man's body was shipped today from the morgue in Manaus back to the States. His remains are due to be examined tomorrow at a private research facility sponsored by MEDEA."

"MEDEA?" Manny asked. "Why does that name sound familiar?"

Kelly answered from where she was studying topographic maps tacked on the wall. "MEDEA's been active in rain forest conservation since its inception back in 1992."

"What is MEDEA?" Nathan asked, placing the photos on the desk.

"Back in 1989, there were congressional hearings on whether or not the classified data gathered by the CIA through its satellite surveillance systems might be useful in studying and monitoring global environmental changes. As a result, MEDEA was formed in 1992. The CIA recruited more than sixty researchers in various environmental-related fields into a single organization to analyze classified data in regard to environmental concerns."

"I see," Nathan said.

Frank spoke up, "Our mother was one of the original MEDEA founders, with a background in medicine and hazardous-waste risks. She was hired by my father when he was deputy director of the CIA. She'll be overseeing the autopsy of Agent Clark."

Manny frowned. "Your father is the deputy director of the CIA?"

"*Was*," Frank said bitterly.

Kelly turned from the maps. "He's now director of the CIA's Environmental Center. A division that was founded by Al Gore in 1997 at the behest of MEDEA. Frank works in this division, as well."

"And you?" Nathan asked. "Are you CIA, too?"

Kelly waved away his question.

"She's the youngest member of MEDEA," Frank said with a bit of pride in his voice. "Quite the distinguished honor. It was why we were chosen to head this operation. I represent the CIA. She represents MEDEA."

"Nothing like keeping it all in the family," Kouwe said with a snort.

"The fewer who know about the mission the better," Frank added.

"Then how does Tellux Pharmaceuticals play a role in all this?" Nathan asked.

Kouwe answered before either of the O'Brien siblings. "Isn't it obvious? Your father's expedition was financed by Eco-tek and Tellux, which are now one and the same. They own any proprietary intelligence gained from the expedition. If the team discovered some compound out there with regenerative properties, Tellux owns the majority rights to it."

Nathan glanced to Kelly, who stared at her toes.

Frank simply nodded. "He's right. But even at Tellux, only a handful of people know the true purpose of our mission here."

Nate shook his head. "Great, just great." Kouwe placed a sympathetic hand on his shoulder.

"All that aside," Manny said, "what's our first step?"

"Let me show you." Kelly turned once again to the maps on the back wall. She pointed to the centermost one. "I'm sure Dr. Rand is familiar with this map."

He stared at it and did indeed recognize it like the lines on his own palm. "It's the recorded route my father's team took four years ago."

"Exactly," Kelly said, tracing her finger along the dotted course that led in haphazard fashion from Manaus south along the Madeira River until it reached the town of Pôrto Velho, where it angled north into the heart of the Amazon basin. From there, the team crisscrossed the area until they bridged into the little-explored region between the southern and northern tributaries of the Amazon. Her finger stopped at the small cross at the end of the line. "Here is where all radio contact with the team ceased. And where all searches originated— both those sponsored by the Brazilian government and those financed privately." She glanced significantly at Nathan. "What can you tell us about the searches?"

Nate circled around the desk to stare at the map. A familiar creeping despair edged through the core of his being. "It was December, the height of the rainy season," he whispered dully. "Two major storm systems had moved through the region. It was one of the reasons no one was initially concerned. But when an update from the team grew to be almost a week late and the storms had abated, an alarm went up. At first, no one was really that worried. These were people who had lived their lives in the jungle. What could go wrong? But as search teams began tentatively looking, it was realized that all trace of the expedition was gone, erased by the rains and the flooded forests. This spot"—Nathan placed a finger on the black *X*—"was found to be underwater when the first team arrived."

He turned to the others. "Another week went by, then another. Nothing. No clues, no further word . . . until one last frantic signal. 'Send help . . . can't last much longer. Oh, God, they're all around us.'" Nate took a deep breath. The memory of those words still haunted him deeply. "The signal was so full of static that it was impossible to discern who even spoke. Maybe it was this Agent Clark." But in his heart, Nathan knew it had been his father. He had listened over and over to that last message. The last words of his father.

Nathan stared at the photos and documents strewn across the desktop. "For the next three months, the searchers swept throughout the region, but storms and floods made any progress difficult. There was no telling in which direction my father's team had headed: east, west, north, south." He shrugged. "It was impossible. We were searching a region larger than the state of Texas. Eventually everyone gave up."

"Except you," Kelly said softly.

Nathan clenched a fist. "And a lot of good that did. No further contact was ever heard."

"Until now," Kelly said. She gently drew him around and pointed to a small red circle he had not noticed before. She pointed to it. It lay about two hundred miles due south of São Gabriel, near the river of Jarurá, a branch of the Solimões, the mighty southern tributary of the Amazon. "This is the mission of Wauwai, where Agent Clark died. This is where we're heading tomorrow."

"And what then?" Manny asked.

"We follow Gerald Clark's trail. Unlike the earlier searches, we have an advantage."

"What is that?" Manny asked.

Nathan spoke up, leaning close to the wall map. "We're at the end of the dry season. There hasn't been a major storm through here in a month." He glanced over his shoulder. "We should be able to track his movements."

"Hence, the urgency and speed of organizing this mission." Frank stood. He leaned one hand on the wall and nodded to the map. "We hope to follow any clues before the wet season begins and the trail is washed away. We're also hoping Agent Clark was sound enough in mind to leave some evidence of his route— marks on a tree, piles of rock—some way to lead us back to where he had been held these past four years."

Frank turned back to the desk and slid out a large folded sheet of sketch paper. "In addition, we've employed Anna Fong so we can communicate with any natives of the region: peasants, Indians, trappers, whoever. To see if anyone has seen a man with these markings pass by." Frank unfolded and smoothed the paper. A hand-sketched drawing was revealed. "This was tattooed across Agent Clark's chest and abdomen. We hope that we'll find isolated folk who might have seen a man with this marking."

Professor Kouwe flinched.

His reaction did not go unnoticed by those in the room.

"What is it?" Nathan asked.

Kouwe pointed to the sketch paper. It delineated a complex serpentine pattern that spiraled out from a single stylized handprint.

"This is bad. Very bad." Kouwe fumbled in his pocket and pulled out his pipe. He lifted a questioning eye at Frank.

The redheaded man nodded.

Kouwe slipped out a pouch and tamped some locally grown tobacco into the pipe, then lit it with a single match. Nathan noted his uncharacteristically trembling fingers.

"What is it?"

Kouwe puffed on his pipe and spoke slowly. "It's the symbol for the Ban-ali. The Blood Jaguars."

"You know this tribe?" Kelly asked.

The shaman blew out a long stream of smoke and sighed, then shook his head. "No one *knows* this tribe. It is what's whispered among village elders, stories passed from one generation to another. Myths of a tribe that mates with jaguars and whose members can vanish into thin air. They bring death to all who encounter them. It is said they are as old as the forest and that the very jungle bends to their will."

"But I've never heard of them," Nathan said, "and I've worked with tribes throughout the Amazon."

"And Dr. Fong, the Tellux anthropologist," Frank said. "She didn't recognize it either."

"I'm not surprised. No matter how well you're accepted, a nontribesman will always be considered *pananakiri*, an alien to the Indians of the region. They would never speak of the Ban-ali to you."

Nate couldn't help but feel a bit insulted. "But I—"

"No, Nathan. I don't mean to slight your own work or abilities. But for many tribes, names have power. Few will speak the name Ban-ali. They fear to draw the attention of the Blood Jaguars." Kouwe pointed to the drawing. "If you take this symbol with you, it must be shown with care. Many Indians would slay you for possessing such a paper. There is no greater taboo than allowing that symbol into a village."

Kelly frowned. "Then it's doubtful Agent Clark passed through any villages."

"If he did, he wouldn't have walked out alive."

Kelly and Frank shared a concerned look, then the doctor turned to Nathan. "Your father's expedition was cataloging Amazonian tribes. If he had heard of these mysterious Ban-ali or had found some clue of their existence, perhaps he sought them out."

Manny folded the sketched drawing. "And perhaps he found them."

Kouwe studied the glowing tip of his pipe. "Pray to God he did not."

A little later, with most of the details settled, Kelly watched the trio, escorted by a Ranger, cross the room and exit the warehouse. Her brother Frank was already at the portable satellite uplink to report the day's progress to his superiors, including their father.

But Kelly found her gaze following Nathan Rand. After their antagonistic exchange in the hospital, she was still slightly put off by his demeanor. But he was hardly the same oily-haired, foul-smelling wretch she had seen hauling the girl on a stretcher. Shaved and in clean clothes, he was certainly handsome: sandy-blond hair, dark complexion, steel-blue eyes. Even the way one eyebrow would rise when he was intrigued was oddly charming.

"Kelly!" her brother called. "There's someone who'd like to say hi."

With a tired sigh, Kelly joined her brother at the table. All around the room, final preparations and equipment checks were being finished. She leaned both palms on the table and stared into the laptop's screen. She saw two familiar faces, and a warm smile crossed her face.

"Mother, Jessie's not supposed to be up this late." She glanced to her own wristwatch and did a quick calculation. "It must be close to midnight."

"Actually after midnight, hon."

Kelly's mother could have been her sister. Her hair was as deep an auburn as her own. The only sign of her age was the slightly deeper crinkles at the corners of her eyes and the small pair of glasses perched on her nose. She had been pregnant with Kelly and Frank when she was only twenty-two, still in med school herself. Giving birth to fraternal twins was enough of a family for the med student and the young navy surveillance engineer. Kelly's mother and father never had any more children.

But that didn't stop Kelly from following in her mother's footsteps, getting pregnant in her fourth year of medical school at Georgetown. Yet unlike her mother, who remained married to the father of her children, Kelly divorced Daniel Nickerson when she found him in bed with a fellow residency student. He at least had enough decency not to contest Kelly's demand for custody of their one-year-old daughter, Jessica.

Jessie, now six years old, stood at her grandmother's shoulder, dressed in a yellow flannel nightgown with Disney's Pocahontas on the front. Her tousled red hair looked as if she had just climbed out of bed. She waved at the screen. "Hi, Mommy!"

"Hi, sweetheart. Are you having a good time with Grandma and Grandpa?"

She nodded vigorously. "We went to Chuck E. Cheese's today!"

Kelly's smile broadened. "That sounds like fun. I wish I could've been there."

"We saved a piece of pizza for you."

In the background, her mother's eyes rolled with the exasperation of all grandparents who've had encounters with the giant Chuck E. Cheese's rodent.

"Did you see any lions, Mommy?"

This earned a chuckle. "No, hon, there are no lions here. That's Africa."

"How about gorillas?"

"No, that's Africa, too—but we did see some monkeys."

Jessica's eyes grew round. "Can you catch one and bring one home? I always wanted a monkey."

"I don't think the monkey would like that. He has his own mommy here."

Her mother placed an arm around Jessica. "And I think it's time we let your mommy get some sleep. She has to get up early like you do."

Jessica's face fell into a pout.

Kelly leaned closer to the screen. "I love you, Jessie."

She waved at the screen. "Bye, Mommy."

Her mother smiled at her. "Be careful, hon. I wish I could be there."

"You've got enough work of your own. Did the . . . um . . ." Her eyes flicked to Jessie. ". . . *package* arrive safely?"

Her mother's face drifted to a more serious demeanor. "It cleared customs in Miami about six o'clock, arrived here in Virginia about ten, and was trucked to the Instar Institute. In fact, your father's still over there, making sure all is in order for tomorrow's examination."

Kelly nodded, relieved Clark's body had arrived in the States safely.

"I should get Jessie to bed, but I'll update you tomorrow night during the evening uplink. You be careful out there."

"Don't worry. I've got a crack team of ten Army Rangers as bodyguards. I'll be safer than on the streets of downtown Washington."

"Still, you two watch each other's backs."

Kelly glanced to Frank, who was talking to Richard Zane. "We will."

Her mother swept her a kiss. "I love you."

"Love you too, Mom." Then the screen went dead.

Kelly closed the laptop, then slumped to a chair by the table, suddenly exhausted. She stared at the others. Her gear was already packed and stored on the Huey. Free from any responsibilities for the moment, her mind drifted back to the red serpentine tattoo wrapped around a blue palm, the symbol of the Ban-ali, the ghost tribe of the Amazon.

Two questions nagged her: Did such a tribe exist, a tribe with these mythic powers? And if so, would ten armed Rangers be enough?

THREE

The Doctor and the Witch

Louis Favre was often described as a bastard and drunkard, but never to his face. *Never.* The unfortunate sot who had dared now sat on his backside in the alley behind the Hotel Seine, a great decaying colonial edifice that sat on a hill overlooking the capital city of French Guiana.

A moment ago, in the hotel's dark bar, the miscreant at his feet had been hassling a fellow regular, a man in his eighties, a survivor of the dreaded penal colony of Devil's Island. Louis had never spoken to the old man, but he had heard his tale from the barkeep. As with many of the prisoners shipped here from France, he had been doubly sentenced: for every year spent in the island hellhole ten miles off the coast, the fellow was forced to spend an equal number of years in French Guiana afterward. It was a way to ensure a French presence in the colony. And as the government had hoped, most of these pitiable souls ended up staying here. What life did they have back in France after so long?

Louis had often studied this fellow, a kindred soul, another exile. He would watch the man sip his neat bourbons, reading the lines in his aged and despairing face. He valued these quiet moments.

So when the half-drunk Englishman had tripped and bumped into the old man's elbow, knocking over his drink, and then simply tottered on past without the courtesy of apology or acknowledgment, Louis Favre had gained his feet and confronted the man.

"Piss off, Frenchie," the young man had slurred in his face.

Louis continued to block the man's exit from the bar. "You'll buy my dear friend another drink, or we'll have it out, monsieur."

"Bugger off already, you drunk wanker." The man attempted to shove past.

Louis had sighed, then struck out with a fist, bashing the man's nose bloody, and grabbed him by the lapels of his poor suit. Other patrons turned their attention to their own drinks. Louis hauled the rude young man, still dazed from the blow and a night of heavy drinking, through a back door into the alley.

He set to work on earning an apology from the man, not that he could really talk with a mouthful of bloody teeth. By the time Louis was done kicking and beating the man, he lay in a ruin of piss and blood in the alley's filth. He gave the man one final savage kick, hearing a satisfying crack of ribs. With a nod,

Louis retrieved his white Panama hat from atop a rubbish bin and straightened his linen suit. He stared at his shoes, ivory patent leather. Frowning, he plucked out a pristine handkerchief and wiped the blood from the tip of his shoes. He scowled at the Englishman, thought about kicking him one last time, but then studied his newly polished shoes and decided better.

Positioning his hat in place, he reentered the smoky bar and signaled the barman. He pointed to the old gent. "Please refresh my friend's drink."

The Spanish barkeep nodded and reached for a bottle of bourbon.

Louis met his gaze and wagged a finger at him.

The barman bit his lip at the faux pas. Louis always went for the best, even when buying drinks for friends. Duly admonished, the man reached for a bottle of properly aged Glenlivet, the best in the house.

"*Merci.*" With matters rectified, Louis headed for the entrance to the hotel's lobby, almost running into the concierge.

The small-framed man bowed and apologized profusely. "Dr. Favre! I was just coming to find you," he said breathlessly. "I have an overseas call holding for your attention." He passed Louis a folded note. "They refused to leave a message and stressed the call was urgent."

Louis unfolded the slip and read the name, printed neatly: *St. Savin Biochimique Compagnie*. A French drug company. He refolded the paper and tucked it into his breast pocket. "I'll take the call."

"There is a private salon—"

"I know where it is," Louis said. He had taken many of his business calls down here.

With the concierge in tow, Louis strode to the small cubicle beside the hotel's front desk. He left the man at the door and sat in the small upholstered chair that smelled of mold and a mélange of old cologne and sweat. Louis settled to the seat and picked up the phone's receiver. "Dr. Louis Favre," he said crisply.

"*Bonjour*, Dr. Favre," a voice spoke on the other end of the line. "We have a request for your services."

"If you have this number, then I assume you know my pricing schedule."

"We do."

"And may I ask what class of service you require?"

"*Première*."

The single word caused Louis's fingers to tighten on the receiver. First class. It meant a payment over six figures. "Location?"

"The Brazilian rain forest."

"And the objective?"

The man spoke rapidly. Louis listened without taking notes. Each number was fixed in his mind, as was each name, especially *one*. Louis's eyes narrowed. He sat up straighter. The man finished, "The U.S. team must be tracked and whatever they discover must be obtained."

"And the other team?"

There was no answer, just the static of the other line.

"I understand and accept," Louis said. "I'll need to see half the fee in my usual account by close of business tomorrow. Furthermore, any and all details of the U.S. team and its resources should be faxed to my private line as soon as possible." He gave the number quickly.

"It will be done within the hour."

"Très bon."

The line clicked dead, the business settled.

Louis slowly replaced the receiver in its cradle and sat back. The thoughts of the money and the thousand details in setting up his own team were pushed back for now. At this moment, one name shone like burning magnesium across his mind's eye. His new employer had glossed over it, unaware of the significance. If he had been, St. Savin's offer probably would have been considerably less. In fact, Louis would have taken this job for the cost of a cheap bottle of wine. He whispered the name now, tasting it on his tongue.

"Carl Rand."

Seven years ago, Louis Favre had been a biologist employed by the Base Biologique Nationale de Recherches, the premier French science foundation. With a specialty in rain forest ecosystems, Louis had worked throughout the world: Australia, Borneo, Madagascar, the Congo. But for fifteen years, his specialty had been the Amazon rain forest. He had journeyed throughout the region, establishing an international reputation.

That is, until he ran into the damnable Dr. Carl Rand.

The American pharmaceutical entrepreneur had found Louis's methods of research to be a bit suspect, after stumbling upon Louis's interrogation of a local shaman. Dr. Rand had not believed cutting off the man's fingers, one by one, had been a viable way of gleaning information from the stubborn Indian, and no amount of money would convince the simpering American otherwise. Of course, the pile of endangered black caiman carcasses and jaguar pelts found in the village had not helped matters. Dr. Rand seemed incapable of understanding that supplementing one's work with black market income was simply a lifestyle choice.

Unfortunately, Carl and his Brazilian forces had outnumbered his own team. Louis Favre was captured and incarcerated by the Brazilian army. Luckily, he had connections in France and enough money to ply the palms of a few corrupt Brazilian officials in order to slip away with no more than a slap on the wrist.

However, it was the figurative slap to his face that had stung worse. The incident had blackened his good name beyond repair. Penniless, he was forced to flee Brazil for French Guiana. There, always resourceful and with previous contacts in the black market, he scrounged together a mercenary jungle force. During the past five years, his group had protected drug shipments from Colombia, hunted down various rare and endangered animals for private collectors, eliminated a troublesome Brazilian government regulator for a gold-mining operation, even wiped out a small peasant village whose inhabitants objected to a logging company's intrusion onto their lands. It was good business all around.

And now this latest offer: to track a U.S. military

team through the jungle as they searched for Carl Rand's lost expedition and steal whatever they discovered. All in order to be the first one to obtain some regenerative compound believed to have been discovered by Rand's group.

Such a request was not unusual. In the past few years, the race for new rain forest drugs had become more and more frantic, a multibillion-dollar industry. The search for "green gold," the next new wonder drug, had spurred a new "gold rush" here in the Amazon. And in the trackless depths of the forest, where millions of dollars were cast into an economy of dirt-poor farmers and unschooled Indians, betrayals and atrocities were committed daily. There were no spying eyes and no one to tell tales. Each year, the jungle alone consumed thousands from disease, from attack, from injuries. What were a few more—a biologist, an ethnobotanist, a drug researcher?

It was a financial free-for-all.

And Louis Favre was about to join the game, championed by a French pharmaceutical company. Smiling, he stood up. He had been delighted when he heard about Carl Rand's disappearance four years ago. He had gotten drunk that night, toasting the man's misfortune. Now he would pound the final nail in the bastard's coffin by stealing whatever the man had discovered and laying more lives upon his grave.

Unlocking the salon's door, Louis stepped out.

"I hope everything was satisfactory, Dr. Favre," the concierge called politely from his desk.

"Most satisfactory, Claude," he said with a nod. "Most satisfactory indeed." Louis crossed to the hotel's small elevator, an antique cell of wrought iron and wood. It hardly fit two people. He pressed the button for the sixth floor, where his apartment suite lay. He was anxious to share the news.

The elevator clanked, groaned, and sighed its way up to his floor. Once the door was open, Louis hurried down the narrow hall to the farthest room. Like a handful of other guests who had taken up permanent residence in the Hotel Seine, Louis had a suite of rooms: two bedrooms, a cramped kitchen, a broad sitting room with doors that opened upon a wrought-iron balcony, and even a small study lined with bookshelves. The suite was not elaborate, but it suited his needs. The staff was discreet and well accustomed to the eccentricities of the guests.

Louis keyed open his door and pushed inside. Two things struck him immediately. First, a familiar and arousing scent filled the room. It came from a pot on the small gas stovetop, boiling ayahuasca leaves that produced the powerful hallucinogenic tea, *natem*.

Second, he heard the whine of the fax machine coming from the study. His new employers were certainly efficient.

"Tshui!" he called out.

He expected no answer, but as was customary among the Shuar tribespeople, one always announced one's presence when entering a dwelling. He noticed the door to the bedroom slightly ajar.

With a smile, he crossed to the study and watched another sheet of paper roll from the machine and fall to the growing stack. The details of the upcoming mission. "Tshui, I have marvelous news."

Louis retrieved the topmost printout from the faxed pile and glanced at it. It was a list of those who would comprise the U.S. search team.

10:45 P.M. UPDATE from Base Station Alpha

I. **Op. AMAZONIA: Civilian Unit Members**
   (1) Kelly O'Brien, M.D.—MEDEA
   (2) Francis J. O'Brien—Environmental Center, CIA
   (3) Olin Pasternak—Science and Technology Directorate, CIA
   (4) Richard Zane, Ph.D.—Tellux Pharmaceutical research head
   (5) Anna Fong, Ph.D.—Tellux Pharmaceutical employee

II. **Op. AMAZONIA: Mil. Support: 75th Army Ranger Unit**
   CAPTAIN: Craig Waxman
   STAFF SERGEANT: Alberto Kostos
   CORPORALS: Brian Conger, James DeMartini, Rodney Graves, Thomas Graves, Dennis Jorgensen, Kenneth Okamoto, Nolan Warczak, Samad Yamir

III. **Op. AMAZONIA: Locally Recruited**
   (1) Manuel Azevedo—FUNAI, Brazilian national
   (2) Resh Kouwe, Ph.D.—FUNAI, Indigenous Peoples Representative
   (3) Nathan Rand, Ph.D.—Ethnobotanist, U.S. citizen

Louis almost missed the last name on the list. He gripped the faxed printout tighter. *Nathan Rand*, the son of Carl Rand. Of course, it made sense. The boy would not let this team search for his father without accompanying them. He closed his eyes, savoring this boon. It was as if the gods of the dark jungle were aligning in his favor. The revenge he had failed to mete upon the father would fall upon the shoulders of the son. It was almost biblical.

As he stood there, he heard a slight rustle coming from the next room, the master bedroom. He let the paper slip from his fingers back to the pile. He would have time later to review the details and formulate a plan. Right now, he simply wanted to enjoy the serendipity of the moment.

"Tshui!" he called again and crossed to the bedroom door.

He slipped the door open and found the room beyond lit with candles and a single incense burner. His mistress lay naked on the canopy bed. The queen-sized bed was draped in white silk with its mosquito net folded back. The Shuar woman reclined upon pillows atop the ivory sheets. Her deep-bronze skin glowed in the candlelight. Her long black hair was a fan around her, while her eyes were heavy-lidded from both passion and *natem* tea. Two cups lay on the small nightstand, one empty, the other full.

As usual, Louis found his breath simply stolen from him at the sight of his love. He had first met the beauty three years ago in Equador. She had been the wife of a Shuar chieftain, until the fool's infidelity had enraged her. She slew him with his own machete. Though such acts—both the infidelity and the murder—were common among the brutal Shuar, Tshui was banished from the tribe, sent naked into the jungle. None, not even the chieftain's kinsmen, would dare touch her. She was well known throughout the region as one of the rare female shamans, a practitioner of *wawek*, malevolent sorcery. Her skill at poisons, tortures, and the lost art of *tsantza*, headshrinking, was both respected and feared. In fact, the only article of adornment she had worn as she left the village was the shrunken head of her husband, hung on a twined cord and resting between her breasts.

This was how Louis found the woman, a wild, beautiful creature of the jungle. Though he had an estranged wife back in France, Louis had taken the woman as his own. She had not refused, especially when he and his mercenaries slew every man, woman, and child in her village, marking her revenge.

Since that day, the two had been inseparable. Tshui, an accomplished interrogator and wise in the ways of the jungle, accompanied him on all his missions. She continued to collect trophies from each venture.

Around the room, aligned on shelves on all four walls, were forty-three *tsantza*, each head no more than a wizened apple—the eyes and lips sewn closed, the hair trailing over the shelf edges like Spanish moss on trees. Her skill at shrinking heads was amazing. He had watched the entire process once.

Once was enough.

With the skill of a surgeon, she would flay the skin in one piece from the skull of her victim, sometimes while he or she was still alive and screaming. She truly was an artist. After boiling the skin, hair and all, and drying it over hot ashes, she used a bone needle and thread to close the mouth and eyes, then filled the inside with hot pebbles and sand. As the leathery skin shrank, she would mold its shape with her fingers. Tshui had an uncanny ability to sculpt the head into an amazing approximation of the victim's original face.

Louis glanced to her latest work of art. It rested on the far bedside table. It was a Bolivian army officer who had been blackmailing a cocaine shipper. From his trimmed mustache to the straight bangs hanging over his forehead, the detail of her work was amazing. The collection was worthy of the finest museum. In fact, the staff of the Hotel Seine thought Louis was a university anthropologist, collecting these specimens for just such a museum. If any thought otherwise, they knew to keep silent.

"*Ma chérie,*" he said, finding his breath again. "I have wonderful news."

She rolled toward him, reaching in his direction. She made a small sound, encouraging him to join her. Tshui seldom spoke. A word here or there. Otherwise, like some jungle cat, she was all eyes, motions, and soft purrs.

Louis could not resist. He knocked off his hat and slipped from his jacket. In moments, he was as naked as she. His own body was lean, muscled, and crisscrossed with scars. He swallowed the draught of *natem* laid out for him while Tshui lazily traced one of his scars down his belly to his inner thigh. A shiver trembled up his back.

As the drug swept through him, heightening his senses, he fell upon his woman. She opened to him, and he sank gratefully into her warmth. He kissed her deeply, while she raked his back with sharpened nails.

Soon, colors and lights played across his vision. The room spun slightly from the alkaloids in the tea. For a moment, it seemed the scores of shrunken heads were watching their play, the eyes of the dead upon him as he thrust into the woman. The audience aroused him further. He pinned Tshui under him, his back arching as he drove into her again and again, a scream clenched in his chest.

All around him were faces staring down, watching with blind eyes.

Louis had one final thought before being consumed fully by his passion and the exquisite pain. A final trophy to add to these shelves, a memento from the son of the man who had ruined him: *the head of Nathan Rand.*

ACT TWO

Under the Canopy

PERIWINKLE
family: *Apocynaceae*
genus: *Vinca*
species: *Minor, Major*
common names: *Periwinkle, Cezayirmeneksesi,*
Common Periwinkle, Vincapervinc
parts used: *Whole Plant*
properties/actions: *Analgesic, Antibacterial, Antimicrobial,*
Antiinflammatory, Astringent, Cardiotonic, Carminative,
Depurative, Diuretic, Emmenagogue, Febrifuge, Hemostat,
Hypotensive, Lactogogue, Hepatoprotective, Sedative,
Sialogogue, Spasmolytic, Stomachic, Tonic, Vulnerary

FOUR

Wauwai

AUGUST 7, 8:12 A.M.
EN ROUTE OVER THE AMAZON JUNGLE

Nathan stared out the helicopter's windows. Even through the sound-dampening earphones, the roar of the blades was deafening, isolating each passenger in his own cocoon of noise.

Below, a vast sea of green spread to the horizon in all directions. From this vantage, it was as if the entire world were just forest. The only breaks in the featureless expanse of the continuous canopy were the occasional giant trees, the emergents, that poked their leafy crowns above their brethren, great monsters of the forest that served as nesting sites for harpy eagles and toucans. The only other breaks were the half-hidden dark rivers, snaking lazily through the forest.

Otherwise, the jungle remained supreme, impenetrable, endless.

Nathan leaned his forehead against the glass. Was

his father down there somewhere? And if not, were there at least answers?

Deep inside, Nathan felt a seed of anxiety, bitter and sour. Could he handle what he discovered? After four years of not knowing, Nate had learned one thing. Time did indeed heal all wounds, but it left a nasty, unforgiving scar.

After his father's disappearance, Nate had isolated himself from the world, first in the bottom of a bottle of Jack Daniel's, then in the embrace of stronger drugs. Back in the States, his therapists had used phrases such as *abandonment issues*, *trust conflicts*, and *clinical depression*. But Nate experienced it as a faithlessness in life. With the exception of Manny and Kouwe, he had formed no deep friendships. He had become too hard, too numb, too scarred.

Only after returning to the jungle had Nate found some semblance of peace. But now this . . .

Was he ready to reopen those old wounds? To face that pain?

The earphone radio clicked on with a rasp of static, and the pilot's voice cut momentarily through the rotor's roar. "We're twenty klicks from Wauwai. But there's smoke on the horizon."

Nathan peered ahead, yet all he could see was the terrain below and to the side. Wauwai would serve as a secondary field base for the search team, a launching-off point from which to supply and monitor those trekking through the forest. Two hours ago, the three Hueys, along with the sleek black Comanche, had set off from São Gabriel, carrying the initial supplies, gear, armament, and personnel. After the expedition proceeded into the jungle later today, the Hueys would serve as a flying supply chain between Wauwai and São Gabriel, ferrying additional supplies, men, and fuel. Meanwhile, the Comanche would remain at Wauwai, a black bird reserved in case of an emergency. Its armament and long-range capabilities would help protect the team from the air if necessary.

That had been the plan.

"The smoke appears to be coming from our destination," the pilot continued. "The village is burning."

Nathan pulled away from the window. *Burning?* He glanced around the cabin. In addition to the two O'Briens, he shared the space with Professor Kouwe, Richard Zane, and Anna Fong. The seventh and final passenger was the hard-faced man who had sat across the conference table from Nathan during the debriefing, the one with the ugly scar across his neck. He had been introduced this morning as Olin Pasternak, another CIA agent, one associated with the administration's Science and Technology division. He found the man's ice-blue eyes staring right back at him, his face an unreadable stoic mask.

To his side, he watched Frank pull a microphone up to his lips. "Can we still land?"

"I can't be sure from this distance, sir," the pilot answered. "Captain Waxman is proceeding ahead to survey the situation."

Nathan watched one of the helicopters break formation and speed forward as their own craft slowed. As they waited, the Huey banked around, and Nathan spotted a column of smoke rising from the blanket of greenery near the horizon. It climbed high into the blue skies. The other passengers shifted closer to peer out the port-side windows.

Kelly O'Brien leaned near his shoulder, eyes on the smoke. He watched her lips move, but the noise and the earphones blocked her words. She pulled back and caught him staring at her.

Her eyes flicked away, and a slight blush reddened her cheeks.

The pilot came on over the radio. "Folks, it looks like we have an okay to proceed from the captain. The landing field is upwind of the fires. Please ready yourselves for landing."

Everyone settled back into their seats and snapped their buckles into place. In short order, the bevy of helicopters was circling the village. Each pilot was careful to keep the wash from his rotor from blowing the smoke toward the landing field. Though still unable to see the source of the flames, Nathan watched a chain of people passing buckets from the river as the helicopter aligned for landing.

As they descended, a clapboard church with a whitewashed steeple came into view. The source of the fire was on its far side, and someone stood on the church's roof, soaking down its shingles.

Then the skids of the helicopter settled to the ground with a slight bump, and Frank signaled for everyone to disembark.

Nathan tugged off his earphones and was assaulted by the growl of the rotors. He unbuckled his shoulder harness and climbed from the helicopter. Once clear of the rotors, he stretched and surveyed the area. The last of the Hueys settled to earth on the far side of the field. The tilled soil and barren rows were telltale signs that the landing field must once have been the village's garden.

Across the yard, the Rangers were already busy. A handful were offloading gear and supplies, while most of the others trotted toward the front of the church to help with the fires.

Slowly, the noise of the helicopters dissipated, and voices could be heard again: shouted orders, yells from beyond the church, the chatter of soldiers hauling equipment.

Kelly stepped to Nathan's side with Frank in tow. "We should see if we can find the padre who found Agent Clark. Interview him, so we can be on our way."

Frank nodded, and the two headed for the rear door of the church.

Someone clapped Nate on the shoulder. It was Professor Kouwe. "Let's go help," the older man said, pointing toward the smoke.

Nathan followed the professor through the fields and around the side of the church. What he found on the far side was chaos: people running with buckets and shovels, smoke billowing in every direction, flames rampant.

"My God," Nate said.

A village of a hundred or so small homes lay between the church and the river. Three-quarters of them were burning.

He and the professor hurried forward, adding the strength of their backs to the water brigade. Working around them were a mix of brown-skinned Indians, white missionaries, and uniformed Rangers. After about an hour of laboring, they all looked the same, just soot-covered rescuers choking and coughing on the smoke.

Nathan ran with buckets, dousing flames, concentrating on maintaining a fire break around the burning section of the village. It was up to them to hold the flames at bay. Inside the fire zone, the blaze consumed all the palm-thatched structures, turning homes into torches in mere seconds. But with the additional men, the fire was contained at last. The conflagration quickly died down as all the homes were consumed within the fire zone. Only a few glowing embers dotted the smoky ruined landscape.

During the crisis, Nate had lost track of the professor and now found himself resting beside a tall, broad-shouldered Brazilian. The man looked close to tears. He mumbled something in Portuguese that sounded like a prayer. Nate guessed he was one of the missionaries.

"I'm sorry," Nate said in Portuguese, tugging away the scrap of cloth that had been shielding his nose and mouth. "Was anyone killed?"

"Five. All children." The man's voice cracked. "But many others were sickened by the smoke."

"What happened here?"

The missionary wiped the soot from his face with a handkerchief. "It was m . . . my fault. I should've known better." He glanced over his shoulder to the steepled church. Aside from being stained with ash and smoke, it stood unharmed. He covered his eyes, and his shoulders shook. It took him another moment to speak. "It was my decision to send the man's body to Manaus."

Nathan suddenly realized to whom he was speaking. "Padre Batista?" It was the mission's leader, the one who had found Gerald Clark.

The tall Brazilian nodded. "May God forgive me."

Nate guided Garcia Luiz Batista away from the blackened ruins of the village and into untouched green fields. He quickly introduced himself as he led the man back to his church. En route, he passed one of the Rangers, covered in soot and sweat, and asked him to send the O'Briens to the church.

With a sharp nod, the Ranger took off.

Nate walked the padre up the wooden steps and through the double doors. The interior was dark and cool. Varnished wooden pews lined the way to the altar and giant mahogany crucifix. The room was mostly empty. A few Indians lay sprawled, exhausted, both on the floor and on pews. Nate led the church's leader toward the front and settled him in the first pew.

The man sagged into his seat, his eyes fixed on the crucifix. "It's all my fault." He bowed his head and lifted his hands in prayer.

Nathan remained quiet, giving the man a private moment. The church door swung open, and he spotted Frank and Kelly. Professor Kouwe was with them. All three were covered in ash from head to toe. He waved them over.

The arrival of the other three drew Padre Batista's attention from his prayers. Nathan made introductions all around. Once done, he sat beside the padre. "Tell me what happened. How did the fires start?"

Garcia glanced around at the others, then sighed heavily and looked at his toes. "It was my own short-sightedness."

Kelly sat on the man's other side. "What do you mean?" she asked softly.

After a moment more, the padre spoke again. "On the night the poor man stumbled out of the forest, a shaman of the Yanomamo tribe scolded me for taking the man into the mission. He warned me that the man's body must be burned." The padre glanced to Nathan. "How could I do that? He surely had family. Maybe he was even a Christian."

Nathan patted his hand. "Of course."

"But I should not have so easily dismissed the Indians' superstitions. I had put too much faith in their conversion to Catholicism. They'd even been baptized." The padre shook his head.

Nate understood. "It's not your fault. Some beliefs are too ingrained to be washed away in a single baptism."

Padre Batista sagged. "At first, all seemed well. The shaman was still angered at my decision not to burn the body, but he accepted that at least it was gone from the village. This seemed to appease him."

"What changed that?" Kelly asked.

"A week later, a couple of children in the village developed fevers. It was nothing new. Such ailments are commonplace. But the shaman decided these illnesses were the sign of a curse from the dead man."

Nate nodded. He had seen firsthand such assessments himself. In most Indian tribes, illness was considered not only due to injury or disease, but often to a spell cast by the shaman of another village. Wars had broken out over such accusations.

"There was nothing I could do to dissuade him. In another few days, three more children fell ill, one of them from the Yanomamo *shabano*. The whole village grew tense. In fear, entire families packed up and left. Every night, drums beat and chanting could be heard." Garcia closed his eyes. "I radioed for medical assistance. But when a doctor arrived from Junta four days later, none of the Indians would let the man examine their children. The Yanomamo shaman had won them over. I tried to plead, but they refused any medical help. Instead, they left the little ones in the care of that witch doctor."

Nathan bristled at this term. He glanced to Professor Kouwe, who gave a small shake of his head, indicating Nate should remain silent.

The padre continued. "Then last night, one of the children died. A great wailing consumed the village. To cover up his failure, the shaman declared the village cursed. He warned that all should leave here. I tried my best to calm the panic, but the shaman had the others under his spell. Just before dawn, he and his fellow Yanomamo tribesmen set fire to their own roundhouse, then fled into the jungle." Garcia was now openly weeping. "The . . . the monster had left the sick children inside. He burned them all alive."

The padre covered his face with his hands. "With so few still in the village to help fight the fire, the flames spread through the huts. If you all had not come and helped, we could have lost everything. My church, my flock."

Nathan placed a hand on the man's shoulder. "Don't despair. We can help you rebuild." He glanced over to Kelly's brother for confirmation.

Frank cleared his throat. "Of course. A contingent of Rangers and researchers are going to remain here after we head into the jungle. As guests here, I'm sure they'll be more than willing to haul in supplies with their helicopters and lend you manpower to rebuild the village out of the ashes."

The man's words seemed to strengthen the padre. "God bless you." He wiped his eyes and nose with his handkerchief.

"We'll do all we can," Kelly assured him. "But, padre, time is of the essence for us, too. We hope to begin tracking the dead man's trail before it grows any colder."

"Of course, of course . . ." Garcia said in a tired voice, and stood. "I'll tell you all I know."

It was a short talk. The padre explained as he led them past the altar to the common rooms of the church. The dining room had been converted into a makeshift hospital for smoke-inhalation victims, but no one appeared seriously injured. Garcia related how he had convinced a few Indians to track the dead man's trail, in case the fellow had any companions out there. The trail led to one of the tributaries of the Jarurá River. No boat was found, but the tracks seemed to follow the offshoot's course, heading west into the most remote sections of the rain forest. The Indian trackers feared going any farther.

Kelly leaned on a window overlooking the rear garden. "Can someone show us this tributary?"

Garcia nodded. He had washed his face and seemed to have collected himself. Steel had entered his voice and demeanor as the initial shock wore away. "I can get my assistant, Henaowe, to show you." He pointed to a small Indian.

Nathan was surprised to see the man was Yano-mamo.

"He was the only one of the tribe who remained behind," Garcia said with a sigh. "At least the love of our Lord Jesus was able to save one of them."

The padre waved his assistant over and spoke rapidly in Yanomamo. Nathan was surprised at how fluent the priest was in the dialect.

Henaowe nodded, agreeing, but Nathan saw the fear in his eyes. Saved or not, deep-seated superstitions still ruled the man.

The group proceeded back outside, the damp heat falling upon them like a wet wool blanket. They skirted around the helicopters to find the Rangers had been busy. A line of rucksacks, heavily packed, lay in the dirt. A Ranger was positioned behind each one.

Captain Waxman was inspecting both his men and their gear. He spotted the group and straightened. "We're ready to head out whenever you give the go." Waxman, in his forties, was pure military: stone-faced, broad-shouldered, his field uniform crisp with pressed creases. Even his brown hair had been shaved to a stubble atop his head.

"We're ready now," Frank said. "We've got some-one here to set us on the right trail." He nodded to the small Indian.

The captain nodded and turned sharply. "Load up!" he called to his men.

Kelly led their group to another row of back-packs, each about half the size of the Rangers' ruck-sacks. There, Nathan found the last members of the expedition. Anna Fong was in deep conversation with Richard Zane, both in matching khaki outfits with the Tellux logo emblazoned on the shoulders. To their side stood Olin Pasternak, sporting a clean but clearly well-worn set of gray coveralls with black boots. He bent down to pick up the largest of the packs. Nate knew it contained their satellite communication gear. But as he hoisted the pack, the man's attention was not on the fragile gear, but on the expedition's final member . . . or rather *members*.

Nate smiled. He had not seen Manny since they had left from São Gabriel. The Brazilian biologist had been on one of the other Hueys. The reason for the separate flight was clear. Manny waved to Nate, a whip in one hand, the other holding a leather leash.

"So how did Tor-tor handle the flight?" Nathan asked.

Manny patted the two-hundred-pound jaguar with the side of his whip. "Like a kitten. Nothing like the wonders of modern chemistry."

Nathan watched the cat wobble a little from the aftereffects of the tranquilizer. Stretching forward to sniff at Nate's pant leg, Tor-tor seemed to recognize his scent, and nuzzled him half drunkenly.

"The big fellow's always had a thing for you," Manny said with a chuckle.

Nate bent to one knee and rubbed the cat's jowls, cuffing him lightly under the chin. This earned him a growled purr of appreciation. "God, he is so much bigger than the last time I saw him."

Olin Pasternak scowled at the beast, then mumbled under his breath and turned away, clearly unimpressed by the newest addition to the team.

Nathan straightened. Tor-tor's inclusion had

been a hard sell, but Manny had persisted. Tor-tor was close to being sexually mature and needed to log more jungle time. This trek would be of benefit to the cat. Additionally, the jaguar had been well trained by Manny and could prove of use—both in protection and in tracking.

Nathan had added his own support. If the team wished to convince any Indians into cooperating, the presence of Tor-tor could go a long way toward winning them over. The jaguar was revered by all Indians. To have one accompany the expedition would give the team instant validity.

Anna Fong had agreed.

Slowly Frank and Captain Waxman had been worn down, and Tor-tor was allowed to join the expedition.

Kelly eyed the cat from a safe distance. "We should gear up."

Nathan nodded and picked up his own small pack. It contained only the essential supplies: hammock, mosquito netting, a bit of dry rations, a change of clothes, machete, water bottle, and filter pump. He could travel months in the jungle with little else. What with the wealth of the forest readily available— from various fruits and berries to roots and edible plants to abundant game and fish—there was little need to haul additional food.

Still, there was one other essential piece of equipment. Nathan hooked his own short-barreled shotgun over a shoulder. Though the team was backed by the Rangers' weaponry, Nate preferred to have a little firepower of his own.

"Let's get going," Kelly said. "We've already lost

the morning putting out the fires." The slender
woman hefted her own pack to her shoulders, and
Nate couldn't help but stare at her long legs. He
forced his gaze upward. Her pack had a large red
cross printed on its back, marking the team's medical
supplies.

Frank ran down the line of civilian team members,
making sure all was in readiness. He stopped in front
of Nate, pulled out a faded baseball cap from a back
pocket, and tugged it in place.

Nate recognized it as the same one from when he
had first seen the man at São Gabriel's hospital. "Fan?"
he asked, pointing to the Boston Red Sox logo.

"And a good-luck charm," Frank added, then
turned to the group. "Let's set out!"

In short order, the eighteen-man team tromped
into the jungle, led for the moment by a small, wide-
eyed Indian.

Kelly had never been in a jungle. In preparation for
this trip, she had scanned books and articles, but the
first sight of the rain forest was not what she had
expected.

As she followed the four Rangers in the lead, she
craned around in wonder. Contrary to old movies,
the understory of the Amazon rain forest was not a
clotted mass of clinging vines and overgrown vegetation. Instead, it was more like they were marching
through a green cathedral. A dense canopy of woven
tree branches arched overhead, absorbing most of the
sunlight and casting everything in a greenish glow.
Kelly had read that less than 10 percent of the sun's
light pierced through the unbroken green tent to

reach the jungle floor. Because of this, the lowest level of the forest, where they walked now, was surprisingly clear of vegetation. Here the jungle was a world of shadow and decomposition, the domain of insects, fungi, and roots.

Still, the lack of green vegetation didn't necessarily make trekking through the pathless forest an easy journey. Rotted logs and branches lay everywhere, frosted with yellow mold and white mushrooms. Under her boots, a slick mulch of decaying black leaves threatened her footing, while buttress roots that supported the gigantic trees in the thin soil snaked under the leaves and added to the risk of a twisted ankle.

And though the vegetation down at this level was scant, it was not nonexistent. The floor was festooned with fan-tailed ferns, thorny bromeliads, graceful orchids, and slender palms, and everywhere around were draped the ubiquitous ropelike vines called lianas.

The sound of a slap drew her attention around.

Her brother rubbed at his neck. "Damn flies."

Kelly reached into a pocket and passed a plastic bottle of insect repellent to Frank. "Put more on."

He doused his exposed limbs and rubbed some on his neck.

Nathan stepped beside her. He had donned an Australian bush hat, and looked like some cross between Indiana Jones and Crocodile Dundee. His blue eyes sparkled with amusement in the jungle gloom. "You're wasting your time with that repellent," he said to Frank. "Anything you put on will be sweated off your skin in minutes."

Kelly couldn't argue with that. After just fifteen minutes of trekking, she felt damp everywhere. The humidity under the canopy had to be close to a hundred percent. "Then what do you suggest for the bugs?"

Nathan shrugged, wearing a crooked grin. "You surrender. You ignore them. It's a battle you can't win. Here it's an eat-or-be-eaten world, and sometimes you have to simply pay the price."

"With my own blood?" Frank asked.

"Don't complain. That's getting off cheap. There are much worse insects out there, and I don't just mean the big ones, like bird-eating spiders or foot-long black scorpions. It's the little ones that'll get you. Are you familiar with the assassin bug?"

"No, I don't think so," Frank said.

Kelly shook her head, too.

"Well, it has the unpleasant habit of biting and defecating at the same time. Then when the victim scratches the wound, he drives the feces loaded with the protozoan *Tripanozoma crusii* into the bloodstream. Then in anywhere from one to twenty years you die due to damage to the brain or heart."

Frank paled and stopped scratching at the fly bite on his neck.

"Then there are the blackflies that transmit worms to the eyeball and cause a disease called river blindness. And sand flies that can trigger Leishmaniasis, a leprosy type of disease."

Kelly frowned at the botanist's attempt to shake her brother. "I'm well familiar with the transmittable diseases out here. Yellow fever, dengue fever, malaria, cholera, typhoid." She hiked her medical pack higher on her shoulders. "I'm prepared for the worst."

"And are you prepared for the candiru?"

Her brow crinkled. "What type of disease is that?"

"It's not a disease. It's a common little fish in the waters here, sometimes called the toothpick fish. It's a slender creature, about two inches long, and lives parasitically in the gills of larger fish. It has the nasty habit of swimming up the urethras of human males and lodging there."

"Lodging there?" Frank asked, wincing.

"It spreads its gill spines and embeds itself in place, blocking the bladder and killing you most excruciatingly in about twenty-four hours."

"How do you get rid of it?"

By now, Kelly had recognized the little fish's description and nasty habits. She had indeed read about them. She turned to her brother and said matter-of-factly, "The only cure is to cut the victim's penis off and extract the fish."

Frank flinched, half covering himself. "Cut his penis off?"

Nate shrugged. "Welcome to the jungle."

Kelly scowled at him, knowing the man was only trying to spook them. But from his grin, she could tell it was mostly all in good fun.

"Then there are the snakes . . ." Nate continued.

"I think that's enough," Professor Kouwe said behind them, rescuing the siblings from Dr. Rand's further lecturing. He stepped forward. "While the jungle must be respected as Nathan has suggested so eloquently, it's as much a place of beauty as danger. It contains the ability to cure as well as sicken."

"And that's why we're all out here," a new voice said behind them.

Kelly turned. It was Dr. Richard Zane. Over his shoulder, she noticed Anna Fong and Olin Pasternak deep in conversation. And beyond them, Manuel Azevedo stalked with his jaguar alongside the Rangers at the rear.

She turned around and saw that the grin on Nate's face had vanished. His expression had hardened at the intrusion by the Tellux representative. "And what would you know of the jungle?" Nate asked. "You've not set foot out of the main offices of Tellux in Chicago in over four years . . . about the time my father vanished, as I recall."

Richard Zane rubbed his small trimmed goatee and maintained his casual countenance, but Kelly had not missed the flash of fire in the man's eyes. "I know what you think of me, Dr. Rand. It was one of the reasons I *volunteered* for this expedition. You know I was a friend of your—"

Nathan took a fast step in the man's direction, one hand balled into a fist. "Don't say it!" he spat out. "Don't say you were a *friend* of my father! I came to you, begged you to continue the search after the government stopped. And you refused. I read the memo you dispatched from Brasilia back to the States: 'I see no further benefit in extending Tellux's financial resources in a futile search for Dr. Carl Rand. Our monies are better spent in new endeavors.' Do you remember those words, words that damned my father! If you had pressed the corporate office—"

"The result would've been the same," Zane said between clenched teeth. "You were always so naive. The decision was made long before I gave my report."

"Bullshit," Nathan said.

"Tellux was hit by over three hundred separate lawsuits after the expedition's disappearance. From families, from underwriters, from insurance companies, from the Brazilian government, from the NSF. Tellux was under assault from all sides. It was one of the reasons we had to merge Eco-tek's assets. It helped insulate us from other rapacious pharmaceutical companies. They were circling like sharks around our financially bleeding carcass. We could not continue funding a search that seemed hopeless. We had a bigger fight on our hands."

Nathan continued to glower.

"The decision *had* already been made."

"You'll excuse me if I don't shed tears for Tellux."

"If we had lost our battle, thousands of families would have lost their jobs. Hard decisions had to be made, and I won't apologize for them."

Nate and Zane continued to stare each other down.

Professor Kouwe attempted to mediate. "For now, let the past lie in the past. If we're to succeed here, I suspect we'll all need to work together. I suggest a truce."

After a pause, Zane held out a hand.

Nathan glanced to the open palm, then turned away. "Let's go."

Zane shook his head and lowered his hand. He met the professor's eyes. "Thanks for trying."

Kouwe watched Nate's departing back. "Give him time. Though he tries to hide it, he's still in a lot of pain."

Kelly stared after Nathan. He walked stiffly, shoulders back. She tried to imagine losing her mother, then her father, but it was a loss she could not comprehend. It was a well of pain from which she didn't know if she could have emerged. Especially alone.

She glanced to her brother, suddenly glad he was here.

A call rang out from far ahead. One of the Rangers. "We've reached the river!"

As the team continued along, paralleling the river, Nathan found himself lagging behind the others. To his right, glimpses of the river peeked from the tangle of vegetation that bordered the small brown tributary. They had been following it now for almost four hours. Nathan estimated they had traveled about twelve miles. The going was slow while one of the Rangers, a corporal named Nolan Warczak, a skilled tracker, kept them on the proper trail.

An Indian guide could have moved with more assurance and set a faster pace. But after reaching the tributary, the small Yanomamo tribesman from Wauwai had refused to go any farther. He had pointed to clear footprints in the loam that led deeper into the forest, following the watercourse.

"You go," he had mumbled in stilted Portuguese. "I stay here with Padre Batista."

So they had set off, determined to cover as much distance as possible before nightfall. But Corporal

Warczak was a cautious tracker, proceeding at a snail's pace. This left much time for Nathan to review his heated outburst with Richard Zane. It had taken him this long to cool off and consider the man's words. Maybe he had been narrow-minded and had not considered all the factors involved.

Off to his left, the crackle of dead twigs announced Manny's approach. He and Tor-tor had kept a bit of distance between themselves and the rest. When the large cat was nearby the Rangers were edgy, fingering their M-16s. The only one of the unit who showed curiosity about the jaguar was Corporal Dennis Jorgensen. He accompanied Manny now, asking questions about the cat.

"So how much does he eat in a day?" The tall corporal took off his slouch hat and swiped the sweat from his brow. He had shockingly white hair and pale blue eyes, clearly of some Nordic descent.

Manny patted the cat. "Somewhere around ten pounds of meat, but he's been living a pretty sedentary life with me. Out in the wild, you almost have to double that amount."

"And how are you going to keep feeding him out here?"

Manny nodded to Nathan as he joined him. "He'll have to hunt. It was the reason I brought him along."

"And if he fails?"

Manny glanced to the soldiers behind them. "There's always other sources of meat."

Jorgensen's face paled a bit, then realized Manny was joking and nudged him with an elbow. "Very funny." He fell back to join the others in his unit.

Manny turned his attention to Nate. "So how're you holding up? I heard about that row with Zane."

"I'm fine," he said with a long sigh. Tor-tor nudged his leg with a furry muzzle, and Nate scratched the jaguar behind the ear. "Just feeling damn foolish."

"Nothing to feel foolish about. I trust that guy about as far as it would take Tor-tor to run his sorry ass down. Which, believe me, wouldn't be far." He pointed a hand forward. "Did you see that dandy outfit he's wearing? Has he ever been in the real jungle?"

Nate smiled, cheered by his friend.

"Now that Dr. Fong. She looks damn fine in her outfit." Manny glanced to him with one eyebrow raised. "I wouldn't kick her out of my hammock for eating crackers. And Kelly O'Brien—"

A commotion ahead interrupted Manny. Voices were raised, and the group was stopped, gathered near a bend in the river. Manny and Nate hurried forward.

As Nate stepped into the throng, he found Anna Fong and Professor Kouwe bent near a dugout canoe that had been pulled fully onto the bank and clumsily covered with palm fronds.

"The trail led here," Kelly said.

Nathan glanced at her. The doctor's face, covered in a sheen of sweat, was almost aglow. Her hair had been pulled back with a rolled green handkerchief that served as a headband.

Professor Kouwe stood with a palm frond in his hand. "These were torn from a *mwapu* palm." He flipped to show the ragged end of the branch. "Not cut, torn."

Kelly nodded. "Agent Clark had no knives with him when he was found."

Professor Kouwe ran a finger along the dried and yellowing tips of the fronds. "And from the rate of decay, this was torn from the living plant around two weeks ago."

Frank bent closer. "Around the time when Gerald Clark stumbled into the village."

"Exactly."

Kelly's voice grew excited. "Then there's no doubt he must have used this boat to get here."

Nathan stared out at the small river. Both banks were thick with dense walls of vegetation: vines, palms, bushes, mosses, stranglers, and ferns. The river itself was about thirty feet across, a featureless silty brown flow. Near the shores, the waters were clear enough to see the muddy, rocky riverbed, but within a few feet visibility vanished.

Anything could be lurking under the water: snakes, caimans, piranhas. There were even catfish so large that they were known to bite the feet off unsuspecting swimmers.

Captain Waxman shoved forward. "So where do we go from here? We can airlift boats to our position, but then what?"

Anna Fong raised a hand. "I think I might be able to answer that." She shoved off more of the palm fronds. Her small fingers ran along the inside of the canoe. "From the pattern in which this canoe was chopped, and from the painted red edges, this had to come from a Yanomamo tribe. They're the only ones who construct canoes in such a manner."

Nate knelt down and ran his own hands along the interior of the canoe. "She's right. Gerald Clark must have obtained or perhaps stolen this canoe from the tribe. If we travel upriver, we can ask any of the Ya-nomamo Indians if they've seen a white man pass through or if any of their canoes have gone missing." He turned to Frank and Kelly. "From there, we can begin tracking again."

Frank nodded and turned to Captain Waxman. "You mentioned boats."

He nodded sharply. "I'll radio in our position and have the Hueys airlift in the pontoons. It'll eat up the remaining daylight, so we might as well set up an early camp for today."

With a plan in place, everyone began to busy them-selves setting up their homestead a short distance from the river. A fire was started. Kouwe collected a few hogplums and sawari nuts from the nearby forest, while Manny, after sending Tor-tor into the jungle to hunt, used a pole and net to catch a few jungle trout.

Within the course of the next hour, the roar of he-licopters rattled the forest, causing birds and monkeys to screech and holler, flitting and leaping through the canopy. Three large crates were lowered into the wa-ter and pulled to shore by ropes. Packed inside were self-inflating pontoons with small outboard motors, what the Rangers called "rubber raiders." By the time the sun had begun to set, the three black boats were tethered to shoreside trees, ready for tomorrow's travel.

As the Rangers worked, Nathan had set up his own hammock and was now skillfully stretching his mosquito netting around it. He saw Kelly having trouble and went to her aid.

"You want to make sure the netting is spread so that none of it touches the hammock, or the night feeders will attack you right through the fabric."

"I can manage," she said, but her brow was furrowed in frustration.

"Let me show you." He used small stones and bits of forest flotsam to pin her netting away from her hammock, creating a silky canopy around her bed.

Off to the side, Frank was fighting his own netting. "I don't know why we can't just use sleeping bags. They were fine whenever I went camping."

"This is the jungle," Nate answered. "If you sleep on the ground, you'll find all sorts of nasty creatures sharing your bed by morning. Snakes, lizards, scorpions, spiders. But be my guest."

Frank grumbled but continued to wrestle with his own bed site. "Fine, I'll sleep in the damn hammock. But what's so important about the netting anyway? We've been plagued by mosquitoes all day."

"At night, they're a thousand times worse. And if the bugs don't bleed you dry, the vampire bats will."

"Vampire bats?" Kelly asked.

"They're all over the place here. At night, you want to be careful even sneaking off to the latrine. They'll attack anything warm-blooded."

Kelly's eyes grew wide.

"You're vaccinated against rabies, right?" he asked. She nodded slowly.

"Good."

She glanced over the bed he had helped make,

then turned to him, her face only inches from his as he straightened from his crouch. "Thanks."

Nathan was again struck by her eyes, an emerald green with a hint of gold. "Y . . . You're welcome." He turned to the fire and saw that others were gathering for an early evening meal. "Let's see what's for dinner."

Around the campfire, the flames were not the only thing heating up. Nathan found Manny and Richard Zane in midargument.

"How could you possibly be against placing constraints on the logging industry?" Manny said, stirring his filleted fish in the frying pan. "Commercial logging is the single largest destroyer of rain forests worldwide. Here in the Amazon we're losing one acre of forest every *second*."

Richard Zane sat on a log, no longer wearing his khaki jacket. His sleeves were rolled up, seemingly ready to fight. "Those statistics are greatly exaggerated by environmentalists. They're based on bad science and generated more by a desire to scare than to educate. More realistic evidence from satellite photography shows that ninety percent of the Brazilian rain forest is still intact."

Manny was near to blustering now. "Even if the rate of deforestation is exaggerated as you claim, whatever is lost is lost forever. We're losing over a hundred species of plants and animals every single day. Lost forever."

"So you say," Richard Zane said calmly. "The idea that a cleared rain forest can't grow back is an outdated myth. After eight years of commercial logging in the rain forests of Indonesia, the rate of recovery of both native plants and animals far exceeded expectations. And here in your own forests, the same is true. In 1982, miners cleared a large tract of forest in western Brazil. Fifteen years later, scientists returned to find that the rejuvenated forest is virtually indistinguishable from the surrounding forest. Such cases suggest that sustainable logging is possible, and that man and nature can coexist here."

Nate found himself drawn into the discussion. *How can the jackass actually advocate rain forest destruction?* "What about peasants burning forestland for grazing and agriculture? I suppose you support that, too."

"Of course," Zane said. "In the forests of western America, we think it's healthy for fires to burn periodically through a mature forest. It shakes things up. Why is it any different here? When dominant species are removed by either logging or burning, it allows for the growth of what are termed 'suppressed species,' the smaller shrubs and plants. And it is in fact these very plants that are of the most medicinal value. So why not allow a little burning and logging? It's good for all concerned."

Kelly spoke into the stunned silence. "But you're ignoring the global implications. Like the greenhouse effect. Aren't the rain forests the proverbial 'lungs of the planet,' a major source of oxygen?"

"'Proverbial' is the key word, I'm afraid," Zane said sadly. "Newest research from weather satellites shows that the forests contribute little if any to the world's oxygen supply. It's a closed system. While the greenery of the canopy produces abundant oxygen, the supply is totally consumed by the fire of decomposition below, resulting in no net oxygen production. Again, the only real areas of positive production are in those regions of secondary forest growth, where new young trees are producing abundant oxygen. So in fact, controlled deforestation is beneficial to the world's atmosphere."

Nathan listened, balanced between disbelief and anger. "And what of those who live in the forest? In the past five hundred years, the number of indigenous tribes has dwindled from over ten million to under two hundred thousand. I suppose that's good, too."

Richard Zane shook his head. "Of course not. That's the true tragedy here. When a medicine man dies without passing on his experience, then the world loses great volumes of irreplaceable knowledge. It's one of the reasons I kept pushing for funds to finance your own research among the fading tribes. It's invaluable work."

Nathan narrowed his eyes with suspicion. "But the forest and its people are intertwined. Even if what you say is true, deforestation does destroy some species. You can't argue against that."

"Sure, but the green movement exaggerates the true number lost."

"Still, even a single species can be significant. Such as the Madagascan periwinkle."

Zane's face reddened. "Well, that surely is a rare exception. You can hardly think that such a discovery is common."

"The Madagascan periwinkle?" Kelly asked, confusion in her eyes.

"The rosy periwinkle of Madagascar is the source

of two potent anticancer drugs—vinblastine and vincristine."

Kelly's brows rose with recognition. "Used in the treatment of Hodgkin's disease, lymphomas, and many childhood cancers."

Nate nodded. "These drugs save thousands of children every year. But the plant that generated this life-saving drug is now extinct in Madagascar. What if these properties of the rosy periwinkle hadn't been discovered in time? How many children would have needlessly died?"

"Like I said, the periwinkle is a rare finding."

"And how would you know? With all your talk of statistics and satellite photography, it comes down to one fact. Every plant has the potential to cure. Each species is invaluable. Who knows what drug could be lost through unchecked deforestation? What rare plant could hold the cure to AIDS? To diabetes? To the thousands of cancers that plague mankind?"

"Or perhaps even to cause limbs to regenerate?" Kelly added pointedly.

Richard Zane frowned and stared into the flames. "Who can say?"

"My point exactly," Nate finished.

Frank stepped up to the flames, seemingly oblivious to the heated debate that had been waged over the campfire. "You're burning the fish," the tall man said, pointing to the black smoke rising from the forgotten frying pan.

Manny chuckled and pulled the pan off the fire. "Thank goodness for the practical Mr. O'Brien, or we'd be eating dry rations tonight."

Frank nudged Kelly. "Olin almost has the satellite feed hooked to the laptop." He checked his watch. "We should be able to connect stateside in another hour."

"Good." Kelly glanced over to where Olin Pasternak was busy around a compact satellite dish and computer equipment. "Perhaps we'll have some answers from the autopsy on Gerald Clark's body. Something that will help."

Nate listened. Maybe it was because he was staring into the flames, but he had a strange foreboding that maybe they all should have heeded the Yanomamo shaman and burned the man's body. As Richard Zane had said just a moment ago, the Indians were wiser than anyone in the ways and dark paths of the jungle. *Na boesi, ingi sabe ala sani.* In the jungle, the Indian knows everything.

He glanced to the darkening forest as the sun sank away.

Here, with the jungle awakening in a chorus of echoing hoots and lonely calls, the myths of the deep forest gained substance and form. Anything could be possible in the lost tracts of the jungle.

Even the curse of the Ban-ali.

FIVE

Stem Cell Research

Lauren O'Brien sat hunched over her microscope when the call came from the morgue. "Damn it," she mumbled at the interruption. She straightened, slipped her reading glasses from her forehead to the bridge of her nose, and hit the speaker phone.

"Histology here," she said.

"Dr. O'Brien, I think you should come down and see this." The voice belonged to Stanley Hibbert, the forensic pathologist from Johns Hopkins and a fellow member of MEDEA. He had been called in to consult on the post mortem of Gerald Clark.

"I'm somewhat busy with the tissue samples. I've just started reviewing them."

"And was I right about the oral lesions?"

Lauren sighed. "Your assessment was correct. Squamous cell carcinoma. From the high degree of mitosis and loss of differentiation, I'd grade it a type one malignancy. One of the worst I've ever seen."

"So the victim's tongue had *not* been cut out. It had rotted away from the cancer."

Lauren suppressed a nonprofessional shudder. The dead man's mouth had been rank with tumors. His tongue had been no more than a friable bloody stump, eaten away by the carcinoma. And this was not the extent of the man's disease. During the autopsy, his entire body was found to be riddled with cancers in various stages, involving lungs, kidneys, liver, spleen, pancreas. Lauren glanced to the stack of slides prepared by the histology lab, each containing sections of various tumors or bone marrow aspirates.

"Any estimate of the onset of the oral cancer?" the pathologist asked.

"It's hard to say with certainty, but I'd estimate it started between six to eight weeks ago."

A whistle of appreciation sounded over the line. "That's damn fast!"

"I know. And so far, most of the other slides I've reviewed show a similar high degree of malignancy. I can't find a single cancer that looks older than three months." She fingered the stack before her. "But then again, I've still got quite a few slides to review."

"What about the teratomas?"

"They're the same. All between one to three months. But—"

Dr. Hibbert interrupted. "My God, it makes no sense. I've never seen so many cancers in one body. Especially teratomas."

Lauren understood his consternation. Teratomas

were cystic tumors of the body's embryonic stem cells, those rare germ cells that could mature into any bodily tissue: muscle, hair, bone. Tumors of these cells were usually only found in a few organs, such as the thymus or testes. But in Gerald Clark's body, they were everywhere—and that wasn't the oddest detail.

"Stanley, they aren't just terato*mas*. They're terato-*carcinomas*."

"What? All of them?"

She nodded, then realized she was on the phone. "Every single one of them." Teratocarcinomas were the malignant form of the teratoma, a riotous cancer that sprouted a mix of muscle, hair, teeth, bone, and nerves. "I've never seen such samples. I've found sections with partly formed livers, testicular tissue, even ganglia spindles."

"Then that might explain what we found down here," Stanley said.

"What do you mean?"

"Like I said when I first called, you really should come and see this for yourself."

"Fine," she said with an exasperated sigh. "I'll be right down."

Lauren ended the connection and pushed away from the microscope table. She stretched the kink out of her back from the two hours spent stooped over the slides. She considered calling her husband, but he was surely just as busy over at CIA headquarters. Besides, she'd catch up with him in another hour when they conferenced with Frank and Kelly in the field.

Grabbing her lab smock, Lauren headed out the door and descended the stairs to the institute's morgue. A bit of trepidation coursed through her. Though she was a doctor and had worked as an ER clinician for ten years, she still grew queasy during gross necropsies. She preferred the clean histology suite to the morgue's bone saws, stainless steel tables, and hanging scales. But she had no choice today.

As she crossed down the long hall toward the double doors, she distracted herself with the mystery of the case. Gerald Clark had been missing for four years, then walked out of the jungle with a new arm, undoubtedly a miraculous cure. But contrarily, his body had been ravaged by tumors, a cancerous onslaught that had started no more than three months prior. So why the sudden burst of cancer? Why the preponderance of the monstrous teratocarcinomas? And ultimately, where the hell had Gerald Clark been these past four years?

She shook her head. It was too soon for answers. But she had faith in modern science. Between her own research and the fieldwork being done by her children, the mystery would be solved.

Lauren pushed into the locker room, slipped blue paper booties over her shoes, then smeared a dab of Vicks VapoRub under her nose to offset the smells and donned a surgical mask. Once ready, she entered the lab.

It looked like a bad horror movie. Gerald Clark's body lay splayed open like a frog in biology class. Half the contents of his body cavities lay either wrapped in red-and-orange hazardous-waste bags or were resting atop steel scales. Across the room, samples were being prepped in both formaldehyde and liquid nitrogen. Eventually Lauren would see the end result as a pile of neatly inscribed microscope slides, stained and ready for her review, just the way she preferred it.

As Lauren entered the room, some of the stronger smells cut through the mentholated jelly: bleach, blood, bowel, and necrotic gases. She tried to concentrate on breathing through her mouth.

Around her, men and women in bloody aprons worked throughout the lab, oblivious to the horror. It was an efficient operation, a macabre dance of medical professionals.

A tall man, skeletally thin, lifted an arm in greeting and waved her over. Lauren nodded and slipped past a woman tilting a hanging tray and sliding Gerald Clark's liver into a waste bag.

"What did you find, Stanley?" Lauren asked as she approached the worktable.

Dr. Hibbert pointed down, his voice muffled by his surgical mask. "I wanted you to see this before we cut it out."

They stood at the head of the slanted table holding Gerald Clark's body. Bile, blood, and other bodily fluids flowed in trickles to the catch bucket at the other end. Closer at hand, the top of Gerald Clark's skull had been sawed open, exposing the brain beneath.

"Look here," Stanley said, leaning closer to the purplish brain.

With a thumb forceps, the pathologist carefully pulled back the outer meningeal membranes, as if drawing back a curtain. Beneath the membranes, the gyri and folds of the cerebral cortex were plainly visible, traced with darker arteries and veins.

"While dissecting the brain from the cranium, we found this."

Dr. Hibbert separated the right and left hemispheres of the cerebrum. In the groove between the two sections of the brain lay a walnut-size mass. It seemed to be nestled atop the corpus callosum, a whitish channel of nerves and vessels that connected the two hemispheres.

Stanley glanced at her. "It's another teratoma . . . or maybe a teratocarcinoma, if it's like all the others. But watch this. I've never seen anything like this." Using his thumb forceps, he touched the mass.

"Dear God!" Lauren jumped as the tumor flinched away from the tip of his forceps. "It . . . it's moving!"

"Amazing, isn't it? That's why I wanted you to see it. I've read about this property of some teratomic masses. An ability to respond to external stimuli. There was one case even of a well-differentiated teratoma that had enough cardiac muscle to beat like a heart."

Lauren finally found her voice. "But Gerald Clark's been dead for two weeks."

Stanley shrugged. "I imagine, considering where it's located, that it's rich with nerve cells. And a good portion of them must still be viable enough to respond weakly to stimulation. But I expect this ability will quickly fade as the nerves lose juice and the tiny muscles exhaust their reserve calcium."

Lauren took a few deep breaths to collect her thoughts. "Even so, the mass must be highly organized to develop a flinch reflex."

"Undoubtedly . . . quite organized. I'll have it sectioned and slides assembled ASAP." Stanley straightened. "But I thought you'd appreciate personally seeing it in action first."

Lauren nodded. Her eyes shifted from the tumor in the brain to the corpse's arm. A sudden thought rose in her mind. "I wonder," she mumbled.

"What?"

Lauren pictured how the mass had twitched. "The number of the teratomas and the mature development of this particular tumor could be clues to the mechanism by which Clark's arm grew back."

The pathologist's eyes narrowed. "I'm not following you."

Lauren faced him, glad to find something else to stare at than the ravaged body. "What I'm saying is—and this is just a conjecture, of course—what if the man's arm is just a teratoma that grew into a fully functioning limb?"

Stanley's brows rose high. "Like some form of controlled cancer growth? Like a living, functioning tumor?"

"Why not? That's pretty much how we all developed. From one fertilized cell, our bodies formed through rapid cellular proliferation, similar to cancer. Only this profusion of cells differentiated into all the proper tissues. I mean, isn't that the goal of most stem cell research? To discover the mechanism for this controlled growth? What causes one cell to become a bone cell and its neighbor a muscle cell and the one after that a nerve cell?" Lauren stared at the splayed corpse of Gerald Clark, not in horror any longer but in wonder. "We may be on our way to answering that very mystery."

"And if we could succeed in discovering the mechanism . . ."

"It would mean the end of cancer and would revolutionize the entire medical field."

Stanley shook his head and swung away, returning to his bloody work. "Then let's pray your son and daughter succeed in their search."

Lauren nodded and retreated back across the morgue. She checked her watch. Speaking of Frank and Kelly, it was getting close to the designated conference call. Time to compare notes. Lauren glanced back one last time to the ruin that was left of Gerald Wallace Clark. "Something's out in that jungle," she mumbled to herself. "But what?"

AUGUST 7, 8:32 P.M.
AMAZON JUNGLE

Kelly stood off from the others, trying her best to assimilate the news her mother had reported. She stared out into the jungle, serenaded by the endless chorus of locusts and river frogs. Firelight failed to penetrate more than a few yards into the shadowed depths of the forest. Beyond the glow, the jungle hid its mysteries.

Closer at hand, a group of Rangers knelt, setting up the camp's perimeter motion-sensor system. The laser grid, rigged a few feet off the ground and established between the jungle and the camp, was meant to keep any large predator from wandering too near without being detected.

Kelly stared beyond their labors to the dark forest. *What had happened to Agent Clark out there?*

A voice spoke near her shoulder, startling her. "Gruesome news indeed."

Kelly glanced over and found Professor Kouwe standing quietly at her side. How long had he been there? Clearly the shaman had not lost his innate abilities to move noiselessly across the forest floor. "Y . . . Yes," she stammered. "Very disturbing."

Kouwe slipped out his pipe and began stoking it with tobacco, then lit it with a fiery flourish. The pungent odor of smoky tobacco welled around them. "And what of your mother's belief that the cancers and the regenerated arm might be connected?"

"It's intriguing . . . and perhaps not without merit."

"How so?"

Kelly rubbed the bridge of her nose and gathered her thoughts. "Before I left the States to come here, I did a literature search on the subject of regeneration. I figured it might better prepare me for anything we find."

"Hmm . . . very wise. When it comes to the jungle, preparation and knowledge can mean the difference between life and death."

Kelly nodded and continued with her thoughts, glad to express them aloud and bounce them off someone else. "While conducting this research, I came across an interesting article in the *Proceedings of the National Academy of Sciences*. Back in 1999, a research team in Philadelphia raised a group of mice with damaged immune systems. The mice were to be used as a model to study multiple sclerosis and AIDS. But as they began working with the immune-compromised creatures, an odd and unexpected phenomenon developed."

Kouwe turned to her, one eyebrow raised. "And what was that?"

"The researchers had punched holes in the mice's ears, a common way of marking test animals, and discovered that the holes healed amazingly fast, leaving no trace of a wound. They had not just scarred over, but had regenerated cartilage, skin, blood vessels, even nerves." Kelly let this news sink in, then continued. "After this discovery, the lead researcher, Dr. Ellen Heber-Katz, tried a few experiments. She amputated a few mice's tails, and they grew back. She severed optic nerves, and they healed. Even the excision of a section of spinal cord grew back in less than a month. Such phenomenal regeneration had never been seen in mammals."

Kouwe removed his pipe, his eyes wide. "So what was causing it?"

Kelly shook her head. "The only difference between these healing mice and ordinary mice was their defective immune systems."

"And the significance?"

Kelly suppressed a grin, warming to the subject, especially with such an astute audience. "From the study of animals with the proven ability to regenerate limbs—starfish, amphibians, and reptiles—we do know their immune systems are rudimentary at best. Therefore, Dr. Heber-Katz hypothesized that eons ago, mammals made an evolutionary trade-off.

To defend against cancers, we relinquished the ability to regenerate bodily limbs. You see, our complex immune systems are designed specifically to eliminate inappropriate cell proliferation, like cancers. Which is beneficial, of course, but at the same time, such immune systems would also block a body's attempt to regenerate a limb. It would treat the proliferation of poorly differentiated cells necessary to grow a new arm as cancerous and eliminate it."

"So the complexity of our immune systems both protects and damns us."

Kelly narrowed her eyes as she concentrated. "Unless something can safely turn off the immune system. Like in those mice."

"Or like in Gerald Clark?" Kouwe eyed her. "You're suggesting something turned off his immune system so he was able to regenerate his arm, but this phenomenon also allowed multiple cancers to sprout throughout his body."

"Perhaps. But it has to be more complicated than that. What's the mechanism? Why did all the cancers arise so suddenly?" She shook her head. "And more important, what could trigger such a change?"

Kouwe nodded toward the dark jungle. "If such a trigger exists, it might be found out there. Currently three-quarters of all anticancer drugs in use today are derived from rain forest plants. So why not one plant that does the opposite—one that *causes* cancer?"

"A carcinogen?"

"Yes, but one with beneficial side effects . . . like regeneration."

"It seems improbable, but considering Agent Clark's state, anything might be possible. Over the next few days, at my request, the MEDEA researchers will be investigating the status of Gerald Clark's immune system and examining his cancers more closely. Maybe they'll come up with something."

Kouwe blew out a long stream of smoke. "Whatever the ultimate answer is, it won't come from a lab. Of that I'm certain."

"Then from where?"

Instead of answering, Kouwe simply pointed the glowing bowl of his pipe toward the dark forest.

Hours later, deeper in the forest, the naked figure crouched motionless in the murk of the jungle, just beyond the reach of the firelight. His slender body had been painted with a mix of ash and *meh-nu* fruit, staining his skin in a complex pattern of blues and blacks, turning him into a living shadow.

Ever since first dark, he had been spying upon these outsiders. Patience had been taught to him by the jungle. All *teshari-rin*, tribal trackers, knew success depended less on one's actions than on the silence between one's steps.

He maintained his post throughout the night, a dark sentinel upon the camp. As he crouched, he studied the giant men, stinking with their foreignness, while they circled around and around the site. They spoke in strange tongues and bore clothing most odd.

Still, he watched, spying, learning of his enemy.

At one point, a cricket crawled across the back of his hand as his palm rested in the dirt. One eye watched the camp, while the other watched the small insect scratch its hind legs together, a whisper of characteristic cricket song.

A promise of dawn.

He dared wait no longer. He had learned all he could. He rose smoothly to his feet, the motion so swift and silent that the cricket remained on the back of his steady hand, still playing its last song of the night. He raised the hand to his lips and blew the surprised insect from its perch.

With a final glance to the camp, he fled away into the jungle. He had been trained to run the forest paths without disturbing a single leaf. None would know he had passed.

Moreover, the tracker knew his ultimate duty.

Death must come to all but the Chosen.

SIX

The Amazon Factor

AUGUST 11, 3:12 P.M.
AMAZON JUNGLE

Nate kept one finger fixed to his shotgun's trigger, the muzzle pointed ahead. The caiman had to be almost twenty feet long. It was a huge specimen of *Melanosuchus niger*, the black caiman, the king of the giant crocodilian predators of the Amazon rivers. It lay atop the muddy bank, sunning in the mid-afternoon heat. Black armored scales shone dully. Its maw gaped slightly open. Jagged yellow teeth, longer than Nate's own palm, lined the cavity. Its bulging, ridged eyes were solid black, cold and dead, the eyes of a prehistoric monster. Stone still, it was impossible to tell if the great beast even acknowledged the trio of approaching boats.

"Will it attack?" Kelly whispered behind him.

Nate shrugged without looking back. "They're unpredictable. But if we leave it alone, it should leave us alone."

Nate crouched in the prow of the middle pontoon boat. He shared the craft with the two O'Briens, Richard Zane, and Anna Fong. A single soldier, Corporal Okamoto, manned the small outboard engine in the boat's stern. The stocky Asian corporal had developed the habit of whistling almost nonstop, which after four days of motoring up the wide tributary had grown to be excruciating. But at least the giant monster lounging on the bank had squelched the man's tuneless noise.

Ahead, the lead boat puttered past the beast, sticking close to the opposite shore. The starboard pontoon bristled with M-16s, all pointing toward the black caiman.

Each boat held a complement of six team members. The lead boat carried three soldiers and the rest of the civilians: Professor Kouwe, Olin Pasternak, and Manny, who lounged with his pet jaguar in the center of the boat. Tor-tor had been on boats before and seemed to enjoy this means of transportation, tail lazily flicking, ears pricked for noises, eyes mostly in a half-lidded drowse.

The rear boat held the other six Rangers, anchored by Captain Waxman.

"They should just shoot the damn thing," Frank said.

Nate glanced to the man. "It's an endangered species. In the last century, they were poached to near extinction. Only lately have their numbers grown."

"And why does this news not please me?" Frank muttered, glancing to the waters around them. He tugged the bill of his baseball cap lower as if he were trying to hide behind it.

"The caimans kill hundreds every year," Zane mumbled, hunched down beside his pontoon. "They've swamped boats, attacking anything. I read about a black caiman found dead with two outboard motors in its belly, swallowed whole. I'm with Mr. O'Brien. A few well-placed shots . . ."

By now, the lead boat was past the beast's sunning spot, and Nate's boat followed next, moving slowly against the sludgy current as it passed the caiman, motor rumbling.

"Marvelous," Nate said. He faced the creature, no farther away than thirty yards. It was monstrous, a creature from another time. "It's bloody beautiful."

"A male, isn't it?" Anna Fong asked, staring avidly.

"From the ridge lines and shape of the nostrils, I'd agree."

"Shh!" Frank hissed at them.

"It's moving!" Kelly yelped, shifting from her seat to the far side of the boat. She was quickly followed by Richard Zane.

The armored head swung slowly, now following their boat.

"It's waking up," Frank said.

"It was never asleep," Nate corrected as they glided safely past. "It's just as curious about us as we are about it."

"I'm sure as hell *not* curious," Frank said, clearly glad to be past the monster. "In fact, it can just kiss my hairy—"

The giant caiman suddenly lunged, lightning quick, diving smoothly across the slick mud to vanish under the brown water. The third boat had just been drawing abreast of it. A few shots were fired by the soldiers aboard. But the crocodile's speed and sudden movement had caught them all by surprise. It was already gone by the time the few shots peppered the muddy bank.

"Stop!" Nate called out. "It's just running!" With nothing to protect, the caiman's first reaction was to flee from the unknown—that is, unless aroused . . . or threatened.

One of the Rangers, a tall black corporal named Rodney Graves, stood halfway up in the boat, searching the waters, gun pointed. "I don't see—"

It happened fast. The rear boat jarred about three feet in the air. Nate caught the barest glimpse of the thick scaled tail. The soldier who had been standing tumbled headfirst into the water. The others grabbed rubber handholds and held tight. The boat slammed back to the river.

Captain Waxman crouched by the outboard motor. "Graves!"

The fallen corporal suddenly popped out of the water, ten meters downstream from the trio of boats, carried by the current. The man's hat was gone, but he still had his gun. He began to kick and swim toward the nearest boat.

Behind him, like a submarine rising, the head of the caiman crested the waters, its eyes two periscopes.

The Rangers scrambled to bring their weapons to bear. But before a single shot was fired, the caiman had sunk away again.

Nate imagined the giant creature slashing its thick tail, sweeping through the muddy depths toward the kicking soldier, drawn by the man's thrashing. "Damn it," he said under his breath, then yelled with all his lungs. "Corporal Graves! *Don't move!* Stop kicking!"

He was not heard. By now, everyone was yelling for the man to hurry. His panicked thrashing grew worse. Captain Waxman motored the boat backward, trying to meet the frantic swimmer.

Nate yelled again, "Stop swimming!" Finally, more in frustration at not being heard than any true bravery, Nate tossed his gun aside and dove into the river. He glided smoothly, eyes open. But the murky depths hid everything beyond a few feet. He gave one solid kick and sweep of his arms, then simply let his momentum and the current propel him forward. Under the water, he heard the motor of the rear boat pass off to the left.

Arching up, his head broke the surface. Rodney Graves was only a yard to his right. "Corporal Graves! Quit kicking! You've gotta play dead." Nate kept his own limbs unmoving. He half floated on his back.

The soldier turned to him, his eyes wide with panic. "Fuck . . . that!" he screamed between gasping breaths. He continued to thrash and kick. The rescue boat was now only three yards away. Already others were stretching out to grab him up.

Nate sensed movement nearby, a sudden surge against the current. It swept between him and the corporal. Something large and swift.

Oh, God . . .

"Graves!" he cried out one last time.

One of the Rangers—Nate recognized him as the swimmer's brother, Thomas Graves—leaned far over the pontoon. He was supported by two others holding his belt. Tom lunged out with both arms, straining with every muscle in his body, his face a mask of fear for his brother.

Rodney kicked and reached, fingers scrambling out.

Tom caught his hand. "Got him!" he yelled. The muscles of his forearm bulged like corded iron.

The two soldiers yanked Tom back as he hauled Rodney forward. With his free arm, Tom snatched a handful of his brother's soaked field jacket for extra purchase, then fell backward, yanking his brother over the pontoon.

Rodney flew up out of the water, landing belly-first onto the pontoon. He laughed in relief. "Goddamn crocodile!"

He twisted to pull his feet out of the water when giant jaws, already gaped wide open, shot out of the water and swallowed both booted legs up to his thighs. The jaws clamped over their captured prey, then fell back into the river. The ton of armored beast could not be fought. Rodney was torn out of his brother's hands, a cry on his lips.

Rodney disappeared under the water, but his last scream echoed over the river. Soldiers, on their knees, had rifles pointed toward the river, but no one shot. Any blind round could take out their fellow unit member rather than the caiman. Yet from their expressions, Nate knew they all understood the truth. Corporal Rodney Graves was gone. They all had seen the size of the monster, had seen the jaws snap him away.

And Nate knew they were right.

The caiman would take its prey deep and merely hold it clamped until the waters drowned its victim. Then it would either eat or store the body in the submerged mangrove roots where it would rot and be easier to tear apart.

There was no way to rescue the man.

Nate remained floating in the water, keeping his limbs still. The caiman was probably content with its meal, but where there was one, there might be other predators, especially once the blood flowed down the current. He took no chances. He rolled to his back and floated quietly until he felt hands grab him and haul him back aboard the boat.

He found himself staring into the stricken face of Tom Graves. The corporal was staring at his hands, as if blaming them for not being strong enough to hold his brother.

"I'm sorry," Nate said softly.

The man glanced up, and Nate was shocked to see the flash of anger in the man's eyes, *anger* that Nate had survived, *anger* that his brother had been taken instead. Tom turned away stiffly.

Another of the unit was not so reticent. "What in God's name were you trying to do?" It was Captain Waxman, his face almost purple with rage. "What sort of asinine stunt was that? You trying to get yourself killed, too?"

Nate swept the wet locks of hair out of his eyes. It was the second time in a week he had dived into the Amazon's waters to rescue someone. Without doubt, it was becoming a bad habit. "I was trying to help," he mumbled.

The fire in Captain Waxman's voice burned down to dull coals. "We were sent to protect *you*. Not the other way around."

By now, Nate's own boat had drawn abreast of the Rangers'. He clambered over the pontoons to resume his original seat.

Once settled, Captain Waxman waved an arm for them to continue forward. The pitch of the motors rose.

Nathan heard a protest raised by Tom Graves. "Captain . . . my brother . . . his body."

"Gone, Corporal. He's gone."

So the trio of boats continued on. Nate caught Professor Kouwe's gaze across the waters from the other boat. Kouwe shook his head sadly. In the jungle, no amount of military training or arsenal could completely protect you. If the jungle wanted you, it was going to take you. It was called the Amazon Factor. All who traveled the mighty green bower were at the jungle's mercy and whim.

Nate felt a touch on his knee. He turned and saw Kelly seated beside him. She sighed, staring forward, then spoke. "That was a stupid thing to do. It really was, but"—she glanced at him—"I'm glad you tried."

After the sudden tragedy, Nate didn't have the strength to muster more than a simple nod, but her words helped warm the cold hollowness inside him. She took her hand from his knee.

The rest of the day's journey was made in silence. There was no more whistling by Corporal Okamoto as he manned the craft's outboard motor. They traveled until the sun was near the horizon, as if trying to put as much distance as possible between them and the death of Rodney Graves.

As the camp was prepared, the news was passed back to the base at Wauwai. The somber mood stretched through a dinner of fish, rice, and a platter of jungle yams Professor Kouwe had found near the campsite.

The only topic of discussion was the sugary yams. Nathan had asked from where such an abundance had come. "It's unusual to find so many plants." The professor had returned with an efficiently constructed backpack of palm leaves filled to the brim with wild yams.

Kouwe nodded toward the deeper forest. "I suspect the site where I found these was an old Indian garden. I saw a few avocado trees and stumpy pineapple plants in the same area."

Kelly straightened with a fork half-raised. "An Indian garden?"

For the past four days, they had not encountered a single soul. If Gerald Clark had obtained his canoe from a Yanomamo village, they had no clue where he got it.

"It was long abandoned," Kouwe said, dashing the hope that had briefly shone in Kelly's eyes. "Such sites dot the riverways throughout the Amazon. Tribes, especially the Yanomamo, are nomadic. They plant gardens, stay a year or two, then move on. I'm afraid a garden's presence here does not mean anything significant."

"Still, it's at least something," Kelly said, refusing to dismiss this bit of hopeful news. "Some sign that others are out there."

"And besides, these yams are damn good," Frank added, munching a mouthful. "I was already getting sick of the rice."

Manny grinned, running his fingers through his jaguar's ruff. Tor-tor had feasted on a large catfish and lay stretched by the fire.

The Rangers had set up a second campfire a short distance away. At sunset, they held a short service for their fallen comrade. Now they were sullen. Only a few muttered words were shared among them. It was unlike the previous nights when the soldiers were full of ribald jokes and loud guffaws before settling to their own hammocks and posts. Not this night.

"We should all get to sleep," Kelly finally said, pushing to her feet. "We have another long day to-morrow."

With murmured assents and a few groans, the party dispersed to their separate hammocks. When returning from the latrine, Nate found Professor Kouwe smoking near his hammock.

"Professor," Nate said, sensing Kouwe wanted to speak to him in private.

"Walk with me a moment. Before the Rangers activate the motion sensors." The shaman led the way a short distance into the forest.

Nate followed. "What is it?"

Kouwe simply continued until they were deep within the jungle's gloom. The camp's two fires were only greenish glows through the bushes. He finally stopped, puffing deeply on his pipe.

"Why did you bring me out here?"

Kouwe flicked on a small flashlight.

Nate stared around. The jungle ahead was clear

of all but a few trees: short breadfruit palms, oranges, figs. Bushes and low plants covered the forest
floor, unnaturally dense. Nate realized what he was
seeing. It was the abandoned Indian garden. He even
spotted a pair of bamboo poles, staked among the
plantings and burned at the top. Normally these
torches were filled with *tok-tok* powder and lit during
harvest times as a smoky repellent against hungry
insects. Without a doubt, Indians had once labored
here.

Nate had seen other such cultivations during his
journeys in the Amazon, but now, here at night,
with the patch overgrown and gone wild, it had a
haunted feeling to it. He could almost sense the eyes
of the Indian dead watching him.

"We're being tracked," Kouwe said.

The words startled Nate. "What are you talking
about?"

Kouwe led Nate into the garden. He pointed his
flashlight toward a passion fruit tree and pulled down
one of the lower branches. "It's been picked bare."
Kouwe turned to him. "I'd say about the same time as
when we were hauling and securing the boats. Several of the plucked stems were still moist with sap."

"And you noticed this?"

"I was watching for it," Kouwe said. "The past
two mornings, when I've gone off to gather fruit for
the day's journey, I noticed some places that I'd
walked the night before had been disturbed. Broken
branches, a hogplum tree half empty of its fruit."

"It could be jungle animals, foraging during the
night."

Kouwe nodded. "I thought so at first, too. So I kept

silent. I could find no footprints or definite proof. But now the regularity of these occurrences has convinced me otherwise. Someone is tracking us."

"Who?"

"Most likely Indians. These are their forests. They would know how to follow without being seen."

"The Yanomamo."

"Most likely," Kouwe said.

Nate heard the doubt in the professor's voice. "Who else could it be?"

Kouwe's eyes narrowed. "I don't know. But it strikes me as odd that they would not be more careful. A true tracker would not let his presence be known. It's almost too sloppy for an Indian."

"But you're an Indian. No white man would've noticed these clues, not even the Army Rangers."

"Maybe." Kouwe sounded unconvinced.

"We should alert Captain Waxman."

"That's why I pulled you aside first. Should we?"

"What do you mean?"

"If they are Indians, I don't think we should force the issue by having an Army Ranger team beating the bushes in search of them. The Indians, or whoever is out there, would simply vanish. If we wish to contact them, maybe we should let them come to us. Let them grow accustomed to our strangeness. Let them make the first move rather than the other way around."

Nate's first instinct was to argue against such caution. He was anxious to forge ahead, to find answers to his father's disappearance after so many years. Patience was hard to swallow. The wet season would begin soon. The rains would start again, washing away all hopes of tracking Gerald Clark's trail.

But then again, as he had been reminded today by the caiman's attack, the Amazon was king. It had to be taken at its own pace. To fight, to thrash, only invited defeat. The best way to survive was to flow with the current.

"I think it's best if we wait a few more days," Kouwe continued. "First to see if I'm correct. Maybe you're right. Maybe it's just jungle animals. But if I'm right, I'd like to give the Indians a chance to come out on their own, rather than scare them away or force them here at gunpoint. Either way, we'd get no information."

Nate finally conceded, but with a condition. "We'll give it another two days. Then we tell someone."

Kouwe nodded and flicked off his flashlight. "We should be getting to bed."

The pair hiked the short distance back to the glowing campfires. Nate pondered the shaman's words and insight. He remembered the way Kouwe's eyes had narrowed, questioning if it was Indians out there. *Who else could it be?*

Arriving back at the site, Nate found most of the camp already retired to their hammocks. A few soldiers patrolled the perimeter. Kouwe wished him good night and strode to his own mosquito-netted hammock. As Nate kicked out of his boots, he heard a mumbled moan from Frank O'Brien in a nearby hammock. After today's tragedy, Nate expected everyone would have troubled dreams.

He climbed into his hammock and threw an arm

over his eyes, blocking out the firelight. Like it or not, there was no fighting the Amazon. It had its own pace, its own hunger. All you could do was pray you weren't the next victim. With this thought in mind, it was a long time until sleep claimed Nate. His final thought: Who *would* be next?

Corporal Jim DeMartini was quickly growing to hate this jungle. After four days traveling the river, DeMartini was sick of the whole damned place: the eternal moist air, the stinging flies, the gnats, the constant screams of monkeys and birds. Additionally, closer to home, mold seemed to grow on everything—on their clothes, on their hammocks, on their rucksacks. All his gear smelled like sweaty gym socks abandoned in a locker for a month. And this was after only *four* days.

Pulling patrol, he stood in the woods near the latrine, leaning on a tree, his M-16 resting comfortably in his arms. Jorgensen shared this shift with him but had stopped to use the latrine. From only a few yards away, DeMartini could hear his partner whistling as he zipped down.

"Fine time to take a shit," DeMartini groused.

Jorgensen heard him. "It's the damn water . . ."

"Just hurry it up." DeMartini shook out a cigarette, his mind drifting back to the fate of his fellow unit member Rodney Graves. DeMartini had been in the lead boat with a few of the civilians, but he had been close enough to see the monstrous caiman rise out of the river and rip Graves from the other boat. He gave an involuntary shudder. He was no plebe. He had seen men die before: gunshots, helicopter crashes, drowning. But nothing compared to what he had witnessed today. It was something out of a nightmare.

Glancing over his shoulder, he cursed Jorgensen. *What's taking the bastard so long?* He took a deep drag on the cigarette. *Probably jerking off.* But then again, he couldn't blame Jorgensen if he was. It was distracting with the two women among them. After setting up camp, he had covertly spied upon the Asian scientist as she had stripped out of her khaki jacket. Her thin blouse beneath had been damp from sweat and clung invitingly to her small breasts.

He shoved back these thoughts, ground out his smoke, and stood straighter. In the dark, the only light came from the flashlight taped on the underside of his rifle. He kept it pointed forward, toward the nearby river.

Deeper in the woods, past the laser motion sensors, small lights winked and flitted. Fireflies. He had been raised in southern California, where there were no such insects. So the blinking of the bugs kept him further on edge. The flashes kept drawing his eye, while around him the jungle sighed with the rustle of leaves. Larger branches creaked like old men's joints. It was as if the jungle were a living creature and he was swallowed inside it.

DeMartini swung his light all around. He firmly believed in the buddy system—and even more so right now in this cursed black jungle. There was an old adage among the Rangers: *The buddy system is essential to survival—it gives the enemy somebody else to shoot at.*

Slightly spooked for his buddy's company, he called back to the latrine. "C'mon, Jorgensen!"

"Give me half a break," his partner snapped irritably from a few yards away.

As DeMartini turned back around, something stung his cheek. He slapped at the insect, squashing it under his palm. An even fiercer sting struck his neck, just under the line of his jaw. Grimacing, he reached to brush the fly or mosquito away, and his fingers touched something still clinging to his neck. Startled, he batted it away in horror.

"What the fuck!" he hissed, stepping back. "Goddamn bloodsuckers!"

Jorgensen laughed from nearby. "At least you aren't bare-assed!"

Staring around the jungle with distaste, he pulled the collar of his jacket higher, offering less of a target to the bloodthirsty insects. As he turned, the splash of his flashlight revealed something bright in the mud at his feet. He bent to pick it up. It was a tied bunch of feathers around a pointed dart. The tip was wet with blood, his own blood.

Shit!

He dropped into a crouch and opened his mouth to shout a warning, but all that came out was a silent gurgle. He tried to take a deep breath but realized he couldn't seem to get his chest to move. His limbs grew leaden. Suddenly weak, he fell onto his side.

Poisoned . . . paralyzed, he realized with panic.

His hand still had enough motor control to scrabble like a spider over the stock of his rifle, struggling to reach the trigger. If he could fire his M-16 . . . warn Jorgensen . . .

Then he sensed someone standing over him, watching him from the dark jungle. He couldn't turn his head to see, but the prickle of some primal instinct sent warnings through his body.

Further panicked, he strained for the M-16's trigger, praying, wordlessly begging. His finger finally reaching the trigger guard. If he could have gasped, he would have done so in relief. As darkness blackened the edges of his sight, he fed all his remaining energy into his single finger—and pulled the trigger.

Nothing happened.

In despair, he realized the rifle's safety was still on. A single tear of defeat rolled down his cheek as he lay in the mud. Paralyzed, he could not even close his eyelids.

The lurker finally stepped over his prone body. In the glow of his weapon's light, he saw a sight that made no sense.

It was a woman . . . a naked woman, a sleek creature of wondrous beauty, with long smooth legs, gentle curves leading to full hips, firm and rounded breasts. But it was her large, dark eyes—full of mystery, full of hunger—that held his attention as he slowly suffocated. She leaned over him, a cascading fall of black hair over his slack face.

For a moment, it felt as if she were breathing into him. He felt something course through him, something warm and smoky.

Then he was gone, darkness swallowing him away.

Kelly startled awake. Voices shouted all around her. She sat up too quickly and tumbled out of her hammock, crashing to her knees. "Damn it!" She glanced up.

More branches had been tossed on the two camp-fires. Flames climbed higher, spreading smoke and a fiery light all around. In the distance, flashlights bobbled through the forests, clearly searching. Shouts and orders echoed out of the jungle.

Gaining her feet, Kelly struggled to find her way through the tangled mosquito netting. She spotted Nate and Manny nearby. Both men were barefooted, dressed in boxers and T-shirts. The large jaguar sat between them. "What's going on?" she called, finally freeing herself of the netting.

The other civilians were now all beginning to gather in various states of undress and confusion. Kelly quickly noticed that all the green canvas hammocks of the Rangers were empty. A single corporal stood between the two fires. His rifle was held at ready.

Nate answered her question, bending down to tug on his boots. "One of the soldiers on patrol has gone missing. We're to stay here until the others secure the area."

"Missing? Who? How?"

"Corporal DeMartini."

Kelly remembered the man: slick black hair, wide nose, eyes that constantly squinted with suspicion. "What happened?"

Nate shook his head. "No one knows yet. He simply vanished."

A sharp shout arose from near the river. Most of the bobbling flashlights converged toward the site.

Professor Kouwe joined them. Kelly noticed an odd look pass between the two men. Something unspoken, something they shared.

Frank suddenly appeared on the far side of the camp. Flashlight in hand, he rushed toward them. He arrived out of breath, the freckles on his cheeks standing out against his ashen face. "We've found the missing man's weapon." His eyes flicked among Nate, Manny, and Kouwe. "You all know more about the jungle than anyone. There's something we could use your opinion about. Captain Waxman has asked for you to come take a look."

The whole group of civilians stepped toward Frank, intending to follow.

He held up a hand. "Just these three."

Kelly pushed forward. "If the man was injured, I may be of help, too."

Frank hesitated, then nodded.

Richard Zane moved to follow, his mouth open to protest, but Frank shook his head. "We don't want the site trampled any more than necessary."

With the matter settled, the group hurried past the fires toward the river. The jaguar kept to its master's side, padding silently with them. They crossed into the dense growth that fringed the tributary. Here was the true mythic jungle: a tangle of vines, bushes, and trees. Single file, the group trekked into the thick growth, approaching the glow of many flashlights ahead.

Kelly followed behind Nate. For the first time, she noticed the spread of his shoulders—and how well he moved through the woods. For such a tall man, he slipped under liana vines and around bushes with a casual ease. She trod in his steps and tried to mimic his moves, but she kept stumbling in the dark.

Her heel slid on something slippery. Her feet went out from under her. She fell sideways, hands out to break her fall.

Then Nate's arms were around her, catching her. "Careful."

"Th . . . thanks." Blushing, she reached toward a vine to pull herself up, but before she could grip it, Nate yanked her away. Only her fingers brushed the vine.

"What are you—*ow!*" Her fingertips began to burn. She rubbed them on her untucked blouse, but the sting grew even worse. It felt as if her fingers were on fire.

"Hold still," Professor Kouwe said. "Rubbing will spread it." He snatched a handful of thick leaves from a slender tree. Crushing them in his hands, he grabbed Kelly's wrist and smeared the oily moisture over her fingers and hand.

Instantly the sting faded. Kelly stared in wonder at the crushed leaves.

"*Ku-run-yeh,*" Nate said behind her. "Of the violet family. A potent analgesic."

Kouwe continued to rub her fingers until the pain was gone.

In the glow of her brother's flashlight, she saw that a couple of blisters had formed on the tips of her fingers.

"Are you okay?" Frank asked.

She nodded, feeling stupid.

"Keep applying the *ku-run-yeh* and you'll heal faster," Kouwe said, giving her arm a fatherly squeeze.

Nate helped her to her feet. He pointed to the grayish vine. "It's named 'fire liana.' And not without reason." The vine draped from a tree and lay tangled near the trunk's base. She would've fallen into the nest of vines if Nate hadn't caught her. "The vine exudes a potent irritant to keep insects away."

"A form of chemical warfare," Kouwe added.

"Exactly." Nate nodded for Frank to continue ahead, then waved an arm. "It's going on all around you all the time here. It's what makes the jungle such a potent medicinal storehouse. The ingenuity and variety of chemicals and compounds waged in this war far outwit anything human scientists could invent in a lab."

Kelly listened, not feeling particularly appreciative of being a casualty in this chemical war.

After a few more yards, they reached the Rangers, gathered in a ring around one section of forest. A couple of men stood off to the side, weapons on their shoulders, night-vision goggles in place over their faces.

Corporal Jorgensen stood at attention before the unit's captain. "Like I said, I was just using the latrine. DeMartini was standing guard by a nearby tree."

"And this?" Captain Waxman held up the butt of a cigarette under the man's nose.

"Okay, I heard him light up, but I didn't think he left. When I zipped and turned around, he was gone. He didn't say a word that he was going to wander over to the river."

"All for a goddamn smoke," Captain Waxman grumbled, then waved an arm. "Dismissed, corporal."

"Yes, sir."

After taking a deep breath, Captain Waxman

crossed to them, fire still in his eyes. "I need your expertise on this," he said, his gaze sweeping over Nate, Kouwe, and Manny. Turning, he swung his light toward an area of trampled jungle grasses. "We found DeMartini's weapon abandoned here, and this stubbed cigarette, but no sign of what happened to his body. Corporal Warczak has searched for any prints leading from here. There aren't any. Just this trampled and shredded area of grasses that leads back to the river."

Kelly saw that the disturbed area did indeed lead all the way to the water's edge. The tall green reeds lining the bank were parted and crushed.

"I'd like to examine this more closely," Professor Kouwe said.

Captain Waxman nodded, passing Kouwe his flashlight.

Nate and Kouwe moved forward. Manny followed, but his pet jaguar stopped at the edge of the area, growling deep in the back of his throat as it sniffed at the grasses.

Hand on his whip, Manny tried to coax the cat to follow. "C'mon, Tor-tor." The jaguar refused, even retreated a step.

Kouwe glanced back to them. The professor had stopped to crouch at a spot, examining something near the reeds. He sniffed at his fingers.

"What is it?" Nate asked.

"Caiman feces." He wiped his hand clean on some grasses, then nodded to the growling jaguar. "I think Tor-tor agrees."

"What do you mean?" Kelly asked.

Manny answered, "Wild cats have the ability to

sense the size of an animal from just the smell of its excrement or urine. In fact, elephant urine is sold throughout the western United States as a repellent against bobcats and cougars. They won't go near a site marked with elephant urine, freaked by the smell of such a huge animal."

Kouwe clambered through the reeds to the river's edge. He was careful to pluck aside a few broken stalks, then waved Captain Waxman over. Kelly followed.

Kouwe shone his light on a spot of muddy bank. Clawed prints were clear in the riverbank mud. "Caiman."

Kelly heard an odd note of relief in Kouwe's voice. Again Nate and the professor shared a secretive glance.

Straightening, Kouwe explained, "Caimans will often hunt the riverbanks, snatching tapir and wild pigs as they come to drink. Your corporal must have come too close to the river and was grabbed."

"Could it be the same one that attacked Corporal Graves?" Waxman asked.

Kouwe shrugged. "Black caimans are fairly intelligent. After learning that our boats are a source of food, it might have followed the rumble of our motors, then lay in wait until nightfall."

"Goddamn that motherfucker!" Waxman spat, a fist clenched. "Two men in one day."

Staff Sergeant Kostos stepped forward. The tall swarthy Ranger wore a tight expression. "Sir, I can call for reinforcements. The Hueys could be here by morning with two more men."

"Do it," he snapped. "And from here on out, I want two patrols every shift. Two men in each patrol! I don't want anyone—civilian or soldier—walking this jungle alone. Ever! And I want the river side of every camp set up with motion sensors, not just the jungle."

"Yes, sir."

Captain Waxman turned to them. There was no warmth in his words, only dismissal. "Thank you for your assistance."

The group wound back through the forest. As they marched, Kelly felt numb. Another man gone . . . so suddenly. She hiked past the nest of fire liana vines and eyed them warily. It wasn't only chemical warfare going on out here, but a savage feeding frenzy, where the strong consumed the weak.

Kelly was glad to reach the campsite with its roaring fires—the warmth, the light. In a small way, the flames were reassuring, temporarily driving back the dark heart of the forest.

She found the eyes of the other teammates upon them. Anna Fong stood with Richard Zane. Frank's fellow operative, Olin Pasternak, stood near the fires, warming his hands.

Manny quickly explained what they had found. As he talked, Anna covered her mouth with her hand and turned away. Richard shook his head. And as usual, Olin remained his stoic self, staring into the flames.

Kelly barely noticed their reactions. Standing by the campfire, her attention remained focused on Nate and Kouwe. The pair had moved to the side, near

Nate's hammock. From the corner of her eye, she watched them. No words were exchanged between the two men, but she caught the inquiring look on Kouwe's face. An unspoken question.

Nate answered with a small shake of his head.

With some secret settled between them, Kouwe reached to his pipe and moved a few steps away, clearly needing a moment alone.

Kelly turned, giving the older man his privacy, and found Nate staring at her.

She glanced back to the fires. She felt foolish and oddly frightened. She swallowed and bit her lower lip, remembering the man's strong arms catching her, saving her. She sensed Nate still staring at her, his gaze like the sun's heat on her skin. Warm, deep, and tingling.

Slowly the feeling faded.

What was he hiding?

SEVEN

Data Collection

AUGUST 12, 6:20 A.M.
LANGLEY, VIRGINIA

Lauren O'Brien was going to be late for work. "Jessie!" she called as she nestled an orange beside a peanut-butter-and-jelly sandwich in a lunch box. "Hon, I need you down here . . . *now*." The day-care center was a twenty-minute drive out of her way, followed by the usual fight through morning traffic into Langley.

She checked her watch and rolled her eyes. "Marshall!"

"We're coming," a stern voice answered.

Lauren leaned around the corner. Her husband was leading their granddaughter down the stairs. Jessie was dressed, though her socks didn't match. *Close enough*, she thought to herself. She had forgotten what it was like to have a child in the house again. Patterns and schedules had to be altered.

"I can take her to day care," Marshall said, reaching

the bottom stairs. "I don't have a meeting until nine o'clock."

"No, I can do it."

"Lauren . . ." He crossed and gave her a quick peck on the cheek. "Let me help you."

She returned to the kitchen and snapped shut the lunch box. "You should get into the office as soon as possible." She tried to keep the tension out of her voice.

But Marshall heard it anyway. "Jessie, why don't you get your sweater?"

"'Kay, Grandpa." The girl skipped toward the front door.

Marshall turned back to Lauren. "Frank and Kelly are fine. If there was any change, we would know it right away."

Lauren nodded, but she kept her back toward him. She did not want Marshall to see the threatening tears. Last night, they had heard about the first Army Ranger being attacked by a crocodile. Then, a few hours past midnight, the phone had rung. From Marshall's tone as he spoke, Lauren had known it was more bad news. A call this late could only mean one thing—something horrible had happened to either Frank or Kelly. She was sure of it. After Marshall had hung up the phone and explained about the second dead soldier, Lauren had cried with selfish relief. Still, deep inside, a seed of dread had been planted that she could not shake. *Two dead . . . how many more?* She had been unable to sleep the rest of the night.

"Another two Rangers are being airlifted to their campsite as we speak. They have plenty of protection."

She nodded and sniffed back tears. She was being foolish. She had spoken with the twins last night. They were clearly shaken by the tragedy, but both were determined to continue onward.

"They're tough kids," Marshall said. "Resourceful and cautious. They're not going to take any foolish chances."

With her back still turned to her husband, she mumbled, "Foolish chances? They're out there, aren't they? That's foolish enough."

Marshall's hands settled on her shoulders. He brushed aside the hair from the back of her neck and kissed her gently. "They'll be fine," he whispered in her ear calmly.

At fifty-four, Marshall was a striking man. His black-Irish hair was going to silver at the temples. He had a strong jaw, softened by full lips. His eyes, a bluish hazel, caught her and held her.

"Kelly and Frank will be fine," he said succinctly. "Let me hear you say it."

She tried to glance down, but a fingertip moved her chin back up.

"Say it . . . please. For me. I need to hear it, too."

She saw the glimmer of pain in his eyes. "Kelly and Frank . . . will be fine." Though her words were muttered, speaking them aloud was somehow reassuring.

"They will be. We raised them, didn't we?" He smiled at her, the pain fading in his eyes.

"We sure did." She slipped her arms around her husband and hugged him.

After a moment, Marshall kissed her on the forehead. "I'll take Jessie to day care."

She didn't object. After giving her grandchild a long hug by the front door, she allowed herself to be guided to her BMW. The forty-minute drive to the Instar Institute was a blur. When she arrived, she was glad to grab her briefcase and head through the cipher-locked doors into the main building. After such a disturbing night, it was good to be busy again, to have something to distract her from her worries.

She crossed to her office, greeting familiar faces in the hall. The complete immunology report was due today, and she was anxious to test Kelly's theory about an alteration to Gerald Clark's immune status. Preliminary results, coming piecemeal, were not terribly helpful. With the degree of cancerous processes ravaging the body, assessment was difficult.

Reaching her office, Lauren found a stranger standing by her door.

"Good morning, Dr. O'Brien," the man said, holding out a hand. He was no older than twenty-five, slender, with a shaved head, and dressed in blue scrubs.

Lauren, as head of the MEDEA project, knew everyone involved on the research, but not this man. "Yes?"

"I'm Hank Alvisio."

The name rang a bell. Lauren shook his hand while racking her brain.

"Epidemiology," he said, clearly reading her momentary confusion.

Lauren nodded. "Of course, I'm sorry, Dr. Alvisio." The young man was an epidemiologist out of Stanford. She had never met him in person. His field of expertise was the study of disease transmission. "How can I help you?"

He lifted a manila folder. "Something I'd like you to see."

She checked her watch. "I have a meeting with Immunology in about ten minutes."

"All the more reason you should see this."

She unlocked her office door with a magnetic ID card and ushered him inside. Switching on the lights, she crossed to her desk and offered Dr. Alvisio a seat on the other side. "What have you got?"

"Something I've been working on." He fiddled through his folder. "I've turned up some disturbing data that I wanted to run past you."

"What data?"

He glanced up. "I've been reviewing Brazilian medical records, looking for any other cases similar to Gerald Clark's."

"Other people with strange regenerations?"

He grinned shyly. "Of course not. But I was trying to put together an epidemiological assessment of cancers among those living in the Brazilian rain forests, with particular concentration in the area where Gerald Clark died. I thought maybe, by tracking cancer rates, we could indirectly track where the man had traveled."

Lauren sat up. This was an intriguing angle, even ingenious. No wonder Dr. Alvisio had been hired. If he could discover a cluster of similar cancers, then it might narrow the search parameters, which in turn could shorten the time Kelly and Frank would need to trek the jungle on foot. "And what did you find?"

"Not what I expected," he said with a worried look in his eyes. "I contacted every city hospital, medical facility, and jungle field clinic in the area. They've been sending me data covering the past decade. It's taken me this long to crunch the information through my computer models."

"And did you discover any trends in cancer rates in the area?" Lauren asked hopefully.

He shook his head. "Nothing like the cancers seen in Gerald Clark. He seems to be a very unique case."

Lauren hid her disappointment but could not keep a touch of irritation from entering her voice. "Then what did you discover?"

He pulled out a sheet of paper and passed it to Lauren. She slipped on her reading glasses.

It was a map of northwestern Brazil. Rivers snaked across the region, all draining toward one destination—the Amazon River. Cities and towns dotted the course, most sticking close to channels and waterways. The black-and-white map was dotted with small red *X*'s.

The young doctor tapped a few of the marks with the tip of a pen. "Here are all the medical facilities that supplied data. While working with them, I was contacted by a staff doctor at a hospital in the city of Barcellos." His pen pointed to a township along the Amazon, about two hundred miles upriver from Manaus. "They were having a problem with a viral outbreak among the city's children and elderly. Something that sounded like some form of hemorrhagic fever. Spiking temperatures, jaundice, vomiting, oral ulcerations. They had already lost over a dozen children to the disease. The doctor in Barcellos said he had never seen anything like it and asked for my assistance. I agreed to help."

Lauren frowned, slightly irked. The epidemiologist had been hired and flown here to work specifically and solely on this project. But she kept silent and let him continue.

"Since I already had a network of contacts established in the region, I utilized them, sending out an emergency request for any other reports of this outbreak." Dr. Alvisio pulled out a second sheet of paper. It appeared to be the same map: rivers and red X's. But on this map, several of the X's were circled in blue, with dates written next to them. "These are the sites that reported similar cases."

Lauren's eyes widened. There were so many. At least a dozen medical facilities were seeing cases.

"Do you see the trend here?" Dr. Alvisio said.

Lauren stared, then slowly shook her head.

The epidemiologist pointed to one X with a blue circle. "I've dated each reported case. This is the earliest." He glanced up from the paper and tapped the spot. "This is the mission of Wauwai."

"Where Gerald Clark was found?"

The doctor nodded.

She now recalled reading the field report from the expedition's first day. The Wauwai mission had been razed by superstitious Indians. They'd been frightened after several village children had become inexplicably sick.

"I checked with local authorities," Dr. Alvisio continued. He began to tap down the line of blue-circled X's. "The small steamboat that transported Clark's body stopped at each of these ports." The epidemiologist continued to tap the riverside towns. "Every site where the body passed, the disease appeared."

"My God," Lauren mumbled. "You're thinking the body was carrying some pathogen."

"At first. I thought it was one of several possibilities. The disease could have spread out from Wauwai through a variety of carriers. Almost all transportation through the region is by river, so *any* contagious disease would've followed a similar pattern. The pattern alone wasn't conclusive evidence that the body was the source of the contagion."

Lauren sighed, relieved. "It couldn't be the body. Before being shipped from Brazil, my daughter oversaw the disposition of the remains. It was tested for a wide variety of pathogens: cholera, yellow fever, dengue, malaria, typhoid, tuberculosis. We were thorough. We checked for every known pathogen. The body was clean."

"But I'm afraid it wasn't," Dr. Alvisio said softly.

"Why do you say that?"

"This was faxed this morning." He slid a final paper out of his folder. It was a CDC report out of Miami. "Clark's body was inspected in customs at Miami International. Now three cases of the disease have been reported in local children. All of them from families of airport employees."

Lauren sank into her chair as the horror of the man's words struck her. "Then whatever the disease is, it's here. We brought it here. Is that what you're saying?" She glanced over to Dr. Alvisio.

He nodded.

"How contagious is it? How virulent?"

The man's voice became suddenly mumbled. "It's hard to say with any certainty."

Lauren knew the man, even at such a young age, was a leader in his field or he wouldn't be here. "What is your cursory assessment? You have one, don't you?"

He visibly swallowed. "From the initial study of transmission rates and the disease's incubation period, it's a bug that's a hundredfold more contagious than the common cold . . . and as virulent as the Ebola virus."

Lauren felt the blood drain from her face. "And the mortality rate?"

Dr. Alvisio glanced down and shook his head.

"Hank?" she said hoarsely, her voice hushed with fear.

He lifted his face. "So far no one has survived."

AUGUST 12, 6:22 A.M.
AMAZON JUNGLE

Louis Favre stood at the edge of his camp, enjoying the view of the river at sunrise. It was a quiet moment after a long night. Kidnapping the corporal from under the other camp's nose had taken hours to prepare and execute, but as usual, his team had performed without fail.

After four days, the job of shadowing the other team was reduced to a routine. Each night, runners would slip ahead of the Rangers' team, trekking through the deep jungle to set up spy positions in well-camouflaged roosts in emergent trees that towered above the forest canopy. While spying, they maintained contact with the mercenary team via radio. During the day, Louis and the bulk of his forces followed in a caravan of canoes, trailing ten kilometers behind the others. Only at night had they crept any nearer.

Louis turned from the river and crossed into the deeper wood. Hidden among the trees, the camp was hard to spot until you were on top of it. He stared around while his forty-man team began to break camp. It was a motley group: bronze-skinned Indians culled from various tribes, lanky black Maroons out of Suriname, swarthy Colombians hired from the drug trade. Despite their differences, all the men had one thing in common: they were a hardened lot, marked by the jungle and forged in its bloody bower.

Rifles and guns, wrapped in sailcloth, lay in an orderly spread beside sleeping sites. The armament was as varied as his crew: German Heckler & Koch MP5s, Czech Skorpions, stubby Ingram submachine guns, Israeli-manufactured Uzis, even a few obsolete British Sten guns. Each man had his favorite. Louis's weapon of choice was his compact Mini-Uzi. It had all of the power of its bigger brother but measured only fourteen inches long. Louis appreciated its efficient design, small but deadly, like himself.

In addition to the munitions, a few men were sharpening machetes. The scrape of steel on rock blended with the morning calls of waking birds and barking monkeys. In hand-to-hand combat, a well-turned blade was better than a gun.

As he surveyed the camp, his second-in-command,

a tall black Maroon tribesman named Jacques, approached. At the age of thirteen, Jacques had been exiled from his village after raping a girl from a neighboring tribe. The man still bore a scar from his boyhood journey through the jungle. One side of his nose was missing from an attack by a piranha. He nodded his head respectfully. "Doctor."

"Yes, Jacques."

"Mistress Tshui indicates that she is ready for you."

Louis sighed. *Finally.* The prisoner had proven especially difficult.

Reaching into a pocket, Louis pulled free the dog tags and jangled them in his palm. He crossed to the lone tent set near the edge of the camp. Normally the camouflaged tent was shared by Louis and Tshui, but not this past night. During the long evening, Tshui had been entertaining a new guest.

Louis announced himself. "Tshui, my dear, is our visitor ready for company?" He pulled back the flap and bowed his way through the opening.

It was intolerably hot inside. A small brazier was burning in a corner. His mistress knelt naked before the small camp stove, lighting a bundle of dried leaves. Aromatic smoke spiraled upward. She rose to her feet. Her mocha skin shone with a sleek layer of sweat.

Louis stared, drinking her in. He longed to take her then and there, but he restrained himself. They had a guest this morning.

He turned his attention to the naked man staked spread-eagle on the bare-earth floor. The only bit of clothing he wore was a ball gag. Louis kept his eyes diverted from the bloody ruin of the corporal's body.

Still holding the man's dog tags, Louis crossed to a folding camp chair and sat down. He glanced to the name etched on the tags. "Corporal James DeMartini," he said in crisp English, reading the name, then looking up. "I've heard it from good authority that you're ready to cooperate."

The man moaned, tears flowed from his eyes.

"Is that a yes?"

The Ranger, a beaten and tortured dog, nodded with a pained wince. Louis studied the man. *What hurt more*, he wondered, *the torture? Or the actual moment you finally broke?*

With a tired sigh, he pulled the man's gag free. Louis needed information. Over the years, he had learned that the difference between success and failure lay in the details. He had reams of facts on the opposing team—not only information supplied directly by St. Savin, but also timely intelligence gained from a closer source.

Still Louis hadn't been satisfied.

He had kidnapped the young corporal because his other resources had proved woefully lacking in specific details about the Army Ranger unit: their firepower, their radio codes, their timetables. Furthermore, there was always the unspoken military objective, orders meant only for military ears. And last, Louis had arranged the abduction simply as a challenge, a small test of his forces.

The maneuver had gone flawlessly. Equipped with night-vision glasses, a small team had snuck in via the river. Once the chance arose, they had poisoned one of the Rangers with a special curare dart prepared by Tshui. Afterward, they had covered their tracks, setting up a false trail beside the river with caiman dung and prints. His mistress had then kept the kidnapped man alive by breathing mouth-to-mouth until he could be revived back at their camp with a special antidote.

But Tshui's true talents were proven during the long night. Her art of torture was without equal, plying pain and pleasure in a strange hypnotic rhythm until finally her prey's will broke.

"Please kill me," the man begged, hoarse, blood dribbling from his lips.

"Soon enough, *mon ami* . . . but first a few questions." Louis leaned back as Tshui walked around the corporal, waving her smoking bundle of dried leaves through the air. He noticed the broken soldier flinch from the woman, his terrified eyes following her every move.

Louis found this extremely arousing, but he kept himself focused. "Let's first go over a few numbers." Over the next few minutes, he extracted all the codes and time schedules of the army unit. He did not have to write any of it down, setting all the frequencies and numbers to memory. The information would greatly facilitate eavesdropping on the other team's communications. Next, he collected the details on the Ranger force's strength: number and types of weapons, skill levels, weaknesses, means of air support.

The man proved most talkative. He babbled on and on, giving out more information than requested.

". . . Staff Sergeant Kostos has a secret stash of whiskey in his rucksack . . . two bottles . . . and in Captain Waxman's boat, there's a crate that holds a cradle of napalm minibombs . . . and Corporal Conger has a *Penthouse* mag—"

Louis sat up. "Hold on, monsieur. Let's back up. Napalm bombs?"

"Minibombs . . . an even dozen . . ."

"Why?"

The corporal looked confused.

"James," he said sternly.

"I . . . I don't know. I suppose if we need to clear a section of jungle. Something that blocks our way."

"How large a region would one of those bombs clear?"

"I . . ." The man choked back a sob. "I'm not sure . . . maybe an acre . . . I don't know."

Louis leaned his elbows on his knees. "Are you telling me the truth, James?" He wiggled a finger for Tshui, who had grown bored with the conversation and sat cross-legged, busy laying out a new set of tools.

On his signal, she rose from her work and crawled like some jungle cat toward the naked soldier.

"No," the corporal cried, mewling, "no, I don't know anything more."

Louis shifted back in his seat. "Do I believe you?"

"Please . . ."

"I think I will believe you." Standing, he turned to his mistress. "We're done here, *ma chérie*. He's all yours."

She slid smoothly to her feet, offering a cheek to be kissed as he passed.

"No," the man on the ground moaned, pleading.

"Don't dawdle," he said to Tshui. "The sun is almost up, and we'll need to be under way shortly."

She smiled, smoky and full of hidden lusts. As he stepped to the tent's threshold, he saw her bend down and collect her bone needle and thread from the spread of tools. Lately, Tshui had been trying a new approach in preparing her specimens for head-shrinking. She now liked to sew her victims' eyelids closed while they were yet alive. To better capture their essence, he supposed. The Shuar shamans placed special significance in the eyes, a path to the spirit.

A sharp scream arose behind him.

"Tshui, don't forget the man's gag," Louis scolded. He made the mistake of glancing over his shoulder.

Tshui squatted above the face of Corporal James, her thighs on either side of his head, holding the squirming man in place as she busied herself with her needle and thread. He lifted an eyebrow in surprise. It seemed Tshui was trying something new.

"*Pardon, ma chérie*," he said, bowing out of the tent. Apparently he had scolded her too soon. The gag truly wasn't necessary.

Tshui was already sewing the corporal's lips shut.

ACT THREE

Survival of the Fittest

BRAZIL NUT
family: *Lecythidaceae*
genus: *Bertholletia*
species: *Excelsa*
common names: *Brazil Nut, Castanheiro do Para, Para-Nut,
Creamnut, Castana-de-Para, Castana-de-Brazil*
parts used: *Nut, Seed Oil*
properties/actions: *Emollient, Nutritive,
Antioxidant, Insecticide*

EIGHT

Village

Frowning, Nate caught the line and secured it to a mangrove tree. "Careful," he warned his boat mates. "It's swampy here. Watch your footing." He helped Kelly climb over the pontoon and onto the firmest section of the bank. He himself was muddy up to his knees and soaked everywhere else.

He lifted his face to the drizzle of rain from the cloudy skies. A storm had blown in overnight, starting with a fierce downpour, then fading into a steady misty drizzle within the last hour. The day's journey so far had been dreary. They had taken turns with a hand pump to bilge the water out of the boat all morning. Nate was glad when Captain Waxman had called a halt for lunch.

After helping everyone off their boats, Nate climbed the muddy bank onto higher ground. The jungle wept all around him, dripping, sluicing, and trickling from the leafy canopy overhead.

Professor Kouwe seemed unperturbed. With a pack hastily constructed of palm leaves, he was already heading out into the forest to forage for edibles, accompanied by a sodden Corporal Jorgensen. From the sour expression on the soldier's face, the tall Swede seemed little interested in a jungle trek. But Captain Waxman insisted that no one, not even the experienced Kouwe, walk the jungles alone.

Around the camp, the mood of the entire group remained sullen. Word of a possible contagion associated with Gerald Clark's body had reached them yesterday. Quarantines had been set up in Miami and around the institute where the body was being examined. Additionally, the Brazilian government had been informed and quarantine centers were being established throughout the Amazon. So far only children, the elderly, and those with compromised immune systems were at risk. Healthy adults seemed resistant. But much was still unknown: the causative agent, modes of transmission, treatment protocols. Back in the States, a Level Four containment had been set up at the Instar Institute to research these questions.

Nate glanced over to Frank and Kelly. Frank had his arm around his sister. She was still pale. Their entire family, including Kelly's daughter and the families of other scientists and workers at Instar, had been put into quarantine at the institute. No one was showing any symptoms, but the worry etched in Kelly's face was clear.

Nate turned away, giving them their privacy, and continued on.

The only bright spot in the last forty-eight hours was that no additional members of their party had fallen prey to the jungle. After losing Corporal DeMartini two days ago, everyone had kept alert, minding Nate's and Kouwe's warnings about jungle hazards, respecting their native lore. Now, before disembarking from a boat or bathing, everyone checked the shallows for buried stingrays in the mud or hidden electric eels. Kouwe gave lessons on how to avoid scorpions and snakes. No one put on a boot in the morning without first thoroughly shaking it out.

Nate checked the camp, walking the periphery, searching for any other hazards: fire liana, ant nests, hidden snakes. It was the new routine.

He spotted the two new members of the team, replacements for those lost. They were gathering wood. Both were ranked private first class, newly commissioned Rangers: a battle tank of a man with a thick Bronx accent, Eddie Jones, and, surprisingly, a woman, one of the first female Rangers, Maria Carrera. Special Forces had only started accepting women applicants six months before, after an amendment to Title 10 restrictions had passed Congress. But these new female recruits were still limited from front-line combat, assigned to missions like this one.

The morning after the nighttime attack, the two soldiers had been flown in from the field base at Wauwai, sliding down ropes from a hovering Huey. Afterward, small tanks of fuel and additional supplies were lowered.

It was a critical shipment, their last one. From that morning on, the team would be motoring beyond the range of the Hueys, beyond the range of air support. In fact, as of today, they had traveled close to four hundred miles. The only craft with enough range to reach them now was the black Comanche. But the sleek attack helicopter would only be utilized in case of emergency, such as the evacuation of an injured team member or in case an aerial assault was needed. Otherwise from here on out, they were on their own.

Finished with his survey, Nate crossed back to the center of the camp. Corporal Conger was hunched over a pile of twigs. With a match, he was trying to light a pile of dead leaves under a steeple of twigs. A drip of water from overhead doused his flame. "Damn it," the young Texan swore, tossing the match aside in disgust. "Everything's friggin' waterlogged. I could break out a magnesium flare and try to light it."

"Save them," Captain Waxman ordered from a step away. "We'll just make a cold camp for lunch."

Manny groaned from nearby. He was soaked to the skin. The only team member who looked even more dejected was Tor-tor. The jaguar stalked sullenly around its master, fur dripping water, ears drooped. Nothing was more piteous than a wet cat, even a two-hundred-pound one.

"I think I might be able to help," Nate said.

Eyes glanced to him.

"I know an old Indian trick."

He crossed back to the forest, searching for a particular tree he had noted during his survey of the campsite. He was followed by Manny and Captain Waxman. He quickly found the tall tree with characteristic bumpy gray bark. Slipping out his machete, he pierced the bark. A thick rusty resin flowed out. He fingered the sap and held it toward Waxman's nose.

The captain sniffed it. "Smells like turpentine."

Nate patted the tree. "It's called *copal*, derived from the Aztec word for resin, *copalli*. Trees in this family are found throughout the rain forests of Central and South America. It's used for a variety of purposes: healing wounds, treating diarrhea, alleviating cold symptoms. It's even used today in modern dentistry."

"Dentistry?" Manny asked.

Nate lifted his sticky finger. "If you ever had a cavity filled, you have some of this stuff in your mouth."

"And how is this all supposed to help us?" Waxman asked.

Nate knelt and pawed through the decaying leaves at the base of the tree. "Copal is rich in hydrocarbons. In fact, there has been some research recently into using it as a fuel source. Copal poured into a regular engine will run cleaner and more efficiently than gasoline." Nate found what he was searching for. "But Indians have known of this property for ages."

Standing, Nate revealed a fist-sized hardened lump of sap. He speared it atop a sharp stick like a marshmallow. "Can I borrow a match?"

Captain Waxman removed one from a waterproof container.

Nate struck the matchhead on the bark and held

the flame to a corner of the resin ball. Immediately it ignited into a bright blue flame. He held it out and marched toward the site of the failed campfire. "Indian hunters have been using this sap for centuries to light campfires during rainstorms. It'll burn for hours, acting as a starter to light wet wood."

Other eyes were drawn to the flame. Frank and Kelly joined the group as Nate settled the flaming resin ball into a nest of leaves and twigs. In a short time, the tinder and wood took the flame. A decent blaze arose.

"Good job," Frank said, warming his hands.

Nate found Kelly staring at him with a trace of a smile. It was her first smile in the past twenty-four hours.

Nate cleared his throat. "Don't thank me," he mumbled. "Thank the Indians."

"We may be able to do just that," Kouwe said suddenly from behind them.

Everyone turned.

The professor and Corporal Jorgensen crossed quickly toward them.

"We found a village," Jorgensen said, his eyes wide. He pointed in the direction that the pair had gone in search of foodstuffs. "Only a quarter mile upstream. It's deserted."

"Or appears to be," Kouwe said, staring significantly at Nate.

Nate's eyes grew wide. *Were these the same Indians who had been secretly dogging their trail?* Hope surged in Nate. With the rainstorm, he had been worried that any trail left by Gerald Clark would be washed away. This storm was but the first to mark the beginning of the Amazonian wet season. Time grew short. *But now . . .*

"We should investigate immediately," Captain Waxman said. "But first, I want a three-man Ranger team to recon the village."

Kouwe raised an arm. "It might be better if we approached less aggressively. By now, the Indians know we're here. I believe that's why the village is deserted."

Captain Waxman opened his mouth to disagree, but Frank held up a hand. "What do you suggest?"

Kouwe nodded to Nate. "Let the two of us go first . . . alone."

"Certainly not!" Waxman blurted. "I won't have you going in unprotected."

Frank took off his Red Sox cap and wiped his brow. "I think we should listen to the professor. Swarming in with heavily armed soldiers will only make the Indians fear us. We need their cooperation. But at the same time, I share Captain Waxman's concern about the two of you going in on your own."

"Then only one Ranger," Nate said. "And he keeps his gun on his shoulder. Though these Indians may be isolated, most are well aware of rifles."

"I'd like to go, too," Anna Fong said. The anthropologist's long black hair lay plastered to her face and shoulders. "A woman among the group may appear less hostile. Indian raiding parties don't bring women with them."

Nate nodded. "Dr. Fong is right."

Captain Waxman scowled, clearly not keen on letting civilians lead the way into an unknown encampment.

"Then perhaps I should be the one to go as their backup." Gazes turned to Private Carrera, the female Ranger. She was strikingly beautiful, a dark-skinned Latina with short-cropped black hair. She faced Captain Waxman. "Sir, if women are viewed as less hostile, I would be best suited for this mission."

Waxman finally agreed grudgingly. "Fine. I'll trust Professor Kouwe's assessment for now. But I want the rest of my forces set within a hundred yards of their position. And I want constant radio contact."

Frank glanced to Nate and Kouwe.

They nodded.

Satisfied, Frank cleared his throat. "Then let's move."

Kelly watched the camp fracture into various units. Nate, Kouwe, Anna Fong, and Private Carrera were already motoring their pontoon boat into the current, while Captain Waxman selected three of his men and led them to a second rubber raider. They would paddle a hundred yards behind the first boat, keeping a safe distance away yet close enough for a rapid response. Additionally, three more Rangers would travel overland with Corporal Jorgensen in command. This team would take up a position a hundred yards from the village. In preparation, they painted their faces in jungle camouflage.

Manny had attempted to join this last party, but he'd been rebuffed by Captain Waxman. "All other civilians stay here."

With the matter settled, Kelly could only watch

as the others set off. Two Rangers—the newly arrived Private Eddie Jones and Corporal Tom Graves—remained at the camp as bodyguards. Once the others were launched and on their way, Kelly overheard Jones grumble to Graves, "How did we end up minding the friggin' sheep?"

Corporal Graves did not respond, staring dully into the drizzle, clearly grieving for his brother Rodney.

Alone now, Kelly crossed to Frank's side. As the nominal leader of this operation, her brother had the right to insist on joining either of the departing groups, but he had chosen to remain behind—not out of fear, she knew, but concern for his twin sister.

"Olin has the satellite link hooked up," Frank said, taking his sister under his arm. "We can reach the States when you're ready."

She nodded. Not far from the fire, under a rain tarp, Olin sat hunched before a laptop and a satellite dish. He tapped busily at the keyboard, his face scrunched in concentration. Richard Zane stood over his shoulder watching him work.

Finally, Olin glanced to them and nodded. "All set," he said. Kelly heard the trace of his Russian accent. It was easy to miss unless one's ears were tuned for it. Olin was ex-KGB, once a member of their computer surveillance department before the fall of the communist regime. He had defected to the States only months before the Berlin Wall tumbled. His background in technology and his knowledge of Russian systems earned him a low-level security position in the CIA's Directorate of Science and Technology.

Frank guided Kelly to a camp chair before the laptop computer. Since learning of the contagion, Kelly had insisted they be updated twice daily now. Her excuse was to keep both sides fully apprised, but in reality, she had to know her family was still okay. Her mother, her father, her daughter. All three were at ground zero.

Kelly sat on the camp chair, eyeing Olin askance as he moved aside. She was never fully at ease around the man. Maybe because he was ex-KGB and she had grown up with a father in the CIA. Or maybe it was that ropy scar that stretched from ear to ear across his throat. Olin had claimed to be no more than a Russian computer geek for the KGB. But if that were true, how had he obtained that scar?

Olin pointed to the screen. "We should be up-linked in thirty seconds."

Kelly watched the small timer on the computer screen count downward. When it reached zero, her father's face blinked onto the screen. He was dressed casually, his tie half undone, no jacket.

"You look like a drowned rat" were his first words from the flickering image.

With a small smile, Kelly lifted a hand to her wet hair. "The rains have started."

"So I see." Her father returned her grin. "How are things out there?"

Frank leaned forward into the view. He gave a quick overview of their discovery.

As he talked, Kelly listened to the echoing whine of Nate's boat. The waters here and the overhanging jungle played tricks with acoustics. It sounded like the boat was still nearby, but then the noise suddenly choked off. They must have reached the village already.

"Watch out for your sister, Frank," her father said, finishing their talk.

"Will do, sir."

Now it was Kelly's turn. "How're Mother and Jessie?" she asked, holding her fists clenched in her lap.

Her father smiled reassuringly. "Both in the pink of health. We all are. The entire institute. So far no cases have been reported in the area. Any risk of contamination has been successfully quarantined, and we've converted the west wing of the institute into temporary family housing. With so many MEDEA members here, we've got around-the-clock doctors."

"How's Jessie handling it?"

"She's a six-year-old," he said with a shrug. "At first she was a bit scared at being uprooted. But now she's having a ball with the other staff's children. In fact, why don't you ask her yourself?"

Kelly sat straighter as her daughter's face came into view, a small hand waving. "Hi, Mommy!"

Tears welled. "Hi, sweetheart. Are you having fun?"

Her daughter nodded vigorously, climbing into her grandfather's lap. "We had chocolate cake, and I rode a pony!"

Choking back a laugh, her father spoke over the top of his granddaughter's head. "There's a small farm nearby, in the quarantine zone. They brought a pony over to entertain the kids."

"That sounds like fun, honey. I wish I could've been there."

Jessie squirmed in her seat. "And you know what else? A clown is coming over and is gonna make animal balloons."

"A clown?"

Her father whispered to the side. "Dr. Emory from histopathology. He's damn good at it, too."

"I'm gonna ask him to make me a monkey," Jessie said.

"That's wonderful." Kelly leaned closer, soaking up the view of both her father and her daughter.

After a bit more elaboration on clowns and ponies, Jessie was lifted off her grandfather's knee. "It's time for Ms. Gramercy to take you back to class."

Jessie pouted but obeyed.

"Bye, honey," Kelly called. "I love you!"

She waved again, using her entire arm. "Bye, Mommy! Bye, Uncle Frankie!"

Kelly had to restrain herself from touching the screen.

Once Jessie was gone, her father's face grew grim. "Not all the news is so bright."

"What?" Kelly asked.

"It's why your mother isn't here. While we seem to have things contained, the outbreak in Florida is spreading. Overnight, there's been another six cases reported in Miami hospitals, and another dozen in outlying county hospitals. The quarantine zone is being widened, but we don't think we secured the area in time. Your mother and others are monitoring reports from across the country."

"My God," Kelly gasped.

"In the last twelve hours, the number of cases has

now climbed to twenty-two. The fatalities to eight. Scenarios calculated by the best epidemiologists in the country have these numbers doubling every twelve hours. In fact, along the Amazon, the death toll is already climbing toward the five hundred mark."

As Kelly calculated in her head, her face blanched. Frank's hand on her shoulder tightened. In just a few days, the number in the U.S. could climb into the tens of thousands.

"The president has just signed an order to mobilize the National Guard in Florida. The official story is an outbreak of a virulent South American flu. Specifics on how it got here are being kept under wraps."

Kelly leaned back, as if distance would lessen the horror. "Has any protocol for treatment been established?"

"Not as of yet. Antibiotics and antivirals don't seem to be of any help. All we can offer is symptomatic care—intravenous fluids, drugs to combat fever, and pain relievers. Until we know what is causing the disease, fighting it's an uphill battle." Her father leaned closer to the screen. "That's why your work out in the field is so critical. If you can find out what happened to Agent Clark, you may discover a clue to this disease."

Kelly nodded.

Frank spoke, his voice a hoarse whisper. "We'll do our best."

"Then I'd better let you all get back to your work." After a sober good-bye, her father signed off.

Kelly glanced to her brother. She saw that Manny stood to one side of him, Richard Zane to the other.

"What have we done?" Manny asked. "Maybe someone should have listened to that Indian shaman back in Wauwai. Burned Clark's body after he died."

Zane shook his head and mumbled, "It wouldn't have mattered. The disease would've eventually broken out of the forest. It's just like AIDS."

"What do you mean?" Kelly asked, turning in her seat.

"AIDS started after a highway was built into the African jungle. We come disturbing these ancient ecosystems, and we don't know what we stir up."

Kelly pushed out of the camp chair. "Then it's up to us to stop it. The jungle may have produced AIDS, but it also offered our best treatments against the disease. Seventy percent of AIDS drugs are derived from tropical plants. So if this new disease came out of the jungle, why not the cure, too?"

"That's if we can find it," Zane said.

Off to the side, Manny's jaguar suddenly growled. The great cat swung around and crouched, ears pricked, eyes fixed on the jungle behind them.

"What's wrong with him?" Zane asked, backing a step away.

Manny squinted at the shadowed rain forest as Tortor continued a deep warning growl. "He's caught a scent . . . something's out there."

Nate crossed down the narrow trail toward the small Indian village, which consisted of a single large roundhouse, open to the sky in the middle. As he approached the structure, he heard none of the usual noises coming from the *shabano*. No arguing *huyas*, no women yelling for more plantains, no laughter of children. It was ghostly quiet and unnerving.

"The construction is definitely Yanomamo," Nathan said softly to Kouwe and Anna Fong. "But small. It probably houses no more than thirty villagers."

Behind them marched Private Carrera, her M-16 held in both hands, muzzle pointed at the ground. She was whispering into her radio's microphone.

Anna stared wide-eyed at the *shabano*.

Nate stopped her from continuing through the roundhouse's small doorway and into the village proper. "Have you ever been among the Yanomamo?"

Anna shook her head.

Nate cupped his mouth. *"Klock, klock, klock,"* he yelled. Then softer to Anna, he explained, "Whether it seems deserted or not, you never approach a Yanomamo village without first announcing yourself. It's a good way to get an arrow in your back. They have the tendency to shoot first and ask questions later."

"Nothing wrong with that policy," Carrera mumbled behind him.

They stood near the entrance for a full minute, then Kouwe spoke. "No one's here." He waved an arm behind him. "No canoes by the river, no nets or fishing gear either. No *yebis* squawking in alarm."

"Yebis?" their Ranger escort asked.

"The gray-winged trumpeter," Nate said. "Sort of an ugly chicken really. The Indians use them like feathered guard dogs. They raise a ruckus when anyone approaches."

The Ranger nodded. "So no chickens, no Indians."

She turned in a slow circle, surveying the forest around them. The woman refused to let down her guard. "Let me go first."

Lifting her weapon higher, she paused near the short entrance. Bowing low, she ducked her head through. After a moment, she slid through the bamboo-framed entrance, sticking close to the banana-leaf wall, then barked to them, "All clear. But stick behind me."

Carrera moved toward the center of the circular structure. She kept her weapon ready, but as Nate had suggested, she kept the rifle's muzzle pointing at the ground. Among the Yanomamo, an arrow nocked and aimed at a fellow tribesman was a call to war. Since Nate didn't know how familiar these particular Indians were with modern weapons, he wanted no misinterpretations on this point.

As a group, Nate, Kouwe, and Anna entered the *shabano*.

Around them, the individual family units were sectioned off from their neighbors by drapes of tobacco leaves, water gourds, and baskets. Woven hammocks, all empty, hung from the roof beams. A pair of stone bowls lay toppled in the central clearing beside a grinding stone, manioc flour spilled onto the dirt.

A sudden burst of color startled them all as a parrot took wing. It had been roosting atop a pile of brown bananas.

"I don't like this," Kouwe said.

Nate knew what he meant and nodded.

"Why?" asked Carrera.

"When the Yanomamo migrate to a new site,

they either burn the old *shabano* or at least strip it of all useful items." Kouwe pointed around him. "Look at all these baskets, hammocks, and feather collections. They wouldn't leave these behind."

"What could make them leave so suddenly?" Anna asked.

Kouwe slowly shook his head. "Something must have panicked them."

"Us?" Anna stared around her. "Do you think they knew we were coming?"

"If the Indians had been here, I'm sure they would've been well aware of our approach. They keep a keen watch on their forest. But I don't think it was our party that made them abandon this *shabano* so quickly."

"Why do you say that?" Nate asked.

Kouwe crossed around the edge of the living sites. "All the fires are cold." He nudged the pile of bananas upon which the parrot had been feeding. "They're half rotten. The Yanomamo would not have wasted food like this."

Nate understood. "So you think the village was abandoned some time ago."

"At least a week, I'd estimate."

"Where did they go?" Anna asked.

Kouwe stood in place and turned in a slow circle. "It's hard to say, but there's one other detail that may be significant." He glanced to Nate to see if he had noticed it, too.

Frowning, Nate studied the dwellings. Then it dawned on him. "All the weapons are gone." Among the abandoned wares, there was not a single arrow, bow, club, or machete.

"Whatever spooked them to run," Kouwe said, "they were scared for their lives."

Private Carrera edged closer to them. "If you're right, if this place is long deserted, I should call in my unit."

Kouwe nodded.

She stepped away, mumbling into her radio.

Kouwe silently waved Nate aside so they could speak privately. Anna was busy examining an individual dwelling, picking through the goods left behind.

Kouwe whispered. "It was not these Yanomamo who were tracking our party."

"Then who?"

"Some other group . . . I'm still not sure it was even Indians. I think it's time we informed Frank and Captain Waxman."

"Are you thinking that whatever spooked the Indians is what's now on our trail?"

"I'm not sure, but whatever could frighten the Yanomamo from their homes is something we should be wary of."

By now, the constant drizzle had stopped. The cloud banks began to break apart, allowing cracks of afternoon sunlight to pierce through in dazzling rays. After so long in the misty murk, the light was bright.

In the distance, Nate heard a single engine roar to life. Captain Waxman and his Rangers were coming.

"You're certain we should tell them?" Nate asked.

Before Kouwe could answer, Anna had wandered over. She pointed to the skies off to the south. "Look at all those birds!"

Nate glanced to where she pointed. With the rains dying away, various birds were rising from the canopy to dry their wings and begin the hunt for food again. But a half mile away, a huge flock of black birds rose from the canopy like a dark mist. Thousands of them.

Oh, God. Nate crossed quickly to Private Carrera. "Let me have your binoculars."

The Ranger's eyes were on the strange dance of black birds, too. She unsnapped a compact set of binoculars from her field jacket and passed them to Nate. Holding his breath, he peered through the glasses. It took him a moment to focus on the birds. Through the lenses, the flock broke down to individuals, a mix of large and small birds. Many were fighting among themselves in the air, tearing at each other. But despite their differences, the various birds all shared one common trait.

"Vultures," Nate said, lowering the binoculars.

Kouwe edged nearer. "So many . . ."

"Turkey vultures, yellow-heads, even king vultures."

"We should investigate," Kouwe said. In his eyes, Nate saw the worry shared by all. The missing Indians . . . the vultures . . . It was a dire omen.

"Not until the unit gets here," Private Carrera warned.

Behind them, the roaring of the other boat drew abreast of their location and choked out. In a few minutes, Captain Waxman and another three Rangers were entering the *shabano*. Private Carrera quickly updated the others.

"I've sent the Rangers stationed in the woods

back to camp," Captain Waxman said. "They'll gather everyone here. In the meantime, we'll scout what lies out there." He pointed to three of his unit: Private Carrera, Corporal Conger, and Staff Sergeant Kostos.

"I'd like to go with them," Nate said. "I know this jungle better than anyone."

After a short pause, Captain Waxman sighed. "So you've proven." He waved them off. "Keep in radio contact."

As they left, Nate heard Kouwe approach Waxman. "Captain, there is something I think you should be made aware of . . ."

Nate ducked out of the *shabano*'s low door, glad to escape. He imagined Captain Waxman would not be pleased that he and Kouwe had kept hushed about the nighttime prowlers around their campsites. Nate was more than happy to leave such explanations to the diplomatic professor.

Out in the woods, the two men, Conger and Kostos, took the point, leaving Private Carrera to dog Nate's steps and maintain a rear guard.

They half trotted through the wet woods, careful of the slippery mud and dense layers of sodden leaves. A small stream that drained toward the river behind them seemed to be heading in the same direction. They found an old game trail paralleling it and made better time.

Nate noticed footprints along the trail. Old prints almost obscured by the rain. *Barefooted*. He pointed one out to Private Carrera. "The Indians must've fled this way."

She nodded and waved him onward.

Nate pondered this oddity. *If panicked, why flee on foot? Why not use the river?*

The scouting party climbed the trail, following the streambed. Despite the hard pace, Nate kept up with the Rangers in the lead. The forest around them was unusually quiet, almost hushed. It was eerie, and suddenly Nate regretted leaving his shotgun back at camp.

So occupied was he with keeping his footing and watching for any hidden dangers that Nate almost missed it. He stumbled to a stop with a gasp.

Private Carrera almost collided into him. "Damn it. Give some warning."

The other two Rangers, failing to notice the pair had halted, continued up the trail.

"Need a rest?" Carrera asked with a bit of playful disdain.

"No," Nate said, panting heavily to catch his breath. "Look."

Soaked and pinned to a small branch was a scrap of faded yellow material. It was small, half the size of a standard playing card and roughly square. Nathan pulled it free.

"What is it?" Carrera peered over his shoulder. "Something from the Indians?"

"No, not likely." He fingered the material. "It's polyester, I think. A synthetic." He checked the branch upon which the scrap had been impaled. The thin limb had been cut, not naturally broken. As he examined the end, crude markings on the tree's trunk caught his attention. "What's this?"

He reached and brushed rainwater from the trunk. "My God . . ."

"What?"

Nathan stood clear so his escort could see. Deeply inscribed into the bark of the tree's trunk was a coded message.

$$\nwarrow_{SW}$$

$$17/5 \; \substack{G \\ C}$$

Private Carrera whistled appreciatively and leaned closer. "This *G* and *C* near the bottom . . ."

"Gerald Clark," Nathan finished her thought. "He signed it. The arrow must indicate where he had come from . . . or at least where his next marker might lie."

Carrera checked her wrist compass. "Southwest. It's pointing the right way."

"But what about the numbers? Seventeen and five."

The Ranger scrunched up her face. "Maybe a date, done the military way. The day, followed by the month."

"That would make it May seventeenth? That's nearly three months ago." Turning, Nate started to question her assessment, but Carrera had a palm raised toward him. Her other hand pressed her radio earpiece more firmly in place.

She spoke into her radio. "Roger that. We're on our way."

Nate raised an inquiring eyebrow.

"Conger and Kostos," she said. "They've found bodies ahead."

Nate felt a sickening lurch in his belly.

"Come on," Carrera said stiffly. "They want your opinion."

Nodding, Nate continued up the trail. Behind him, as they marched, Private Carrera reported their discovery to her captain.

As Nate hurried, he glanced down and realized he still held the bit of faded yellow material. He remembered Gerald Clark had stumbled out of the jungle barefoot, wearing only pants. Had the man used the scraps of his own shirt to flag these sites? Like a trail of bread crumbs back to wherever he had come from?

Nate rubbed the bit of cloth between his fingers. After four years, here was the first tangible bit of proof that at least some of his father's team had survived. Up to this point, Nate had not entertained any hope that his father was still alive. In fact, he had refused even to contemplate that possibility, not after so long, not after coming to some semblance of peace with his father's death. The pain of losing his father a second time would be more than he could handle. Nate stared at the scrap in his hand for a second longer, then stuffed it into a pocket.

As he trekked up the trail, he wondered if there were more such flags out there. Though he had no way of knowing, Nate knew one thing for certain. He would not stop looking, not until he discovered the truth of his father's fate.

Carrera swore behind him.

Nathan glanced back. Carrera had an arm over her nose and mouth. Only then did Nate notice the stench in the air. Rancid meat and offal.

"Over here!" a voice called out. It was Staff Sergeant Kostos. The older Ranger stood only ten yards farther down the trail. In full camouflage, he blended well with the dappled background.

Nate crossed to him and was immediately assaulted by a horrible sight.

"Jesus Christ," Carrera gasped behind him.

Corporal Conger, the young Texan, was farther down the trail, a handkerchief over his face, in the thick of the slaughterhouse. He waved off vultures with his M-16 as swarms of flies rose around him.

Bodies lay sprawled everywhere: on the trail, in the woods, some draped halfway in the stream. Men, women, children. All Indians from the look of them, but it was difficult to say for sure. Faces had been chewed away, limbs gnawed to bone, entrails ripped from bellies. The carrion feeders had made quick work of the bodies, leaving the rest to flies, other insects, and burrowing worms. Only the diminutive sizes of the corpses suggested they were Yanomamo, the missing villagers. And from the number, probably the *entire* village.

Nathan closed his eyes. He pictured the villagers with whom he had worked in the past: little Tama, noble Takaho. With a sudden burst, he rushed off the trail and hunched over the stream. He breathed deeply, fighting in vain the rising gorge. With a sickening groan, his stomach spasmed. Bile splattered into the flowing water, swelled by the recent rains. Nate remained crouched, hands on his knees, breathing hard.

Kostos barked behind him. "We don't have all

day, Rand. What do you think happened here? An attack by another tribe?"

Nate could not move, not trusting his stomach.

Private Carrera joined him, placing a sympathetic hand on his shoulder. "The sooner we get this done," she said softly, "the sooner we can leave."

Nathan nodded, took a final deep breath, and forced himself to climb back within view of the slaughter. He studied the area from a few steps away, then moved closer.

"What do you think?" Carrera asked.

Gulping back bile, Nate spoke quietly. "They must've fled during the night."

"Why do you say that?" Kostos asked.

Nate glanced to the sergeant, then nudged a stick near one of the corpses. "A torch. Burned to char at the end. The village took flight in full darkness." He studied the bodies, recognizing a pattern to the carnage. He pointed an arm as he spoke. "When the attack came, the men tried to protect the women and children. When they failed, the women were a second line of defense. They tried to run with the children." Nate indicated a woman's corpse deeper in the woods. In her arms rested a dead child. He turned away.

"The attack came from across the stream," Nate continued. His hand shook as he pointed to the number of male bodies piled near or in the stream. "They must have been caught by surprise. Too late to put up an adequate defense."

"I don't care in what order they were killed," Kostos said. "Who the hell killed them?"

"I don't know," Nate said. "None of the bodies are pierced by arrows or spears. But then again, the enemy might have collected their weapons after the attack—to conserve their arsenal and to leave no evidence behind. With the bodies so torn apart, it's impossible to tell which wounds are from weapons and which from the carrion feeders."

"So in other words, you have no damn clue." Kostos shook his head and swung around. From a few steps away, he spoke into his radio.

Nate wiped his damp forehead and shivered. What the hell *had* happened here?

Finally, Kostos stepped forward, raising his voice. "New orders everyone. We're to collect a body for Dr. O'Brien to examine—one that's chewed up the least—and return it to the village. Any volunteers?"

No one answered, which earned a mean snicker from the sergeant. "Okay," Kostos said. "I didn't think so." He pointed to Private Carrera. "Why don't you take our fragile little doctor back to camp? This is *men's* work."

"Yes, sir." Carrera waved Nate to the path, and together they continued down toward the village. Once out of earshot, Carrera grumbled under her breath. "What an asshole . . ."

Nate nodded, but truthfully, he was only too glad to leave the massacre site. He couldn't care less what Sergeant Kostos might think. But he understood Carrera's anger. Nate could only imagine the hassles the woman had to endure from the all-male force.

The remainder of the journey down the trail was made in silence. As they neared the *shabano*, voices could be heard. Nathan's pace quickened. It would be good to be among the living again. He hoped someone had thought to light a fire.

Circling around the *shabano*, Nathan approached Private Eddie Jones, who stood guard by the entrance. Beyond him, limned against the water, a pair of Rangers was posted by the river.

As he and Carrera reached the roundhouse's door, Eddie Jones greeted them and blurted out the news. "Hey, you guys ain't gonna fuckin' believe what we fished out of the jungle."

"What?" Carrera asked.

Jones thrust a thumb toward the door. "Go see for yourselves."

Carrera waved her rifle's barrel for Nate to go first.

Within the *shabano*, a small congregation was clustered in the roundhouse's open central yard. Manny stood somewhat to the side with Tor-tor. He lifted an arm when he spotted Nate, but there was no greeting smile.

The voices from the others were raised in argument.

"He's my prisoner!" Captain Waxman boomed. He stood with three Rangers, who all had their weapons on their shoulders pointing at someone out of sight behind the group of civilians.

"At least remove the cuffs on his wrists," Kelly argued. "His ankles are still bound. He's just an old man."

"If you want cooperation," Kouwe added, "this is no way to go about it."

"He'll answer our questions," Waxman said with clear menace.

Frank stepped in front of Waxman. "This is still my operation, Captain. And I won't tolerate abuse of this prisoner."

By now, Nate had crossed the yard and joined them. Anna Fong glanced to him, her eyes scared.

Richard Zane stood slightly to the side, a satisfied smirk on his face. He nodded to Nathan. "We caught him lurking in the jungle. Manny's big cat helped hunt him down. You should have heard him screaming when the jaguar had him pinned against a tree."

Zane stepped aside, and Nate saw who had been captured. The small Indian lay in the dirt, his ankles and wrists bound in strips of thick plastic zip ties. His shoulder-length white hair clearly marked him as an elder. He sat before the others, mumbling under his breath. His eyes flicked between the rifles pointed at him and Tor-tor pacing nearby.

Nate listened to his muttered words. *Yanomamo.* He moved closer. It was a shamanic prayer, a warding against evil. Nate realized the prisoner must be a shaman. *Was he from this village? A survivor of the slaughter?*

The Indian's eyes suddenly flicked to Nate, his nostrils flaring. "Death clings to you," he warned, in his native dialect. "You know. You saw."

Nate realized the man must smell the stench of the massacre on his clothes and skin. He knelt nearer and spoke in Yanomamo. "*Haya.* Grandfather. Who are you? Are you from this village?"

He shook his head with a deep scowl. "This village is marked by *shawari.* Evil spirits. I came here to deliver myself to the Ban-ali. But I was too late."

Around Nate, the arguing had stopped as they watched the exchange. Kelly whispered behind him. "He's not spoken a word to anyone, not even Professor Kouwe."

"Why do you seek the Blood Jaguars, the Ban-ali?"

"To save my own village. We did not heed their ways. We did not burn the body of the *nabe*, the white man marked as a slave of the Ban-ali. Now all our children sicken with evil magic."

Nate suddenly understood. The white man marked by the Ban-ali had to be Gerald Clark. If so, that meant . . . . "You're from Wauwai."

He nodded and spit into the dirt. "Curse that name. Curse the day we ever set foot in that *nabe* village."

Nate realized this was the shaman who had tried to heal the sick mission children, then burned their village down in an attempt to protect the others. But by his own admission, the shaman must have failed. The contagion was still spreading through the Yanomamo children.

"Why come here? How did you get here?"

"I followed the *nabe*'s tracks to his canoe. I saw how it was painted. I know he came from this village, and I know the trails here. I came to seek the Ban-ali. To give myself to them. To beg them to lift their curse."

Nate leaned back. The shaman, in his guilt, had come to sacrifice himself.

"But I was too late. I find only one woman still alive." He glanced toward the site of the massacre. "I give her water, and she tells me the tale of her village."

Nate sat up straighter.

"What is he saying?" Captain Waxman asked.

Nate waved off his question. "What happened?"

"The white man was found by hunters three moons ago, sick and bony. They saw his markings. In terror, they imprisoned the man, fearing he would come to their village. They stripped him of all his belongings and tethered him in a cage, deep in the woods, intending to leave him for the Blood Jaguars to collect. The hunters fed and cared for him, fearing to harm what belonged to the Ban-ali. But the *nabe* continued to sicken. Then, a moon later, one of the hunter's sons grew ill."

Nate nodded. The contagious disease had spread.

"The shaman here declared them cursed and demanded the death of the *nabe*. They would burn his body to appease the wrath of the Ban-ali. But that morning when the hunters reached the cage, he was gone. They thought the Ban-ali had claimed him and were relieved. Only later that day would they discover one of their canoes was missing. But by then it was too late."

The Indian grew quiet. "Over the next days, the hunter's child died, and more in the village grew ill. Then a week ago, a woman returning from gathering bananas from the garden found a marking on the outer wall of the *shabano*. No one knew how it got there." The Indian nodded to the southwest section of the roundhouse. "It is still there. The mark of the Ban-ali."

Nate stopped the story and turned to the others. He quickly recounted what the Indian shaman had told him. Their eyes grew wide with the telling.

Afterward, Captain Waxman sent Jorgensen to check that section of the outer wall.

As they waited for him to return, Nate convinced Captain Waxman to slice the wrist bindings off the prisoner. He agreed, since the man was clearly cooperating. The shaman now sat in the dirt with a canteen in hand, sipping from it gratefully.

Kelly knelt beside Nathan. "His story makes a certain sense from a medical standpoint. The tribe, when they kept Clark isolated in the jungle, almost succeeded in quarantining him. But as Clark's disease progressed, either the man became more contagious . . . or perhaps the hunter, whose son got sick, had somehow contaminated himself. Either way, the disease leaped here."

"And the tribe panicked."

Behind them, Jorgensen ducked back into the *shabano*, his face grim. "The old guy's right. There's a scrawled drawing on the wall. Just like the tattoo on Agent Clark's body." His nose curled in distaste. "But the damn thing smells like it was drawn with pig shit or something. Stinks something fierce."

Frank frowned and turned back to Nate. "See if you can find out what else the shaman knows."

Nate nodded and turned back to the shaman. "After finding the symbol, what happened?"

The shaman scrunched up his face. "The tribe fled that same night . . . but . . . but something came for them."

"What?"

The Indian frowned. "The woman who spoke to me was near to death. Her words began to wander. Something about the river coming to eat them.

They fled, but it followed them up the little stream and caught them."

"What? What caught them? The Ban-ali?"

The shaman gulped from the canteen. "No, that's not what the woman said."

"Then what?"

The shaman stared Nate in the eye to show he spoke truthfully. "The jungle. She said the jungle rose out of the river and attacked them."

Nathan frowned.

The shaman shrugged. "I know no more. The cursed woman died, and her spirit went to join her tribe. The next day, this day, I hear you coming up the river. I go to see who you are." He glanced over to Manny's jaguar. "But I am found. Death scent clings to me, like it does to you."

Nathan sat back on his heels. He stared over at Manny. The biologist had Tor-tor on a leash, but the cat was clearly agitated, pacing around and around with his hackles raised. Spooked.

Kouwe finished translating for the others. "That's all he knows."

Waxman waved for Jorgensen to slice the shaman's ankle restraints, too.

"What do you make of his story?" Kelly asked, still kneeling at his side.

"I don't know," he mumbled, picturing the spread of bodies up the trail. He had thought something had attacked from the stream's far side, but if the woman's story was true, the attack had come from the stream itself.

Kouwe joined them. "The story is consistent with

the myths of the Ban-ali. They're said to be able to bend the very jungle to their will."

"But what could come from the river and kill all those tribesmen?" Kelly asked.

Kouwe slowly shook his head. "I can't even imagine."

A commotion near the *shabano*'s door drew their attention. Staff Sergeant Kostos pushed inside, dragging a travois behind him. A dead body lay atop it. One of the massacred.

Behind them, the shaman let out a piercing cry.

Nate swung around.

The Indian, his eyes wide with terror, backed away. "Do not bring the cursed here! You will call the Ban-ali upon us!"

Jorgensen tried to restrain the man, but even at his age, the Indian was wiry with muscle. He slipped out of the Ranger's grip, fled to one of the dwellings, then, using a hammock as a ladder, scrambled to the encircling roof of the *shabano*.

One of the Rangers raised his rifle.

"Don't shoot!" Nathan called.

"Lower your weapon, Corporal," Waxman ordered.

The shaman paused atop the roof and turned to them. "The dead belong to the Ban-ali! They will come to collect what is theirs!" With these final words, the shaman dove off the roof and into the surrounding jungle.

"Go fetch him," Waxman ordered two of the Rangers.

"They'll never find him," Kouwe said. "As scared as he is, he'll vanish into these jungles."

The professor's words proved prophetic. The Yanomamo shaman was never found. As afternoon closed toward evening, Kelly ensconced herself in a corner of the *shabano* and worked to discover what had killed the tribesman. Nate took Captain Waxman and Frank over to the tree with the carved directions left behind by Gerald Clark.

"He must have written this just before being captured," Frank said. "How awful. He was so close to reaching civilization, then was captured and imprisoned." Frank shook his head. "For almost three months."

As they returned to the *shabano*, the rest of the team prepared to set up for the night: lighting fires, setting up guard shifts, preparing food. The plan tomorrow was to leave the river and to begin the overland journey, following Gerald Clark's trail.

With the sun setting and a meal of fish and rice being prepared, Kelly finally left her makeshift morgue. She settled to a camp chair with a long, tired sigh and stared into the flames as she gave her report. "As near as I can tell, he was poisoned by something. I found evidence of a convulsive death. Tongue chewed through, signs of contracted stricture of spine and limbs."

"What poisoned him?" Frank asked.

"I'd need a tox lab to identify it. I couldn't even tell you how it was delivered. Maybe a poisoned spear, arrow, or dart. The body was too macerated by the carrion feeders to judge adequately."

Watching the sun set, Nate listened as the discussions continued. He remembered the words of the vanished shaman—*they will come to collect what is theirs*—and pondered the massacre up the nearby trail and the disease spreading here and through the States. As he did so, Nate could not escape the sinking sensation that time was running out for them all.

NINE

Night Attack

AUGUST 14, 12:18 A.M.
AMAZON JUNGLE

Kelly woke from a nightmare, bolting up from her hammock. She didn't remember the specifics of her dream, only a vague sense of corpses and a chase. She checked her watch. The glowing dial put the time after midnight.

All around the *shabano*, most of the others were asleep. A single Ranger stood by the fire; his partner was guarding the door. Kelly knew another pair patrolled outside the roundhouse. Otherwise, the rest were snuggled in their hammocks after the long, horrible day.

It was no surprise she had nightmares: the massacre, the ravaged body she had examined, the ongoing tension. All of it overshadowed by the ever-present fear for her family back in Virginia. Her subconscious had plenty of fodder to mull through during her REM sleep.

Yesterday's evening report from the States had not been any cheerier than the lunchtime update. Another twelve cases had been reported in the U.S., and another three deaths—two children and an elderly matron from Palm Beach. Meanwhile, across the Amazon basin, disease and death were spreading like fire through dry tinder. People were barricading themselves indoors or leaving cities. Bodies were being burned in the streets of Manaus.

Kelly's mother had reported that so far no cases had yet arisen among the research team at Instar. But it was too soon to say they were out of the woods. The newest data, gathered mostly from cases in the Amazon, where the disease had a longer track record, suggested that the incubation period could be as short as three days or as long as seven. It all depended on the initial health of the victim. Children with poorer nutrition or parasitic conditions became sick faster.

As to the cause of the disease, a bacterial pathogen had been firmly ruled out by the CDC, but various viral assays were still continuing. So far, the culprit had not yet been identified.

Still, even as grim as the report was, there was worse news. Her mother had looked pale as she had spoken over the satellite link. "We now know that the transmission of the disease can be strictly airborne. It does not require physical contact." Kelly knew what this meant. With such ease of transmission, a pathogen like this was one of the hardest to quarantine. And with the mortality rates so high . . .

"There's only one hope," her mother had said at the end. "We need a cure."

Kelly reached to her canteen beside her hammock and took a long slow drink. She sat for a moment and knew sleep would not come. Moving quietly, she climbed from her hammock.

The guard by the fire noticed her movement and turned toward her. Still in the clothes she had worn yesterday—a gray T-shirt and brown trousers—she simply slipped on her boots. She pointed toward the entrance, wanting to stretch her legs but not wishing to disturb the others sleeping.

The Ranger nodded.

Kelly walked quietly to the *shabano*'s entrance. Ducking through, she found Private Carrera standing guard.

"Just needed some fresh air," Kelly whispered.

The female Ranger nodded and pointed her weapon toward the river. "You're not the only one."

Kelly saw a figure standing a few yards down the path by the river. From his silhouette, Kelly knew it was Nathan Rand. He was alone, except for two Rangers positioned a short distance upriver, easily spotted by their flashlights.

"Keep a safe distance from the water," Private Carrera warned. "We didn't have enough motion sensors to secure the perimeter and the river."

"I will." Kelly remembered too well what had happened to Corporal DeMartini.

Walking down the path from the roundhouse, Kelly listened to the jungle hum of locust song, accompanied by the soft croaking of countless frogs. It was a peaceful sound. In the distance, fireflies danced in the branches and zipped in graceful arcs over the river.

The lone spectator heard Kelly's approach. Nathan turned. He had a cigarette hanging from his lips, its tip a red spark in the night.

"I didn't know you smoked," Kelly said, stepping next to him and staring at the river from atop the bank.

"I don't," he said with a grin, puffing out a long stream of smoke. "At least not much. I bummed it from Corporal Conger." He thumbed in the direction of the pair on patrol. "Haven't touched one in four or five months, but . . . I don't know . . . I guess I needed an excuse to come out here. To be moving."

"I know what you mean. I came out here for the proverbial fresh air." She held out her hand.

He passed his cigarette.

She took a deep drag and sighed out the smoke, releasing her tension. "Nothing like fresh air." She passed the cigarette back to him.

He took one last puff, then dropped it and stamped it out. "Those things'll kill you."

They stood in silence as the river quietly flowed by. A pair of bats glided over the water, hunting fish, while somewhere in the distance, a bird cried out a long mournful note.

"She'll be okay," Nate finally said, almost a whisper.

Kelly glanced to him. "What?"

"Jessie, your daughter . . . she'll be okay."

Stunned for a moment, Kelly had no breath to reply.

"I'm sorry," Nate mumbled. "I'm intruding."

She touched his elbow. "No, I'm grateful . . . really. I just didn't think my worry was so plain."

"You may be a great physician, but you're a mother first."

Kelly remained quiet for a bit, then spoke softly. "It's more than that. Jess is my only child. The only child I'll ever have."

"What do you mean?"

Kelly couldn't say exactly why she was discussing this with Nate, only that it helped to voice her fears aloud. "When I gave birth to Jessie, there were complications . . . and an emergency surgery." She glanced to Nate, then away. "Afterward, I couldn't bear any more children."

"I'm sorry."

She smiled tiredly. "It was a long time ago. I've come to terms with it. But now with Jessie threatened . . ."

Nate sighed and settled to a seat on a fallen log. "I understand all too well. Here you are in the jungle, worrying about someone you love deeply, but having to continue on, to be strong."

Kelly sank beside him. "Like you, when your father was first lost."

Nate stared at the river and spoke dully. "And it's not just the worry and fear. It's guilt, too."

She knew exactly what he meant. With Jessie at risk, what was she doing here, traipsing through the jungle? She should be searching for the first flight home.

Silence again fell between them, but it grew too painful.

Kelly asked a question that had been nagging her since she had first met Nate. "Why are you here then?"

"What do you mean?"

"You lost both your mother and your father to the Amazon. Why come back? Isn't it too painful?"

Nate rubbed his palms together, staring down between his toes, silent.

"I'm sorry. It's none of my business."

"No," he said quickly, glancing to her, then away. "I . . . I was just regretting stamping out that cigarette. I could use it right now."

She smiled. "We can change the subject."

"No, it's okay. You just caught me by surprise. But your question's hard to answer, and even harder to put into words." Nate leaned back. "When I lost my father, when I truly gave up on ever finding him, I *did* leave the jungle, vowing to never come back. But in the States, the pain followed me. I tried to drown it away in alcohol and numb it away with drugs, but nothing worked. Then a year ago, I found myself on a flight back here. I couldn't say why. I walked into the airport, bought a ticket at the Varig counter, and before I knew it, I was landing in Manaus."

Nathan paused. Kelly heard his breath beside her, heavy and deep, full of emotion. She tentatively placed a hand on his bare knee. Without speaking, he covered it with his own palm.

"Once back in the jungle, I found the pain less to bear, less all-consuming."

"Why?"

"I don't know. Though my parents died here, they also *lived* here. This was their true heartland." Nate shook his head. "I'm not making any sense."

"I think you are. Here is where you still feel the closest to them."

She felt Nate stiffen beside her. He remained silent for the longest time.

"Nate?"

His voice was hoarse. "I couldn't put it into words before. But you're right. Here in the jungle, they're all around me. Their memories are strongest here. My mother teaching me how to grind manioc into flour . . . my father teaching me how to identify trees by their leaves alone . . ." He turned to her, his eyes bright. "This is my home."

In his face, she saw the mix of joy and loss. She found herself leaning closer to him, drawn by the depth of his emotion. "Nate . . ."

A small explosion of water startled them both. Only a few yards from the bank, a narrow geyser shot three feet above the river's surface. Where it blew, something large hunched through the water and disappeared.

"What was that?" Kelly asked, tense, half on her feet, ready to bolt.

Nate put his arm around her shoulders and pulled her back down. "It's nothing to be afraid of. It's just a *boto*, a freshwater dolphin. They're abundant, but pretty shy. You'll mostly find them in remote areas like this, traveling in small packs."

Proving his point, another pair of geysers blew, casting spray high into the air. Ready this time, and less panicked, Kelly spotted small dorsal fins arcing through the water, then diving back down. They were moving swiftly.

"They're fast," she said.

"Probably hunting."

As they settled back to their log, a whole procession of dolphins sped by, arcing, spraying. Frantic clicks and whistles echoed out eerily. Soon it seemed the whole river was full of dolphins racing down the current.

Nate frowned and stood.

"What's wrong?" Kelly asked.

"I don't know." A single dolphin shot through the shallows near their feet. It struck the mud bank, almost beaching itself, then, with a flip of its tail, fled to deeper waters. "Something's panicking them."

Kelly got up and joined him. "What?"

Nate shook his head. "I've never seen them display this behavior before." He glanced over to where the two patrolling Rangers stood guard. They also stared at the parade of dolphins. "I need more light."

Nate hurried along the top of the bank toward the soldiers. Kelly followed, her blood beginning to race. The guards were positioned where a small stream emptied into the river.

"Corporal Conger, could I borrow your flashlight?" Nate asked.

"They're just dolphins," said the other soldier. It was Staff Sergeant Kostos. The swarthy man scowled at them. "We've seen lots of the damned things while patrolling at night. But, oh yeah, that was while you all were sleeping in your beds, all tucked away."

The younger Ranger was more cooperative. "Here, Dr. Rand," Corporal Conger said, passing his flashlight.

With a mumbled thanks, Nathan accepted the light. He moved down the bank, shining the light upriver. Dolphins continued to pass but not in as great a number. As Kelly looked on, Nate widened the cone of the light, splashing it down the river.

"Damn," Nate said.

Almost at the reach of his light, the river's surface seemed to be churning, like white-water rapids over sharp rocks, frothing and gurgling. Only these rapids were moving toward them, flowing down the current.

"What is that?" Kelly asked.

Another dolphin bumped into the shallows, bellying into the mud, but this one didn't quickly flip away. It rolled against the bank, squealing a high-pitched wail. Nate swung the light. Kelly gasped and took a couple steps back.

The tail end of the dolphin was gone. Its belly had been ripped open. Intestines trailed. The current rolled the pitiful creature back into the river.

Nathan swung his light back upstream. The churning white water was already much closer.

"What is it?" Corporal Conger asked, his Texas drawl thicker. "What's happening?"

From up the river, the piercing squeal of a pig woke the night. Nesting birds took wing. Monkeys, startled awake, barked in irritation.

"What's going on?" the Texan repeated.

"I need your night-vision goggles," Nate ordered.

Kelly stood behind his shoulder. "What is it?"

Nate grabbed the Ranger's glasses. "I've seen rivers churn like this a few times before—but *never* this much."

"What's causing it?" Kelly asked.

Nate lifted the goggles. "Piranhas . . . in a feeding frenzy."

* * *

Through the night-vision lenses, the world both brightened and dissolved into a monochrome green. It took Nate a moment to focus on where the waters churned. He fingered the telescopic lenses to bring the image closer. Within the roiling waters, he spotted flashes of large fins—dolphins caught by the razor-toothed predators—and in brief flickers, the silvery flash of the deadly fish themselves as they fought over their meal.

"What's the threat?" Kostos said with thick disdain. "Let the dumb fucks chew up the dolphins. They ain't gonna get us on dry land."

The sergeant was right, but Nate remembered the bodies of the massacred Indians . . . and their fear of the river. Was this the threat? Were the waters here so thick with piranhas that the Indians themselves feared to travel the rivers at night? Was that why they had fled on foot? And this behavior, attacking dolphins . . . it made no sense. Nate had never heard of such a slaughter.

Motion at the edge of his goggles drew his eye. He turned from the churning water, and spotted a carcass lying on the bank. It appeared to be a peccary, a wild pig. Was it the same one that had screamed a moment ago? Something smaller, several of them, hopped around the carcass, like huge bullfrogs, except these seemed to be tearing into the dead pig and dragging it toward the water.

"What the hell . . ." Nate mumbled.

"What?" Kelly asked. "What do you see?"

Nate clicked the telescopic lenses up a few notches, zeroing in. He watched more of the bullfroglike creatures leap out of the water and attack the carcass. Others joined it, flying high over the bank to disappear into the riverside foliage. As he watched, a large capybara burst from the jungle and ran along the muddy bank. It looked like a hundred-pound guinea pig racing beside the river. Then it suddenly fell as if tripping over its own feet. Its body began to convulse. From the waters, the creatures flopped and hopped, leaping at this new meal.

Nate suddenly knew what he was seeing. It was what the village Indians must have seen. He remembered the shaman's words. *The jungle rose out of the river and attacked them.* Down the bank, the capybara ceased writhing as death claimed it. Hadn't Kelly mentioned something about the corpse she had examined showing signs of a convulsive event?

He ripped off the goggles. The line of white water was now only thirty yards away. "We need to get everyone away from the river! Away from all waterways."

Sergeant Kostos scoffed. "What the hell are you talking about?"

Corporal Conger retrieved his glasses. "Maybe we should listen to Dr.—" Something knocked the corporal's helmet askew, hitting with a wet plop. "Jesus Christ."

Nathan shone his light down. Sitting in the mud was a strange creature, slightly stunned. It looked like a monstrous tadpole, but in the stage where its muscular hind legs had developed.

Before anyone could react, the creature leaped again, latching onto Conger's thigh with its jaws. Gasping, the corporal bludgeoned it away with the stock of his rifle and took a few shaky steps away. "Damn thing has teeth."

Kostos slammed his boot heel atop the creature, squashing it and shooting entrails down the bank. "Not any longer it doesn't."

As a group, they scurried away from the river. Conger fingered the pant leg of his fatigues, hopping along. A hole had been torn in the fabric, and when he lifted his hand, Nate spotted blood on the corporal's fingertips. "Practically tore a chunk out of me," Conger said with a nervous laugh.

In no time, they were back at the *shabano*'s entrance.

"What's going on?" Private Carrera asked.

Nate pointed back to the river. "Whatever got the Indians is coming our way. We need to clear out of here."

"For now, maintain your post," Kostos ordered Carrera. "Conger, you get that leg looked at while I go report to Captain Waxman."

"My med pack is inside," Kelly said.

Conger leaned against a beam of bamboo. "Sarge, I'm not feeling so good."

All eyes turned to the man.

"Everything's gone sort of blurry."

Kelly reached to help him. Nathan saw ropes of drool begin to flow from the corner of the man's lips. Then his head fell back, followed by his body, already convulsing.

Sergeant Kostos caught him. "Conger!"

"Get him inside!" Kelly snapped, ducking through the entrance.

The Ranger hauled the soldier toward the *shabano*'s

door, but was having difficulty as the man thrashed. Private Carrera shouldered her rifle and bent to help. "Maintain your post, soldier!" Kostos barked, then turned to Nate. "Grab his goddamn legs!"

Nate dropped and hooked Conger's ankles under his arms. It was like holding the end of a downed power line as the man's body snapped and seized. "Go!"

As a team, they hauled the soldier through the narrow doorway.

Others came rushing up, awakened by the yelling.

"What happened?" Zane asked.

"Stand out of the way!" Kostos hollered, bowling the man over as he ran with the fallen soldier.

"Over here!" Kelly called. She already had her pack open and a syringe in hand. "Lay him down and hold him still."

After lowering Conger to the dirt, Nate was elbowed aside. Two Rangers took his place, pinning the soldier's legs to the ground.

Kostos knelt on the corporal's shoulders, holding him in place. But the man's head continued to bang up and down as if he were trying to knock himself unconscious. Froth foamed from his lips, bloody from where he half chewed through his own lip. "Jesus Christ! Conger!"

Kelly sliced open the man's right sleeve with a razor blade, then quickly slid a needle into Conger's arm. She injected the syringe's contents and knelt back to watch their effect, holding his wrist clamped in her fingers. "C'mon . . . c'mon . . ."

Suddenly the man's contorted form relaxed.

"Thank God," Kostos sighed.

Kelly's reaction wasn't as relieved. "Damn it!" She pounced on his form, checking his neck for a pulse, then pushed the soldiers aside as she began CPR on his chest. "Someone start mouth-to-mouth."

The Rangers were too stunned for a moment to move.

Nathan bumped Kostos aside, wiped the bloody froth from Conger's mouth, then began to breathe in sync with Kelly's labors. Nate's focus narrowed down to the rhythm of their work. He vaguely heard the concerned chatter of the others.

"Some damn frog thing or fish," Kostos explained. "It hopped out and bit Conger on the leg."

"Poisoned!" Kelly huffed as she worked. "It must have been venomous."

"I've never heard of such a creature," Kouwe said.

Nathan wanted to agree, but was too busy breathing for the dying soldier.

"There were thousands," Kostos continued, "chewing their way downstream toward here."

"What are we going to do?" Zane asked.

Captain Waxman's voice drowned everyone else out. "First of all, we're not going to panic. Corporal Graves and Private Jones . . . . join Carrera in securing the perimeter."

"Wait!" Nate gasped between breaths.

Waxman turned on him. "What?"

Nate spoke in stilted breaths between attempts to resuscitate Conger. "We're too close to the stream. It runs right past the *shabano*."

"So?"

"They'll come for us from the stream . . . like the Indians." Nate was dizzy from hyperventilating. He breathed into Corporal Conger's mouth, then was up again. "We have to get away. Away from the waterways until daybreak. Nocturnal . . ." Down he went to breathe.

"What do you mean?"

Professor Kouwe answered. "The Indians were attacked at night. Now this assault. Nathan believes these creatures may be nocturnal. If we could avoid their path until sunrise, we should be safe."

"But we have shelter and a secure area here. They're just fish or frogs or something."

Nate remembered the black-and-white view through the night-vision goggles: the creatures leaping from the river, bounding high into the trees. "We're not secure here!" he gasped out. He bent down again, but he was stopped by a hand on his shoulder.

"It's useless," Kelly said, pulling him up. "He's gone." She faced the others. "I'm sorry. The poison spread too quickly. Without an antivenom . . ." She shook her head sadly.

Nate stared at the still form of the young Texan. "Damn it . . ." He stood up. "We have to get away. Far away from the waters. I don't know how far from the streams and rivers these creatures can travel, but the one I saw had gills. They probably can't stay out of the water for long."

"What do you suggest?" Frank asked.

"We travel to higher ground. Avoid the river and the little stream. I think the Indians believed it was just the river they needed to fear, but the predators followed the stream and ambushed them."

"You're speaking as if the creatures are intelligent."

"No, I can't imagine they are." Nate remembered the way the dolphins were fleeing, while none of the larger river fish were bothered. He pictured the attack on the pig and the capybara. A theory slowly jelled. "Maybe they're simply focused on warm-blooded creatures. I don't know . . . maybe they can zone in on body heat or something, scouring both the water and the river's edges for prey."

Frank turned to Waxman. "I say we heed Dr. Rand."

"So do I," Kelly said, standing. She pointed to Corporal Conger. "If a single bite can do this, we can't take the risk."

Waxman turned on Frank. "You may be the head of operations, but in matters of security, my word is law."

Private Carrera ducked her head through the roundhouse's doorway. "Something's happening out here. The river is frothing something fierce. One of the boats' pontoons just blew."

Beyond the walls of the *shabano*, the jungle awoke with monkey howls and screeching birds.

"We're running out of options," Nate said fiercely. "If they come up the stream and flank us, cutting us off from higher ground, many more will die like Conger . . . like the Indians."

Nate found support in the most unlikely of places. "The doctor's right," Sergeant Kostos said. "I saw those buggers. Nothing'll stop them from attacking." He waved an arm. "Definitely not this flimsy place. We're sitting ducks in here, sir."

After a pause, Waxman nodded. "Load up the gear."

"What about the motion sensors outside?" Kostos asked.

"Leave 'em. Right now, I don't want anyone out there."

Kostos nodded and turned to obey.

In short order, everyone was shouldering packs. Two Rangers dug a shallow grave for Corporal Conger's body.

Carrera stood crouched by the doorway. She wore night-vision goggles and stared out toward the river and jungle. "The commotion by the river's died down, but I hear rustling in the brush."

Beyond the walls, the jungle had grown silent.

Nate crossed to the door and knelt on one knee beside Carrera. He was already packed and ready, his stubby-nosed shotgun clutched in his right hand. "What do you see?"

Carrera adjusted her goggles. "Nothing. But the jungle is too dense to see far."

Nate leaned out the door. He heard a branch snap. Then a small forest deer, a spotted fawn, shot out of the jungle and dashed past where Nate and the Ranger crouched. Both gasped and ducked inside before realizing there was no danger.

"Christ," Carrera said with a choked laugh.

The deer paused near the edge of the roundhouse, ears pricked.

"Shoo!" the Ranger called, waving her M-16 threateningly.

Then something dropped out of the trees and landed on the fawn's back. The deer suddenly squealed in pain and terror.

"Get inside!" Nate ordered Carrera.

As she rolled through the door, Nate covered her with his shotgun. Another creature pounced from the jungle's edge toward the deer. A third leaped from the underbrush. The fawn skittered a few steps, then fell on its side, legs kicking.

A single motion sensor blared from the direction of the side stream.

"They're here," Nathan mumbled.

By his side, Carrera had torn off her night-vision goggles and clicked on her flashlight. The brightness spread down the jungle trail to the river. The jungle to either side remained dark, blocking the light. "I don't see—"

Something plopped into the trail, only a few yards away.

From this angle, the creature appeared to be all legs with a long finned tail dragging behind it. It took a small hop toward them. From under two globular black eyes, its mouth gaped open. Teeth glinted in the bright light, like some cross between a tadpole and a piranha.

"What the hell is it?" Carrera whispered.

It leaped toward her voice.

Nate pulled the trigger of his shotgun. The spray of pellets shredded the creature, blowing it backward. That's what Nate appreciated about a shotgun in the jungle. It didn't require precision aim. Perfect for small threats—poisonous snakes, scorpions, spiders—and apparently against venomous amphibians, too.

"Get back," he said and swung the small door shut. It was no more than a woven flap of banana leaves, but it would temporarily block the creatures.

"That's the only way out," Carrera said.

Nate stood and unhooked his machete with his

left hand. "Not in a *shabano*." He pointed the blade toward the far wall, the side opposite both river and stream. "You can make a doorway wherever you want."

Frank and Captain Waxman joined him as he crossed to the central yard. Waxman was folding a field map.

"They're already out there," Nate said. He reached the far wall, raised his machete, and began hacking through the woven palm and banana leaves. "We have to leave now."

Waxman nodded, then shouted and waved an arm in the air. "We're hauling out! Now!"

Nate cleared a ragged hole through the rear wall, kicking debris aside.

Waxman waved Corporal Okamoto to take the point. Nate saw an unusual weapon in the soldier's hands. "Flamethrower," Okamoto explained, hefting the weapon. "If necessary we'll burn a way through the bastards." He pressed the trigger and a steam of orange fire shot from the muzzle like the flickering tongue of a snake.

"Excellent." Nate patted the corporal's shoulder. After so many days on the river, Nate had grown fond of his boat's motorman, although the Asian corporal's off-tune whistling still drove him crazy.

With a wink to Nathan, Okamoto ducked through the arch without hesitation. As he passed, Nate spotted the small fuel tank strapped to the corporal's back.

Another four Rangers followed: Warczak, Graves, Jones, and Kostos. All had outfitted their M-16s with grenade launchers. They spread to the right and left of their point man. New alarms blared as the Rangers tripped the perimeter's motion-sensor lasers.

"Now the civilians," Waxman ordered. "Stay close. Always keep a Ranger between you and the forest."

Richard Zane and Anna Fong hurried through. Next Olin and Manny followed, trailed by Tor-tor. Last, Kelly, Frank, and Kouwe passed.

"C'mon," Kelly said to Nate.

He nodded, glancing back to the *shabano*. Waxman oversaw the last of the Rangers, who would guard their rear. Two soldiers were gathered over something in the middle of the yard.

"Let's move, ladies!" Waxman ordered.

The Rangers stood. One, a corporal named Samad Yamir, gave a thumbs-up sign to Waxman. The corporal seldom spoke, and when he did, his voice was thick with a Pakistani accent. There was only one other fact Nate knew about Yamir. He was the unit's demolitions expert.

Nate eyed the device left in the yard with suspicion.

Waxman found Nate staring. The captain pointed his rifle toward the opening. "Waiting for a personal invitation, Dr. Rand?"

Nate licked his lips and followed after Frank and Kelly.

Again he found Private Carrera marching behind him. She was now outfitted with a flamethrower, too. She studied the dark forest with narrowed eyes. Beyond her, Waxman and Yamir were the last to leave the *shabano*.

"Stay close!" Waxman yelled. "Frag or fry anything that moves."

Carrera spoke at Nate's shoulder. "We're going to make for a knoll about five klicks ahead."

"How do you know it's there?"

"Topographic map." Her voice sounded unsure.

Nate glanced over his shoulder questioningly.

Carrera lowered her voice and nodded to the side. "The stream wasn't on the map."

Kelly glanced over, looking sick, but she remained silent.

Nate sighed. He was not surprised at the inaccuracy of the map. The waterways through the deep jungle were unpredictable. While the boundaries of lakes and swamps varied according to the rainfall, the smaller rivers and streams were even more changeable. Most remained unnamed and uncharted. But at least the knoll was on the map.

"Keep moving!" Waxman ordered behind them.

As a group, the team fled into the jungle. Nate stared around him, his ears pricked for any suspicious rustle. In the distance, he heard the babble of the small stream. He imagined the Indian villagers racing up the nearby footpath, unaware of the danger lurking so close, oblivious of the death that lay ahead.

Nate tromped after Frank and Kelly. A flicker of flame lit up the jungle ahead as Corporal Okamoto led the way. Few words were shared as the group scaled the gentle slope away from the river. All eyes watched the jungle around them.

After about twenty minutes of climbing, Waxman spoke to the soldier at his side. "Light the candle, Yamir."

Nate turned. Samad Yamir swung around and faced the way they had come. He shouldered his M-16 and loosened a handheld device.

"Radio transmitter," Carrera explained.

Yamir raised the device and pressed a button, triggering a red light to blink rapidly.

Nate frowned. "What is—?"

A soft *boom* sounded. A section of forest blew upward in a ball of fire. Flames shot high into the night sky and mushroomed through the surrounding forest.

Stunned, Nate stumbled back. Shouts of surprise arose from the other civilians. Nate watched the sphere of flames die away, collapsing in on itself, but leaving a good section of the forest burning. Through the hellish red glow, a scorched hole in the forest was evident, every tree stripped of leaf and branch. At least an acre. There was no sign of the *shabano*. Even the motion-sensor alarms had gone silent, fried by the explosion.

Nate was too dumbstruck to speak—but his eyes, furious, met Waxman's gaze.

The captain waved them all on. "Keep moving."

Carrera urged Nate forward. "Fail-safe method. Burning everything behind us."

"What was that?" Kouwe asked.

"Napalm bomb," the corporal explained dourly. "New jungle munition."

"Why weren't we told . . . at least warned?" Frank asked loudly, walking half backward.

Captain Waxman answered, marching and waving them on. "It was my call. My order. I wanted no arguments about it. Security is my priority."

"Which I appreciate, captain," Richard Zane called back from up ahead. "I, for one, commend your actions. Hopefully you've annihilated the venomous bunch."

"That doesn't appear to be the case," Olin said with narrowed eyes. Their Russian teammate pointed to the stream, now visible due to the blaze. A section of the waterway on their side of the fires frothed with the leaping, racing bodies of thousands of small creatures. A roiling stampede climbed up the stream, like salmon spawning.

"Get moving!" Waxman yelled. "We need to reach higher ground!"

The pace of the party accelerated. They scrambled up the slope, less concerned with watching the forest than with speed. The creatures were flanking them off to the right.

Flashes of fire marked the point man ahead. "I've got water here!" Okamoto called.

The group converged toward him.

"Dear Lord," Kelly said.

Fifty yards ahead, another stream cut across their path. It was only ten yards wide, but was dark and still. Beyond it, the land continued to rise toward the knoll, their destination.

"Is this the same stream?" Frank asked.

One of the Rangers, Jorgensen, pushed out of the forest. He had his night-vision glasses in his hand. "I've scouted down a ways. It's an offshoot of the other stream. This one feeds into the other."

"Fuck," Waxman swore. "This place is a god-damn water maze."

"We should cross while we still can," Kouwe said. "The creatures will surely come this way soon."

Waxman stared at the slowly flowing water with clear trepidation. He moved beside Okamoto. "I need some light."

The Ranger fired his flamethrower across the waters. It did little to reveal what lay in the murky depths.

"Sir, I'll go across first," Okamoto volunteered. "See if it can be crossed safely."

"Careful, son."

"Always, sir."

Taking a deep breath, Okamoto kissed a crucifix around his neck, then stepped into the water. He waded into it, his weapon held chest high. "Current's sluggish," he said softly, "but deep." Halfway across, the waters had climbed to his waist.

"Hurry up," Frank mumbled. He had a fist clenched to his belly.

Okamoto climbed to the far side and out of the water. He turned with a grin. "It appears to be safe."

"For now," Kouwe said. "We should hurry."

"Let's go!" Waxman ordered.

As a group, they splashed through the waters. Frank held Kelly's hand. Nate helped Anna Fong. "I'm not a good swimmer," Anna said to no one in particular.

The Rangers followed, guns held above their heads.

On the far side, the party climbed the steep slope. With wet boots and the mud still slick from the rains yesterday, trekking was treacherous. Their progress slowed. The tight group began to stretch apart.

Jorgensen appeared out of the gloom, night scope in hand. "Captain," he said, "I've checked the other stream. The waters seem to have calmed. I don't see any more of the creatures."

"They're out there," Nate said. "They're just not in a frenzy any longer."

"Or maybe now that the fires have died down, they fled back to the main river channel," Jorgensen offered hopefully.

Waxman frowned. "I don't think we should count—"

A sharp cry interrupted the captain. Off to the left, a body slid down the slick, muddy slope. It was a Ranger. Eddie Jones. His limbs flailed as he tried to break his fall. "Fuck!" he screamed in frustration. He tried to grasp a bush, but its roots ripped out of the thin soil. Then he hit a bump in the slope, and went cartwheeling, his weapon flying from his fingers, and landed in the stream.

A pair of Rangers—Warczak and Graves—ran to his aid.

He popped out, coughing water and choking. "Goddamn it!" He clambered to the stream's edge. "Fuck this jungle!" As he straightened his helmet, more colorful obscenities flowed. He climbed out of the stream.

"Smooth, Jones . . . very smooth," Warczak said, running his flashlight up and down the man's soaked form. "I'd give you a perfect ten in the jungle slalom."

"Cram it up your ass," Jones said, bending to finger a rope of sticky algae from his pant leg. "Ugh."

Corporal Graves was the first to spot it: something moving atop the other man's pack. "Jones . . ."

Still half crouched, the man glanced up. "What?"

The creature leaped, latching onto the soft flesh under Jones's jaw. He jerked. "What the hell!" He tore the creature from his neck, blood spurting. "Ahhhhh . . ."

The small stream suddenly frothed and burst forth with another dozen of the creatures. They leaped at the man, attacking his legs. Jones fell backward, his face twisted in agony. He hit the stream with a loud splash.

"Jones!" Warczak stepped nearer.

Another of the creatures leaped from the water and plopped in the wet mud at the corporal's feet, gill flaps vibrating. Warczak scrambled backward, as did Graves.

In the shallow stream, Jones writhed. It was as if he had been thrown in boiling water. His body jerked and spasmed.

"Get back!" Waxman yelled. "Everyone uphill!"

Warczak and Graves were already running. From the stream, more of the creatures leaped and bounded in pursuit.

The group tossed caution aside and scrambled up the slope, some half crawling on hands and knees. Kelly's legs suddenly went out from under her. Her muddy hand slipped out of her brother's grip. She began a deadly slide.

"Kelly!" Frank called out.

But Nate was a couple yards behind her. He caught her one-handed by the waist, falling on top of her, holding his shotgun in his other arm. Manny came to their aid, hauling both back to their feet. Tor-tor paced anxiously back and forth behind him.

The Brazilian waved the jaguar ahead. "Move your furry ass."

By now, the three were the last of the group. Frank waited a few yards up.

Only Private Carrera was still with them. She stood and sprayed a jet of fire behind them, her flamethrower roaring dully. "Let's pick up the pace," she said tensely, backing up the slope, herding them upward.

"Thanks," Kelly said, her eyes swiveling to encompass the entire group.

Frank met them and took his sister in hand. "Don't do that again."

"I'm not planning on it."

Nate kept a watch behind them. He met Carrera's gaze. He saw the fear in her eyes. This momentary distraction was all it took. One of the creatures sprang at the Ranger from the surrounding underbrush. It had slipped past her firewall.

Carrera fell backward, fire spitting into the sky.

The creature had latched onto her belt, but squirmed for a meatier purchase.

Before anyone else could react, a sharp *crack* split the night. The creature was flung away, the two halves of its body sailing high. Both Carrera and Nate turned to see Manny snapping his short bullwhip back into ready position.

"Are you just gonna sit there gawking?" Manny asked.

Carrera scrambled up with Nate's help. The group sped up the hill. At last they reached the summit. Nate hoped putting the rise between them and the amphibious creatures would be enough.

He found the others gathered on top.

"We should keep moving," Nate said. "Keep as much land between us and them as possible."

"That's a good theory," Kouwe said. "But putting it into practice is another thing altogether." The shaman pointed down the knoll's far side.

Nathan stared. From this height, the stream below shone silver in the moonlight. Groaning, he realized it was the same stream they had been avoiding all along. Nate turned in a slow circle, recognizing their predicament. They had made a fatal error.

The small waterway they had crossed a few minutes ago was not a feeder draining into the larger stream, but actually a *part* of the same stream.

"We're on an island," Kelly said with dismay.

Nate stared upstream and saw that the flow of the waterway split and ran around both sides of the knoll. Once past the hill, it joined to become a single stream again. The party indeed stood on an island, in the middle of the deadly stream, water all around.

Nate felt sick. "We're trapped."

2:12 A.M.
WEST WING OF THE INSTAR INSTITUTE
LANGLEY, VIRGINIA

Lauren O'Brien sat at the small table in the communal galley, hunched over a cup of coffee. At this late hour, she had the place to herself. All the other quarantined MEDEA members were either asleep in their makeshift bedrooms or working in the main labs.

Even Marshall had retired to their room with Jessie hours ago. He had an early morning conference call with the CDC, two Cabinet heads, and the director of the CIA. He had eloquently described the meeting as "a preemptive strike before the political shitstorm hits the fan." Such were the ways of government. Rather than attacking the problem aggressively, everyone was still pointing fingers and running for cover. Marshall's goal tomorrow was to shake things up. A decisive plan of action was needed. So far, the fifteen outbreak zones were being managed fifteen different ways. It was chaos.

Sighing, Lauren stared at the reams of papers and printouts spread atop her table. Her team was still struggling with one simple question. *What was causing the disease?*

Testing and research were ongoing in labs across the country—from the CDC in Atlanta all the way to the Salk facility in San Diego. But the Instar Institute had become scientific ground zero for the disease.

Lauren pushed away a report from a Dr. Shelby on utilizing monkey kidney cells as a culture medium. He had failed. *Negative response.* Up to this point, the contagious agent continued to thwart all means of identification: aerobic and anaerobic cultures, fungal assays, electron microscopy, dot hybridization, polymerase chain reaction. As of today, no progress had been made. Each study ended with similar tags: *negative response, zero growth, indeterminate analysis.* All fancy ways of saying failure.

Her beeper, resting beside her now-cold cup of coffee, began to buzz and dance across the Formica countertop. She snatched it before it fell off the table.

"Who the heck is paging me at this hour?" she mumbled, glancing at the beeper's screen. The Caller ID feature listed the number as *Large Scale Biological Labs*. She didn't know the facility, but the area code placed it somewhere in northern California. The call was probably just some technician requesting their fax number or submission protocol. Still . . .

Lauren stood, pocketed her beeper, and headed over to the phone on the wall. As she picked up the receiver, she heard a door open behind her. Over her shoulder, she was surprised to see Jessie standing in her pajamas, rubbing at her eyes blearily.

"Grandma . . ."

Lauren replaced the receiver and crossed to the child. "Honey, what are you doing up? You should be in bed."

"I couldn't find you."

She knelt before the girl. "What's wrong? Did you have another scary dream?" The first few nights here, Jessie had awoken with nightmares, triggered by the quarantine and the strange environment. But the child had seemed to adjust rapidly, making friends with several of the other kids.

"My tummy hurts," she said, her eyes sheening with threatening tears.

"Oh, honey, that's what you get for eating ice cream so late." Lauren reached out and pulled the girl into a hug. "Why don't I get you a glass of water, and we'll get you tucked back into—"

Lauren's voice died as she realized how warm the child was. She reached a palm to Jessie's forehead. "Oh, God," she mumbled under her breath.

The child was burning up.

2:31 A.M.
AMAZON JUNGLE

Louis stood by his tent as Jacques strode up from the river. His lieutenant carried something wrapped in a sodden blanket under his arms. Whatever it was, it appeared no larger than a watermelon.

"Doctor," the Maroon tribesman said stiffly.

"Jacques, what did you discover?" He had sent the man and two others to investigate the explosion that had occurred just after midnight. The noise had woken his own camp mere minutes after they had settled in for the night. Earlier, at sunset, Louis had learned of the discovery of the Indian *shabano* and the fate of the villagers. Then hours later the explosion . . .

What was going on over there?

"Sir, the village has been incinerated . . . as has much of the surrounding forest. We could not get too close due to the remaining fires. Maybe by morning."

"And the other team?"

Jacques glanced to his toes. "Gone, sir. I dropped Malachim and Toady ashore to scout after them."

Louis clenched a fist and cursed his overconfidence. After the successful abduction of one of their soldiers, he had grown complacent with his prey. But now this! One of his team's trackers must have been spotted. Now that the fox had been alerted to the hounds, Louis's mission was far more complicated. "Gather the other men. If the Rangers are running from us, we don't want them to get too far away."

"Yes, sir. But, Doctor, I'm not sure the others are fleeing from us."

"What makes you think that?"

"As we paddled up to the fire zone, we saw a body float out from a side stream."

"A body?" Louis feared it was his mole, dispatched and sent downriver as a message.

Jacques unrolled the sodden blanket in his arms and dropped its content to the leafed floor of the jungle. It was a human head. "We found it floating near the remains."

Frowning, Louis knelt and examined the head, what little there was of it. The face had been all but chewed away, but from the shaved scalp, it was clearly one of the Rangers.

"The body was the same," Jacques said, "gnawed to the bone."

Louis glanced up. "What happened to him?"

"Piranhas, I'd say, from the bite wounds."

"Are you sure?"

"Pretty damn sure." Jacques fingered the scarred half of his nose, reminding Louis that, as a boy, his lieutenant had had intimate experience with the voracious river predators.

"Did they feed on him after he was dead?"

Jacques shrugged. "If he wasn't, I pity the poor bastard."

Louis climbed to his feet. He stared out toward the river. "What the hell is happening out there?"

TEN

Escape

Atop the island knoll, Nate stood with the other civilians, ringed by the Ranger team, which was now down to eight members. *One for each of the civilians*, Nate thought, *like personal bodyguards.*

"How about using another of your napalm bombs to clear a path through the buggers?" Frank asked, standing near Captain Waxman. "Roll it down the slope, then duck for cover."

"We'd all be dead. If the heat blast didn't fry us, then we'd be pinned down between a burning forest and the poisonous bastards."

Frank sighed, staring out into the dark forests. "How about your grenades? We could lob them in series, creating a swath through them."

Waxman frowned. "It'd be risky to deploy them so close to us, and no guarantee that it would kill enough of the bastards among all these tree trunks. I say we hold the hill, try to last until daybreak."

Frank crossed his arms, little pleased with this plan.

Around the knoll, occasional fiery blasts from the flamethrowers ignited the night as Corporal Okamoto and Private Carrera maintained sentry posts on either slope. Though it had been half an hour since sighting one of them, the beasts were still out there. The surrounding forests had gone deathly quiet, no monkey calls, no birdsong. Even the insects seemed to have died down to a whispery buzz and whine. But beyond the reach of their flashlights, the leaves still rustled as unseen lurkers crept through the underbrush.

Night scopes focused on the surrounding waters revealed creatures still hopping into and out of the stream. Nathan's earlier assessment seemed to be accurate. The creatures, gill-breathers, needed to return to the waters occasionally to revive themselves.

Nearby, Manny knelt in the leaf-strewn dirt, working by flashlight. Kelly and Kouwe stood behind his shoulder. Earlier, Manny had risked his life to dash into the forest's fringe to collect one of the beasts stunned by a blast of flame. Though partially charbroiled, it was a decent specimen. The creature was about a foot long from the tip of its tail to its razor-toothed mouth. Large black eyes protruded, giving it a nearly 360-degree view of its surroundings. Strong articulated limbs ended in webbed and suckered toes almost as long as the body itself.

As the others watched, Manny was performing a rapid dissection. The Brazilian biologist worked deftly with a scalpel and forceps from Kelly's med kit.

"This thing is amazing," Manny finally mumbled.

Nate joined Kelly and Kouwe as the biologist explained.

"It's clearly some form of chimera. An amalgam of more than one species."

"How so?" Kelly asked.

Manny shifted aside and pointed with his thumb forceps. "Nathan was right. Though its skin is not scaled like a fish, it definitely has the breathing system of an aquatic species. Gills, no lungs. But its legs—notice the banding on the skin—are definitely amphibious. The striping pattern is very characteristic of *Phobobates trivittatus*, the striped poison-dart frog, the largest and most toxic member of the frog family."

"So you're saying it's some mutated form of this species?" Nate asked.

"I thought so at first. It looks almost like a tadpole whose growth was arrested at the stage where gills were still present and only its hind legs had formed. But as I dissected further, I became less convinced. First, and most obvious, is that its size is way out of proportion. This thing must weigh close to five pounds. Monstrously gigantic for even the largest species of dart frog."

Manny rolled the dissected creature over and pointed to its eyes and teeth. "Additionally, its skull structure is all misshapen. Rather than flattened horizontally like a frog's, the cranium is flattened vertically, more like a fish's. In fact, the skull conformation, jaw, and teeth are almost identical in size and shape to a common Amazonian river predator—*Serrasalmus rhombeus*." Manny glanced up from his handiwork. "The black piranha."

Kelly leaned away. "That's impossible."

"If this thing weren't right in front of me, I'd agree." Manny sat back. "I've worked with Amazonian species all my life, and I've seen nothing like it. A true chimera. A single creature that shares the biological features of both frog and fish."

Nate eyed the creature. "How could that be?"

Manny shook his head. "I don't know. But how does a man regenerate a limb? I think the presence of such a chimera suggests we're on the right trail. Something is out there, something your father's expedition discovered, something with a distinct mutating ability."

Nate stared at the dissected ruins. *What the hell was out there?*

A call arose from Private Carrera. Her sentry post faced the northern slope of the knoll. "They're on the move again!"

Nate straightened. The rustling from her side of the forest had grown louder. It sounded as if the entire jungle were stirring.

Carrera flamed the lower slope. Her fiery jets pushed back the darkness. Reflected in the fire were hundreds of tiny eyes, covering both the forest floor and the trees. One of the creatures sprang from its perch on the limb of a palm tree and bounded into the fire zone. There was a short chatter of automatic rifle fire, and the creature was shredded to a bloody mush.

"Everybody back!" Carrera called. "They're coming!"

From the trees and underbrush, small bodies started to leap and bound toward them, oblivious to the fire and bullets. The creatures were determined to overrun them with their sheer numbers.

Nate flashed back on the Indian massacre site. It was happening all over again. He swung his shotgun from his shoulder, aimed, and blasted a creature in midair as it leaped from a branch over Carrera's head. Gobbets of flesh rained down.

As a group, they were forced to vacate the knoll's summit and retreat down the southern face. Gunfire and flames lit the night. Flashlights danced, making every shadow shift and jerk.

Leading the charge down the southern slope, Corporal Okamoto swathed jets of fire before them. "It still looks clear this way!" he called out.

Nate risked a peek his way. Distantly through the forest, he could make out the other fork of the stream below as it swept around the southern flank of the hill.

"Why aren't any of the creatures on this side of the hill?" Anna asked, her face flushed.

Zane answered, his eyes wide as he kept glancing behind him. "They probably rallied all their numbers on the far side for this final assault."

Nate stared toward the stream below. It was wide, smooth, and quiet, but he knew better. He remembered the large capybara rodent flushed from the forest and racing along the river, where it was set upon by the predators. "They're herding us," he mumbled.

"What?" Kelly asked.

"They want us close to the water. The pack is driving us to the river."

Manny heard him. "I think Nate's right. Despite their ability to move on land for short distances, they're basically aquatic. They'd want their meal as close to water as possible before taking it down."

Kelly looked behind her to the line of Rangers flaming and firing along their back trail. "What choice do we have?"

Down the slope, Okamoto slowed as they neared the river, clearly suspicious of the water, too. The corporal turned to Captain Waxman behind him. "Sir, I'll try to cross first. Like last time."

Waxman nodded. "Careful, corporal."

Okamoto headed for the stream.

"No!" Nate called. "I'm sure it's a trap."

Okamoto glanced to him, then to his captain, who waved him forward again.

"We have to get off this island," Waxman said.

"Wait," Manny said, stepping forward, his voice pained. "I . . . I can send Tor-tor instead."

The others were now all gathered around.

Waxman stared at the jaguar, then nodded. "Do it."

Manny guided his jaguar toward the dark waters.

Nate's mind spun. It was suicide to enter those waters. He knew this as certainly as he knew the sun would rise tomorrow. But Waxman was right. They had to find a way across. He ran through various scenarios in his head.

A rope bridge over the stream. He quickly ruled that out. Even if they could somehow string a bridge up, the aquatic creatures were adept at leaping great heights. They'd all just be so much bait strung on a line.

Maybe grenades tossed in the water to stun them. But the stream was long. Any creatures killed by the concussion would be quickly replaced by those upstream. They would sweep down the sluggish current, attacking the team as they tried to rush across. No, what was needed was something that could strip this entire fork of the creatures—but what could do that?

Then it dawned on him. He had seen the answer demonstrated just a few days back.

By now, Manny and Tor-tor were only a couple of yards from the stream. Okamoto was with them, flames lighting the way.

"Wait!" Nate called. "I have an idea!"

Manny paused.

"What?" Waxman asked.

"According to Manny, these things are basically fish."

"So?"

Nate ignored the captain's glare and turned to Kouwe. "You have powdered *ayaeya* vine in your medicine kit, don't you?"

"Certainly, but what—?" Then the professor's eyes grew rounder with understanding. "Brilliant, Nate. I should've thought of that."

"What?" Waxman asked, growing frustrated.

Behind them, up the slope, the line of Rangers held the creatures momentarily at bay with rifles and fire. Down slope, Okamoto stood ready by the river.

Nate quickly explained. "Indians use crushed *ayaeya* vine to fish." He remembered the small fishing scene he had witnessed as he canoed with Tama and Takaho to São Gabriel: a woman dusting the river with a black powder, while downstream the men gathered stunned fish with spears and nets. "The vine contains a potent rotenone, a toxin that literally chokes and suffocates the fish. The effect is almost instantaneous."

"So what are you proposing?" Waxman asked.

"I'm familiar with the compound. I'll take the satchel upstream and poison the stream. As the toxin flows down this fork, it should stun any and all of the creatures in the river."

Waxman's eyes narrowed. "This powder will do this?"

Kouwe answered, digging in his pack. "It should. As long as the creatures are true gill-breathers." The professor glanced to Manny.

The biologist nodded, clear relief in his eyes. "I'm sure of it."

Sighing, Waxman waved Okamoto and Manny away from the stream. As the captain turned back to Nate, an explosion sounded behind them.

Dirt, leaves, and branches blew high into the air. Someone had fired a grenade. "They're breaking through!" Sergeant Kostos yelled.

Waxman pointed to Nate. "Move!"

Nate turned.

Professor Kouwe pulled a large leather satchel from his pack and tossed it to Nate. "Be careful."

Nate caught the bag of powder one-handed, swinging around with his shotgun in the other.

"Carrera!" Waxman called and pointed to Nate. "Cover him."

"Yes, sir." The private backed down the slope with her flamethrower, leaving her post to Okamoto.

"When you first start to see fish float to the surface," Nate instructed the others, "haul ass across. Though the current here is slow, I'm not sure how long the effect will last before the toxin is swept away."

"I'll make sure we're ready," Kouwe said.

Nate glanced around the group. Kelly's eyes met his, a fist clutched to her throat. He offered her a small, confident smile, then turned away.

Together, he and Private Carrera sprinted upstream, keeping a wary distance from the water.

Nate trailed behind the soldier as she strafed the way ahead with continual bursts from her flamethrower. They crashed through the smoking underbrush and raced ahead. Nate searched behind. The encampment of his fellow teammates had dwindled down to a green glow in the forest.

"The buggers must know something's up," Carrera said, gasping with exertion. She pointed a free arm toward the stream. A couple splashes marked where creatures were beginning to hop out of the water in pursuit of the pair.

"Keep moving," Nate urged. "It's not much farther."

They rushed on, accompanied by tiny splashes and the sound of crashing bodies hitting the underbrush.

At last they reached the place where the main stream forked into the northern and southern branches, encircling the knoll. Here the channel was narrower, the current swifter, rumbling over rocks in a frothy white foam. More of the creatures leapt from the current, slick bodies glistening in the glow of the firelight.

Nate stopped as Carrera laid down a protective spray of flame. Creatures sizzled in the muddy bank, some fleeing back into the river, skin smoking. "Now or never," Carrera said.

Shouldering his shotgun, Nate slipped in front of her, the satchel of powder in hand. He quickly loosened the pouch's leather tie.

"Just lob the whole thing in," the Ranger recommended.

"No, I have to make sure it disperses evenly." Nate took another step nearer the river.

"Careful." Carrera followed, jetting bursts of flame around them to discourage the predators.

Nate reached the edge of the stream, standing now only a foot away.

Carrera half knelt and strafed fire over the water's surface, ready to incinerate anything that dared pop out. "Do it!"

With a nod, Nate leaned over the stream, extending his arm, his fingers clutching the satchel. Attracted by the movement, something sprang from the water. Nate jerked his arm back in time to miss getting bitten. Instead, the creature latched its razored teeth into the cuff of his shirt sleeve, hanging there.

Nate whipped his arm back, fabric ripped, and the creature went flying far into the woods. "Damn it!" Not waiting, Nate quickly powdered the river with the crushed *ayaeya* vine, sprinkling it slowly, ensuring a good spread.

Behind him, Carrera was busy protecting their rear. The beasts from the stream were now converging on them.

Nate shook the last of the powder from the satchel, then tossed it into the stream. As he watched the pouch drift downstream rapidly, he prayed his plan would work. "Done," he said, turning.

Carrera glanced over to him. Past her shoulder, Nate spotted bodies leaping from branches in the deeper jungle. "We have a problem," the Ranger said.

"What?"

The Ranger lifted her flamethrower and shot a jet of fire toward the jungle. As he watched, the line of fire drizzled back to the weapon's muzzle, like a hose draining after the spigot had been turned off.

"Out of fuel," she said.

Frank O'Brien stood by his twin sister, guarding her. At times, he swore that he could read her mind. Like now. Kelly stared at the river, watching with Kouwe and Manny for any sign that Rand's plan might work. But he noticed how she kept peering into the jungle, her eyes drawn to the path the ethnobotanist and soldier had taken. He also saw the glint in her eyes.

An explosion momentarily drew his attention around. Another grenade. The rain of debris rattled through the canopy. Gunfire was now almost continuous, all around them. The line of Rangers was slowly being driven back to the cluster of civilians. Soon they would have no choice but to retreat toward the stream and closer to whatever skulked in its watery depths.

Nearby, Anna Fong stood with Zane, guarded by Olin Pasternak, who stood with a 9mm Beretta pistol in hand. It was a poor weapon against such small, fast-moving targets, but it was better than nothing.

A growl suddenly rumbled behind him, from Manny's jaguar.

"Look!" Kelly called out.

Frank turned. His sister stood with her flashlight pointed toward the stream. Then he saw it, too, lit by the reflection of her flashlight. Small glistening objects began to bob up from the water's depths, floating, drifting with the current.

"Nate did it!" Kelly said, a smile on her face.

At her side, Professor Kouwe stepped nearer the streambed. One of the piranha-frogs burst from the water toward him, but landed on its side in the mud. It flopped for a couple seconds, then lay still. Stunned. Kouwe glanced to Frank. "We must not lose this chance. We must cross now."

Frank turned and spotted Captain Waxman a short distance up the slope. He yelled to be heard above the gunfire. "Captain Waxman! Rand's plan is working!" Frank waved an arm. "We can cross! Now!"

Waxman acknowledged his words with a nod, then his voice boomed. "Bravo unit! Retreat toward the stream!"

Frank touched the brim of his lucky baseball cap and stepped to Kelly. "Let's go."

Manny hurried past them. "Tor-tor and I'll still go first. It was my dissection upon which this plan was based." He didn't wait for a reply. He and his pet stepped to the stream's edge. He paused for half a breath, then waded into the stream. This fork was clearly deeper. Midstream, the water reached Manny's chest. Tor-tor had to swim.

But shortly the biologist was climbing out the far side. He turned. "Hurry! It's safe for the moment!"

"Move it!" Waxman ordered.

The civilians crossed together, strung along the current.

Frank went with Kelly, holding her hand. By now, hundreds of creatures bobbed in the water. They had to wade through the deadly forms, bumping them aside, avoiding sharp teeth that glistened from slack mouths. Horrified, Frank held his breath, praying for them to remain inert.

They reached the far side and scrambled, half panicked, out of the water. The Rangers followed next, rushing across in full gear, oblivious to what floated around them. As they clambered up to dry land, the first of the advancing creatures began to appear on the far side of the stream, hurtling out of the jungle. A couple piranha-frogs approached the stream but stopped at the water's edge, gill flaps trembling.

They must sense the danger, Frank thought. But they had no choice. On land they were suffocating. As if obeying some silent signal, the mass of mutated piranhas fled into the water.

"Back away!" Waxman ordered. "We can't count on the water still being tainted."

The group fled from the stream into the jungle-covered heights. Flashlights remained fixed on the water and banks. But after several minutes, it was clear the pursuit was over. Either the waters were still toxic to the beasts or they had given up their chase.

Frank sighed. "It's over."

Kelly remained quietly focused beside him, using her flashlight to scan the far bank of the stream. "Where's Private Carrera?" she asked softly, then turned to Frank. "Where's Nate?"

Upriver, a blast sounded, echoing through the forest.

Kelly's eyes widened as she stared at Frank. "They're in trouble."

Nate raised his shotgun and blasted another of the creatures that ventured too close. Carrera had shrugged off her weapon's fuel canister and was bent over it. "How much longer?" Nate asked, eyes wide, trying to watch everything at once.

"Almost done."

Nate glanced to the stream at his back. In the glow from Carrera's flashlight, he saw that the poison in the water was working. Downstream, bodies floated to the surface, but the current was rapidly carrying them away. The narrow streambed behind them was empty of bodies and could not be trusted. The current, as swift as it was, had surely swept the powdered poison away from here and down the length of the stream. It was not safe. They needed to backtrack along the trailing toxin in the water and seek a secure place to cross, where the current was more sluggish, somewhere where the poison was still active—but between them and safety lay a small legion of the creatures, entrenched in the forest, blocking their way.

"Ready," Carrera said, standing.

She hauled her handiwork from the jungle floor

and tightened the canister's lid, leaving a primer cord draping from it. The tank contained only a bit of fuel, not enough to service the weapon, but enough for their purposes. At least he hoped.

Nate held his position with his shotgun. "Are you sure this will work?"

"It had better."

Her words were not exactly the vote of confidence Nate was seeking.

"Point out the target again," she said, moving beside him.

He shifted his shotgun's muzzle and pointed at the gray-barked tree about thirty yards downstream.

"Okay." Carrera lit the end of the primer cord with a butane lighter. "Get ready." She swung her arm back and, using all the strength in her body, lobbed the canister underhanded.

Nate held his breath. It arced end-over-end—and landed at the foot of the targeted tree.

"All those years of women's softball finally paid off," Carrera mumbled, then to Nate: "Get down!"

Both dropped to the leafy floor. Nate fell, keeping his shotgun pointed ahead of him. And he was lucky he did. One of the creatures leaped from a bush, landing inches from his nose. Nate rolled and batted it away with the stock of his shotgun. He rolled back to his belly and glanced to the Ranger beside him. "Varsity baseball," he mumbled. "Senior year."

"Down!" Carrera reached and smashed his head to the dirt.

The explosion was deafening, shrapnel ripped through the canopy overhead. Nate glanced over. Carrera's trick had indeed worked. She had transformed the near-empty fuel tank into a large Molotov cocktail. Flames lit the night.

Carrera got to her knees. "What about—?"

Now it was Nate's turn to tug her down.

The second explosion sounded like a lightning strike: splintering wood accompanied by a low *boom*. The nearby jungle was shredded apart, followed by a rain of flaming copal resin.

"Damn it!" Carrera swore. Her sleeve was on fire. She patted it out in the loam.

Nate stood, relieved to see that the plan had worked. The tree, their target, was now just a blasted wreck, bluish flames dancing atop the stump. As Nate expected, the sap, rich in hydrocarbons, had acted as fuel, causing the makeshift Molotov cocktail to turn the tree into a natural bomb, and torch the entire riverbank as well.

"C'mon!" Nate called, bounding up with Carrera.

Together, they ran along the flaming and shredded section of the forest, paralleling the stream until they overtook the poison trailing through the water. Bodies of the creatures and other fish filled the channel.

"This way!" Nate ran into the river, half swimming, half clawing his way across. Carrera followed.

In no time, they were scrambling up the far bank.

"We did it!" the Ranger said with a laugh.

Nate sighed. Off in the distance, he spotted the shine of the others' flashlights. The team had made it across, too. "Let's go see if everyone else is okay."

They helped each other up and stumbled away from the stream, aiming for the other camp.

When they marched out of the forest, a cheer

went up. "Way to go, Carrera," Kostos said, a true smile on his lips.

Nate's greeting was no less earnest. As soon as he arrived, Kelly threw her arms around his neck and hugged him tight. "You made it," she mumbled in his ear. "You did it."

"And not a minute too soon," Nate said with a nod.

Frank patted him on the back.

"Well done, Dr. Rand," Captain Waxman said stoically, and turned to organize his troops. No one wanted to remain this close to the stream, poisoned or not.

Kelly dropped her arms, but not before planting a soft kiss on his cheek. "Thanks . . . thanks for saving us. And thanks for returning safely."

She swung away, leaving Nate somewhat bewildered.

Carrera nudged him with an elbow and rolled her eyes. "Looks like someone made a friend."

10:02 A.M.
AMAZON JUNGLE

Louis stood in the center of the blasted region near the river's edge. He could still smell the acrid tang of napalm in the air. Behind him, his team was offloading the canoes and loading up backpacks. From here, the journey would be on foot.

With the dawn, clouds had rolled in, and a steady drizzle fell from the sky, dousing the few fires that still smoldered. A smoky mist clung to the dead pocket of jungle, ghostly white and thick.

Off to the side, his mistress wandered around the site, a wounded expression on her face, as if the damage to the forest were a personal injury. She slowly circled a pole planted in the ground with a speared creature impaled on it. It was one of the strange beasts that had attacked the other group. Louis had never seen anything of its ilk before. And from Tshui's expression, neither had she. Tshui eyed the beast, cocking her head like a bird studying a worm.

Jacques stepped up behind Louis. "You have a radio call . . . on your coded frequency."

"Finally," he sighed.

Earlier, just before dawn, one of his two scouts had returned, badly frightened and wild-eyed. He had reported that his partner, a squat Colombian who went by the name of Toady, had been attacked by one of these beasts and died horribly. Malachim had barely made it back alive. Unfortunately, the man's report of the other team's whereabouts was thready at best. It seemed the Rangers' group, chased across a tributary stream, had fled these same beasts, and was now heading in a southwesterly direction. But toward where?

Louis had a way of finding out. He accepted the radio from Jacques. It was a direct link to a tiny scrambled transmitter held by a member of the opposing team, a little mole planted under the Rangers' noses at significant expense.

"Thank you, Jacques." Radio in hand, Louis stepped a few yards away. He had already had one previous call this morning, from his financiers, St. Savin Pharmaceuticals in France. It seemed some disease was spreading across the Amazon and the United

States, something associated with the dead man's body. Stakes were now higher. Louis had argued to raise his own fee, on the grounds that his work was now more hazardous. St. Savin had accepted, as he knew they would. A cure to this disease would be worth billions to his employer. What were a few more francs tossed his way?

Louis lifted the radio. "Favre here."

"Dr. Favre." The relief was clear in the other's voice. "Thank God, I reached you."

"I've been awaiting your call." A bit of menace entered Louis's tone. "I lost a good man last night because someone did not have the foresight to inform us of these venomous little toads."

There was a long pause. "I . . . I'm sorry. In all the commotion, I could hardly sneak off and place a call. In fact, this is the first chance I've had to slip away to the latrine alone."

"Fine. So tell me about this *commotion* last night."

"It was horrible." His spy blathered in his ear for the next three minutes, giving Louis an overview of what happened. "If it wasn't for Rand's use of some powdered fish toxin, we would all have surely died."

Louis's fingers gripped the radio tighter at the mention of Rand's name. The family name alone bristled the small hairs on his neck. "And where are you all now?"

"We're still heading in a southwesterly direction, searching for Gerald Clark's next marker."

"Very good."

"But—"

"What is it?"

"I . . . I want out."

"Pardon, mon ami?"

"Last night I was almost killed. I was hoping that you could . . . I don't know . . . pick me up if I wandered off. I would be willing to pay for my safe delivery back to civilization."

Louis closed his eyes. It seemed his mole was getting cold feet. He would have to warm the little mouse up. "Well, if you vacate your post, I will certainly find you."

"Th . . . thank you. I would—"

He interrupted. "And I'd be sure, when I found you, that your death would be long, painful, and humiliating. If you're familiar with my dossier, I'm sure you know how *creative* I can be."

There was silence on the other end. Louis could imagine his little spy blanching and quivering with fear.

"I understand."

"Excellent. I'm glad we've settled this matter. Now on to more important matters. It seems our mutual benefactor in France has placed a request upon our services. Something, I'm afraid, you'll have to accomplish."

"Wh . . . what?"

"For security purposes and to ensure their proprietary rights to what lies ahead, they wish to choke off the team's communication to the outside world, preferably as soon as possible without raising suspicion."

"How am I supposed to do that? You know I was supplied the computer virus to degrade the team's satellite uplink, but the Rangers have their own communication equipment. I wouldn't be able to get near it."

"No *problème*. You get that virus planted and leave the Rangers to me."

"But—"

"Have faith. You are never alone."

The line was silent again. Louis smiled. His words had not reassured his agent.

"Update me again tonight," Louis said.

A pause. "I'll try."

"Don't try . . . *do*."

"Yes, Doctor." The line went dead.

Louis lowered the radio and strode to Jacques. "We should be under way. The other team has a good start on us."

"Yes, sir." Jacques retreated to gather and organize his men.

Louis noticed that Tshui still stood by the impaled creature. If he wasn't mistaken, there was a trace of fear in the woman's eyes. But Louis wasn't sure. How could he be? He had never seen such an emotion displayed by the Indian witch. He crossed to her and pulled her into his arms.

She trembled ever so slightly under his hand.

"Hush, *ma chérie*. There is nothing to fear."

Tshui leaned against him, but her eyes flicked to the stake. She pulled tighter to him, a slight moan escaping her lips.

Louis frowned. Maybe he should heed his lover's unspoken warning. From here, they should proceed with more caution, more stealth. The other team had almost been destroyed by these aquatic predators, something never seen before. A clear sign they were probably on the right path. *But what if there are more hidden dangers out there?*

As he pondered this risk, he realized his team possessed a certain inherent advantage. Last night, it had taken all his opponents' cunning and ingenuity to survive the assault—a battle which inadvertently had opened a safer path for Louis's group to follow. So why not again? Why not let the other team flush out any other threats?

Louis mumbled, "Then we'll waltz in over their dead bodies and collect the prize." Pleased once again, he leaned and kissed the top of Tshui's head. "Fear not, my love. We cannot lose."

10:09 A.M.
HOSPITAL WARD OF THE INSTAR INSTITUTE
LANGLEY, VIRGINIA

Lauren O'Brien sat beside the bed, a book forgotten in her lap. Dr. Seuss's *Green Eggs and Ham*, Jessie's favorite. Her grandchild was asleep, curled on her side. Her fever had broken with the rising of the sun. The cocktail of antiinflammatories and antipyretics had done the job, slowly dropping the child's temperature from 102 back to 98.6. No one was sure if Jessie had contracted the jungle contagion—childhood fevers were common and plentiful—but no one was taking any chances.

The ward in which her granddaughter now slept was a closed system, sealed and vented against the spread of any potential germ. Lauren herself wore a one-piece disposable quarantine suit, outfitted with a self-breathing mask. She had refused at first, fearing the garb would further alarm Jessie. But policy dictated that all hospital staff and visitors wear proper isolation gear.

When Lauren had first entered the room, all suited up, Jessie had indeed appeared frightened, but the clear faceplate of the mask and a few reassuring words calmed her. Lauren had remained bedside all morning as Jessie was examined, blood samples collected, and drugs administered. With the resilience of the young, she now slept soundly.

A slight *whoosh* announced a newcomer to the room. Lauren awkwardly turned in her suit. She saw a familiar face behind another mask. She placed the book on a table and stood. "Marshall."

Her husband crossed to her and enveloped her in his plastic-clad arms. "I read her chart before coming in," he said, his voice sounding slightly tinny and distant. "Fever's down."

"Yes, it broke a couple of hours ago."

"Any word yet on the lab work?" Lauren heard the fear in his voice.

"No . . . it's too soon to tell if this is the plague." Without knowing the causative agent, there was no quick test. Diagnosis was made on a trio of clinical signs: oral ulcerations, tiny submucosal hemorrhages, and a dramatic drop in total white blood cell counts. But these symptoms typically would not manifest until thirty-six hours after the initial fever. It would be a long wait. Unless . . .

Lauren tried to change the subject. "How did your conference call go with the CDC and the folks in the Cabinet?"

Marshall shook his head. "A waste of time. It'll be days until all the politicking settles and a true course of action can be administered. The only good news is that Blaine at the CDC supported my idea to close Florida's border. That surprised me."

"It shouldn't," Lauren said. "I've been sending him case data all week, including what's happening in Brazil. The implications are pretty damn frightening."

"Well, you must have shaken him up." He squeezed her hand. "Thanks."

Lauren let out a long rattling sigh as she stared at the bed.

"Why don't you take a break? I can watch over Jessie for a while. You should try to catch a nap. You've been up all night."

"I'll never be able to sleep."

Marshall put his arm around her waist. "Then at least get some coffee and a little breakfast. We have the midday call with Kelly and Frank scheduled in a couple hours."

Lauren leaned against him. "What are we going to tell Kelly?"

"The truth. Jessie has a fever, but it's nothing to panic about. We still don't know for sure if it's the disease or not."

Lauren nodded. They remained silent for a bit, then Marshall guided her gently to the door. "Go."

Lauren passed through the air-locked doors and crossed down the hall to the locker room, where she stripped out of the suit and changed into scrubs. As she left the locker room, she stopped by the nurses' station. "Did any of the labs come back yet?"

A small Asian nurse flipped a plastic case file to her. "These were faxed just a minute ago."

Lauren flipped the file open and thumbed to the page of blood chemistries and hematology results. Her finger ran down the long list. The chemistries were all normal, as expected. But her nail stopped at the line for the total white blood cell count:

TWBC: 2130 (L)   6,000–15,000

It was low, significantly low, one of the trio of signs expected with the plague.

With her finger trembling, she ran down the report to the section that detailed the different white blood cell levels. There was one piece of news that the team's epidemiologist, Dr. Alvisio, had mentioned to her late last night, a possible pattern in the lab data that his computer model for the disease had noted: an unusual spike of a specific line of white blood cells, *basophils*, that occurred early in the disease as the total white blood cell levels were dropping. Though it was too soon to say for certain, it seemed to be consistent in all cases of the disease. It was perhaps a way to accelerate early detection.

Lauren read the last line.

BASOPHIL COUNT: 12 (H)   0–4

"Oh, God." She lowered the chart to the nurses' station. Jessie's basophil levels were spiked above normal, well above normal.

Lauren closed her eyes.

"Are you okay, Dr. O'Brien?"

Lauren didn't hear the nurse. Her mind was too full of a horrifying realization: Jessie had the plague.

11:48 A.M.
AMAZON JUNGLE

Kelly followed the line of the others, bone tired but determined to keep moving. They had been walking all night with frequent rest breaks. After the attack, they had marched for a solid two hours, then made a temporary camp at dawn while the Rangers contacted the field base in Wauwai. They had decided to push on until at least midday, when they would use the satellite link to contact the States. Afterward, the team would rest the remainder of the day, regroup, and decide how to proceed.

Kelly glanced at her watch. Noon approached. *Thank God.* Already she heard Waxman grumbling about choosing a site for the day's camp. "Well away from any waterways," she heard him warn.

All day long, the team had been wary of streams and pools, skirting them or crossing in a mad rush. But there were no further attacks.

Manny had offered a reason. "Perhaps the creatures were local to just that small territory. Maybe that's why the buggers were never seen before."

"If so, good riddance," Frank had voiced sourly.

They had trudged onward, the morning drizzle drying slowly to a thick humid mist. The moisture weighed everything down: clothes, packs, boots. But no one complained about the march. All were glad to put distance between them and the horror of the previous night.

From up ahead, a Ranger scout called back. "A clearing!" It was Corporal Warczak. As the unit's tracker, his scouting served double duty. He was also watching for any physical evidence of Gerald Clark's passage. "The spot looks perfect for a campsite!"

Kelly sighed. "About time."

"Check it out!" Waxman said. "Make sure there are no close streams."

"Yes, sir! Kostos is already reconnoitering the area."

Nate, just a couple steps ahead of her, called forward, "Be careful! There could be—"

A pained shout rose from ahead.

Everyone froze, except Nate who rushed forward. "Damn it, doesn't anyone listen to what I tell them?" he muttered as he ran. He glanced back to Kelly and Kouwe and waved an arm. "We'll need your help! Both of you."

Kelly moved to follow. "What is it?" she asked Kouwe.

The Indian professor was already slinging his pack forward and working the straps loose. "*Supay chacra*, I'd imagine. The devil's garden. C'mon."

Devil's garden? Kelly did not like the sound of that.

Captain Waxman ordered the bulk of his Rangers to remain with the other civilians. He and Frank joined in following Nate.

Kelly hurried forward and saw a pair of Rangers on the ground ahead. They seemed to be fighting, one rolling in the dirt, the other striking him with the flat of his hand.

Nate ran toward them.

"Get these goddamn shits off me!" the Ranger on

the ground yelled, rolling through the underbrush. It was Sergeant Kostos.

"I'm trying," Corporal Warczak replied, continuing to slap at the man.

Nate knocked the corporal aside. "Stop! You're only making them angrier." Then to the soldier on the ground, he ordered, "Sergeant Kostos, lie still!"

"They're stinging me all over!"

Kelly was now close enough to see that the man was covered with large black ants, each about an inch long. There had to be thousands of them.

"Quit moving and they'll leave you alone."

Kostos glanced to Nate, eyes burning and angry, but he did as told. He stopped thrashing in the brush and lay panting.

Kelly noticed the blistered welts all over his arms and face. It looked as if he had been attacked with a burning cigarette butt.

"What happened?" Captain Waxman asked.

Nate held everyone away from Kostos. "Stand back."

Kostos trembled where he lay. Kelly saw the tears of pain at the corners of the man's eyes. He must be in agony. But Nate's advice proved sound. As he lay, unmoving, the ants stopped biting and crawled from his arms and legs, disappearing into the leafy brush.

"Where are they going?" Kelly asked.

"Back home," Kouwe said. "They were the colony's soldiers." He pointed past a few trees. A few yards ahead a jungle clearing opened, so empty and bare it looked as if someone had taken a broom and hedge clippers to the area. In the center stood a massive tree, its branches spread through the space, a solitary giant.

"It's an ant tree," the professor continued to explain. "The ant colony lives inside it."

"Inside it?"

Kouwe nodded. "It's just one of the many ways rain forest plants have adapted to animals or insects. The tree has evolved with special hollow branches and tubules that serve the ants, even feeding the colony with a special sugary sap. The tree in turn is serviced by the ants. Not only does the colony's debris help fertilize the tree, but they're active in protecting it, too—from other insects, from birds and animals." Kouwe nodded to the clearing. "The ants destroy anything that grows near the tree, trimming away stranglers or climbers from the branches themselves. It's why such spots in the jungle are called *supay chacra*, or a devil's garden."

"What a strange relationship."

"Indeed. But the relationship is mutually beneficial to both species—tree and insect. In fact, one cannot live without the other."

Kelly stared toward the clearing, amazed at how intertwined life was out here. A few days back, Nate had shown her an orchid whose flower was shaped like the reproductive parts of a certain species of wasp. "In order to lure the insect over to pollinate it." Then there were others that traded sugary nectars to lure different pollinators. And such relationships weren't limited to insect and plant. The fruit of certain trees *had* to be consumed by a specific bird or animal and pass through its digestive tract before it could root and grow. So much strangeness, all life dependent and twined with its neighbors in a complex evolutionary web.

Nate knelt beside the sergeant, drawing back her attention. By now, the ants had vacated the soldier's body. "How many times have I warned you to watch what you lean against?"

"I didn't see them," Kostos said, his voice pained and belligerent. "And I needed to take a leak."

Kelly saw the man's zipper was indeed down.

Nate shook his head. "Against an ant tree?"

Kouwe explained as he rummaged through his pack. "Ants are tuned to chemical markers. The man's urine would have been taken as an assault on the colony living in the tree."

Kelly broke out a syringe of antihistamine, while Kouwe removed a handful of leaves from his own pack and began to rub them together. She recognized the leaves and the scent of the oily compound. "*Ku-run-yeh?*" she asked.

The Indian smiled at her. "Very good." It was the same medicinal plant that Kouwe had used to treat her blistered fingers when she had touched the fire liana vine. A potent analgesic.

The two doctors began to work on their patient. As Kelly injected a combination of an antihistamine and a steroidal antiinflammatory, Kouwe smeared some of the *ku-run-yeh* extract on the soldier's arm, showing him how to apply it.

The sergeant's face reflected the immediate soothing relief. He sighed and took the handful of leaves. "I can do the rest myself," he said, his voice hard with embarrassment.

Corporal Warczak helped his sergeant stand.

"We should skirt around this area," Nate said. "We don't want to camp too near an ant tree. Our food might draw their scouts."

Captain Waxman nodded. "Then let's get going. We've wasted enough time here." His glance toward the limping sergeant was not sympathetic.

Over the next half hour, the group wound again under the forest canopy, accompanied by the hoots and calls of capuchin and wooly monkeys. Manny pointed out a tiny pigmy anteater nestled atop a branch. Frozen in place by fear, it looked more like a stuffed animal with its large eyes and silky coat. And of more menace, but appearing just as artificial due to its fluorescent-green scales, was a forest pit viper, wrapped and dangling from a palm frond.

At last, a shout arose from up ahead. It was Corporal Warczak. "I've found something!"

Kelly prayed it wasn't another ant tree.

"I believe it's a marker from Clark!"

The group converged toward the sound of his voice. Up a short hill, they found a large Brazil nut tree. Its bower shaded a great area littered with old nuts and leaves. Upon the trunk, a small strip of torn cloth hung, soaked and limp.

The others approached, but Corporal Warczak waved them all away. "I've found boot tracks," he said. "Don't trample them."

"Boot tracks?" Kelly said in a hushed voice as the soldier slowly circled the tree, then stopped on the far side.

"I see a trail leading here!" he called back.

Captain Waxman and Frank crossed over to him.

Kelly frowned. "I thought Gerald Clark came out of the forest barefooted."

"He did," Nate answered as they waited. "But the Yanomamo shaman we captured mentioned that the Indian villagers had stripped Clark of his possessions. They must have taken his boots."

Kelly nodded.

Richard Zane pointed toward the tree. "Is there another message?"

They all waited for the okay to enter the area. Captain Waxman and Frank returned, leaving Corporal Warczak crouched by the trail.

The group was waved forward. "We'll camp here," Waxman declared.

Sounds of relief flowed, and the team approached the tree, decaying nuts crackling underfoot. Kelly was one of the first to the trunk. Again, deeply incised in the bark were clear markings.

"*G. C.*: Clark again," Nate said. He pointed in the direction of the arrow. "Due west. Just like the boot trail Warczak found. Dated May seventh."

Olin leaned against the tree. "May seventh? That means it took Clark ten days to reach the village from here? He must have been moving damn slowly."

"He probably didn't make a beeline like we did," Nate said. "He probably spent a lot of time searching for some sign of habitation or civilization, tracking back and forth."

"Plus he was getting sick by this time," Kelly added. "According to my mother's examination of his remains, the cancers would've been starting to spread through his body. He probably had to rest often."

Anna Fong sighed sadly. "If only he could've reached civilization sooner . . . been able to communicate where he'd been all this time."

Olin shoved away from the tree. "Speaking of communication, I should get the satellite uplink set up. We're due to conference in another half hour."

"I'll help you," Zane said, heading off with him.

The rest of the group dispersed to string up hammocks, gather wood, and scrounge up some local fruits. Kelly busied herself with her own campsite, spreading her mosquito netting like a pro.

Frank worked beside her. "Kelly . . . ?" From her brother's tone, she could tell he was about to tread on cautious ground.

"What?"

"I think you should go back."

She stopped tugging her netting and turned. "What do you mean?"

"I've been talking to Captain Waxman. When he reported the attack this morning to his superiors, they ordered him to trim nonessential personnel after a safe camp had been established. Last night was too close. They don't want to risk additional casualties. Plus the others are slowing the Rangers down." Frank glanced over his shoulder. "To expedite our search, it's been decided to leave Anna and Zane here, along with Manny and Kouwe."

"But—"

"Olin, Nate, and I will continue with the Rangers."

Kelly turned fully around. "I'm *not* nonessential, Frank. I'm the only physician here, and I can travel just as well as you."

"Corporal Okamoto is a trained field medic."

"That doesn't make him an M.D."

"Kelly . . ."

"Frank, don't do this."

He wouldn't meet her eyes. "It's already been decided."

Kelly circled to make him look at her. "*You* decided this. You're the leader of this operation."

He finally looked up. "Okay, it was my decision." His shoulders sagged, and he swung away. "I don't want you at risk."

Kelly fumed, trembling with frustration. But she knew the decision was indeed ultimately her brother's.

"We'll send out a GPS lock on our current position and leave two Rangers as guards. Then a team will evacuate you as soon as a Brazilian supply helicopter with the range to reach camp can be coordinated. In the meantime, the remaining party—the six Rangers and the three of us—will strike out from here."

"When?"

"After a short rest break. We'll leave this afternoon. March until sundown. Now that we're on Clark's trail, a smaller party can travel faster."

Kelly closed her eyes, huffing out a sigh. The plan was sound. And with the contagion spreading here and in the States, time was essential. Besides, if something was found, a scientific research team could always be airlifted to the site to investigate. "I guess I have no choice."

Frank remained silent, cinching his hammock for his short rest break.

A call broke the tension. Olin, busy establishing the satellite uplink, shouted, "We're ready here!"

Kelly followed Frank to the laptop, again protected under a rain tarp.

Olin hunched over the keyboard, tapping rapidly. "Damn it, I'm having trouble getting a solid feed." He continued working. "All this dampness . . . ah, here we go!" He sat up. "Got it!"

The ex-KGB agent slid to the side. Kelly crouched with Frank. A face formed on the screen, jittering and pixellating out of focus.

"It's the best I can manage," Olin whispered from the side.

It was their father. Even through the interference, his hard face did not look pleased. "I heard about last night," he said as introduction. "It's good to see you're both safe."

Frank nodded. "We're fine. Tired but okay."

"I read the report from the army, but tell me yourselves what happened."

Together Frank and Kelly quickly related the attack by the strange creatures.

"A chimera?" her father said as they finished, eyes narrowed. "A mix of frog and fish?"

"That's what the *biologist* here believes," Kelly said pointedly, glancing to Frank, stressing that even Manny had proven useful to the expedition.

"Then that settles matters," her father said, straightening and staring directly at Kelly. "An hour ago I was contacted by the head of Special Forces out of Fort Bragg and was informed of the revised plan."

"What revised plan?" Zane asked behind them.

Frank waved away his question.

Their father continued, "Considering what's happening with this damn disease, I totally concur with General Korsen. A cure must be found, and time has become a critical factor."

Kelly thought about protesting her expulsion, but bit her lip, knowing she would find no ally in her father. He had not wanted his little girl to come out here in the first place.

Frank leaned closer to the screen. "What's the condition in the States?"

Their father shook his head. "I'll let your mother answer that." He slid aside.

She looked exhausted, her eyes shadowed with fatigue. "The number of cases . . ." Lauren coughed and cleared her throat. "The number of cases has trebled in the last twelve hours."

Kelly cringed. *So fast . . .*

"Mostly in Florida, but we're now seeing cases in California, Georgia, Alabama, and Missouri."

"What about in Langley?" Kelly asked. "At the Institute?"

A glance was shared between her parents.

"Kelly . . ." her father began. His tone sounded like Frank's from a moment ago, cautionary. "I don't want you to panic."

Kelly sat up straighter, her heart already climbing

into her throat. Don't panic? Did those words *ever* calm someone? "What is it?"

"Jessie's sick—"

The next few words were lost on Kelly. Her vision darkened at the corners. She had been dreading hearing those words since first learning of the contagion. *Jessie's sick* . . .

Her father must have noticed her falling back in her seat, pale and trembling. Frank put his arm around her, holding her.

"Kelly," her father said. "We don't know if it's the disease. It's just a fever, and she's already responding to medications. She was eating ice cream and chattering happily when we came to make this call."

Her mother placed a hand on her father's shoulder, and they exchanged a look. "It's probably not the disease, is it, Lauren?"

Their mother smiled. "I'm sure it's not."

Frank sighed. "Thank God. Is anyone else showing symptoms?"

"Not a one," her father assured them.

But Kelly's eyes were fixed on her mother. Her smile now looked sickly and wan. Her gaze slipped down.

Kelly closed her own eyes. *Oh, God* . . .

"We'll see you soon," her father concluded.

Frank nudged her.

She nodded. "Soon . . ."

Zane again spoke behind her. "What did your father mean that he'd see you soon? What's this about revised plans? What's going on?"

Frank gave Kelly a final squeeze. "Jessie's fine," he

whispered to her. "You'll see when you get home." He then turned to answer Zane's question.

Kelly remained frozen before the laptop as the arguments began to rage behind her. In her mind's eye, she again saw her mother's smile fade, her eyes lower in shame. She knew her mother's moods better than anyone, possibly even better than her father did. Her mother had been lying. She had seen the knowledge hidden behind the reassuring words.

Jessie had the disease. Her mother believed it. Kelly knew this with certainty. And if her mother believed it . . .

Kelly could not stop the tears. Busily arguing about the change in plans, the others failed to notice her.

She covered her face with her hand. *Oh, God . . . no . . .*

ELEVEN

Aerial Assault

AUGUST 14, 1:24 P.M.
AMAZON JUNGLE

Nate could not sleep. As he lay in his hammock, he knew he should be resting for the next leg of the journey. In only another hour, his group was due to depart, but questions still persisted. He stared around the campsite. While half the camp napped, the other half were still quietly arguing about the split-up.

"We can just follow them," Zane said. "What are they going to do, shoot us?"

"We should mind their orders," Kouwe said calmly, but Nate knew the older professor was no more pleased with being abandoned than the Tellux rep.

Nate turned his back on them, but he understood their frustration. If he had been one of those left behind, they would've had to hog-tie him to stop him from continuing on his own.

From this new vantage, he spotted Kelly lying in

her hammock. She was the only one who had not protested. Her concern for her daughter was clearly foremost in her mind. As he watched, Kelly rolled over and their gazes met. Her eyes were puffy from tears.

Nate gave up trying to nap and slid from his hammock. He crossed to her side and knelt. "Jessie will be fine," he said softly.

Kelly stared at him in silence, then spoke through her pain, her voice small. "She has the disease."

Nate frowned. "Now that's just your fear talking. There's no proof that—"

"I saw it in my mother's eyes. She could never hide anything from me. She knows Jessie has the disease and is trying to spare me."

Nate didn't know what to say. He reached through the netting and rested a hand on her shoulder. He quietly comforted her, willing her strength, then spoke with his heart, softly but earnestly, "If what you say is true, I'll find a cure out there somewhere. I promise."

This earned a tired smile. Her lips moved, but no words came out. Still, Nate read those lips easily. *Thank you.* A single tear rolled from her eyes before she covered her face and turned away.

Nate stood, leaving her to her grief. He noticed Frank and Captain Waxman conferring over a map splayed across the ground and headed toward them. With a glance back at Kelly, he silently repeated his promise. *I will find a cure.*

The map the two were surveying was a topographic study of the terrain. Captain Waxman drew a finger across the map. "Following due west of here, the land elevates as it approaches the Peruvian border. But it's a broken jumble of cliffs and valleys, a veritable maze. It'll be easy to get lost in there."

"We'll have to watch closely for Gerald Clark's signposts," Frank said, then looked up to acknowledge Nate's presence. "You should get your pack ready. We're gonna head out shortly and take advantage of as much daylight as we can."

Nate nodded. "I can be ready in five minutes."

Frank stood. "Let's get moving then."

Over the next half hour, the team was assembled. They decided to leave the Rangers' SATCOM radio equipment with the remaining party, who needed to coordinate the retrieval effort by the Brazilian army. The group heading out would continue to use the CIA's satellite array to maintain contact.

Nate hoisted his shotgun to one shoulder and shifted his backpack to a comfortable spot. The plan was to move swiftly, with few rest breaks, until sunset.

Waxman raised an arm and the group headed off into the forest, led by Corporal Warczak.

As they left, Nate looked behind him. He had already said good-bye to his friends, Kouwe and Manny. But behind the pair stood the two Rangers who would act as guards: Corporal Jorgensen and Private Carrera. The woman lifted her weapon in farewell. Nate waved back.

Waxman had originally slated Corporal Graves to remain behind, to be evacuated out, on account of the death of his brother Rodney. But Graves had argued, "Sir, this mission cost my brother's life along with my fellow teammates. With your permission, I'd like to see it through to the end. For the honor of my brother . . . for all my brothers."

Waxman had consented.

With no further words, the group set off through the jungle. The sun had finally broken through the clouds, creating a steam bath under the damp canopy. Within minutes, everyone's face shone with sweat.

Nate marched beside Frank O'Brien. Every few steps, the man slid off his baseball cap and wiped the trickling dampness from his brow. Nate wore a handkerchief as a headband, keeping the sweat from his own eyes. But he couldn't keep the black flies and gnats, attracted by the salt and odor, from plaguing him.

Despite the heat, humidity, and constant buzzing in their ears, they made good progress. Within a couple of hours, Nathan estimated they had covered over seven miles. Warczak was still finding boot-prints in the bare soil as they headed west into the jungle. The prints were barely discernable, pooled with water from yesterday's rains.

Ahead of him marched Corporal Okamoto, whistling his damn tune again. Nate sighed. *Didn't the jungle offer enough aggravations?*

As they continued, Nate kept wary watch for any perils: snakes, fire liana, ant trees, anything that might slow them down. Each stream was crossed with caution. But no sign of the piranha-frogs appeared. Overhead, Nate saw a three-toed sloth amble along a branch high in the canopy, oblivious to the intrusion. He watched its passage, glancing over his shoulder as he walked under it. Sloths seemed slow and amiable, but when injured, they were known to gut those who came too close. Their climbing claws were dagger-sharp. But this great beast just continued its arboreal journey.

Turning back around, Nate caught the barest flicker of something reflecting from high in a tree, about half a mile back. He paused to study it.

"What is it?" Frank asked, noticing Nate had stopped.

The flickering reflection vanished. He shook his head. Probably just a wet leaf fluttering in the sunlight. "Nothing," he said and waved Frank on. But throughout the remainder of the afternoon, he kept glancing over his shoulder. He could not escape the feeling that they were being watched, spied upon from on high. The feeling grew worse as the day wore on.

Finally, he turned to Frank. "Something's bothering me. Something we neglected to address after the attack back at the village."

"What?"

"Remember Kouwe's assessment that we were being tracked?"

"Yeah, but he wasn't a hundred percent sure. Just some picked fruit and bushes disturbed during the night. No footprints or anything concrete."

Nate glanced over his shoulder. "Let's say the professor was correct. If so, who's tracking us? It couldn't have been the Indians at the village. They were dead before we even entered the jungle. So who was it?"

Frank noticed the direction of Nate's stare. "You

think we're still being tracked. Did you see something?"

"No, not really . . . just an odd reflection in the trees a while back. It's probably nothing."

Frank nodded. "All the same, I'll let Captain Waxman know. It wouldn't hurt to be on extra guard out here." Frank dropped back to speak with the Rangers' leader, who was marching with Olin Pasternak.

Alone, Nate stared into the shadowy forest around him. He was suddenly less sure that leaving the others behind was such a wise move.

5:12 P.M.

Manny ran a brush through Tor-tor's coat. Not that the bit of hygiene was necessary. The jaguar did a good enough job with his own bristled tongue. But it was a chore that both cat and human enjoyed. Tor-tor responded with a slow growl as Manny groomed the cat's belly. Manny wanted to growl himself, but not in contentment and pleasure.

He hated being left behind by the others.

Hearing a rustle at his side, Manny glanced up. It was the anthropologist, Anna Fong. "May I?" She pointed to the jaguar.

Manny lifted an eyebrow in mild surprise. He had noticed the woman eyeing the cat before, but he had thought it was with more fear than interest. "Sure." He patted the spot next to him. She knelt, and he handed her the brush. "He especially likes his belly and ruff worked over."

Anna took the brush and bent over the sleek feline. She stretched her arm, cautiously wary as Tortor watched her. She slowly lowered the brush and drew it through his thick coat. "He's so beautiful. Back at home, in Hong Kong, I watched the cats stalk back and forth in their cages at the zoo. But to raise one of them yourself, how wonderful that must be."

Manny liked the way she talked, soft with a certain stilted diction, oddly formal. "Wonderful, you say? He's been eating through my household budget, chewed through two sofas, and shredded I don't know how many throw rugs."

She smiled. "Still . . . it must be worth it."

Manny agreed, but he was reluctant to speak it aloud. It was somehow unmanly to express how much he loved the great big lug. "I'll have to release him soon."

Though he tried to hide it, she must have heard the sorrow in his words. Anna glanced up to him, her eyes supportive. "I'm sure it's still worth it."

Manny grinned shyly. *It sure was.*

Anna continued to massage the cat with the brush. Manny watched her from the side. One fall of her silky hair was tucked behind an ear. Her nose crinkled ever so slightly as she concentrated on the cat's grooming.

"Everyone!" a voice called out, interrupting them. They both turned.

Nearby, Corporal Jorgensen lowered the radio's receiver and shook his head. He turned and faced the camp. "Everyone. I've got good news and bad news."

A universal grumbling met the soldier's attempt at joviality.

"The *good* news is that the Brazilian army has rousted up a helicopter to fly us out of here."

"And the bad?" Manny asked.

Jorgensen frowned. "It won't be here for another two days. With the plague spreading through the region, the demand for aircraft is fierce. And for the moment, our evac is a low priority."

"Two days?" Manny spoke up, accepting the brush back from Anna. Irritation entered his voice. "Then we could've traveled with the others until then."

"Captain Waxman had his orders," Jorgensen said with a shrug.

"What about the Comanche helicopter stationed at Wauwai?" Zane asked. He had been lounging in his hammock, quietly fuming.

Private Carrera answered from where she was cleaning her weapon. "It's a two-seater attack chopper. Besides, the Comanche's held in reserve to back up the other team as necessary."

Manny shook his head and furtively glanced at Kelly O'Brien. She sat in her hammock, eyes tired, dull, defeated. The waiting would be the worst for her. Two more days lost before she could join her sick daughter.

Kouwe spoke from near the large Brazil nut tree. He had been examining the crude markings knifed in the bark by Clark, and now had his head cocked questioningly. "Does anyone else smell smoke?"

Manny sniffed, but the air seemed clear.

Anna crimped her brow. "I smell something . . ."

Kouwe swung around the base of the large Brazil nut tree, nose half raised. Though long out of the forests, the professor's Indian senses were still keen. "There!" he called out from the far side.

The group followed after him. Carrera quickly slapped her M-16 back together, hauling it up as she stood.

To the south of their camp, about a hundred feet into the forest, small flames flickered in the shadows, low to the ground. Through breaks in the canopy, a thin column of gray smoke drifted skyward.

"I'll investigate," Jorgensen said. "The rest hang back with Carrera."

"I'm going with you," Manny said. "If anyone's out there, Tor-tor will scent them."

As answer, Jorgensen unstrapped the M-9 pistol from his belt and passed it to Manny. Together they cautiously passed into the deeper jungle. Manny signaled with his hand, and Tor-tor trotted ahead of them, taking the point.

Back behind them, Carrera ordered everyone together. "Keep alert!"

Manny followed after his cat, walking abreast of Corporal Jorgensen. "The fire's burning on the ground," Manny whispered.

As they neared the spot, the corporal signaled for silence.

Both men's senses were stretched, watching for any shift of shadows, listening for the telltale snap of a twig, searching for any sign of a hidden threat. But with the twittering of birds and mating calls of monkeys, it was difficult work. Their steps slowed as they neared the smoldering glow.

Ahead Tor-tor edged closer, his natural feline curiosity piqued. But once within a few yards of the smoky fire, he suddenly crouched, growling. He stared at the flames and slowly backed away.

The men stopped. Jorgensen lifted a hand, a silent warning. *The jaguar sensed something.* He motioned for Manny to sink lower and take up a guard position. Once set, Jorgensen proceeded ahead. Manny held his breath as the corporal moved silently through the forest, stepping carefully, weapon ready.

Manny kept watch all around them, unblinking, ears straining. Tor-tor backed to his side, now silent, hackles raised, golden eyes aglow. Beside him, Manny heard the cat chuffing at the air. Manny remembered the cat's reaction to the caiman urine beside the river. *He smells something . . . something that has him spooked.*

With adrenaline doped in Manny's blood, his own senses were more acute. Alerted by the jaguar, Manny now recognized an odd scent to the smoke: metallic, bitter, acrid. It was not plain wood smoke.

Straightening, Manny wanted to warn Jorgensen, but the soldier had already reached the site. As the soldier eyed the burning patch, Manny saw the man's shoulders jerk with surprise. He slowly circled the smoldering fire, rifle pointed outward. Nothing came out of the forest to threaten. Jorgenson maintained his watch for a full two minutes, then waved Manny over.

Letting out his held breath, Manny approached. Tor-tor hung back, still refusing to approach the fire.

"Whoever set this must have run off," Jorgensen said. He pointed at the fire. "Meant to scare us."

Manny moved close enough to see the spread of

flames on the forest floor. It was not wood that burned, but some thick oily paste painted atop a cleared section of dirt. It cast a fierce brightness but little heat. The smoke rising from it was redolent and cloying, like some musky incense. But it was not the smoke nor the strange fuel of this fire that sent icy chills along Manny's limbs—it was the pattern.

Painted and burning on the jungle floor was a familiar serpentine coiled symbol—the mark of the Ban-ali, burning bright under the canopy's gloom.

Jorgensen used the tip of his boot to nudge the oily substance. "Some combustible paste." He then used his other foot to kick dirt over the spot, smothering the flames. He worked along the burning lines, and with Manny's help, they doused the fire. Once they were done, Manny stared up, following the smoke into the late afternoon sky.

"We should get back to camp."

Manny nodded. They retreated to the bower under the large Brazil nut tree. Jorgensen reported what they discovered. "I'll radio the field base. Let them know what we found." He crossed to the bulky radio pack and picked up the receiver. After a few moments, the soldier swore and slammed the receiver down.

"What is it?" Manny asked.

"We've missed SATCOM's satellite window by five minutes."

"What does that mean?" Anna asked.

Jorgensen waved an arm at the radio unit, then at the sky overhead. "The military's satellite transponders are out of range."

"Until when?"

"Till four o'clock tomorrow morning."

"What about reaching the other team?" Manny asked. "Using your personal radios?"

"I already tried that, too. The Sabers only have a range of six miles. Captain Waxman's team is beyond our reach."

"So we're cut off?" Anna asked.

Jorgensen shook his head. "Just until morning."

"And what then?" Zane paced nervously, eyes on the forest. "We can't stay here for two more days waiting for that damned helicopter."

"I agree," Kouwe said, frowning deeply. "The village Indians found the same mark on their *shabano* the very night they were assaulted by the piranha creatures."

Private Carrera turned to him. "What are you suggesting?"

Kouwe frowned. "I'm not sure yet." The professor's eyes were fixed on the smoggy smudge in the sky. The forest still reeked of the bitter fumes. "But we've been marked."

5:33 P.M.

Frank was never happier to see the sun sink toward the horizon. They should be stopping soon. Every muscle ached from so many hours of hiking and so little sleep. He stumbled in step with the Ranger ahead of him, Nate marching behind.

Someone yelled a short distance away. "Whoa! Check this out!"

The straggling team members increased their pace. Frank climbed a short rise and saw what had triggered the startled response. A quarter mile ahead, the jungle was flooded by a small lake. Its surface was a sheet of silver from the setting sun to the west. It blocked their path, spreading for miles in both directions.

"It's an *igapo*," Nate said. "A swamp forest."

"It's not on my map," Captain Waxman said.

Nate shrugged. "Such sections dot the Amazon basin. Some come and go according to the rainfall levels. But for this region still to be so wet at the end of the dry season suggests it's been here a while." Nate pointed ahead. "Notice how the jungle breaks down here, drowned away by years of continual swamping."

Frank indeed noticed how the dense canopy ended ahead. What remained of the jungle here were just occasional massive trees growing straight out of the water and thousands of islands and hummocks. Otherwise, above the swamp, the blue sky was open and wide. The brightness after so long in the green gloom was sharp and biting.

The group cautiously hiked down the long, low slope that headed toward the swamp. The air seemed to grow more fecund and thick. Around the swamp, spiky bromeliads and massive orchids adorned their view. Frogs and toads set up a chorus, while the chattering of birds attempted to drown out their amphibious neighbors. Near the water's edges, spindly-limbed wading birds, herons and egrets, hunted fish. A handful of ducks took wing at their noisy approach.

Once within fifty feet of the water's edge, Captain Waxman called a halt. "We'll search the bank for any sign of a marker, but first we should make sure the water is safe to be near. I don't want any surprises."

Nate moved forward. "We may be okay. According to Manny, those predatory creatures were part piranha. Those fish don't like standing water like this. They prefer flowing streams."

Captain Waxman glanced to him. "And the last time I checked, piranhas didn't chase their prey onto dry land either."

Frank saw Nate blush slightly and nod.

Waxman sent Corporal Yamir forward toward the swamp's edge. "Let's see if anything stirs up."

The Pakistani soldier raised his M-16 and shot a grenade from its attached launcher toward the shallows off to the side. The explosion geysered water high into the air, startling birds and monkeys from their perches. Water and bits of lily pads rained down upon the forest.

The party waited for ten minutes, but nothing responded. No venomous predators fled the assault or attacked from the water's edge.

Captain Waxman waved his men forward to begin the search for another tree marker. "Be careful. Stay away from the water's edge and keep your eyes open!"

They didn't have long to wait. Again Corporal Warczak, the team's tracker, raised his voice. "Found it!" He stood only ten yards to the right, not far from the sludgy water.

Upon the bole of a palm that leaned over the

water was the now familiar strip of polyester cloth, nailed to the tree with a thorn. The markings were almost identical to the last one. The initials and an arrow pointing due west again, right toward the swamp. Only the date was different. "May fifth," Olin read aloud. "Two days from the last marker."

Warczak stood a few paces away. "It looks like Clark came from this way."

"But the arrow points across the water," Frank said. He tipped the bill of his baseball cap to shadow his eyes and stared over the water. Distantly, beyond the swamp, he could see the highlands that Captain Waxman had shown him on the topographic map: a series of red cliff faces, broken with jungle-choked chasms and separated into tall forest-crowned mesas.

At his side, Corporal Okamoto passed him a set of binoculars. "Try these."

"Thanks." Frank fitted the scopes in place. Nate was also offered a pair. Through the lenses, the cliffs and mesas grew clearer. Small waterfalls tumbled from the towering heights into the swampy region below, while thick mists clung to the lower faces, obscuring the forested chasms that stretched from the swamp and up into the highlands.

"Those small streams and falls must feed the swamp," Nate said. "Keeping the area wet year round."

Frank lowered his glasses and found Captain Waxman studying a compass.

Nate pointed to the tree. "I wager that this marker points to Clark's next signpost. He must have had to circle around the swamp." Nate stared at the huge boggy spread of the water. "It would've taken him weeks to skirt the water."

Frank heard the despair in Dr. Rand's voice. To hike around the swamp would take them just as long.

Captain Waxman lifted his eyes from the compass and squinted across the swamp. "If the marker lies straight across, that's where we'll go." He pointed an arm. "It'll only take us a day to raft across here, rather than losing a week hiking."

"But we have no rubber raiders," Frank said.

Waxman glanced to him condescendingly. "We're Army Rangers, not Boy Scouts." He waved to the forest. "There are plenty of downed logs, acres of bamboo, and with the rope we have with us and the vines around us, we should be able to lash together a couple of rafts. It's what we're trained to do—improvise with the resources available." He glanced to the distant shore. "It can't be more than a couple miles to cross here."

Nate nodded. "Good. We can shave days off the search."

"Then let's get to work! I want to be finished by nightfall, so we're rested and ready in the morning to cross." Waxman assembled various teams: to roll and manhandle logs to the swamp's edge, to go out with axes and hack lengths of bamboo, and to strip vines for lashing material.

Frank assisted where needed and was surprised how quickly the building material accumulated on the muddy shore. They soon had enough for a flotilla of rafts. The assembling took even less time. Two matching logs were aligned parallel and topped with a solid layer of bamboo. Ropes and vines secured it all together. The first raft was shoved through the slick mud and into the water, bobbing in the shallows.

A cheer rose from the Rangers. Nate grinned approvingly as he sculpted paddles from bamboo and dried palm fronds.

A second raft was soon finished. The entire process took less than two hours.

Frank watched the second raft drift beside its mate. By now, the sun was setting. The western sky was aglow with a mix of reds, oranges, and splashes of deep indigo.

Around him, the camp was being set up. A fire lit, hammocks strung, food being prepared. Frank turned to join them when he spotted a dark streak against the bright sunset. He pinched his eyebrows, squinting.

Corporal Okamoto was passing Frank with an armful of tinder. "Can I borrow your binoculars?" Frank asked.

"Sure. Grab 'em from my field jacket." The soldier shifted his burden.

Frank thanked him and took the glasses. Once Okamoto had continued past, Frank raised the binoculars to his eyes. It took him a moment to find the dark streak rising in the sky. *Smoke?* It rose from the distant highlands. A sign of habitation? He followed the curling black line.

"What do you see?" Nate said.

"I'm not sure." Frank pointed to the sky. "I think it's smoke. Maybe from another camp or village."

Nate frowned and took the glasses. "Whatever it is," he said after a moment, "it's drifting this way."

Frank stared. Even without the binoculars, he

could see that Nate was correct. The column of smoke was arching toward them. Frank lifted a hand. "That makes no sense. The wind is blowing in the opposite direction."

"I know," Nate said. "It's not smoke. Something is flying this way."

"I'd better alert the captain."

Soon everyone was outfitted with binoculars, staring upward. The ribbon of darkness had become a dense black cloud, sweeping directly toward them.

"What are they?" Okamoto mumbled. "Birds? Bats?"

"I don't think so," Nate said. The smoky darkness still appeared to be more cloud than substance, its edges billowing, ebbing, flowing as it raced toward them.

"What the hell are they?" someone mumbled.

In a matter of moments, the dark cloud swept over the campsite, just above tree level, blocking the last of the sunlight. The team was immediately flooded by a high-pitched droning. After so many days in the jungle, it was a familiar sound—but *amplified*. The tiny hairs on Frank's body vibrated to the subsonic whine.

"Locusts," Nate said, craning upward. "Millions of them."

As the cloud passed overhead, the lower edges of the swarm rattled the leafy foliage. The team ducked warily from the creatures, but the locusts passed them without pausing, sweeping east.

Frank lowered his binoculars as the tail end of the cloud droned over them. "What are they doing? Migrating or something?"

Nate shook his head. "No. This behavior makes no sense."

"But they're gone now," Captain Waxman said, ready to dismiss the aerial show.

Nate nodded, but he glanced to the east, one eye narrowed. "Yes, but *where* are they going?"

Frank caught Nate's glance. Something did lie to the east: *the other half of their party.* Frank swallowed back his sudden fear. *Kelly* . . .

7:28 P.M.

As the day darkened into twilight, Kelly heard a strange noise, a sharp whirring or whine. She walked around the Brazil nut tree. Squinting her eyes, she tried to focus on its source.

"You hear it, too?" Kouwe asked, meeting her on the far side of the trunk.

Nearby, the two Rangers stood with weapons raised. Others stood by the camp's large bonfire, feeding more dry branches and bamboo to the flames. With the threat of someone stalking around their camp, they wanted as much light as possible. Stacked beside the fire was a large pile of additional fodder for the flames, enough to last the night.

"That noise . . . it's getting louder," Kelly mumbled. "What is it?"

Kouwe cocked his head. "I'm not sure."

By now, others heard the noise, too. It rose quickly to a feverish pitch. Everyone started glancing to the sky.

Kelly pointed to the rosy gloaming to the west. "Look!"

Cast against the glow of the setting sun, a dark shadow climbed the skies, a black cloud, spreading and sweeping toward them.

"A swarm of locusts," Kouwe said, his voice tight with suspicion. "They'll do that sometimes in mating season, but it's the wrong time of the year. And I've never seen a swarm this big."

"Is it a threat?" Jorgensen asked from a few steps away.

"Not usually. More a pest for gardens and jungle farms. A large enough cloud of locusts can strip leaf, vegetable, and fruit from a spot in mere minutes."

"What about people?" Richard Zane asked.

"Not much of a threat. They're herbivorous, but they can bite a little when panicked. It's nothing more than a pinprick." Kouwe eyed the swarm. "Still . . ."

"What?" Kelly asked.

"I don't like the coincidence of such a swarm appearing after finding the Ban-ali mark."

"Surely there can't be any connection," Anna said at Richard's side.

Manny approached with Tor-tor. The great cat whined in chorus with the locusts, edgy and padding a slow circle around his master. "Professor, you aren't thinking the locusts might be like the piranha creatures? Some new threat from the jungle, another attack?"

Kouwe glanced to the biologist. "First there was the mark at the village, then piranhas. Now a mark here, and a strange swarm rises." Kouwe strode over to his pack. "It's a coincidence that we shouldn't dismiss."

Kelly felt a cold certainty that the professor was right.

"What can we do?" Jorgensen asked. His fellow soldier, Private Carrera, kept watch with him. The front edge of the swarm disappeared into the twilight gloom overhead, one shadow merging with another.

"First shelter . . ." Kouwe glanced up, his eyes narrowing with concentration. "They're almost here. Everyone into their hammocks! Close the mosquito netting tight and keep your flesh away from the fabric."

Zane protested. "But—"

"Now!" Kouwe barked. He began to dig more purposefully in his pack.

"Do as he says!" Jorgensen ordered, shouldering his useless weapon.

Kelly was already moving. She ducked into her tent of mosquito netting, glad that they had set up camp earlier. She closed the opening and positioned a stone atop the flap to hold the cheesecloth netting in place. Once secure, she clambered onto her hammock, tucking her legs and arms tight around herself, keeping her head ducked from the tent's top.

She glanced around her. The rest of her party were digging in, too, each hammock a solitary island of shrouded material. Only one member of the camp was still outside.

"Professor Kouwe!" Jorgensen called from his spot. The soldier began to clamber out of his netted tent.

"Stay!" Kouwe ordered as he rummaged in his pack.

Jorgensen froze with indecision. "What're you doing?"

"Preparing to fight fire with fire."

Suddenly, from clear skies, it began to rain. The canopy rattled with the familiar sounds of heavy drops striking leaves. But it was not water that cascaded from the skies. Large black insects pelted through the dense canopy and dove earthward.

The swarm had reached them.

Kelly saw one insect land on her netting. It was three inches long, its black carapace shining like oil in the firelight. Trebled wings twitched on its back as it fought to keep its perch. She balled her limbs tighter around herself. She had seen locusts and cicadas before, but nothing like this monstrous bug. It had no eyes. Its face was all clashing mandibles, gnashing at the air. Though blind, it was not senseless. Long antennae probed through the netting's mesh, swiveling like a pair of divining rods. Other of its brethren struck the netting with little smacks, clinging with segmented black legs.

A cry of pain drew her attention to Kouwe. The professor stood five yards away, still crouched by the fire. He swatted a locust on his arm.

"Professor!" Jorgensen called out.

"Stay where you are!" Kouwe fought the leather tie on a tiny bag. Kelly saw the blood dripping from his arm from the locust's bite. Even from here, she could tell it was a deep wound. She prayed the bugs were not venomous, like the piranhas. Kouwe crouched closer to the fire, his skin ruddy and aglow. But the flames' intense heat and smoke seemed to keep the worst of the swarm at bay.

All around the forest, locusts flitted and whined. With each breath, more and more filled the space.

"They're chewing through the netting!" Zane cried in panic.

Kelly turned her attention to the bugs closer at hand. The first attacker had retracted its antennae and was indeed gnashing at the netting, slicing through with its razored jaws. Before it could burrow inside, Kelly struck out with the back of her hand and knocked it away. She didn't kill it, but her netting was protected from further damage. She went to work on the other clinging insects.

"Smack them loose!" she yelled back to the others. "Don't give them a chance to bite through!"

Another yelp erupted from nearby. "Goddamn it!" It was Manny. A loud slap sounded, followed by more swearing.

Kelly couldn't get a good look at his position since his hammock was behind hers. "Are you okay?"

"One crawled under the netting!" Manny called back. "Be careful! The buggers pack a vicious bite. The saliva burns with some type of digestive acid."

Again she prayed the insects weren't toxic. She twisted around to get a look at Manny, but all she could make out was Tor-tor pacing at the edge of his master's tent. Clusters of the black insects crawled across the cat's fur, making it look as if his spots were squirming. The jaguar ignored the pests, its dense coat a natural barrier. One landed on the cat's nose, but a paw simply batted it away.

By now, the area buzzed with wings. The constant

whine set Kelly's teeth on edge. In moments, the swarm thickened. It grew difficult to see much outside her tent. It was as if a swirling black fog had descended over them. The bugs coated everything, chewing and biting. Kelly focused her attention on knocking the insects off her netting, but it quickly became a losing battle. The bugs crawled and skittered everywhere.

As she struggled, sweat dripped down her face and into her eyes. Panicked, she batted and swung at the clinging insects and began to lose hope. Then in her mind's eye, she pictured Jessie in a hospital bed, arms stretched out for her missing mother, crying her name. "Damn it!" She fought the insects more vigorously, refusing to give up.

I won't die here . . . not like this, not without seeing Jessie.

A sharp sting flamed from her thigh. Using the flat of her hand, she crushed the insect with a gasp. Another landed on her arm. She shook it away in disgust. A third scrabbled in her hair.

As she fought, a scream built like a storm in her chest. Her tent had been breached. Cries arose from other spots in the camp. They were all under assault.

They had lost.

Jessie . . . Kelly moaned, striking a locust from her neck. *I'm sorry, baby.* New stings bloomed on her calves and ankles. She futilely kicked, eyes weeping in pain and loss.

It soon became hard to breathe. She coughed, choking. Her eyes began to sting worse. A sharp smell filled her nostrils, sweet with resins, like green pine logs in a hearth. She coughed again.

What was happening?

Through her tears, she watched the dense swarm disperse as if blown by a mighty gust. Directly ahead, the camp's bonfire grew clearer. She spotted Kouwe standing on the far side of the flames, waving a large palm frond over the fire, which had grown much smokier.

"*Tok-tok* powder!" Kouwe called to her. His body was covered with bleeding bites. "A headache medicine and, when burned, a powerful insect repellent."

The locusts clinging to her netting dislodged and winged away from the odor. Kelly vaguely remembered Nate telling her how the Indians would stake their gardens with bamboo torches and burn some type of powder an insect repellent to protect their harvest. She silently thanked the Indians of the forest for their ingenuity.

Once the locusts had dwindled to only a few stragglers, Kouwe waved to her, to all of them. "Come here!" he called. "Quickly!"

She climbed from her hammock, and after a moment's hesitation, she slipped through her netting, now ragged and frayed. Ducking low, she crossed to the fire. Others followed in step behind her.

The smoke was choking and cloying, but the insects held back. The locusts had not dispersed. The swarm still whined and whirred overhead in a dark cloud. Occasional bombers would dive toward them and away, chased off by the fire's smoke.

"How did you know the smoke would work?" Jorgensen asked.

"I didn't. At least not for sure." Kouwe panted slightly and continued to waft his palm frond as he explained. "The flaming Ban-ali symbol in the jungle . . . the amount of smoke and the strong scent of it. I thought it might be some sort of signal."

"A smoke signal?" Zane asked.

"No, more of a *scent* signal," Kouwe said. "Something in the smoke drew the locusts here specifically."

Manny grunted at this idea. "Like a pheromone or something."

"Perhaps. And once here, the little bastards were bred to lay waste to anything in the area."

"So what you're saying is that we were marked for death," Anna commented. "The locusts were sent here on purpose."

Kouwe nodded. "The same could be true with the piranha creatures. Something must have drawn them specifically to the village, maybe another scent trace, something dribbled in the water that guided them to the *shabano*." He shook his head. "I don't know for sure. But for a second time, the Ban-ali have called the jungle down upon us."

"What are we going to do?" Zane asked. "Will the powder last till dawn?"

"No." Kouwe glanced to the dark swarm around them.

8:05 P.M.

Nate was tired of arguing. He, Captain Waxman, and Frank were still in the midst of a debate that had been going on for the past fifteen minutes. "We have to go back and investigate," he insisted. "At least send one person to check on the others. He can be there and back before dawn."

Waxman sighed. "They were only locusts, Dr. Rand. They passed over us with no harm. What makes you think the others are at risk?"

Nate frowned. "I have no proof. Just my gut instinct. But I've lived all my life in these jungles and something was unnatural about the way those locusts were swarming."

Frank initially had been on Nate's side, but slowly he had warmed to the Ranger's logic of wait-and-see. "I think we should consider Captain Waxman's plan. First thing tomorrow morning, when the satellites are overhead, we can relay a message to the others and make sure they're okay."

"Besides," Waxman added, "now that we're down to six Rangers, I'm not about to risk a pair on this futile mission—not without some sign of real trouble."

"I'll go myself." Nate balled a fist in frustration.

"I won't allow it." Waxman shook his head. "You're just jumping at shadows, Dr. Rand. In the morning, you'll see they're okay."

Nate's mind spun, trying to find some way past the captain's obstinate attitude. "Then at least let me head out with a radio. See if I can get close enough to contact someone over there. What's the range on your personal radios?"

"Six or seven miles."

"And we traveled roughly fifteen miles. That means I would only have to hike back eight miles to be within radio range of the others. I could be back before midnight."

Waxman frowned.

Frank moved a step closer to Nathan. "Still . . . it's not a totally foolhardy plan, Captain. In fact, it's a reasonable compromise."

Nate recognized the pained set to Frank's eyes. It was his sister out there. So far the man had been balancing between fear for his sister and Waxman's reasonable caution, trying his best to be a logical operations leader while reining in his own concern.

"I'm sure the others *are* okay," Nate pressed. "But it doesn't hurt to be a little extra wary . . . especially after the last couple of days."

Frank was now nodding.

"Let me take a radio," Nate urged.

Waxman puffed out an exasperated breath and conceded. "But you're not going alone."

Nate bit back a shout. *Finally . . .*

"I'll send one of the Rangers with you. I won't risk two of my men."

"Good . . . good." Frank seemed almost to sag with relief. He turned to Nate, a look of gratitude in his eyes.

Captain Waxman turned. "Corporal Warczak! Front and center!"

8:23 P.M.

Manny and the others stood by the fire, smoke billowing around them. The pall from the powder kept the locusts in check. All around, the swarm swirled, a black cocoon, holding them trapped. Manny's eyes stung as he studied the flames. How long would the professor's *tok-tok* powder last? Already the smoke seemed less dense.

"Here!" Kelly said behind him. She passed him a two-foot length of bamboo from the pile of tinder beside the fire, then returned to work, kneeling with Professor Kouwe. The Indian shaman was packing a final piece of bamboo with a plug of *tok-tok* powder.

Manny shifted his feet nervously. The professor's plan was based on too many assumptions for his liking.

Finished with the last stick of bamboo, Kelly and Kouwe stood. Manny stared around the fire. Everyone had packs in place and was holding a short length of bamboo, like his own.

"Okay," Jorgensen said. "Ready?"

No one answered. Everyone's eyes reflected the same mix of panic and fear.

Jorgensen nodded. "Light the torches."

As a unit, each member reached and dipped the ends of their bamboo in the bonfire's flames. The powder ignited along with the dry wood. As they pulled the bamboo free, smoke wafted in thick curls up from their makeshift torches.

"Keep them close, but held aloft," Kouwe instructed, demonstrating with his own torch. "We must move quickly."

Manny swallowed. He eyed the whirring wall of locusts. He had been bitten only twice. But the wounds still ached. Tor-tor kept close to his side, rubbing against him, sensing the fear in the air.

"Keep together," Kouwe hissed as they began to

walk away from the sheltering fire and toward the waiting swarm.

The plan was to use the tiki torches primed with *tok-tok* powder to breach the swarm while holding the locusts at bay. Under this veil of smoky protection, the team would attempt to flee the area. As Kouwe had explained earlier, "The locusts were drawn specifically *here* by the scent from the burning Ban-ali symbol. If we get far enough away from this specific area, we might escape them."

It was a risky plan, but they didn't have much choice. The shaman's supply of powder was meager. It would not keep the bonfire smoking for more than another hour or two. And the locusts seemed determined to remain in the area. So it was up to them—they would have to vacate the region.

"C'mon, Tor-tor." Manny followed after Corporal Jorgensen. Behind and to the side, the group moved in a tight cluster, torches held high. Manny's ears were full of the swarm's drone. As he walked, he prayed Kouwe's assumptions were sound.

No one spoke . . . no one even breathed. The group trod slowly forward, heading west, in the direction the other team had taken. It was their only hope. Manny glanced behind him. The comforting light of their bonfire was now a weak glow as the swarm closed in behind them.

Underfoot, Manny crushed straggling locusts on the ground.

Silently, the group marched into the forest. After several minutes, there was still no end to the cloud of insects. The team remained surrounded on all sides. Locusts were everywhere: buzzing through the air, coating the trunks of trees, scrabbling through the underbrush. Only the smoke kept them away.

Manny felt something vibrating on his pantleg. He glanced down and used his free hand to swat the locust away. The bugs were getting bolder.

"We should be through them by now," Kouwe muttered.

"I think they're following us," Anna said.

Kouwe slowed, and his eyes narrowed. "I believe you're right."

"What are we going to do?" Zane hissed. "These torches aren't gonna last much longer. Maybe if we ran. Maybe we could—"

"Quiet . . . let me think!" Kouwe scolded. He stared at the swarm and mumbled. "Why are they following us? Why aren't they staying where they were summoned?"

Carrera spoke softly at the rear of the group. She held her torch high. "Maybe they're like those piranha creatures. Once drawn here, they caught *our* scent. They'll follow us now until one or the other of us is destroyed."

Manny had a sudden idea. "Then why don't we do what the Ban-ali do?"

"What do you mean?" Kelly asked.

"Give the buggers something more interesting than our blood to swarm after."

"Like what?"

"The same scent that drew the locusts here in the first place." Words tumbled from Manny in his excitement. He pictured the flaming symbol of the Blood Jaguars. "Corporal Jorgensen and I doused the flames that produced the smoky pheromone or whatever—but the fuel is still there! Out in the forest." He pointed his arm.

Jorgensen nodded. "Manny's right. If we could relight it . . ."

Kouwe brightened. "Then the fresh smoke would draw the swarm away from us, keep it here while we ran off."

"Exactly," Manny said.

"Let's do it," Zane said. "What are we waiting for?"

Jorgensen stepped in front. "With our torches burning low, time is limited. There's no reason to risk all of us going back."

"What are you saying?" Manny asked.

Jorgensen pointed. "You all continue on the trail after the others. I'll backtrack and light the fire on my own."

Manny stepped forward. "I'll go with you."

"No. I won't risk a civilian." Jorgensen backed away. "And besides, I can travel faster on my own."

"But—"

"We're wasting time and powder," the corporal barked. He turned to his fellow Ranger. "Carrera, get everyone away from here. Double time. I'll join up with you after I've lit the motherfucker."

"Yes, sir."

With a final nod, Jorgensen turned and began to trot back toward the camp, torch held high. In moments, his form was swallowed away as he dove through the swarm. Just the bobbing light of his torch illuminated his progress, then even that vanished amid the dense mass of swirling insects.

"Move out!" Carrera said.

The group turned and once again headed down

the trail. Manny prayed the corporal succeeded. With a final glance behind him, Manny followed the others.

Jorgensen rushed through the swarm. With only his single torch protecting him, the swarm grew tighter. He was stung a few times by bolder bugs, but he ignored the discomfort. A Ranger went through vigorous training programs across a multitude of terrains: mountains, jungles, swamps, snow, desert.

But never this . . . never a goddamn cloud of carnivorous bugs!

With his weapon on his shoulder, he shrugged his pack higher on his back, both to make it easier to run and to shield him from the swarm overhead.

Though he should have been panicked, an odd surge of zeal fired his blood. This was why he had volunteered for the Rangers, to test his mettle and to experience balls-out action. How many farm boys from the backwaters of Minnesota had a chance to do this?

He thrust his torch forward and forged ahead. "Fuck you!" he yelled at the locusts.

Focusing on the abandoned campfire as a beacon, Jorgensen worked across the dizzying landscape of whirling bugs. Smoke from his torch wafted around him, redolent with the burning powder. He circled around the Brazil nut tree and headed toward where the Ban-ali's burning signature had been set in the forest.

Half blind, he ran past the site before realizing it and doubled back. He fell to his knees beside the spot. "Thank God."

Jorgensen planted his torch in the soft loam, then leaned over and swept free the dirt and scrabbling bugs from the buried resinous compound. Locusts lay thick over this site. Several bites stung his hand as he brushed them away. Leaning close, the residual fumes from the oil filled his nostrils, bitter and sharp. The professor was right. It certainly attracted the buggers.

Working quickly, Jorgensen continued to uncover the original marker. He didn't know how much of the black oil should be lit to keep the swarm's attention here, but he wasn't taking any chances. He didn't want to have to return a second time. Crawling on his knees, his hands sticky with the black resin, he worked around the site. He soon had at least half of the serpentine pattern exposed.

Satisfied, he sat back, pulled free a butane lighter, and flicked a flame. He lowered the lighter to the oil. "C'mon . . . burn, baby."

His wish was granted. The oil caught fire, flames racing down the twists and curls of the exposed symbol. In fact, the ignition was so fiercely combustible that the first flames caught him off guard, burning his fingers.

Jorgensen dropped the lighter and pulled his hand away, his fingers on fire. "Shit!" The smattering of sticky oil on his hand had caught the flames. *"Shit!"*

He rolled to the side and shoved his hands into the loose dirt to stanch the fire. As he did so, his elbow accidentally struck the planted bamboo torch, knocking it into a nearby bush, casting embers in a fiery arc. Jorgensen swore and snatched at the torch—but he was too late. The powder stored in the hollow top of the bamboo had scattered into the dirt and bush, sizzling out. The top of the torch still glowed crimson, but it was no longer smoking.

Jorgensen sprang to his feet.

Behind him, the symbol of the Ban-ali flamed brightly, calling the swarm to its meal.

"Oh, God!"

Kelly heard the first scream, a horrible sound that froze everyone in place.

"Jorgensen . . ." Private Carrera said, swinging around.

Kelly stepped beside the Ranger.

"We can't go back," Zane said, shifting further down the trail.

A second scream, bone-chilling, garbled, echoed from the forest.

Kelly noticed the swarm of locusts whisk from around them, retreating back toward the original campsite. "They're leaving!"

Professor Kouwe spoke at her shoulder. "The corporal must have succeeded in relighting the symbol."

By now, the agonized cries were constant, prolonged, bestial. No human could scream like that.

"We have to go help him," Manny said.

Carrera clicked on a flashlight in her free hand. She pointed it back toward the campsite. Fifty yards away, the condensed swarm was so thick, the trees themselves were invisible, swallowed by the black cloud. "There's not enough time," she said softly and lifted her own bamboo torch. It was already sputtering. "We don't know how long a distraction Jorgensen has bought us."

Manny turned to her. "We could at least still try. He might be alive."

As if hearing him, the distant cries died away.

Carrera glanced to him and shook her head.

"Look!" Anna called out, pointing her arm.

Off to the left, a figure stumbled out of the swarm.

Carrera pointed her flashlight. "Jorgensen!"

Kelly gasped and covered her mouth.

The man was impossible to identify, covered from crown to ankle with crawling locusts. His arms were out, waving, blind. His legs wobbled, and he tripped in the underbrush, falling to his knees. All the while, he remained eerily silent. Only his arms stretched out for help.

Manny took a step in the man's direction, but Carrera held him back.

The swarm rolled back over the kneeling man, swallowing him.

"It's too late," Carrera said. "And we're all running out of time." Punctuating her statement, her own torch cast a final sputter of fiery ash, then dimmed. "We need to get as far from here as possible before we lose our advantage."

"But—" Manny began.

He was cut off by a hard stare from the Ranger. Her words were even harder. "I won't have Jorgensen's sacrifice be meaningless." She pointed toward the deeper wood. "Move out!"

Kelly glanced back as they headed away. The swarm remained behind them, a featureless black cloud. But at its heart was a man who had given his life to save them all. Tears filled her eyes. Her legs were numb with exhaustion and despair, her heart heavy.

Despite the loss of the corporal, one thought, one face remained foremost in Kelly's mind. Her daughter needed her. Her mind roiled with flashes of her child in bed, burning with fever. *I'll get back to you, baby*, she promised silently.

But deep in her heart, she now wondered if it was a pact she could keep. With each step deeper into the forest, more men died. *Graves, DeMartini, Conger, Jones . . . and now Jorgensen . . .*

She shook her head, refusing to give up hope. As long as she was alive, putting one foot in front of the other, she would find a way home.

Over the next hour, the group forged through the forest, following the path the other half of their team had taken the previous afternoon. One by one, their torches flickered out. Flashlights were passed around. So far, no sign of renewed pursuit by the swarm manifested. Maybe they were safe, beyond the interest of the blind locusts, but no one voiced such a hope aloud.

Manny marched close to the Ranger. "What if we miss the other team?" he asked softly. "Jorgensen had our radio equipment. It was our only way of contacting the outside world."

Kelly hadn't considered this fact. With the radio gone, they were cut off.

"We'll reach the others," Carrera said with a steely determination.

No one argued with her. No one wanted to.

They marched onward through the dark jungle, concentrating on just moving forward. As hours ticked by, the tension blended into a blur of bone-weary exhaustion and endless fear. Their passage was marked with hoots and strange cries. Everyone's ears were pricked for the telltale buzz of the locusts.

So they were all startled when the small personal radio hanging from Private Carrera's field jacket squawked with static and a few scratchy words. "This is . . . if you can hear . . . radio range . . ."

Everyone swung to face the Ranger, eyes wide. She pulled her radio's microphone from her helmet to her mouth. "This is Private Carrera. Can you hear me? *Over.*"

There was a long pause, then . . . "Read you, Carrera. Warczak here. What's your status?"

The Ranger quickly related the events in a dispassionate and professional manner. But Kelly saw how the soldier's fingers trembled as she held the microphone to her lips. She finished, "We're following your trail. Hoping to rendezvous with the main team in two hours."

Corporal Warczak responded, "Roger that. Dr. Rand and I are already under way to meet you. Over and out."

The Ranger closed her eyes and sighed loudly. "We're gonna be okay," she whispered to no one in particular.

As the others murmured in relief, Kelly stared out at the dark jungle.

Out here in the Amazon, they were all far from okay.

ACT FOUR

Blood Jaguars

HORSETAIL
family: *Equisetaceae*
genus: *Equisetum*
species: *Arvense*
common name: *Field Horsetail*
ethnic names: *At Quyroughi, Atkuyrugu,
Chieh Hsu Ts'Ao, Cola de Caballo,
Equiseto Menor, Kilkah Asb, Prele, Sugina,
Thanab al Khail, Vara de Oro, Wen Ching*
properties/actions: *Astringent, Antiinflammatory,
Diuretic, Antihemorrhagic*

Blood Jaguars

TWELVE

Lake Crossing

Lauren slid the magnetic security card through the lock on her office door and entered. It was the first chance she'd had to return to her office in the past day. Between stretches in the institute's hospital ward visiting Jessie and meetings with various MEDEA members, she hadn't had a moment to herself. The only reason she had this free moment was that Jessie seemed to be doing very well. Her temperature continued to remain normal, and her attitude was growing brighter with every passing hour.

Cautiously optimistic, Lauren began to hope that her initial diagnosis had been mistaken. Maybe Jessie did *not* have the jungle disease. Lauren was now glad she had kept silent about her fears. She could have needlessly panicked Marshall and Kelly. Lauren may have indeed placed too much confidence in Alvisio's statistical model. But she could not fault the epidemiologist. Dr. Alvisio *had* indeed warned her his results were far from conclusive. Further data would need to be collected and correlated.

But then again, that pretty much defined all the current levels of investigation. Each day, as the disease spread through Florida and the southern states, thousands of theories were bandied about: etiological agents, therapeutic protocols, diagnostic parameters, quarantine guidelines. Instar had become the nation's think tank on this contagion. It was their job to ferret through the maze of scientific conjecture and fanciful epidemiological models to glean the pearls from the rubbish. It was a daunting task as data flowed in from all corners of the country. But they had the best minds here.

Lauren collapsed into her seat and flicked on her computer. The chime for incoming mail sounded. She groaned as she slipped on a pair of reading glasses and leaned closer to the screen. *Three hundred and fourteen messages waited*. And this was just her private mailbox. She scrolled down the list of addresses and skimmed the subject lines, searching through the little snippets for anything important or interesting.

Inbox	
From	Subject
jpcdvm@davis.uc.org	re: simian biosimilarities
trent_magnus@scriabs.com	call for sample standardization
systematica@cdc.gov	prog.report
xreynolds@largebio.com	large scale biological labs
synergymeds@phdrugs.com	pharmacy question
geard@dadecounty.fl.gov	quarantine projection
hrt@washingtonpost.org	request for interview

As she scrolled down, one name caught her eye. It was oddly familiar, but she could not remember exactly why. She brought her computer's pointer to the name: *Large Scale Biological Labs*. She crinkled her nose in thought, then it came to her. The night Jessie's fever developed, she had been paged by this same outfit. Well after midnight, she recalled. But the sick child had distracted her from following up on the page.

It probably wasn't important, but she opened the e-mail anyway, her curiosity now aroused. The letter appeared on the screen. *Dr. Xavier Reynolds*. She smiled, instantly recognizing the name. He had been a grad student of hers years ago and had taken a position at some lab in California, perhaps this same lab. The young man had been one of her best students. Lauren had attempted to recruit him into the MEDEA group here at Instar, but he had declined. His fiancée had accepted an associate professorship at Berkeley, and he had naturally not wanted to be separated.

She read his note. As she did, the smile on her lips slowly faded.

From: xreynolds@largebio.com
Date: 14 Aug 13:48:28
To: lauren_obrien@instar.org
Subject: Large Scale Biological Labs

Dr. O'Brien:

Please excuse this intrusion. I attempted to page you last night, but I assume you're very busy. So I'll keep this brief.

As with many labs around the country, our own is involved in researching the virulent disease, and I think I've come across an intriguing angle, if not a possible answer to the root puzzle: *What is causing the disease?* But before voicing my findings, I wanted to get your input.

As head of the proteonomic team here at Large Scale Biological Labs, I have been attempting to index mankind's protein genome, similar to the Human Genome Project for DNA. As such, my take on the disease was to investigate it backward. Most disease-causing agents— bacteria, viruses, fungi, parasites—do not cause illness by themselves. It is the *proteins* they produce that trigger clinical disease. So I hunted for a unique protein that might be common to all patients.

And I found one! But from its folded and twisted pattern, a new thought arose. This new protein bears a striking similarity to the protein that causes bovine spongiform encephalopathy. Which in turn raises the question: *Have we been chasing the wrong tail in pursuing a viral cause for this disease?*

Has anyone considered a *prion* as the cause?

For your consideration, I've modeled the protein below.

Title: unknown prion (?)
Compound: folded protein w/ double terminal alpha helixes
Model:

Exp. Method: X-ray diffraction
EC Number: 3.4.1.18
Source: Patient #24-b12, Anawak Tribe, lower Amazon
Resolution: 2.00   **R-Value:** 0.145
Space Group: P21 20 21
  Unit cell:
    dim: a 60.34   b 52.02   c 44.68
    angles: *alpha* 90.00   *beta* 90.00   *gamma* 90.00
Polymer chains: 156L   **Residues:** 144
Atoms: 1286

So there you have the twisted puzzle. As I value your expertise, Dr.
O'Brien, I would appreciate your thoughts, opinions, or judgments
before promoting this radical theory.

Sincerely,
Xavier Reynolds, Ph.D.

"A prion." Lauren touched the diagram of the
molecule. *Could this indeed be the cause?*

She pondered the possibility. The word *prion* was

scientific shorthand for "proteinaceous infectious particle." The role of prions in disease had only been documented within the last decade, earning a U.S. biochemist the 1997 Nobel Prize. Prion proteins were found in all creatures, from humans down to single-celled yeast. Though usually innocuous, they had an insidious duality to their molecular structure, a Jekyll-and-Hyde sort of thing. In one form, they were safe and friendly to a cell. But the same protein could fold and twist upon itself, creating a monster that wreaked havoc on cellular processes. And the effect was cumulative. Once a twisted prion was introduced into a host, it would begin converting the body's other proteins to match, which in turn converted its neighbors, spreading exponentially through the host's systems. Worse, this host could also pass the process to another body, a true infectious phenomenon.

Prion diseases had been documented both in animals and man: from scabies in sheep to Creutsfeldt-Jacob disease in humans. The most well-known prion disease to date was one that *crossed* between species. Dr. Reynolds had mentioned it in his letter: bovine spongiform encephalopathy, or more commonly, mad cow disease.

But these human diseases were more of a degenerative nature, and none were known to be transmitted so readily. Still, that did not rule out prions as a possibility here. She had read research papers on prions and their role in genetic mutations and more severe manifestations. Was something like that happening here? And what about airborne transmission? Prions were particulate and subviral in size, so since certain viruses could be airborne, why not certain prions?

Lauren stared at the modeled protein on the computer screen and reached for her desk phone. As she dialed, an icy finger ran up her spine. She prayed her former student was mistaken.

The phone rang on the other end, and after a moment, it was answered. "Dr. Reynolds, proteonomics lab."

"Xavier?"

"Yes?"

"This is Dr. O'Brien."

"Dr. O'Brien!" The man began talking animatedly, thanking her, thrilled.

She cut him off. "Xavier, tell me more about this protein of yours." She needed as much information from him as possible, the sooner the better. If there was even a minute possibility that Dr. Reynolds was correct . . . .

Lauren bit back a shudder as she stared at the crablike molecule on her computer monitor. There was one other fact she knew about prion-triggered diseases.

There were no known cures.

9:18 A.M.

AMAZON JUNGLE

Nate looked over Olin Pasternak's shoulder. The CIA's communications expert was growing ever more frustrated with the satellite computer system. Beads of sweat bulleted his forehead, both from the morning's steaming heat and his own consternation.

"Still no feed . . . goddamn it!" Olin chewed his lower lip, eyes squinting.

"Keep trying," Frank urged on the other side.

Nate glanced to Kelly, who stood beside her brother. Her eyes were haunted and dull. Nate had heard various versions of last night's attack: the strange swarm of giant locusts attracted to the camp by the burning Ban-ali marker. It was too horrible to imagine, impossible, but Jorgensen's death made it all too real.

Once the entire group had been reassembled at the swamp-side camp last night, the Ranger team had remained on guard. The group kept a posted watch throughout the night, in and around the surrounding forest, alert for any danger, watchful for any flare of flames, ears keened for the whine of locusts. But nothing happened. The few hours until dawn had been uneventful.

As soon as the communication satellite was in range, Olin had set about trying to reach the States and to relay messages to the Wauwai field base. It was vital to radio the change in plans to all parties. With unknown hunters dogging their trail, it was decided to continue with the goal of rafting across the swamp. Captain Waxman hoped to get a couple of days' jump on his pursuers, leave their trackers traipsing around the swamp on foot. Once across, Waxman would keep a constant watch on the waters for any Ban-ali canoes and keep the group intact on the far shore until the evac helicopter could arrive. He planned to trade each civilian with another Ranger from the field base at the mission. With these new forces, he would continue on Gerald Clark's trail.

There was only one problem with his plan.

"I'm gonna have to rip the laptop down to the motherboard," Olin said. "Something is damnably fritzed. Maybe a faulty chip or even a loose one knocked out of place by the manhandling these past two days. I don't know. I'll have to tear it down and check it all."

Waxman had been speaking with his staff sergeant, but he overheard Olin. The captain stepped nearer. "We don't have time for that. The third raft is ready, and it'll take a good four hours to cross the waters. We need to get moving."

Nate glanced to the swamp's edge and saw four Rangers positioning the newly constructed raft so that it floated beside the two prepared last night. The additional raft was necessary to carry everyone in their expanded party.

Olin hovered over his computer and satellite dish with a small screwdriver. "But I've not been able to reach anyone. They won't know where we are." He wiped his forehead with the back of his wrist. His features were pale.

Zane stood, shifting his feet uneasily and rubbing at a Band-Aid on his cheek that covered a locust bite. "We could send someone back and retrieve Jorgensen's pack with the military radio," he suggested.

Everyone began talking at once, arguing both sides.

"We'd lose another day waiting." "We'd risk more of our people." "We need to reach *someone*!" "Who knows if his radio will even work, what with all those locusts. They could've chewed through the wiring and—"

Waxman interrupted, his voice booming. "There is no reason to panic!" He directed his comment to all of them. "Even if we can't raise the outside, the field base knows our rough location from yesterday's report. When the Brazilian evac copter comes tomorrow as previously arranged, we'll hear it—even from across the swamp. We can send up orange smoke flares to draw their attention to our new location."

Nate nodded. He had not participated in the argument. In his mind, there was only one way to go—*forward*.

Waxman pointed to Olin. "Pack it up. You can work on the problem once we're on the far side."

Resigned, Olin nodded. He returned his tiny screwdriver to his repair kit.

With the matter settled, the others dispersed to gather their own gear, readying for the day's journey.

"At least we won't have to walk," Manny said, patting Nate on the shoulder as he passed on his way to wake Tor-tor. The jaguar was asleep under a palm, oblivious to the world after last night's trek.

Nate stretched a kink from his neck and approached Professor Kouwe. The Indian shaman stood near the swamp, smoking his pipe. His eyes were as haunted as Kelly's had been. When Nate and Corporal Warczak had met the fleeing group on the trail, the professor had been unusually quiet and somber, more than could be attributed to the loss of Jorgensen.

Nate stood silently beside his old friend, studying the lake, too.

After a time, Kouwe spoke softly, not looking at Nate. "They sent the locusts . . . the Ban-ali . . ." The shaman shook his head. "They wiped out the Yanomamo tribe with the piranha creatures. I've never seen anything like it. It's as if the Blood Jaguar tribe could indeed control the jungle. And if that myth is true, what else?" He shook his head again.

"What's troubling you?"

"I've been a professor of Indian Studies for close to two decades. I grew up in these jungles." His voice grew quiet, full of pain. "I should have known . . . the corporal . . . his screams . . ."

Nate glanced to Kouwe and placed a hand on the man's shoulder. "Professor, you saved everyone with the *tok-tok* powder."

"Not everyone." Kouwe drew on his pipe and exhaled. "I should've thought to relight the Ban-ali symbol before we left the camp. If I had, the young corporal would be alive."

Nate spoke sharply, trying to cut through the man's remorse and guilt. "You're being too hard on yourself. No amount of study or experience could prepare you to deal with the Ban-ali and their biological attacks. Nothing like it has ever been documented before."

Kouwe nodded, but Nate sensed that the man was hardly convinced.

Captain Waxman called from near the water's edge. "Let's load up! Five to a raft!" He began assigning Rangers and dividing the civilians accordingly.

Nate ended up with Kouwe and Manny, along with Tor-tor. Their two mates were Corporal Okamoto and Private Carrera. The group was forced to wade through the shallows to reach the bamboo-and-log constructions. As Nate heaved himself onboard, he appreciated its sturdy construction. Reaching out, Nate helped Manny guide the large cat atop the bobbing raft.

Tor-tor was not pleased about getting wet. As the cat shook the swamp water from its pelt, the rest of the group mounted their own boats.

On the neighboring raft, Kelly and Frank stood with Captain Waxman, along with corporals Warczak and Yamir. The last five teammates climbed onto the farthest raft. Olin was careful to carry his pack with the satellite gear high above his head. Richard Zane and Anna Fong helped him aboard, flanked by a stoic Tom Graves and a scowling Sergeant Kostos.

Once everyone was mounted, lengths of bamboo were used as poles to push away from shore and through the shallows. But the swamp's banks dropped steeply. Within a hundred feet of the shore, the poles no longer touched bottom, and the paddles were taken up. With four paddles per raft, it allowed one person to rotate out and rest. The goal was to continue straight across without a break.

Nate manned the raft's starboard side as the tiny flotilla slowly drifted toward the far bank. Out on the waters, the distant roar of multiple waterfalls, muffled and threatening, echoed over the swamp lake. Nate stared, shading his eyes. The highlands across the way remained shrouded in mist: a mix of green jungle, red cliffs, and a fog of heavy spray. Their goal was a narrow ravine between two tower-

ing, flat-topped mesas, a yawning misty channel into
the highlands. It had been where Clark's last carved
message had pointed.

As they glided, the denizens of the swamp noted
their passage. A snow-white egret skimmed over the
water, a hand span above the surface. Frogs leaped
from boggy hummocks with loud splashes, and *hoa-
tzin* birds, looking like some ugly cross between a
turkey and a pterodactyl, screeched at them as they
circled over their nests atop the palms that grew
from the island hummocks. The only inhabitants
that seemed pleased with their presence were the
clouds of mosquitoes, buzzing with joy at the floating smorgasbord.

"Damned bugs," Manny griped, slapping his
neck. "I've had it with flying insects making a meal
out of me."

To make matters even worse, Okamoto began to
whistle again, tunelessly and without the vaguest
sense of rhythm.

Nate sighed. It would be a long trip.

After an hour, the little muddy islands vanished
around them. In the swamp's center, the water was
deep enough to drown away most of the tiny bits
of land and jungle. Only an occasional hummock,
mostly bare of trees, dotted the smooth expanse of
the swamp's heart.

Here the sun, scorching and bright, shone inces-
santly down on them.

"It's like a steam bath," Carrera said from the
raft's port side.

Nate had to agree. The air was thick with moisture, almost too heavy to breathe. Their speed across

the swamp slowed as exhaustion set in. Canteens were passed around and around the raft. Even Tortor lounged in the middle of the bamboo planking, his mouth open, panting.

The only consolation was being temporarily free of the jungle's snug embrace. Here the horizons opened up, and there was a giddy sense of escape. Nate glanced frequently back the way they had come, expecting to see a tribesman on the bank back there, shaking a fist. But there remained no sign of the Ban-ali. The trackers of the ghost tribe remained hidden. Hopefully the group was leaving them behind and getting a few days head start on their pursuers.

Nate was tapped on the shoulder. "I'll take a shift," Kouwe said, emptying his pipe's bowl of tobacco ash into the water.

"I'm okay," Nate said.

Kouwe reached and took the paddle. "I'm not an invalid yet."

Nate didn't argue any further and slid to the raft's stern. As he lounged, he watched their old campsite get smaller and smaller. He reached back for the canteen and caught movement to the right of their raft. One of the bare hummocks, rocky and black, was sinking, submerging so slowly that not a ripple was created.

What the hell?

Off to the left another was sinking. Nate climbed to his feet. As he began to comment on this unusual phenomenon, one of the rocky islands opened a large glassy eye and stared back at him. Instantly Nate knew what he was seeing.

"Oh, crap!"

With his attention focused, he now recognized the armored scales and craggy countenance of a crocodilian head. It was a caiman! A pair of giants. Each head had to be four feet wide from eye to eye. If its head was that big . . .

"What's wrong?" Private Carrera asked.

Nate pointed to where the second of the two caimans was just slipping under the surface.

"What is it?" the Ranger asked, eyes wide, as confused as Nate had been a moment before.

"Caimans," Nate said, his voice hoarse with shock. "Giant ones!"

By now, his entire raft had stopped paddling. The others stared at him.

Nate raised his voice, yelling so all three rafts could hear him. He waved his arms in the air. "Spread out! We're about to be attacked!"

"From what?" Captain Waxman called from his raft, about fifty yards away. "What did you see?"

As answer, something huge slid between Nate's boat and its neighbor, nudging both rafts and spinning them ever so slightly. Through the swamp's murk, the twin lines of tail ridges were readily evident as the beast slid sinuously past.

Nate was familiar with this behavior. It was called *bumping*. The kings of the caimans, the great blacks, were not carrion eaters. They liked to kill their own food. It was why drifting motionless could often protect someone from the predators. Often they would bump something that they considered a meal, testing to see if it would move.

They had just been *bumped*.

Distantly, the third raft suddenly bobbed and

turned. The second caiman was also testing these strange intruders.

Nate yelled again, revising his initial plan. "Don't move! No one paddle! You'll attract them to attack!"

Waxman reinforced his order. "Do as he says! Weapon up. Grenades hot!"

Manny now crouched beside Nate, his voice hushed with awe. "It had to be at least a hundred feet long, over three times larger than any known caiman."

Carrera had her M-16 rifle in hand and was quickly fitting on her grenade launcher. "No wonder Gerald Clark circled around the swamp."

Okamoto finished prepping his rifle, kissed the crucifix around his neck, then nodded to Professor Kouwe. "I pray you have another one of your magical powders up your sleeve."

The shaman shook his head, eyes wide, unblinking. "I pray you're all good shots."

Okamoto glanced at Nate.

Nate explained, "With their armored body plating, the only sure kill shot is the eye."

"No, there's also through the upper palate," Manny added, pointing a finger toward the roof of his mouth. "But to take that shot, you'd have to be damn close."

"Starboard side!" Carrera barked, kneeling with her rifle on her shoulder.

A rippling line disturbed the flat waters, ominous and long.

"Don't take a shot unless you're sure," Nate hissed, dropping beside her. "You could provoke it. Only shoot if you've got a kill shot."

With everyone dead quiet, Waxman heard Nate's

warning. "Listen to Dr. Rand. Shoot if you have a chance—but make it count!"

Rifles bristled around the periphery of each raft. Nate grabbed up his shotgun with one hand. They all waited, baking in the heat, sweat dripping into eyes, mouths drying. Around and around, the caimans circled, leaving no sign of their passage but ripples. Occasionally a raft would be bumped, tested.

"How long can they hold their breath?" Carrera asked.

"Hours," Nate said.

"Why aren't they attacking?" Okamoto asked.

Manny answered this question. "They can't figure out what we are, if we're edible."

The Asian Ranger looked sick. "Let's hope they don't find out."

The waiting stretched. The air seemed to grow thicker around them.

"What if we shot a grenade far from here?" Carrera offered. "As a distraction, something to draw them off."

"I'm not sure it would help. It might just rile them up, get them snapping at anything that moves, like us."

Zane spoke from the farthest raft, but his words easily reached Nate's boat. "I say we strap some explosives to that jaguar and push it overboard. When one of the crocodiles goes for the cat, we trigger the bomb."

Nate shuddered at this idea. Manny looked sick. But other eyes were glancing their way with contemplative expressions.

"Even if you succeeded in doing that, you'd only kill one of them," Nate said. "The other, clearly its mate, would go into a rampage and attack the rafts. Our best bet is to hope the pair loses interest in us and drifts away, then we can paddle out of here."

Waxman turned to Corporal Yamir, the demolition expert. "In case the crocodiles don't get bored, let's be prepared to entertain them. Prime up a pair of the napalm bombs."

The corporal nodded and turned to his pack.

Once again, the waiting game began. Time stretched.

Nate felt the raft tremble under his knees as one of the pair rubbed the underside of the logs with its thick tail. "Hang on!"

Suddenly the raft bucked under them. The stern was tossed high in the air. The group clung like spiders to the bamboo. Loose packs rolled into the lake with distinct splashes. The raft crashed back to the water, jarring them all.

"Is everyone okay?" Nate yelled.

Murmurs of assent rose.

"I lost my rifle," Okamoto said, his eyes angry.

"Better your gun than you," Kouwe said dolefully.

Nate raised his voice. "They're getting bolder!"

Okamoto reached out to one of their floating packs. "My gear."

Nate saw what he was doing. "Corporal! Stop!"

Okamoto immediately froze. "Shit . . ." He already had the strap of his rucksack in hand, half pulled out of the water.

"Leave it," Nate said. "Get away from the edge."

The corporal released his pack with a slight splash and yanked his arm back.

But he moved too slowly.

The monster lunged up out of the depths, jaws open, water sluicing from its scales. It shot ten feet out of the swamp, a tower of armor plating and teeth as long as a man's forearm. The Ranger was pulled off his feet and shoved high into the air, screaming in shock and terror. The huge jaws clamped shut with an audible crunch of bones. Okamoto's scream changed in pitch to pain and disbelief. His body was shaken like a rag doll, legs flailing. Then the creature's bulk dropped back into the depths.

"Fire!" Waxman called.

Nate had been too stunned to move. Carrera blazed with her M-16. Bullets peppered the underside of the giant, prehistoric caiman, but its yellowed belly scales were as hard as Kevlar. Even at almost point-blank range, it looked like little harm was done. Its weak points, the eyes, were hidden on the far side of its bulk.

Nate swung up his own shotgun, stretched his arm over Manny's head, and fired. A load of pellet sprayed through the empty air as the beast dropped out of range. A wasted, panicked shot.

The caiman was gone. Okamoto was gone.

Everyone was frozen in shock.

Nate's raft bobbed in the wake of the creature's passing. He stared out at the spot where the Ranger had vanished, Okamoto with his damn whistling. A red stain bubbled up from below.

Blood on the water . . . now the monsters know there's food here.

Kelly crouched with her brother in the center of their raft. Captain Waxman and Corporal Warczak knelt with their weapons ready. Yamir was finalizing his prep on two black bombs, each the size of a flat dinner plate with an electronic timer/receiver atop it. The demolitions expert leaned back. "Done," he said with a nod to his captain.

"Retrieve your weapon," Waxman said. "Be ready."

Yamir picked up his M-16 rifle and took up watch on his side of the raft.

A splintering crash sounded behind them. Kelly swung around in time to see the third raft in their flotilla knocked high into the air, the same as Nate's raft had done a moment before. But this time, its occupants were not as lucky. Anna Fong, her grip broken, went flying, catapulted through the air by the sudden attack. The anthropologist struck the water at the same time the raft crashed back down. Zane and Olin had managed to cling to the raft, as had Sergeant Kostos and Corporal Graves.

Anna popped to the surface, coughing and choking on water. She was only yards from the raft.

"Don't move, Anna!" Nate called. "Tuck your arms and legs together and float."

She clearly tried to obey, but her pack, waterlogged, dragged her underwater unless she kicked to keep herself afloat. Her eyes were white with panic; both the fear of drowning and the fear of what lurked in the waters shone bright in her eyes.

Movement drew her attention back to the assaulted raft. Sergeant Kostos was leaning out with one of the long bamboo poles that they had used to propel themselves away from shore.

"Grab on!" Kostos called to her.

Anna reached to the bamboo, fingers scrabbling for a moment, then clinging.

"I'm gonna pull you toward the raft."

"No!" she moaned.

Nate again called. "Anna, it should be okay as long as you don't make any sudden moves. Kostos, pull her very slowly toward you. Try not to raise a ripple."

Kelly trembled. Frank put his arm around her.

Ever so slowly, the sergeant drew Anna back to the raft.

"Good, good . . ." Nate mumbled in a tense mantra.

Then, behind Anna, an armored snout appeared, just the nose, its eyes hidden underwater still.

"No one shoot!" Nate called. "Don't rile it!"

Guns pointed, but there was no kill shot anyway.

Kostos had stopped pulling on the bamboo with the appearance of the caiman. No one moved.

A moan flowed from the woman in the water.

Ever so slowly the snout inched forward, rising slightly as its massive jaws yawned open.

Kostos was forced to slowly draw Anna toward him, keeping her just a couple of feet ahead of the approaching monster.

"Careful!" Nate called.

It was like some macabre slow-motion chase . . . and they were losing.

The snout of the creature was now less than a foot from the woman, the jaws gaping open behind her head. There was no way Anna could be pulled aboard without the creature attacking.

Someone else came to this same realization.

Corporal Graves ran across their raft and leaped over Anna's head like an Olympic long jumper.

"Graves!" Kostos yelled.

The corporal landed atop the creature's open snout, driving its jaws closed and shoving it underwater.

"Pull her aboard!" Graves hollered as he was sucked under by the caiman.

Kostos yanked Anna back to the raft and Olin helped haul her on board.

A moment later, the beast reared up out of the water, Graves still clinging to the top of its wide head. The caiman thrashed, trying to dislodge its strange rider. Its jaws reared open, and a bellow of rage escaped from it.

"Fuck you!" Graves said. "This is for my brother!" Clinging fast with his legs, he yanked something from his field jacket and tossed it down the beast's gullet.

A grenade.

The massive jaws snapped at the Ranger, but he was out of reach.

"Everybody down!" Waxman bellowed.

Graves leaped from his perch, aiming for the raft, a shout on his lips. "Chew on that, you bastard!"

Behind him, the explosion ripped through the silent swamp. The head of the caiman blew apart, shredded by shrapnel.

Graves flew through the air, a roar of triumph flowing from his lips.

Then up from the depths shot the other caiman. Jaws wide, it lunged at the flying corporal, snatching him out of midair, like a dog catching a tossed ball, then crashed away, taking its prey with it. It had all happened in seconds.

The bulk of the slain caiman slowly rose to the surface of the lake, belly up, exposing the gray and yellow scaling of its underside.

The slack body of the huge creature was nudged from below. Ripples slowly circled it as the large beast was examined by the survivor.

"Maybe it'll leave," Frank said. "Maybe the other's death will spook it away."

Kelly knew this wouldn't happen. These creatures had to be hundreds and hundreds of years old. Mates for life, the only pair of its kind sharing this ecosystem.

The ripples faded. The lake grew quiet again.

Everyone kept eyes fixed on the waters around them, holding their breath or wheezing tensely. Minutes stretched. The sun baked everyone.

"Where did it go?" Zane whispered, hovering beside his ashen colleague. Anna, soaked and terrified, just trembled.

"Maybe it did leave," Frank mumbled.

The trio of rafts, rudderless, slowly drifted alongside the bulk of the dead monster. Nate's boat was on the far side of the body. Kelly met his eye. He nodded, trying to convey calm assurance, but even the experienced jungle man looked scared. Behind him, the jaguar crouched beside its master, hackles raised.

Frank shifted his legs slightly. "It must have fled. Maybe—"

Kelly sensed it a moment before it struck: a sudden welling of the water under their raft. "Hang on!"

"What—"

The raft exploded under them—not just bumped up, but driven skyward. Shattering up from the center of the raft jammed the massive armored snout of the angered caiman.

Kelly flew, tumbling through the air. She caught glimpses of the others falling amid the rain of bamboo and packs. "Frank!" Her brother splashed on the far side of the monster.

Then she hit the water—hard, on her stomach. The wind was knocked out of her. She spluttered up, remembering Nate's warning to remain as still as possible. She glanced up in time to see a chunk of the raft's log dropping through the air toward her face.

Dodging, she missed a fatal blow, but the edge of the flying log clipped the side of her head. She collapsed backward, driven underwater, darkness swallowing her away.

From the far side of the dead caiman's bulk, Nate watched Kelly get hit by debris and go under—dead or unconscious, he didn't know. All around the ruined raft, people, packs, and bits of debris floated. "Float as still as possible!" Nate called out, frantically searching for what had happened to Kelly.

The caiman had vanished underwater again.

"Kelly!" Frank called.

His sister bobbed to the surface on the far side of the debris field. She was facedown in the water, limp.

Nate hesitated. *Was she dead?* Then he saw one arm move, flailing weakly. *Alive!* But for how long? As dazed as she was by the blow, she risked drowning.

"Damn it!" He searched for some plan, some way to rescue her. Just beyond her body was one of the small hummocks of land with a single large mangrove tree sprouting up from it. Its thick trunk sprang from a tangle of exposed buttress roots, then fanned out into a branched canopy hanging over the waters. If Kelly could reach there . . .

A shout arose from the waters, drawing back his attention. The caiman's head appeared, rising like a submarine amid the debris. A large eye studied its surroundings. Shots were fired toward it, but it remained low in the water, blocked by the debris and the people. Then it sank quickly away.

Frank finally spotted his sister. "Oh, God . . . Kelly!" He turned, ready to swim to her aid.

"Frank! Don't move!" Nate called. "I'll get to her!" He dropped his shotgun to the bamboo planking.

"What are you doing?" Manny asked.

As answer, Nate leaped across the gap between the raft and the dead caiman. He landed on its exposed belly, landing in a half crouch, then ran down the length of the beast's slippery bulk, trying to get as close to Kelly as possible.

A scream rose on his right. He watched Corporal Yamir, struggling—then suddenly Yamir was yanked under the water, large bubbles trailing down into the depths. The caiman was picking off the survivors in the water.

Time was running out.

Nate ran and leaped from the belly of the floating caiman, flinging his body with all the strength in his legs. Flying out, he dove smoothly for Kelly, reaching her in a heartbeat. He rolled her face out of the water. She struggled weakly against him.

"Kelly! It's Nate! Lie still!"

Something must have registered, for her struggling slowed.

Nate kicked strongly toward the nearby hummock. He scrabbled through the debris. His hand hit something: a black dinner plate decorated with blinking red lights. One of the dead corporal's bombs.

Instinctively, Nate grabbed it up in his free hand and continued to kick.

"Behind you!" Sergeant Kostos called from across the water.

Nate glanced back.

A rippling wake aimed in his direction, then the tip of the snout broke the surface, then more of the bull's black-scaled head. Nate found himself staring eye-to-eye with the beast. He sensed the intelligence behind that gaze. No dumb brute. Playing dead wouldn't work here.

He turned and kicked and paddled with the napalm bomb toward the swamp island. His feet hit muddy ground.

With a strength born of fear and panic, he scooped Kelly under his arm and hauled them through the shallows, climbing the banks.

"It's right on top of you!"

Nate didn't bother to turn. He ran toward the tangle of mangrove roots, shoved Kelly between them, then dove in after her. There was a cramped natural cavity behind the main buttress roots.

Kelly groggily awoke, coughing out gouts of

water and staring around in panic. Nate fell atop her in the small space.

"What . . . ?"

Then, over his shoulder, she must have spotted their pursuer. Her eyes grew large. "Oh, shit!"

Nate rolled around and saw the monster hurling itself up out of the lake, scrabbling up the short bank. It struck like a locomotive hitting a car on the tracks. The whole tree shook. Nate was sure it would crash atop them. But the tree held. The caiman stared at Nate between the roots, mouth gaping open, teeth glinting with menace. It paused, glaring at him, then backpedaled and slid into the waters.

Kelly turned to him. "You saved me."

He glanced to her, their noses almost touching in the cramped root prison. "Or almost got you killed. It's all perspective, really." Nate pushed to his knees. He grabbed one of the roots to haul himself to his feet. "And we're not out of the woods yet."

Nate studied the waters, watching for any telltale ripple. It seemed quiet. But he knew the caiman was still out there, watching. Taking a deep breath, he squeezed back out between the roots.

"Where are you going?"

"There are still others in the water . . . including your brother." Nate shoved the napalm bomb under his shirt and began to climb the mangrove, a plan slowly forming. Once high enough, he picked a good branch, clambered atop it, and slowly crawled down its length to where it hung over the water. As the branch thinned, it began to bend under his weight. He moved more cautiously.

At last, he could risk going no farther. He glanced down and around his perch. This would have to do.

He called to the other raft while pulling out the bomb. "Does anyone know how to arm one of these explosives?"

Sergeant Kostos answered, "Type in the time delay manually! Then hit the red button!"

Waxman yelled from where he floated in the water. Nate had to respect how calm the captain's voice was as he added a warning. "It's got an explosive radius of a couple hundred meters. Blow it wrong and you'll kill us all!"

Nate nodded, staring at the bomb. A simple sealed keyboard glowed atop it, not unlike a calculator. Nate prayed it hadn't been damaged by the dunking or abuse. He set the timer for fifteen seconds. That should be long enough.

Next, Nate cradled the bomb to his chest and snapped free his work knife. Clenching his teeth, he dug the blade into the meat of his thumb and sliced a deep gash. He needed the wound to bleed freely.

Once done, he used a secondary branch as support and climbed to his feet on the swaying perch. He pulled the bomb out with his bloodied hand and made sure he had a good grip. Stretching out over the water, Nate extended his arm, bomb in hand. Blood dripped over the weapon's surface and down to the waters below, plopping in thick drops and sending out ripples.

He held steady, his thumb on the trigger button. "C'mon, damn you." In Australia, he had once visited a live animal park and had seen a thirty-foot saltwater crocodile trained to leap after a freshly decapitated chicken on a pole.

Nate's plan wasn't much different. Only he was the chicken.

He slightly shook his arm, scattering more drops. "Where are you?" he hissed. His arm was getting tired.

Down below, he watched a small pool of his own blood forming on the surface of the water. A caiman could smell blood in the water from miles away. "C'mon!"

Squinting, he risked a peek toward the others still afloat in the debris field. With no way of knowing where the caiman was, neither of the other two rafts dared paddle to their mates' rescue.

Distracted, Nate almost missed the flash of something large heaving through the shallows toward him.

"Nate!" Kelly called.

He saw it.

The caiman lunged out of the water, blasting straight out of the lake and springing toward him, jaws wide open, roaring.

Nate hit the bomb's trigger, then dropped the blood-slick device down the open mouth. He realized at the same time that he had vastly underestimated how *high* a giant swamp caiman could leap.

Nate crouched on his branch, then leaped straight up, propelled by both his legs and the spring in the branch. Crashing through leaves, Nate grabbed a limb overhead. He yanked his feet out of the way just as the monster's jaws snapped shut under the seat of his pants. He felt its huffed breath on his back. Denied its prey, it fell back to the water, shooting spray almost as high as its leap.

Staring down, Nate saw the branch he had been

perched on. It was gone, a stump, cleaved clean through by those mighty jaws. If he had still been standing there . . .

Nate saw the caiman again glide from the shallows into the deeper waters, but now it remained floating on the surface, revealing its length. A male, 120 feet if it was an inch.

Hanging from the branch, Nate caught a frustrated glower directed up at him. It slowly turned toward where the others were floating, giving up on him for the moment and going after easier prey.

Before it could complete its turn, Nate saw the beast suddenly shudder. He had forgotten to count the seconds.

Suddenly the belly of the beast swelled immensely. It opened its maw to scream but all that came out were jets of flame. The caiman had become a veritable flaming dragon. It rolled on its side and sank into the murkier depths, then a huge *whoosh* exploded upward in a column of water, flames, and caiman.

Nate clung to his perch with his arms and legs. Down below in the roots, Kelly yelled in shock.

The blast ended as quickly as it blew. In the aftermath, bits and pieces of flaming flesh showered harmlessly around the swamp. Insulated by the armored bulk of the great giant, the worst of the bomb's effect had been contained.

A shout of triumph arose from the others.

Nate climbed down the tree and retrieved Kelly. "Are you okay?" he asked her.

She nodded, fingering a gash at her hairline. "Head hurts a little, but I'll be fine." She coughed hoarsely. "I must've swallowed a gallon of swamp water."

He helped her down to the water's edge. While Kostos's raft went to collect the swimmers and packs, Nate's own raft, manned by his friends and Ranger Carrera, glided over to the pair to keep them from having to swim.

Carrera helped pull Kelly aboard. Manny grabbed Nate's wrist and hauled him up onto the bamboo planks. "That was some pretty fast thinking, doc," Manny said with a grin.

"Necessity is the mother of invention," Nate said, matching his expression with a tired smile. "But I'll be damned glad to be on dry land again."

"Could there be more of them out there?" Kelly asked as the group paddled toward the other raft.

"I doubt it," Manny said with a strange trace of regret. "Even with an ecosystem this large, I can't imagine there's enough food to support more than two of these gigantic predators. Still, I'd keep a watch out for any offspring. Even baby giants could be trouble."

Carrera kept watch with her rifle as the others paddled. "Do you think that the Ban-ali sent these after us, like the locusts and piranhas?"

Kouwe answered, "No, but I would not put it past them to have nurtured this pair as some de facto gatekeepers to their lands, permanently stationed guards against any who dared to enter their territory."

Gatekeepers? Nate stared at the far shore. The broken highlands were now clear in the afternoon brightness. Waterfalls were splashes of silver flowing down cliffs the color of spilled blood. The jungled summits and valleys were verdant.

If the professor was right about the caiman being gatekeepers, then ahead of them stretched the lands of the Ban-ali, the heart of their deadly territory.

He stared at the other raft, counting heads. *Waxman, Kostos, Warczak, and Carrera.* Only four Rangers remained of the twelve sent out here—and they hadn't even crossed into the true heart of the Ban-ali lands. "We'll never make it," he mumbled as he paddled.

Carrera heard him. "Don't worry. We'll dig in until reinforcements can be flown here. It can't take more than a day."

Nate frowned. *They had lost three men today, elite military professionals.* A day was not insignificant. As he stared at the growing heights of the far shore, Nate was suddenly less sure he wanted to reach dry land, especially *that* dry land. But they had no choice. A plague was spreading through the States, and their small party was as close to an answer to the puzzle as anyone. There was no turning back.

Besides, his father had taken this route, run this biological gauntlet. Nate could not retreat now. Despite the deaths, the dangers, and the risks, he had to find out what had happened to his father. Plague or not, he could only go forward.

Waxman called as they neared the far shore. "Stay alert! Once we pull up, move quickly away from the swamp. We'll set up a base camp a short distance into the forest."

Nate saw the way the captain kept scanning the

swamps. Waxman was clearly worried about other caiman predators. But Nate kept his gaze focused on the jungles ahead. In his blood, he knew that was where the true danger lay—the Ban-ali.

Across the water, Nate heard the captain fall upon Olin Pasternak. "And you, get that uplink running as soon as possible. We have a three-hour window before the satellites are out of range for the night."

"I'll do my best," Olin assured him.

Waxman nodded. Nate caught the look in the captain's eyes: full of grief and worry. Despite his booming confident voice, the leader of the Rangers was as nervous as Nate. And this realization was oddly reassuring. Nervous men kept a keen eye on their surroundings, and Nate suspected that their survival would depend on this.

The pair of rafts reached the shallows and soon were bumping into solid ground. The Rangers offloaded first, rifles ready. They fanned out and checked the immediate forest. Soon, calls of "All clear!" rang out from the dark jungles fringing the swamp.

Nate glanced up as he waited for the okay to disembark from the rafts. Around him, the soft roar of countless waterfalls echoed. To either side, towering cliffs framed the narrow defile ahead, choked with jungle. Down the center of the canyon a wide stream flowed, emptying sluggishly into the swamp.

Warczak shouted from near the forest's edge. "Found it!" The corporal leaned out of the shadowy fringe and waved to his captain. "Another of Clark's markers."

Waxman motioned with his rifle. "Everybody on land!"

Nate did not wait. He hurried with the others toward Warczak. A few steps into the forest, a large Spanish cedar had been pegged with a strip of cloth. And under it, another carved marking. Each member stared at it with a growing sense of dread. An arrow pointed up the defile. The meaning was clear.

"Skull and crossbones," Zane muttered.

Death lay ahead.

3:40 P.M.

"Now that was quite entertaining," Louis said to his lieutenant, lowering his binoculars. "When that caiman exploded . . ." He shook his head. "Resourceful."

Earlier that morning, radioed by his mole, Louis had learned of the Rangers' plan to camp near the far shore until reinforcements could be flown in. He imagined the loss of three more men would cement Captain Waxman's plan. The group was now down to four Rangers. No threat. Louis's team could take the other at any time—and Louis didn't want those odds changed.

He turned to Jacques. "We'll let them rest until midnight, then rouse the little sleepyheads and get them running forward. Who knows what other dangers they'll prepare us for?" Louis pointed to the swamp.

"Yes, sir. I'll have my team suited up and ready by nightfall. We're draining several lanterns now to collect enough kerosene."

"Good." Louis turned his back on the swamp. "Once the others are on the run, we'll follow behind you in the canoes."

"Yes, sir, but . . . ." Jacques bit his lower lip and stared out at the swamp.

Louis patted his lieutenant on the shoulder. "Fear not. If there had been any other beasties lurking in the swamp, they would've attacked the Rangers. You should be safe." But Louis could understand his lieutenant's concern. Louis would not be the one using scuba gear to cross the swamp on motorized sleds, with nothing between him and the denizens of the swamp except a wet suit. Even with the night-vision lamps, it would be a dark and murky crossing.

But Jacques nodded. He would do as ordered.

Louis crossed back into the jungle, heading to the camp. Like his lieutenant, many others were on edge, the tension thick. They all had seen the remains of the Ranger back in the woods. The soldier looked like he had been eaten alive, down to the bone, eyes gone. A scattering of locusts had still crawled around the site, but most of the swarm had dispersed. Alerted by his mole, Louis had carefully kept burners of *tok-tok* powder smoldering as they crossed through the forest this morning, just in case. Luckily Tshui had been able to harvest enough dried liana vines to produce the protective powder.

Despite the threats, Louis's plan was proceeding smoothly. He was not so vain as to think his group moved unseen, but so far the Ban-ali were concentrating all their resources on the foremost group, the Rangers.

Still, Louis could not count on this particular advantage lasting much longer, especially once they entered the heart of the secretive tribe's territory. And he was not alone in these thoughts. Earlier, three mercenaries from his party had attempted to sneak off and flee, abandoning their obligations, fearful of what lay ahead. The cowards had been caught, of course, and Tshui had made an example of them.

Louis reached their temporary jungle campsite. He found his mistress, Tshui, kneeling by his tent. Across the way, strung spread-eagle between various trees, was the AWOL trio. Louis averted his eyes. There was surely artistry to Tshui's work, but Louis had only so strong a stomach.

She glanced up at his approach. She was cleaning her tools in a bowl of water.

Louis grinned at her. She stood, all legs and sinewy muscle. He took her under his arm and guided her toward their tent.

As Tshui ducked past the flap, she growled deep in her chest and, impatient, tugged his hand to draw him into the dark heat of the tent.

For the moment, it seemed rest would have to wait.

THIRTEEN

Shadows

AUGUST 15, 3:23 P.M.
INSTAR INSTITUTE
LANGLEY, VIRGINIA

Lauren knocked on Dr. Alvisio's office door. Earlier this morning, the epidemiologist had requested, rather urgently, a moment with her. But this was the first chance she'd had to break away and meet with him.

Instead, she had spent the entire morning and afternoon in video conference with Dr. Xavier Reynolds and his team at Large Scale Biological Labs in Vacaville, California. The prion protein they had discovered could be the first clue to solving this disease, a contagion that had claimed over sixty lives so far with another several hundred sick. Lauren had arranged for her former student's data to be cross-referenced and double-checked by fourteen other labs. As she waited for confirmation, she had time to meet with the epidemiologist.

The door opened. The young Stanford doctor looked as if he hadn't slept in weeks. A bit of dark stubble shadowed his cheeks, and his eyes were bloodshot. "Dr. O'Brien. Thank you for coming." He ushered her into the room.

Lauren had never been in his office, so she was surprised to see a whole array of computer equipment lining one entire wall. Otherwise, the room was rather Spartan: a cluttered desk, an overflowing bookcase, a few chairs. The only personal touch was a lone Stanford Cardinals banner hanging on the far wall. But Lauren's eye was drawn back to the computer bank. The monitors were full of graphs and flowing numbers.

"What was so urgent, Hank?" she asked him.

He waved her to the computers. "I need you to see this." His voice was grim.

She nodded and took the seat he offered before one of the monitors.

"Do you remember when I told you about the possible signature spike of basophils early in the disease process? How this clinical finding might be a way to detect and specify cases more quickly?"

She nodded, but since hearing his theory, she had already begun to doubt it. Jessie's basophils had spiked, but the child was recovering very well. There had even been talk of letting her out of the hospital ward as soon as tomorrow. This rise in basophils could be something that occurs with many different fevers and is not specific to this disease.

She opened her mouth to say just that, but Dr. Alvisio interrupted, turning to his computer keyboard. He typed rapidly. "It took me a full twenty-four hours to gather data from around the entire country, specifically searching for fever cases in children and the elderly with characteristic basophil spikes. I wanted to run a model for the disease using this new criteria."

On the monitor, a map of the United States appeared in yellow with each state mapped out in black lines. Small pinpoints of red dotted the map, most clustered in Florida and other southern states. "Here is the old data. Each area of red indicates current documented cases of the contagion."

Lauren slipped on her reading glasses and leaned closer.

"But using the basophil spike as the marker for designating cases, here is a truer picture of the disease's present status in the United States." The epidemiologist hit a keystroke. The map bloomed brighter with red dots. Florida was almost a solid red, as were Georgia and Alabama. Other states, empty before, now were speckled with red spots.

Hank turned to her. "As you can see, the number of cases skyrockets. Many of these patients are in unquarantined wards due to the fact that the trio of signs designated by the CDC have not shown up yet. They're exposing others."

Despite her doubts, Lauren felt a sick churn in her belly. Even if Dr. Alvisio was wrong about the basophils, he had made a good point. Early detection was critical. Until then, all feverish children or elderly should be quarantined immediately, even if they weren't in hot zones like Florida and Georgia.

"I see what you're saying," she said. "We should contact the CDC and have them establish nation-wide quarantine policies."

Hank nodded. "But that's not all." He turned back to his computer and typed. "Based on this new basophil data, I ran an extrapolation model. Here is what the disease picture will look like in two weeks." He pressed the ENTER key.

The entire southern half of the country went red.

Lauren sat back in shock.

"And in another month." Hank struck the ENTER key a second time.

The red mottling spread to consume almost the entire lower forty-eight states.

Hank glanced at her. "We have to do something to stop this. Every day is critical."

Lauren stared at the bloodstained screen, her mouth dry, her eyes wide. Her only consolation was that Dr. Alvisio's basis for this model was probably overly grim. She doubted the basophil spike was truly an early marker for the disease. Still, the warning here was important. Every day *was* critical.

Her pager vibrated on her hip, reminding her that the war against this disease had to be fought with every resource. She glanced down to her pager's screen. It was Marshall. He had followed his numeric code with a 911. Something urgent.

"Can I use your phone?" she asked.

"Of course."

She stood and crossed to his desk. Hank returned to his computers and statistical models. She dialed the number. The phone was answered in half a ring.

"Lauren . . ."

"What is it, Marshall?"

His words were rushed, full of fear. "It's Jessie. I'm at the hospital."

Lauren clutched the phone tighter. "What is it? What's wrong?"

"Her temperature is up again." His voice cracked. "Higher than it's ever been. And three other children have been admitted. Fevers, all of them."

"Wh . . . what are you saying?" she stammered, but she knew the answer to her own question.

Her husband remained silent.

"I'll be right there," she finally said, dropping the phone and scrabbling to replace it in its cradle.

Hank turned to her, noticing her reaction. "Dr. O'Brien?"

Lauren could not speak. *Jessie . . . the basophil spike . . . the other children.* Dear God, the disease was here!

Lauren stared glassily at the monitor with the map of the United States mottled entirely in red. The epidemiologist's theory was not a mistake. It wasn't overly pessimistic.

"Is everything all right?" Hank asked softly.

Lauren slowly shook her head, eyes fixed on the screen.

One month.

5:23 P.M.
AMAZON JUNGLE

Kelly sat hunched with her brother, both flanking Olin Pasternak. The Russian computer expert was screwing down the cover piece to reassemble the satellite communication system. He had been working on it all afternoon, trying to raise the States.

"This had better work," he mumbled. "I've torn it down to the motherboard and built it back up. If this doesn't work, I don't know what else to try."

Frank nodded. "Fire it up."

Olin checked the connections one final time, adjusted the satellite dish, then returned his attention to the laptop computer. He switched on the solar power, and after a short wait, the operating system booted up and the screen hummed to life.

"We've got a connection to the HERMES satellite!" Olin said, and sighed with relief.

A cheer went up around Kelly. The entire camp, except for the pair of Rangers on guard by the swamp, was gathered around Olin and his communication equipment.

"Can you get an uplink established?" Waxman asked.

"Keep your fingers crossed," Olin said. He began tapping at the keyboard.

Kelly found herself holding her breath. They needed to reach someone Stateside. Reinforcements were certainly needed here. But more important to her, Kelly couldn't stand not knowing Jessie's status. She had to find a way to get back to her.

"Here we go." Olin struck a final sequence of keys. The familiar connection countdown began.

Richard Zane mumbled behind her. "Please, please work . . ."

His prayer was in all their hearts.

The countdown blipped to zero. The computer

screen froze for an interminably long second, then a picture of Kelly's mother and father appeared. The pair looked shocked and relieved.

"Thank God!" her father said. "We've been trying to reach you for the past hour."

Olin moved aside for Frank. "Computer problems," her brother said, "among many others."

Kelly leaned in. She could not wait a moment longer. "How's Jessie?"

Her mother's face answered the question. Her eyes fidgeted, and she paused before speaking. "She's . . . she's doing fine, dear."

The image on the screen fritzed as if the computer had become a lie detector. Static and snow ate away the picture. Her mother's next words became garbled. "Lead on a cure . . . prion disease . . . sending data as we speak . . ."

Her father spoke, but the interference grew worse. They seemed unaware that their message was corrupted. ". . . helicopter on its way . . . Brazilian army . . ."

Frank hissed to Olin, "Can you fix the reception?"

He leaned in and tapped quickly. "I don't know. I don't understand. We've just received a file. Maybe that's interfering with our downstream feed."

But for each key the man tapped, the signal deteriorated.

Static whined and hissed with occasional words coming through. "Frank . . . losing you . . . can you . . . tomorrow morning . . . GPS locked . . ." Then the entire feed collapsed. The screen gave one final frazzled burst, then froze up.

"Damn it!" Olin swore.

"Get it back up," Waxman said behind them.

Olin bent over his equipment and shook his head. "I don't know if I can. I've troubleshot the motherboard and rebooted all the software."

"What's wrong then?" Kelly asked.

"I can't say for sure. It's almost like a computer virus has corrupted the entire satellite communication array."

"Well, keep trying," Waxman said. "You've got another half hour before the satellite is out of range."

Frank stood, facing everyone. "Even if we can't link up, from what we did hear, it sounds like the Brazilian helicopter may be on its way here. Maybe as soon as tomorrow morning."

Beside him, Olin stared at the frozen screen. "Oh, God."

All eyes turned to the Russian communications expert. He tapped the screen, pointing to a set of numbers in the upper right-hand corner. "Our GPS signal . . ."

"What's the matter?" Waxman asked.

Olin glanced over to them. "It's wrong. Whatever glitched the satellite system must've corrupted the feed to the GPS satellites, too. It sent a wrong signal back to the States." He stared back at the screen. "It places us about thirty miles south of our current position."

Kelly felt the blood rush from her head. "They won't know where we are."

"I've got to get this up and running," Olin said. "At least long enough to correct the signal." He rebooted the computer and set to work.

For the next half hour, Olin worked furiously

with his equipment. Oaths and curses, both in English and Russian, flowed from the man. As he labored, everyone found busy work to occupy the time. No one bothered to try resting. Kelly helped Anna prepare some rice, the last of their supplies. As they worked, they kept looking over to Olin, silently praying.

But for all the man's efforts and their prayers, nothing was gained.

After a time, Frank crossed and placed a hand on Olin's shoulder. He raised his other arm, exposing his wristwatch. "It's too late. The communication satellites are out of range."

Olin sagged over his array, defeated.

"We'll try again in the morning," Frank said, his encouragement forced. "You should rest. Start fresh tomorrow."

Nate, Kouwe, and Manny returned from a fishing expedition by the swamp. Their catch was bountiful, strung on a line between them. They dropped their load beside the fire. "I'll clean," Kouwe said, settling easily to the ground.

Manny sighed. "No argument here."

Nate wiped his hands and stared at Olin and his computer. He crossed toward the man. "There was something I was wondering about while fishing. What about that other file?"

"What are you talking about?" Olin asked blearily.

"You mentioned something about a file being downloaded during the feed."

Olin scrunched his face, then nodded with understanding. "*Da*. Here it is. A data file."

Kelly and Manny hurried over. Kelly now remembered her mother had mentioned sending something just before the system crashed.

Olin brought up the file.

Kelly leaned closer. On the screen appeared a 3-D model of a molecule spinning above pages of data. Intrigued, she settled nearer. Her eyes scanned through the report. "My mother's work," she mumbled, glad to occupy her mind on something other than her own worries. But the topic was troublesome nonetheless.

"What is it?" Nate asked.

"A possible lead on the cause of the disease," Kelly added.

Manny answered, peering over her shoulder. "A prion."

"A what?"

Manny quickly explained to Nate, but Kelly's attention remained focused on the report. "Interesting," Kelly mumbled.

"What?" Manny asked.

"It says here that this prion seems to cause genetic damage." She quickly read the next report.

Manny read over her shoulder. He whistled appreciatively.

"What?" Nate asked.

Kelly spoke excitedly. "This could be the answer! Here's a paper from researchers at the University of Chicago, published in *Nature* back in September of 2000. They hypothesized through the study of yeast that prions may hold the key to genetic mutations, even play a role in evolution."

"Really? How?"

"One of the major mysteries of evolution has been how survival skills that require multiple genetic changes could happen so spontaneously. Such changes are termed *macroevolution*, like the adaptation of certain algae to toxic environments or the rapid development of antibiotic resistance in bacteria. But how such a series of simultaneous mutations could be generated was not understood. But this article offers a possible answer. *Prions*." Kelly pointed to the computer screen. "Here the researchers at the University of Chicago have shown that a yeast's prions can flip an *all-or-nothing* switch in the genetic code, causing massive mutations to develop in unison, to spark an evolutionary jump start, so to speak. Do you know what this suggests?"

Kelly saw realization dawn in Manny's eyes.

"The piranha creatures, the locusts . . ." the biologist mumbled.

"Mutations all of them. Maybe even Gerald Clark's arm!" Kelly said. "A mutation triggered by prions."

"But what does this have to do with the disease?" Nate asked.

Kelly frowned. "I don't know. This discovery is a good start, but we're a long way from a complete answer."

Manny pointed to the screen. "But what about here in the article where it hypothesizes . . ."

Kelly nodded. The two began to discuss the article, speaking rapidly, sharing ideas.

Beside them, Nate had stopped listening. He had scrolled back to the spinning model of the prion protein.

After a time, he interrupted. "Does anyone else see the similarity?"

"What do you mean?" Kelly asked.

Nate pointed to the screen. "See those two spiraling loops at either end?"

"The double alpha helixes?" Kelly said.

"Right . . . and here the corkscrewing middle section," Nate said, tracing the screen with his finger.

"So?" Kelly asked.

Nate turned and reached to the ground beside him. He picked up a stick and drew in the dirt, speaking as he worked. "The middle corkscrew . . . spreading out in double loops at either end." When he was done, he glanced up.

Stunned, Kelly stared at what Nate had drawn in the dirt.

Manny gasped, "The Ban-ali symbol!"

Kelly stared between the two pictures: one, a high-tech computer map; the other, a crude scrawl in the soft dirt. But there was no disputing the similarity. *The corkscrew, the double helixes . . .* It seemed beyond coincidence, even down to the clockwise spin of the molecular spiral.

Kelly turned to Nate and Manny. "Jesus Christ."

The Ban-ali symbol was a stylized model of the same prion.

11:32 P.M.

Jacques still had an unnerving terror of dark waters, born from the piranha attack that had left him disfigured when he was only a boy. Despite these deep fears, he glided through the swamp with nothing but a wet suit between him and the toothy predators of this marsh. He had no choice. He had to obey the doctor. The price of disobedience was worse than any terrors that might lurk in these waters.

Jacques clung to his motorized attack board as the silent fans dragged his body toward the far shore of the swamp. He was outfitted in an LAR V Draeger UBA, gear used by Navy SEALs for clandestine shallow-water operations. The closed-circuit system, strapped to his chest, rather than his back, produced no telltale bubble signature, making his approach undetectable. The final piece of his gear was a night-vision mask, giving him adequate visibility in the murky waters.

Still, the dark waters remained tight around him. His visibility was only about ten yards. He would periodically use a small mirrored device to peek above the water's surface and maintain his bearing.

His two teammates on this mission trailed behind

him, also gliding with tiny motorized sleds held at arms' length.

Jacques checked one last time with his tiny periscope. The two bamboo rafts that the Rangers had used to cross the swamp were directly ahead. Thirty yards away.

In the woods, he spotted the camp's fire, blazing bright. Shadowy figures, even at this late hour, moved around the site. Satisfied, he motioned to his two men to continue on ahead, one to each raft. Jacques would drift behind them, on guard with his scope.

The trio moved slowly forward. The rafts were tethered to the shore and floating in waters less than four feet deep. They would all have to be even more careful from here.

With determined caution, the group converged on the rafts. Jacques watched above and below the surface. His men waited in position, hovering in the shadows of their respective rafts. He studied the woods. He suspected that hidden in the dark jungle were guards, Rangers on patrol. He watched for a full five minutes, then signaled his men.

From under the rafts, the men produced small squeeze bottles full of kerosene. They sprayed the underside of the bamboo planks. Once each bottle emptied, the men gave Jacques a thumbs-up signal.

As his men worked, Jacques continued to watch the woods. So far, there was no sign that anyone had noticed their handiwork. He waited a full minute more, then gave the final signal, a slashing motion across his neck.

Each man lifted a hand above the water and ignited a butane lighter. They lifted the tiny flames to the kerosene-soaked bamboo. Flames immediately leaped and spread over the rafts.

Without waiting, the two men grabbed up their sleds and sped toward Jacques. He turned and thumbed his own motor to high and led his men off in a swooping curve out into the swamp, then back around, aiming for a spot on the shore a half-kilometer from the enemy's camp.

Jacques watched behind him. Men appeared out of the wood, outlined by the burning rafts, weapons pointing. Even underwater, he heard muffled shouts and sounds of alarm.

It had all gone perfectly. The doctor knew the other camp, after the locust attack, would be spooked by fires in the night. They would not likely remain near such a burning pyre.

Still, they were to take no unnecessary chances. Jacques led his men back toward the shallows, and the group slowly rose from the lake, spitting out regulator mouthpieces and kicking off fins. The second part of his mission was to ensure the others did indeed flee.

Slogging out of the water, he breathed a sigh of relief, glad to leave the dark swamp behind. He fingered the unmangled half of his nose, as if making sure it was still there.

Jacques slipped out a pair of night-vision binoculars. He fitted them in place and stared back toward the camp. Behind him, his men whispered, energized from the adventure and the successful completion of their task. Jacques ignored them.

Outlined in the monochrome green of his night

scope, a pair of men—Rangers, to judge by the way they carried their weapons—slipped away from the fiery rafts and called back into the forest. The group was pulling back. In the woods, new lights blinked on. *Flashlights.* Activity bustled around the campfire. Slowly, the lights began to shift away from the fire, like a line of fireflies. The parade marched toward the deeper ravine, up the chasm between the flat-topped highlands.

Jacques smiled. The doctor's plan had worked.

Still spying through his scope, he reached for his radio. He pushed the transmitter and brought the radio to his lips. "Mission successful. Rabbits are running."

"Roger that." It was the doctor. "Canoes heading out now. Rendezvous at their old camp in two hours. Over and out."

Jacques replaced the radio.

Once again, the hunt was on.

He turned to his other men to report the good news—but there was no one behind him. He instantly crouched and hissed their names. "Manuel! Roberto!"

No answer.

The night remained dark around him, the woods even darker. He slipped his night-vision diving mask back over his face. The woods shone brighter, but the dense vegetation made visibility poor. He backed away, his bare feet striking water.

Jacques stopped, frozen between the terrors of what lay behind him and in front of him.

Through his night-vision mask, he spotted movement. For the barest flicker of a heartbeat, it looked like the shadows had formed the figure of a man, staring back at him, no more than ten yards away. Jacques blinked, and the figure was gone. But now all the jungle shadows flowed and slid like living things toward him.

He stumbled backward into the waters, one hand scrambling to shove in his regulator mouthpiece.

One of the shadows broke out of the jungle fringe, outlined against the muddy bank. *Huge, monstrous* . . .

Jacques screamed, but his regulator was in the way. Nothing more than a wet gurgle sounded. More of the dark shadows flowed out of the woods toward him. An old Maroon tribal prayer rose to his lips. He scrambled backward.

Behind his fear of dark waters and piranhas was a more basic terror: *of being eaten alive.*

He dove backward, twisting around to get away.

But the shadows were faster.

11:51 P.M.

With a flashlight duct-taped to his shotgun, Nate followed near the rear of the group. The only ones behind him were Private Carrera and Sergeant Kostos. Everyone had lights, spearing the darkness in all directions. Despite the night, they moved quickly, trying to put as much distance as possible between them and whoever had set the rafts on fire.

The plan, according to Captain Waxman, was to seek a more defensible position. With the swamp on one side of them, the jungle on the other, it was not a secure spot to wait for whatever attack the fires would draw down upon them. And none of their group was delusional enough to think another attack wouldn't come.

Always planning one step ahead, the Rangers had a fallback position already picked out. Corporal Warczak had reported spotting caves in the cliffs a short way up the chasm. That was their goal.

Shelter and a defensible position.

Nate followed the others. Carrera marched at his side. In her arms was a strange shovel-nosed weapon. It looked like a Dustbuster vacuum attached to a rifle stock. She held it out toward the black jungle.

"What is that?" he asked.

She kept her attention on the jungle. "With all we lost in the swamp, we're short on M-16s." She hefted the strange weapon. "It's called a Bailey. Prototype weapon for jungle warfare." She thumbed a switch and a targeting laser pierced the darkness. She glanced over her shoulder to her superior. "Demonstration?"

Staff Sergeant Kostos, armed with his own M-16, grunted. "Testing weapon fire!" he barked forward to alert the others.

Carrera lifted her weapon, pivoting it for a target. She centered the red laser on the bole of a sapling about twenty yards away. "Shine your flashlight here."

Nate nodded and swung his flashlight up. Other eyes turned their way.

Carrera steadied her weapon and squeezed the trigger. There was no blast, only a high-pitched whistle. Nate caught a flash of silver, followed by a ringing crack. The sapling toppled backward, its trunk sliced cleanly through. Beyond it, a thick-boled silk cotton tree shook with the impact of something slamming into its trunk. Nate's flashlight focused on the distant tree. A bit of silver was embedded deep in the trunk.

Carrera nodded toward her target. "Three-inch razor disks, like Japanese throwing stars. Perfect for jungle combat. Set to automatic fire, it can mow down all the loose vegetation around you."

"And anything else in its path," Kostos added, waving the group onward.

Nate eyed the weapon with respect.

The group continued up the jungle-choked ravine, led by Corporal Warczak and Captain Waxman. They were roughly paralleling the small stream that drained down the chasm, but they kept a respectable distance from the water, just in case. After a half hour of trekking, Warczak led them off to the south, heading for the red cliffs.

So far, there appeared to be no evidence of pursuit, but Nate's ears remained alert for any warning, his eyes raking the shadowy jungle. At last the canopy began to thin enough to see stars and the bright glow of the moon. Ahead the world ended at a wall of red rock, aproned by loose shale and crumbled boulders.

At the top of the sloped escarpment, the cliff face was pocked with multiple caves and shadowed cracks.

"Hang back," Captain Waxman hissed, keeping them all hidden in the thicker underbrush that fringed the lower cliffs. He signaled for Warczak to forge ahead.

The corporal flicked off his flashlight, slipped on a pair of night-vision goggles, and ducked into the shadows with his weapon, vanishing almost instantly.

Nate crouched. Flanking him, the two Rangers took firm stances, watching their rear. Nate kept his shotgun ready. Most of the others were also armed. Olin, Zane, Frank, even Kelly had pistols, while Manny bore a Beretta in one hand and his whip in the other. Tor-tor had his own built-in weapons: claws and fangs. Only Professor Kouwe and Anna Fong remained unarmed.

The professor crept backward to Nate's side. "I don't like this," Kouwe said.

"The caves?"

"No . . . the situation."

"What do you mean?"

Kouwe glanced back down toward the swamp. Distantly the two rafts still burned brightly. "I smelled kerosene from those flames."

"So? It could be copal oil. That stuff smells like kerosene and that's abundant around here."

Kouwe rubbed his chin. "I don't know. The fire that drew the locusts was artfully crafted into the Ban-ali symbol. This was sloppy."

"But we were on guard. The Indians had to move fast. It was probably the best they could manage."

Kouwe glanced to Nate. "It wasn't Indians."

"Then who else?"

"Whoever's been tracking us all along." Kouwe leaned in and whispered in an urgent hiss. "Whoever set the flaming locust symbol crept up on our camp in broad daylight. They left no trace of their passage into or out of the area. Not a single broken twig. They were damned skilled. I doubt I could've done it."

Nate began to get the gist of Kouwe's concerns. "And the ones who have been dogging our trail were sloppy."

Kouwe nodded toward the swamp. "Like those fires."

Nate remembered the reflected flash high in the treetops as they hiked through the forest yesterday afternoon. "What are you suggesting?"

Kouwe spoke between clenched teeth. "We have more than one threat here. Whatever lies ahead—a new regenerative compound, a cure for this plague—it would be worth billions. Others would pay dearly for the knowledge hidden here."

Nate frowned. "And you think this other party set those fires? Why?"

"To drive us forward in a panic, like it did. They didn't want to risk us being reinforced with additional soldiers. They're probably using us as a human shield against the natural predatory traps set by the Ban-ali. We're just so much cannon fodder. They'll waste our lives until we are either spent on this trail or reach the Ban-ali. Then they'll sweep in and steal the prize."

Nate eyed the professor. "Why not mention this before we set off?"

Kouwe stared hard at Nate, and the answer to his question dawned in his own mind. "A traitor," Nate whispered. "Someone working with the trackers."

"I find it much too convenient that our satellite feed went on the fritz just as we drew close to these

Ban-ali lands. Plus it then sends off a false GPS signal."

Nate nodded. "Sending our own backup on a wild-goose chase."

"Exactly."

"Who could it be?" Nate eyed the others crouched in the underbrush.

Kouwe shrugged. "Anyone. Highest on the list would be the Russian. It's his system. It would be easy for him to feign a breakdown. But then again both Zane and Ms. Fong have been hovering around the array whenever Olin has stepped away. And the O'Briens have a background tied to the CIA, who have been known to play many sides against one another to achieve their ends. Then, finally, we can't rule out any of the Rangers."

"You're kidding."

"Enough money can sway almost anyone, Nate. And Army Rangers are trained extensively in communications."

Nate swung back around. "That leaves only Manny as someone we can trust."

"Does it?" Kouwe's expression was pained.

"You can't be serious? Manny? He's a friend to both of us."

"He also works for the Brazilian government. And don't doubt that the Brazilian government would want this discovery solely for itself. Such a medical discovery would be an economic boon."

Nate felt a sick sense of dread. *Could the professor be right? Was there no one they could trust?*

Before he could question Kouwe's assessment further, a scream split the night. Something huge came flying through the air. People scattered out of the way. Nate backpedaled with Kouwe in tow.

The large object landed in the middle of the crouched group. Flashlights swung toward the crumpled figure in their midst.

Anna cried out.

Transfixed in the spears of light, Corporal Warczak lay on his back, covered in blood and gore. One arm scrabbled up as if he were drowning in the spreading pool of his own blood. He tried to scream again, but all that came out was a croaking noise.

Nate stared, frozen. He could not tear his eyes from the sight of the ruined corporal.

From the waist down, Warczak's body was gone. He had been bitten in half.

"Weapons ready!" Waxman shouted, breaking through the horrified trance.

Nate dropped to a knee, swinging his shotgun out to the darkness. Kelly and Kouwe dove to aid the downed corporal, but Nate knew it was a futile gesture. The man was already dead.

He pointed his weapon. Throughout the jungle, dark shadows flowed and shifted, jiggled by the play of the group's flashlights. But Nate knew it wasn't all illusion. These shadows were all flowing *toward* the trapped group.

One of the Rangers shot a flare into the sky. The whistling trail arced high and exploded into a magnesium brightness that cast the jungle in silver and black. The sudden brightness gave those who crept up on them reason to pause.

Nate found himself staring into the eyes of a monster, caught in the shine of the flare. It crouched in the lee of a boulder on the cliff's escarpment, a massive creature, the size of a bull, but sleek and smooth. A cat. It studied him with eyes as black and cold as chunks of obsidian. Others lay nestled in the jungle and boulders around them. A pack of the creatures, at least twenty.

"Jaguars," Manny mumbled in shock over his shoulder. "Black jaguars."

Nate recognized the physique similar to Tor-tor's, but these creatures were three times as large, half a ton each. Prehistoric in size.

"They're all around us," Carrera whispered.

In her words, Nate heard the echo of his father's last radioed message: *Can't last much longer . . . oh, God, they're all around us!* Had this been his fate?

For another breath, neither group moved. Nate held his breath, hoping the nighttime prowlers would be intimidated by the flare's brightness and retreat. As if this thought were shared by one of the Rangers, a second flare jetted into the sky and burst with brightness, floating down on a tiny parachute.

"Hold steady," Waxman hissed.

The impasse stretched. The pack was not leaving.

"Sergeant," Waxman said, "on my mark, lay a path of grenades up toward the cliffs. Everyone else, keep weapons ready. Haul ass for the centermost cave on my signal."

Nate's eyes flicked to the yawning cavern in the cliff face. If they could make it there, the group could be attacked from only one direction. It was defensible. Their only hope.

"Carrera, use the Bailey to cover our—"

The sharp crack of a pistol cut off the captain's

order. Off to the side, Zane stumbled backward from the recoil of his smoking gun.

One of the cats spat and leaped in rage. Other jaguars responded, growling low and bounding toward the group.

"Now!" Waxman yelled.

Kostos dropped to one knee, aimed his M-16 toward the cliffs, and fired. Carrera spun with her new weapon, blasting from her hip, laying down a swath of fire across their rear. A flashing arc of flying silver disks flew out, shredding the jungle.

One of the jaguars was caught in midleap, its exposed belly sliced open. It howled and collapsed to the jungle, writhing.

Its cries were cut off as Kostos's grenade barrage began booming, echoing off the cliffs, deafening. Rock dust and dirt flumed up.

Shots were fired all around. Frank guarded his sister and the professor as they knelt beside the slack form of Corporal Warczak. Manny was on one knee beside Tor-tor, whose eyes were wide, hackles raised. Zane and Olin stood with Anna Fong, firing blindly into the dark.

Nate kept his shotgun raised and centered on the giant fellow he had first seen, crouched by the boulder off to the left. Despite the noises and the chatter of rattling rock debris, the creature had remained stone still.

Other shadowy figures fled from the bombarded slope. Others lay unmoving, dead, shredded.

"Go!" Waxman barked sharply, his command cutting through the explosions. "Make for the cave!"

The group lurched through the fringe of brush

and jungle toward the open rocky landscape at the foot of the towering cliffs. Nate kept his shotgun pointed at the cat, finger tensed on the shotgun's trigger. *If it even flicks its tail . . .*

Waxman waved them on, Kostos in the lead. "Get up there before they regroup!" The captain dropped beside Carrera. Behind them, the pack converged along their trail. Several limped or sniffed at a dead mate, but they kept a wary distance now.

Nate sidled past the silent cat off to the left. Only its eyes followed their passage. Nate suspected this was the leader of the pack. Behind that cold gaze, Nate could almost see the thing weighing these strangers, judging them.

Carrera had switched her weapon off automatic, conserving her ammunition. She fired at a lone cat getting too near. Her aim was off. The silver disk shaved the jaguar's ear and whizzed off into the jungle. The wounded cat dropped to its belly, glowering with pain and anger.

"Keep moving!" Waxman yelled.

By now, the cave was in direct sight. The group's tense pace collapsed into a panicked rout. Kostos led the way. He raised a flare pistol and fired it into the opening. A bright trace flashed out of the pistol's muzzle and exploded with light inside the cavern.

The deep cave was illuminated all the way to its rocky end.

"All clear!" Kostos hollered. "Move it!"

Olin, Zane, and Anna were the first to race inside. The sergeant stood at the entrance, M-16 in hand, waving his arm. "Move, move, move . . ."

Frank pushed Kelly ahead of him. Professor Kouwe ran beside him.

As the flares died out overhead, Nate took up a position on the other side of the entrance, shotgun ready.

Manny and Tor-tor followed with Waxman and Carrera on their heels.

They were going to make it, Nate realized.

Then a jaguar leaped from the deepening shadows, landing atop a boulder right beside the last two Rangers. Carrera dropped and aimed her weapon, but before she could fire, a paw struck out and raked into the chest of the team's captain.

Waxman was yanked off his feet, sailing into the air, claws sunk deep into his field jacket and chest. He bellowed, bringing up his own weapon. He fired over his head, striking the cat in the shoulder. The beast toppled backward, dragging the hooked captain with it. His body flew over the boulder, limbs kicking.

Carrera lunged up and ran around the boulder, going to the aid of her captain. Out of sight, Nate heard the characteristic whir of her weapon. Then suddenly she was backing into sight again. On her trail were a pair of jaguars. They were bleeding, embedded bits of silver decorating their flesh. Carrera was obviously struggling with the cartridge to her weapon, out of ammo disks.

Nate leaped away from the cave wall and ran toward her. As he reached her side, he shoved his shotgun to arms' length, the muzzle only a foot away from the snarling face of one of the jaguars.

He pulled the trigger, and the beast flew back, howling.

Carrera unholstered her 9mm pistol. She fired and fired at the other jaguar, unloading the clip. It fell back, then collapsed.

They stumbled up the slope.

Around the other side of the boulder, the captain fell into sight, crawling, one arm gone. His face was a bloody ruin.

"I . . . I thought he was dead," Carrera said with shock, stepping in his direction.

The captain crawled half a step, then a paw shot out and dug into the meat of his thigh. He was pulled back toward the hidden shadows. He screamed, fingers digging at the loose shale, finding no purchase.

A shot cracked. The captain's head flew back, then forward, striking the rock hard. Dead. Nate glanced behind him and saw Kostos crouched with his M-16 in hand, eyes fixed to its sniper scope. The sergeant slowly lowered his weapon, his expression pained and ripe with hard guilt.

"Everyone, get inside!" he yelled.

The party had remained clustered near the entrance.

Nate and Carrera hurried toward the cavern mouth.

Frank and Kostos flanked the threshold, weapons ready. The men were limned against the glare of the dying flare inside the passage. Frank waved to them. "Hurry!"

From Nate's position several yards down the escarpment, he spotted a deeper shadow shift along the base of the rocky cliff. To the left of the cave opening. "Watch out!"

It was the largest of the jaguars, the one Nate had first spotted.

It sprang past the mouth of the cave. Frank was bowled over, flying high into the air and landing on his back. Kostos was slammed into the wall. Then the cat was gone, racing back into the shadows below.

Kelly screamed. "Frank!"

Nate ran with Carrera. Kostos picked himself off the ground, wheezing and holding his chest, dazed.

"Help me!" Kelly yelled.

Frank lay writhing in the shale. Kelly's brother hadn't just been knocked off his feet. Both his legs were gone from the knees down. Blood spurted and jetted across the stones. In those few seconds, the giant jaguar had sheared off the limbs, as cleanly as a guillotine.

Kouwe fell to Frank's other side. Olin helped drag the moaning man into the cave. Kelly followed, yanking tourniquets from her pack. Plastic vials of morphine tumbled to the floor. Nate retrieved them.

Near the entrance, a shot was fired. Light burst outside. Another flare. Nate held out the vials of morphine, feeling useless, stunned.

Kouwe took them. "Go watch our back." He nodded to the entrance.

Olin and Kelly worked on the stricken man. Tears flowed down Kelly's cheeks, but her face was tight with determination and concentration. She refused to lose her brother.

Nate turned with his shotgun and joined Kostos

and Carrera at the cave's opening. The new flare showed that the jungle still moved with shadows. The bouldered slope offered additional cover for the cats.

Manny joined them, pistol in one hand. Tor-tor sniffed at Frank's blood on the rock and growled.

"I count at least another fifteen," Carrera said, face half covered with night-vision goggles. "They're not leaving."

Kostos swore. "If they rush us, we couldn't hope to stop them all. We're down to one grenade launcher, two M-16s, and a handful of pistols."

"And my shotgun," Nate added.

Carrera spoke, "I've fitted a new cartridge into the Bailey. But it's my last."

Manny crouched with his pistol. "There's some old debris blown in the back of the cave—branches, leaves, whatnot. We could light a fire at the entrance."

"Do it," Kostos said.

As Manny turned, a long, low growl rumbled up the slope. Everyone froze. Illuminated by the flare, a large shape revealed itself on the rocky slope. Weapons were raised.

Nate recognized the shadow as the largest cat.

"A female," Manny mumbled.

It remained in plain sight, studying them, challenging them. Behind it, the jungle churned with sleek bodies, muscled and clawed.

"What do we do?" Carrera asked.

"The bitch is trying to psych us out," Kostos grumbled, lowering his eye to the sight on his rifle.

"Don't fire," Nate hissed. "If you shoot now, you'll have the whole pack on us."

"Nate's right," Manny said. "Their blood lust is up. Anything could set them off. At least wait until we have a fire going here."

The cat seemed to hear him and let out a piercing yowl. In a surge of pure muscle, she leaped toward them, charging at an astounding speed, a precision machine.

The Rangers fired, but the she-beast was too fast, gliding with preternatural swiftness. Bullets chewed at the rock, sparking, missing, as if she were a true phantom. A single razored disk whizzed from the Bailey and zinged off a boulder to skitter harmlessly down the slope.

Nate dropped to one knee, shotgun pointed. "Here, kitty-kitty," he hissed under his breath. *Once she was close enough* . . .

Carrera repositioned her weapon, but before she could fire another shot, she was bumped aside. Tor-tor lunged past her, leaping from his master's side to the slope beyond.

"Tor-tor!" Manny called.

The smaller jaguar bounded a few yards down the slope and stopped, digging in, blocking the path of the larger cat. With a sharp snarl, he crouched low, rear haunches raised and bunched to spring, tail flicking with menace. He bared his long yellow claws and sharp fangs.

The giant black jaguar rushed at him, prepared to bowl him over, but at the last moment, she pulled up and stopped in front of Tor-tor, matching his stance, snarling. The two cats hissed and challenged each other.

Kostos lifted his weapon. "You're dead, bitch."

Manny motioned him not to shoot. "Wait!"

The two cats slowly padded around each other, circling, only a yard apart. At one point, the giant female's back was toward them. Nate could tell both Rangers had to restrain themselves not to fire.

"What are they doing?" Carrera asked.

Manny answered, "She can't understand why one of her own species, even a small one like Tor-tor, is protecting us. It has her perplexed."

By now, the two had stopped snarling. They cautiously approached one another, now almost nose to nose. Sharing some silent communication, the circling continued. Raised hackles settled back to sleek fur. A soft chuffing sounded as the larger cat took in the scent of this strange little jaguar.

Eventually they both stopped their dance, once again back to their original positions. Tor-tor crouched between the cave and the giant cat.

With a final grunt, the large jaguar leaned forward and rubbed her jowl against the side of Tor-tor's cheek, some understanding reached, a truce. With a blur of black fur, the giant cat spun and slipped back down the slope.

Slowly Tor-tor straightened from his crouch. His eyes glowed golden. With a feline casualness, he licked a patch of ruffled fur back into perfect place and turned to them. He padded back to the entrance as if he'd just come back from a stroll.

Carrera lowered her weapon and shifted her night-vision goggles. "They're pulling back," she said, amazed.

Manny hugged his pet. "You stupid bastard," he mumbled.

"What just happened?" Kostos asked.

"Tor-tor's close to being sexually mature," Manny said. "A juvenile male. The female, though huge, appears proportionally to be about the same age. And with all the blood in the air, tensions were high, including sexual tension. From their actions, Tor-tor's challenge was construed as both a threat and a sexual display."

Kostos scowled. "So you're saying he was making a play for her ass."

"And she accepted," Manny said, patting his jaguar's side proudly. "Since Tor-tor came out and met her challenge, she probably believes him to be our pack leader. An acceptable mate."

"What now?" Carrera asked. "They've pulled back, but haven't left. As a matter of fact, they seem to be massing down the chasm a bit, blocking any retreat back to the swamp lake."

Manny shook his head. "I don't know what they're doing. But Tor-tor has bought us some time. I say we use it. Get that fire lit and keep our guard up."

Nate watched the bulk of the pack flow down into the jungle chasm. What *were* they doing?

"We've got company," Carrera said, voice tense again. She pointed in the opposite direction, deeper up the canyon.

Nate turned his attention. In that direction, he saw nothing but the dark jungle and the broken landscape of rock at the foot of the cliff. "What did you—"

Then movement caught his eye.

A short way up the chasm, a dark figure stepped more fully out of the jungle fringe and onto the exposed shale. It was a human figure. A man. He was as much a shadow as the cats, black from head to toe. He lifted an arm, then turned and began to walk up the canyon, keeping in plain sight. They watched him, stunned.

"It must be one of the Ban-ali," Nate said.

The figure stopped, turned their way, and seemed to be waiting.

"I think he wants us to follow him," Manny said.

"And the jaguars aren't leaving us much choice," Carrera said. "They've settled into the jungle below us."

The distant figure simply stood.

"What do we do?" Carrera asked.

Nate answered, "We follow him. It's why we came. To find the Ban-ali. Perhaps this was their last test, the jaguar pack."

"Or it could be another trap," Kostos said.

"I don't see we have much choice," Carrera said. "I have a feeling we go or the pack will finish us off."

Nate glanced over his shoulder to the deeper depths of the cave. Ten yards back, Kelly, Kouwe and the others were still gathered around Frank, now stripped to his boxers. The man seemed to be sedated. Anna stood, holding an IV bag at shoulder height. Kelly had one of her brother's stumped limbs already wrapped in a bandage and was tying off a vessel in the other. Kouwe knelt beside her, ready with the bandages for his other limb. Around them, empty syringe wrappers and small plastic drug bottles littered the cave floor.

"I'll see if Frank can be moved."

"We leave no one behind," Kostos said.

Nate nodded, glad to hear it. He crossed to the others. "How's Frank doing?" he asked Kouwe.

"He's lost a lot of blood. Once he's stable, Kelly wants to transfuse him."

Nate sighed. "We may have to move him."

"What?" Kelly asked, tying off a suture. "He can't be moved!" Panic, exhaustion, and disbelief hardened her words.

Nate crouched as Kelly and Kouwe began bandaging the second stump. Frank moaned softly as his leg was jarred.

As they worked, Nate explained what had happened at the cave's entrance. "We've been contacted by the Ban-ali. Perhaps invited to continue on to their village. I suspect the invitation is a one-time offer."

Kouwe nodded. "We must've passed some last challenge, survived some gauntlet," the professor said, parroting Nate's early assessment. "Now we've earned the right to move onward by proving ourselves worthy."

"But Frank . . . ?" Kelly said.

"I can rig up a stretcher out of bamboo and palm fronds," Kouwe said softly, touching Kelly's hand. "Knowing these tribesmen, if we don't move him, he'll be killed. We'll all be killed."

Nate watched the woman's face tighten with fear. Her eyes glazed. *First her daughter, now her brother.*

Nate sank down beside her and put his arm around her. "I'll make sure he gets where we're going safely. Once there, Olin can get the radio up and running." Nate glanced to the Russian.

Olin nodded his head vigorously. "I know I can at least get the GPS working properly to send out a decent signal."

"And once that's done, help will arrive. They'll airlift your brother out. He'll make it. We all will."

Kelly leaned into him, softening against him. "Do you promise?" she said, her voice soft with tears.

He tightened his embrace. "Of course I do." But as Nate stared at the pale face of her brother, with blood slowly seeping through the man's new bandages, he prayed it was a promise he could keep.

Kelly shifted in his hold, and her voice was stronger when she spoke. "Then let's go."

He helped her to her feet.

They quickly began arranging for their departure. Kostos and Manny crossed to the jungle and gathered material to construct the makeshift stretcher, while Kelly and Kouwe stabilized Frank as well as they could. Soon they were ready to head out again into the night.

Nate met Carrera at the cave entrance.

"Our visitor's still out there," she said.

In the distance, the lone shadowy figure stood.

Kostos raised his voice, returning to make sure everything was in order. "Keep together! Keep alert!"

Nate and Carrera separated. The group filed out between them with the sergeant in the lead. Near the end of the line, Manny and Olin carried the stretcher, the patient lashed to the bamboo for extra security. The men in the party would take turns hauling Frank.

As the stretcher passed, Kelly followed last. Then Nate and Carrera moved in step behind her.

Just past the entrance, the toe to Nate's boot knocked an object from the shale, something dusty and discarded. Nate bent to pick it up and inspected it.

They couldn't leave this behind.

He knocked off the dirt and stepped forward. He slipped in front of Manny, wiped the last bit of dust from the brim of Frank's Red Sox cap, and placed it back on the stricken man's head.

As Nate turned to return to his place in line, he found Kelly's eyes on his, tears glistening. She offered him a shadow of a sad smile. He nodded, accepting her silent gratitude.

Nate took his position beside Carrera. He studied the dark jungle and the solitary figure in the distance.

Where did the path lead from here?

FOURTEEN

Habitation

AUGUST 16, 4:13 A.M.
AMAZON JUNGLE

Louis floated in his canoe, awaiting news from his trackers. Dawn was still hours away. Stars shone in the clear sky, but the moon had set, casting the swamp into deep shadows. Through night-vision scopes, Louis watched for any sign of his men.

Nothing.

He grimaced. As he waited in the canoe, he felt his plan crumbling around him. *What was going on out there?* His ruse to get the Ranger team fleeing had been successful. But what now?

At midnight, Louis's team had crossed the swamp in their canoes, hauled overland from the river. As the group neared the far shore, flares had blossomed into the sky farther up the chasm, near the southern cliffs. Shots were fired, echoing down to the swamp.

Using binoculars, Louis had watched a shadowy firefight. The Ranger team was again clearly under attack. But from his vantage, Louis could not see who or what was attacking them. His attempts to contact Jacques's recon team had failed. His lieutenant had gone mysteriously silent.

Needing information, Louis had sent a small team ashore, his best trackers, outfitted with night-vision and infrared equipment, to investigate what was happening. He and the others remained a safe distance offshore in the canoes and waited.

Two hours had passed, and so far, there was no word, not even a radio message from the trackers. Sharing his canoe were three men and his mistress. They all watched the far shore with binoculars.

Tshui was the first to spot a man slip from the jungle. She pointed, making a small sound of warning.

Louis swung his glasses. It was the leader of the tracking team. He waved for them to cross to shore. "At last," Louis mumbled, lowering his scopes.

The convoy of canoes swept to the boggy banks. Louis was one of the first on shore. He silently signaled his men to set up a defensive perimeter, then crossed to the lead tracker.

The dark-haired man, a German mercenary named Brail, nodded in greeting. He was short, no taller than five feet, painted in camouflage and clad in black clothes.

"What did you find?" Louis asked him.

The man spoke with a thick German accent. "Jaguars, a pack of fifteen or so."

Louis nodded, not surprised. Across the swamp, they had heard the strange growls and cries.

"But these were no ordinary jaguars," Brail

continued. "More like monsters. Three times normal size. There's a body I can show you."

"Go on," Louis said, waving this away for now. "What happened to the others?"

Brail continued his report, describing how the trackers had been forced to move with care so as not to be spotted. The rest of his four-man team were positioned in trees up the chasm. "The pack is leaving, heading deeper into the canyon. They appear to be herding the remaining members of the enemy team ahead of them."

Brail held out an open palm. "After the cats left the area, we found these on a mauled corpse." The tracker held two silver bars affixed to a scrap of khaki. They were captain's bars. The leader of the Rangers.

"Why aren't the jaguars attacking the rest?" Louis asked.

Brail touched his night-vision scope. "I spotted someone, an Indian from the look of him, leading them from farther up the canyon."

"One of the Ban-ali?"

The man shrugged.

Who else could it be? Louis wondered. He pondered this newest information. Louis could not let the others get too far ahead, especially if the Rangers had made successful contact with the strange tribe. With the prize so close, Louis dared not lose them now.

But the surviving jaguars could prove a difficulty. They stood between his team and the others. The pack would have to be eliminated as quietly as possible without spooking his true prey.

Louis studied the dark forest. The time of slinking in the others' shadows was nearing an end. Once he knew where the village was located and evaluated its defenses, he could take his plan to its final stage.

"Where are the cats now?" Louis asked. "Are they all heading up the canyon?"

Brail grunted sourly. "For the moment. If there's any change, my scouts will radio back to us. Luckily, with the infrared scopes, the bastards are easy to spot. Large and hot."

Louis nodded, satisfied. "What about any other hostiles?"

"We swept the area, *Herr Doktor*. No heat signatures."

Good. Then at least for the moment, the Rangers were still keeping attention diverted from Louis's team. But this close to the Ban-ali lands, Louis knew such an advantage would not last long. He and his team would have to move quickly from here. But first, for his plan to proceed, the path ahead had to be cleared of the jaguar pack.

He turned and found Tshui standing at his shoulder, as silent and deadly as any jungle cat. He reached and ran a finger tenderly along her cheekbone. She leaned into his touch. His mistress of poisons and potions.

"Tshui, *ma chérie*, it seems once again we must call upon your talents."

5:44 A.M.

Nate's shoulders ached from carrying the stretcher. They had been marching for over two hours. Off to the east, the sky was already glowing a soft rose with the promise of dawn.

"How much farther?" Manny huffed from the head of the stretcher. He voiced the question on all their minds.

"I don't know, but there's no going back from here," Nate said, winded.

"Not unless you want to be someone's morning snack," Private Carrera reminded them, maintaining a vigil on their back trail.

All night long, the jaguar pack had dogged their trail, sticking mostly to the jungles that fringed the cliffs. An occasional bolder individual would stalk the loose shale, a silhouette against the black rock.

Their presence kept Tor-tor on edge. The jaguar would hiss under his breath and pace around and around the stretcher, on guard. His eyes flashed an angry gold.

For them all, the only safe path from here was forward, following the lone figure. The tribesman maintained a quarter-mile lead on them, keeping a pace they could follow.

But exhaustion was quickly setting in. After so many days with so little sleep, everyone was bone tired. The entire team moved at a snail's pace, feet dragging, stumbling often. Still, as hard as the night journey was on all their nerves, one member of their party suffered the most.

Kelly never left her brother's side: constantly checking Frank's vital signs and adjusting his bloody bandages as they walked. Her face remained ashen in the starlight, her eyes scared and exhausted. When she wasn't acting as his doctor, she simply held Frank's hand, just a sister at these moments, clearly trying to will him her own strength.

The only blessing was that the morphine and sedatives were keeping the wounded man in a doped drowse, though he would occasionally moan. Each time this happened, Kelly would tense and her face would twist as if the pain were her own, which Nate suspected was partly true. She clearly suffered as much as her twin brother.

"Attention!" Kostos called from up front. "We're changing direction."

Nate peered ahead. All night they had been trudging along the hard-packed soil where the jungle met the rocky escarpment of the cliffs. He now watched their guide cross the escarpment toward one of the many shattered cracks in the cliff face. It ran from top to bottom, as wide as a two-car garage.

The tribesman stepped to the entrance, turned back to stare at them, then, without a signal or any other sign of welcome, he strode into the chasm.

"I'll check it out first," Kostos said.

The Ranger trotted ahead as they slowed their pace. He had a flashlight secured under his M-16. The light remained steady and fixed on his target. He dashed to the side of the crack's entrance, took a breath, then twisted to shine his light down it. He remained fixed in this position for several seconds, then waved them over with one arm, maintaining his post. "It's a side chute! A steep one."

The group converged upon the Ranger.

Nate squinted up its length. The crack extended the full height of the cliff, open at the top to let starlight shine down it. The way was quite steep, but there appeared to be crude steps climbing the chute.

Professor Kouwe pointed. "It looks like there might be another canyon or valley beyond this one."

Anna Fong stood beside him. "Or perhaps it's a switchback of this same canyon, a shortcut to the upper level."

In the distance, the lone tribesman climbed the stone steps, seemingly unconcerned whether they followed or not. But his nonchalance was not shared by all. Behind them, the jaguar pack drew closer, growling and whining.

"I say we need to make a decision," Carrera said.

Kostos frowned at the tall walls that framed the crude staircase. "It could be a trap, an ambush."

Zane took a step toward the chute. "We're already in a trap, Sergeant. I for one prefer to take my chances with the unknown rather than with what lies behind us."

No one argued. The memory of the deaths of Warczak and Waxman remained fresh and bloody.

Kostos moved on ahead of Zane. "Let's go. Keep alert."

The chute was wide enough that Manny and Nate could walk side by side, the stretcher between them. This made mounting the steep stairs a bit easier. Still, the climb was daunting.

Olin moved down to them. "Do either of you need to be relieved?"

Manny grimaced. "I can last a little longer."

Nate nodded, agreeing.

So they began the long climb. As they progressed,

Nate and Manny were soon lagging behind the others. Kelly kept near them, her face worried. Carrera maintained the rear guard.

Nate's knees ached, his thighs burned, and his shoulders knotted with exhaustion. But he kept on. "It can't be much farther," he said aloud, more to himself than anyone else.

"I hope not," Kelly said.

"He's strong," Manny said, nodding to Frank.

"Strong will only get you so far," she answered.

"He'll pull through this," Nate assured her. "He's got his lucky Red Sox cap, doesn't he?"

Kelly sighed. "He loves that old thing. Did you know he was a shortstop for a farm club? Triple A division." Her voice lowered to a strained whisper. "My father was so proud. We all were. There was even talk of Frank going into the majors. Then he got in a skiing accident, screwed up his knee. It ended his career."

Manny grunted in surprise. "And that's his *lucky* hat?"

Kelly brushed the cap's brim, a trace of a smile on her lips. "For three seasons, he played a game he loved with all his heart. Even after the accident, he was never bitter. He felt himself the luckiest man in the world."

Nate stared down at the cap, envying Frank his moment in the sun. Had life ever been that simple for him? Maybe the man's cap was indeed lucky. And right now, they needed all the luck they could get.

Carrera interrupted their reminiscing. "The jaguars . . . they've stopped following us."

Nate glanced down the stairs. One of the giant cats stood at the entrance. It was the female leader of the pack. She paced back and forth below. Tor-tor stared down at her, eyes flashing. The female stared at the smaller cat for a moment—then, in a shadowy blur, she fled back into the jungle.

"The lower valley must be the pack's territory," Manny said. "Another line of defense."

"But what are they protecting?" Carrera asked.

A call sounded from up ahead. It was Sergeant Kostos. He had stopped ten steps from the end of the chasm and waved them to join him.

As the group gathered, the eastern skies brightened with dawn. Beyond the stepped chute, a valley opened, thick with dense vegetation and towering trees. Somewhere a stream babbled brightly, and in the distance, a waterfall grumbled.

"The Ban-ali lands," Professor Kouwe said.

Olin approached Manny and Nate. He reached for the stretcher. "We'll take over from here."

Nate was surprised to see Richard Zane at the Russian's side. But Nate didn't complain. They passed the stretcher to the new bearers. Relieved of the weight, Nate felt a hundred pounds lighter. His arms felt like they wanted to float up.

He and Manny climbed up to Kostos.

"The Indian disappeared," the sergeant grumbled.

Nate saw that the tribesman had indeed vanished. "Even so, we know where we have to go."

"We should wait until the sun's fully up," Kostos said.

Manny frowned. "The Ban-ali have been tracking us since we first set out into the jungles . . . night and day. Whether the sun is up or not, we won't see a single soul unless they want us to."

"Besides," Nate said, "we have a man down. The sooner we reach a village or whatever, the better Frank's chances. I say we forge on."

Kostos sighed, then nodded. "Okay, but keep together."

The sergeant straightened and led the way from there.

With each step, the new day grew brighter. Sunrise in the Amazon was often sudden. Overhead, the stars were swallowed in the spreading rosy glow of dawn. The cloudless sky promised a hot day to come.

The group paused at the top of the chasm. A thin trail led down into the jungle. But where did it go? In the valley below, there was no sign of habitation. No wood smoke rising, no voices echoing.

Before moving forward, Kostos stood with binoculars, studying the valley. "Damn it," he mumbled.

"What's wrong?" Zane asked.

"This canyon is just a switchback of the one we were in." He pointed to the right. "But it appears this canyon is cut off from the one below it by steep cliffs."

Nate lifted his own binoculars and followed where the sergeant pointed. Through the jungle, he could just make out where a small stream flowed down the canyon's center. He followed its course until it vanished over a steep drop, down into the lower canyon, the one they had been marching through all night, the domain of the giant jaguars.

"We're boxed in here," Kostos said.

Nate swung his binoculars in the opposite direction. He spotted another waterfall. This one tumbled down into this canyon from a massive cliff on the far side. In fact, the entire valley was closed in by rock walls on three sides, and the steep cliff on the fourth.

It's a totally isolated chunk of jungle, Nate realized.

The sergeant continued, "I don't like this. The only way up here is this chute."

As Nate lowered his glasses, the edge of the sun crested the eastern skies, bathing the jungle ahead in sunlight, creating a green glow. A flock of blue-and-gold macaws took wing from a rookery near the misty cliffs and sailed past overhead. The spray from the two waterfalls at either end of the valley made the air almost sparkle in the first rays of the sun.

"Like a bit of Eden," Professor Kouwe said in a hushed voice.

With the touch of light, the jungle awoke with birdsong and the twitter of monkeys. Butterflies as big as dinner plates fluttered at the fringe. Something furry and quick darted back into the jungle. Isolated or not, life had found its way into this verdant valley.

But what else had made its home here?

"What are we going to do?" Anna asked.

Everyone remained silent for several seconds.

Nate finally spoke. "I don't think we have much choice but to proceed."

Kostos scowled, then nodded. "Let's see where this leads. But stay alert."

The group cautiously descended the short slope to the jungle's edge. Kostos led once again, Nate at his side with his shotgun. They marched in a tight bunch down the path. As soon as they entered under the bower of the shadowed forest, the scents of orchids and flowering vines filled the air, so thick they could almost taste it.

Still, as sweet as the air was, the constant tension continued. What secrets lay out here? What dangers? Every shadow was suspect.

It took Nate fifteen minutes of hiking before he noticed something strange about the forest around them. Exhaustion must have dulled his senses. His feet slowed. His mouth dropped open.

Manny bumped into him. "What's the matter?"

His brow furrowed, Nate crossed a few steps off the path.

"What are you doing, Rand?" Kostos asked.

"These trees . . ." Nate's sense of wonder overwhelmed him, cutting through his unease.

The others stopped and stared. "What about them?" Manny asked.

Nate turned in a slow circle. "As a botanist, I recognize most of the plants around here." He pointed and named names. "Silk cotton, laurels, figs, mahogany, rosewood, palms of every variety. The usual trees you'd see in a rain forest. But . . ." Nate's voice died away.

"But what?" Kostos asked.

Nate stepped to a thin-boled tree. It stretched a hundred feet into the air and burst into a dense mass of fronds. Giant serrated cones hung from its underside. "Do you know what this is?"

"It looks like a palm," the sergeant said. "So what?"

"It's not!" Nate slapped the trunk with his palm. "It's a goddamn cycadeoid."

"A what?"

"A species of tree thought long extinct, dating back to the Cretaceous period. I've only seen examples of it in the fossil record."

"Are you sure?" Anna Fong asked.

Nate nodded. "I did my thesis on paleobotany." He crossed to another plant, a fernlike bush that towered twice his height. Each frond was as tall as he was and as wide as his stretched arms. He shook one of the titanic leaves. "And this is a goddamn giant club moss. It's supposed to have gone extinct during the Carboniferous period. And that's not all. They're all around us. Glossopterids, lycopods, podocarp conifers . . ." He pointed out the strange plants. "And that's just the things I can classify."

Nate pointed his shotgun to a tree with a coiled and spiraled trunk. "I have no idea what that thing is." He faced the others, shedding his exhaustion like a second skin, and lifted his arms. "We're in a goddamn living fossil museum."

"How's that possible?" Zane asked.

Kouwe answered, "This place is isolated, a pocket in time. Anything could have sheltered here for eons."

"And geologically this region dates back to the Paleozoic era," Nate added, excited. "The Amazon basin was once a freshwater inland sea before changes in tectonics opened the sea to the greater ocean and drained it away. What we have here is a little peek at that ancient past. It's amazing!"

Kelly spoke up from beside the stretcher. "Amazing or not, I need to get Frank somewhere safe."

Her words drew Nate back to the present, back to their situation. He nodded, embarrassed at his distraction in the face of their predicament.

Kostos cleared his throat. "Let's push on."

The group followed his lead.

Fascinated by the forest, Nate hung back. His eyes studied the foliage around him, no longer peering at the shadows, but fixed on the jungle itself. As a trained botanist, he gaped in disbelief at the riotous flora: stalked horsetails the size of organ pipes, ferns that dwarfed modern-day palms, massive primitive conifers with cones the size of VW bugs. The mix of the ancient and the new was simply astounding, a merged ecosystem unlike any seen before.

Professor Kouwe walked beside him now. "What do you think about all this?"

Nate shook his head. "I don't know. Other prehistoric groves have been discovered in the past. In China, a forest of dawn redwoods was discovered in the eighties. In Africa, a grotto of rare ferns. And most recently, in Australia, an entire stand of prehistoric trees, long thought extinct, was found in a remote rain forest." Nate glanced to Kouwe for emphasis. "So considering how little of the Amazon has been explored, it's actually more surprising that we've *not* found such a grove before."

"The jungle hides its secrets well," Kouwe said.

As they walked, the canopy overhead grew denser, the forest taller. The morning sunlight dwindled to a green glow. It was as if they were walking back into twilight.

Further conversation died as everyone watched the forest. By now, even nonbotanists could tell this jungle was unusual. The number of prehistoric plants began to outnumber the modern-day counterparts. Trees grew huge, ferns towered, strange twisted forms wound among the mix. They passed a spiky bromeliad as large as a small cottage. Massive flowers, as large as pumpkins, grew from vines and scented the air thickly.

It was a greenhouse of amazing proportion.

Kostos suddenly stopped ahead, freezing in place, eyes on the trail, weapon raised and ready. He then slowly motioned them to get down.

The group crouched. Nate shifted his shotgun. Only then did he notice what had startled the Ranger.

Nate stared off to the left, the right, even behind them. It was like one of those computerized pictures that appeared at first to be just a blur of random dots, but when stared at cross-eyed, from a certain angle, a 3-D image suddenly and startlingly appeared.

Nate suddenly and startlingly saw the jungle in a new light.

High in the trees, mounted among the thick branches, platforms had been built, with small dwellings atop them. The roofs of many were woven from the living leaves and branches, offering natural camouflage. These half-living structures blended perfectly with their host trees.

As Nate looked closer, what had appeared to be vines and stranglers crisscrossing between the trees and draping to the ground were in fact natural bridges and ladders. One of these ladders was only a few yards to Nate's right. Flowers grew along its length. It was alive, too.

As he stared around, it was hard to say where

man-made structure ended and living began. Half artificial, half growing plant. The blend was so astounding, the camouflage so perfect.

Without them even knowing it, they had already entered the Ban-ali village.

Ahead, larger dwellings climbed even taller trees, multilevel with terraces and patios. But even these were well camouflaged with bark, vine, and leaf, making them difficult to discern.

As they stared, no one in their party moved. One question was on all their faces: *Where were the inhabitants of these treetop homes?*

Tor-tor growled a deep warning.

Then like the village itself, Nate suddenly saw them. They had been there all along, unmoving, silent, all around. Bits of living shadow. With their bodies painted black, they had melded into the darkness between the trees and under bushes.

One of the tribesmen stepped from his concealing gloom and onto the path. He seemed undaunted by the weapons in their hands.

Nate was certain it was their earlier guide. The one who had led them here. His black hair was braided with bits of leaf and flower in it, adding to the natural camouflage. As he stepped forth, his hands were empty of any weapons. In fact, the tribesman was naked, except for a simple loincloth. He stared at the group, his face hard and unreadable.

Then without a word, he turned and walked down the path.

"He must want us to follow him again," Professor Kouwe said, climbing to his feet. The others slowly stood.

In the woods, more tribesmen remained silent sentinels, bathed in shadows.

Kostos hesitated.

"If they had wanted to kill us," Professor Kouwe added, "we'd be dead already."

Kostos frowned, but the Ranger reluctantly continued on after the tribesman.

As they walked, Nate continued to study the village and its silent inhabitants. He caught occasional glimpses of smaller faces in windows, children and women. Nate glanced to the men half hidden in the forest. *Tribal warriors or scouts*, he guessed.

Their painted faces bore the familiar Amerindian bone structure, slightly Asiatic, a genetic tie to their ancestors who had first crossed the Bering Strait from Asia into Alaska some fifty thousand years ago and settled the Americas. But who were they? How did they get here? Where did their roots trace? Despite the danger and silent threat, Nate was dying to learn more about these people and their history— especially since it was tied to his own.

He stared around the forest. Had his father walked this same path? Considering this possibility, Nate found his lungs tightening, old emotions surfacing. He was so close to discovering the truth about his father.

As they continued, it soon became apparent that the team was being led toward a sunnier clearing in the distance.

The forest around the thin track opened to either side as they reached the clearing. A ring of giant cycads and primitive conifers circled the open glade.

A shallow-banked stream meandered through the sunny space, sparkling and gurgling.

Their guide continued ahead, but the team stopped at the threshold, shocked.

In the center of the clearing, practically filling the entire space, stood a massive tree, a specimen Nate had never seen before. It had to tower at least thirty stories high, its white-barked trunk ten yards in diameter. Thick roots knobbed out of the dark soil like pale knees. A few even spanned the stream beside it before disappearing back into the loam.

Overhead, the tree's branches spread in distinct terraces, not unlike giant redwoods. But instead of needles, this specimen sported wide palmate green leaves, fluttering gently to reveal silver undersides and clusters of husked seed pods, similar to coconuts.

Nate stared, dumbstruck. He didn't even know where to begin classifying this specimen. Maybe a new species of primitive gymnospore, but he was far from sure. The nuts did look a bit like those found on a modern cat's claw plant, but this was a much more ancient specimen.

As he studied the giant, he realized one other thing about the tree. Even this towering hardwood bore signs of habitation. Small clusters of hutlike dwellings rested atop thicker branches or nestled against the trunk. *Constructed to mimic the tree's seed pods*, Nate realized, amazed.

Across the way, their tribal guide slipped between two gnarled roots and disappeared into shadow. Stepping to the side for a better look, Nate realized the shadow was in fact an arched opening into the tree's base, a doorway. Nate stared up at the clustered dwellings. There were no vine ladders here. So how did one reach the dwellings? Was there a tunnel winding through the trunk? Nate began to step forward to investigate.

But Manny grabbed his arm. "Look." The biologist pointed off to the side.

Nate glanced over. Distracted by the white-barked giant, he had failed to notice a squat log cabin across the clearing. It was boxy, but sturdily constructed of logs and a thatched roof. It seemed out of place here, the only structure built on the ground.

"Are those solar cells on its roof?" Manny asked.

Nate squinted and raised his binoculars. Atop the cabin, two small flat black panels glinted in the morning sunshine. They indeed appeared to be solar panels. Intrigued, Nate examined the cabin more thoroughly through his binoculars. The structure was windowless, its door just a flap of woven palm leaves.

Nate's attention caught on something beside the door, a familiar object, bright in the sunshine. It was a tall snakewood staff, polished from years of hard use, crowned by *hoko* feathers.

Nate felt the ground shift under his feet.

It was his father's walking stick.

Dropping his binoculars, Nate stumbled toward the cabin.

"Rand!" Kostos barked at him.

But he was beyond listening. His feet began to run. The others followed him, keeping the group together. Zane and Olin grunted as they struggled with the stretcher.

Nate hurried to the cabin and then skidded to a stop, his breath caught. His mouth grew dry as he stared at the walking stick. Initials were carved in the wood: *C.R.*

Carl Rand.

Tears rose in Nate's eyes. At the time of his father's disappearance, Nate had refused to fathom the man could be dead. He had needed to cling to hope, lest despair cripple him, leaving him unable to pursue the yearlong search. Even when his financial resources had run dry and he was forced to concede his father was gone, he hadn't cried. Over such a prolonged time, sorrow had devolved into a black depression, a pit that consumed his life these past four years.

But now, with a tangible bit of evidence that his father had been here, tears flowed freely down his cheeks.

Nate did not entertain the possibility that his father was still alive. Such miracles were relegated to novels. The structure here bore evidence of long disuse. Dead leaves, blown from the forest, lay windswept into a pile against the cabin's front, undisturbed by any footprints.

Nate stepped forward and pushed open the woven flap. It was dark inside. Grabbing the flashlight from his field jacket, Nate clicked it on. A tailless rat, a *paca*, skittered from a hiding place and dashed through a crack in the far wall. Dust lay thick, tracked with little paw prints, along with rodent droppings.

Nate shone his light around.

Inside, near the back wall, four hammocks lay strung from the raftered ceiling, empty and untouched. Closer still, a small wooden bench had been constructed. Atop it was spread a collection of lab equipment, including a laptop computer.

Like the wooden staff on the porch, Nate recognized the tiny microscope and specimen jars. They were his father's equipment. He stepped into the dark space and opened the laptop. It whirred to electronic life, startling Nate. He stumbled backward.

"The solar cells," Manny said from the doorway. "Still giving it juice."

Nate wiped spiderwebs from his hands. "My father was here," he mumbled, numb. "This is his equipment."

Kouwe spoke a few steps back. "The Indian is returning . . . with company."

Nate stared at the computer for a second more. Dust motes floated in the air, sparkling bright in the morning sunlight streaming through the open flap. The room was aromatic with wood oils and dried palm thatch. But underlying it was an odor of ashes and age. No one had been here for at least half a year.

What had happened to them?

Wiping his eyes, Nate turned to the doorway. Across the glade, he watched the black-painted tribesman march toward the cabin. At his side strode a smaller man, a tiny Indian. He could be no more than four feet tall. His burnished skin was unpainted, except for a prominent design in red on his belly and the familiar blue palm print centered just above the navel.

Stepping back into the sunlight, Nate joined the others.

The newcomer had pierced ears from which hung

feathers, not unlike the typical decorations of the Yanomamo. But he also bore a headband with a prominent beetle decoration in the center. Its black carapace glistened brightly. It was one of the carnivorous locusts that had killed Corporal Jorgensen.

Professor Kouwe glanced over at Nate. His friend had noticed the odd bit of decoration, too. Here was further evidence that the attack truly had originated from this place.

Like a knife through his gut, Nate felt a surge of anger. Not only had this tribe been instrumental in the deaths of half their party, they had held the survivors of his father's expedition prisoner for four years. Fury and pain swelled through him.

Kouwe must have sensed Nate's emotion. "Remain quiet, Nate. Let us see how this plays out."

Their guide led the newcomer to them, then stepped aside, in clear deference to the smaller man.

The tiny Indian glanced at the group, studying each of them, eyes narrowing slightly at the sight of Tor-tor. Finally he pointed to the stretcher, then jabbed at Olin and Zane. "Bring the hurt man," the Indian said in stilted English, then waved an arm at everyone else. "Others stay here."

With these simple commands, the diminutive man turned and headed back to the huge white-barked tree again.

Stunned, no one moved. The shock of hearing spoken English cut through Nate's anger.

Olin and Zane remained standing, not budging.

The taller Indian guide waved an arm angrily, indicating they should follow his fellow tribesman.

"No one's going anywhere," Sergeant Kostos said. Private Carrera moved forward, too. Both had their weapons ready. "We're not splitting up the group."

The tribesman scowled. He pointed at the retreating tiny figure. "Healer," the man said, struggling with the words. "Good healer."

Again the spoken English gave them pause.

"They must have learned the language from your father's expedition," Anna Fong mumbled.

Or from my father himself, Nate thought.

Kouwe turned to Kelly. "I think we should obey. I don't think they mean Frank any harm. But just in case, I can go with the stretcher."

"I'm not leaving my brother's side," Kelly said, stepping closer to the stretcher.

Zane argued, too. "And I'm not going at all. I'm staying where the guns are."

"Don't worry," the professor said. "I'll take your place. It's my turn anyway."

Zane was only too happy to be unburdened of the stretcher. Once free, he quickly scooted into the shadow of Sergeant Kostos, who wore a perpetual scowl.

Kelly moved to Olin at the head of the stretcher. "I'll take the other end." The Russian started to object but was cut off. "You get the GPS working," she ordered. "You're the only one who can get the damned thing fixed."

He reluctantly nodded and let her take the bamboo poles of the stretcher. She struggled with the weight for a moment, then with a heave, got her legs under her.

Nate shifted forward, going to her aid. "I can take Frank," he offered. "You can follow."

"No," she said harshly, teeth clenched. She tossed her head back toward the cabin. "See if you can find out what happened here."

Before any other objections could be raised, Kelly lurched forward. Kouwe followed at his end of the stretcher.

The tribesman looked relieved at their cooperation and hurried ahead, leading them toward the giant tree.

From the dirt porch of the cabin, Nate glanced again at the clusters of dwellings nestled high up the white-barked tree, realizing it was a view his father must have seen. As Nate stood, he sought some connection to his dead father. He remained standing until Kelly and Kouwe disappeared into the tree tunnel.

As the other team members began unhooking packs, Nate returned his attention to the empty cabin. Through the doorway, the laptop's screen shone with a ghostly glow in the dark room. A lonely, empty light.

Nate sighed, wondering again what had happened to the others.

Struggling under the weight of her twin brother, Kelly entered the dark opening in the massive trunk of the tree. Her focus remained divided between Frank's weakening state and the strangeness before her.

By now, Frank's bandages were fully soaked with blood. Flies swarmed and crawled through the gore, an easy meal. He needed a transfusion as soon as possible. In her head, she ran through the additional care needed: a new IV line, fresh pressure bandages, more morphine and antibiotics. Frank had to survive until the rescue helicopter could get here.

Still, as much as horror and fear filled her heart, Kelly could not help but be amazed by what she found beyond the entrance to the tree. She had expected to find a cramped steep staircase. Instead, the path beyond the doorway was wide—a gentle, sweeping course winding and worming its way up toward the treetop dwellings. The walls were smooth and polished to a deep honey color. A smattering of blue handprints decorated the walls. Beyond the entrance, every ten yards down the passage, a thin window, not unlike a castle tower's arrow slit, broke through to the outside, bright with morning sunlight, illuminating the way.

Following their guide, Kelly and Kouwe worked up the winding path. The floor was smooth, but woody enough for good traction. And though the grade was mild, Kelly was soon wheezing with exertion. But adrenaline and fear kept her moving: fear for her brother, fear for them all.

"This tunnel seems almost natural," Kouwe mumbled behind her. "The smoothness of the walls, the perfection of the spiral. It's like this tunnel is some tubule or channel in the tree, not a hewn passage."

Kelly licked her lips but found no voice. Too tired, too scared. The professor's words drew her attention to the floor and walls. Now that he had mentioned it, the passage showed not a single ax or chisel mark. Only the windows were crude, clearly man-made, hacked through to the outside. The difference between the two was striking. Had the tribe stumbled upon this winding tubule within the tree and taken advantage of it? The dwellings they'd seen on the way here proved that the Ban-ali were skilled engineers, incorporating the artificial with the natural. Perhaps the same was true here.

The professor made one last observation: "The flies are gone."

Kelly glanced over her shoulder. The flock of flies nattering and crawling among her brother's bloody bandages had indeed vanished.

"The bugs flew off shortly after we entered the tree," Kouwe said. "It must be some repellent property of the wood's aromatic oils."

Kelly had also noticed the musky odor of the tree. It had struck her as vaguely familiar, similar to dried eucalyptus, medicinal and pleasant, but laced with a deeper loamy smell that hinted at something earthy and ripe.

Staring over her shoulder, Kelly saw how heavily soaked her brother's bandages were. He could not last much longer, not with the continuing blood loss. Something had to be done. As she walked, cold dread iced her veins. Despite her exhaustion, her pace increased.

As they climbed, openings appeared in the tunnel wall. Passing by them, Kelly noted that the passages led either into one of the hutlike dwellings or out onto branches as wide as driveways, with huts in the distance.

And still they were led onward and upward.

Despite her anxiety, Kelly was soon stumbling,

dragging, gasping, eyes stinging with running sweat. She desperately wanted to rest, but she could not let Frank down.

Their guide noticed them drifting farther and farther behind him. He backed down and studied the situation. He moved to Kelly's side.

"I help." He struck a fist on his chest. "I strong." He nudged her aside and took her end of the stretcher.

She was too weak to object, too winded to mumble a thanks.

As Kelly stepped aside, the two men now continued upward, moving faster. Kelly kept pace beside the stretcher. Frank was so pale, his breathing shallow. Relieved of the burden, Kelly's full attention focused back on her brother. She pulled out her stethoscope and listened to his chest. His heartbeat thudded dully, his lungs crackled with rales. His body was rapidly giving out, heading into hypovolemic shock. The hemorrhaging had to be stopped.

Focused on her brother's condition, she failed to notice that they'd reached the tunnel's end. The spiraling passage terminated abruptly at an opening that looked identical to the archway at the base of the giant tree. But instead of leading back into the morning sunshine, this archway led into a cavernous structure with a saucer-shaped floor.

Kelly gaped at the interior, again lit by rough-hewn slits high up the curved walls. The space, spherical in shape, had to be thirty yards across, a titanic bubble in the wood, half protruding out of the main trunk.

"It's like a massive gall," Kouwe said, referring to the woody protuberances sometimes found on oaks or other trees, created by insects or other parasitic conditions.

Kelly appreciated the comparison. But it wasn't insects that inhabited this gall. Around the curved walls, woven hammocks hung from pegs, a dozen at least. In a few, naked tribesmen lay sprawled. Others of the Ban-ali worked around them. The handful of prone men and women were showing various signs of illness: a bandaged foot, a splinted arm, a fevered brow. She watched a tribesman with a long gash across his chest wince as a thick pasty substance was applied to his wound by another of his tribe.

Kelly understood immediately what she was seeing.

A hospital ward.

The tiny-framed tribesman who had ordered them here stood a few paces away. His look was sour with impatience. He pointed to one of the hammocks and spoke rapidly in a foreign tongue.

Their guide answered with a nod and led them to the proper hammock.

Professor Kouwe mumbled as they walked. "If I'm not mistaken, that's a dialect of Yanomamo."

Kelly glanced over to him, hearing the shock in the professor's voice.

He explained the significance. "The Yanomamo language has no known counterparts. Their speech patterns and tonal structures are unique unto themselves. A true lingual isolate. It's one of the reasons the Yanomamo are considered one of the oldest Amazonian bloodlines." His eyes were wide upon the men and women in the woody chamber. "The Ban-ali must be an offshoot, a lost tribe of the Yanomamo."

Kelly merely nodded, too full of worry to appreciate the professor's observation. Her attention remained focused on her brother.

Overseen by the tiny Indian, the stretcher was lowered, and Frank was transferred onto the hammock. Kelly hovered nervously at his side. Jarred by the movement, Frank moaned slightly, eyes fluttering. His sedatives must be wearing off.

Kelly reached down to her med pack atop the abandoned stretcher. Before she could gather up her syringe and bottles of morphine, the tiny healer barked orders to his staff. Their guide and another tribesman began to loosen the bandages over Frank's stumps with small bone knives.

"Don't!" Kelly said, straightening.

She was ignored. They continued to work upon the soaked strips. Blood began to flow more thickly.

She moved to the hammock, grabbing the taller man's elbow. "No! You don't know what you're doing. Wait until I have the pressure wraps ready! An IV in place! He'll bleed to death!"

The stronger man broke out of her grasp and scowled at her.

Kouwe intervened. He pointed at Kelly. "She's our *healer*."

The tribesman seemed baffled by this statement and glanced to his own shaman.

The smaller Indian was crouched by the curved wall at the head of the hammock. He had a bowl in his hand, gathering a flow of thick sap from a trough gouged in the wall. "I am healer here," the small man said. "This is Ban-ali medicine. To stop the bleeding. Strong medicine from the *yagga*."

Kelly glanced to Kouwe.

He deciphered. "*Yagga* . . . it's similar to *yakka* . . . a Yanomamo word for mother."

Kouwe stared around at the chamber. "*Yagga* must be their name for this tree. A deity."

The Indian shaman straightened with his bowl, now half full of the reddish sap. Reaching up, he stoppered the thick flow by jamming a wooden peg into a hole at the top of the trough. "Strong medicines," he repeated, lifting the bowl and striding to the hammock. "The blood of the Yagga will stop the blood of the man." It sounded like a rote maxim, a translation of an old adage.

He motioned for the tribesman to cut away one of the two bandages.

Kelly opened her mouth again to object, but Kouwe interrupted her with a squeeze on her arm. "Gather your bandage material and LRS bag," he whispered to her. "Be ready, but for the moment, let's see what this medicine can do."

She bit back her protest, remembering the small Indian girl at the hospital of São Gabriel and how Western medicine had failed her. For the moment, she would yield to the Ban-ali, trusting not the strange little shaman, but rather Professor Kouwe himself. She dropped to her medical pack and burrowed into it, reaching with deft fingers for her wraps and saline bag.

As Kelly retrieved what she needed, her eyes flicked over to the nearby sap channel. *The blood of the Yagga.* The tapped vein could be seen as a dark ribbon in the honeyed wood, extending up from the top of the trough and arching across the roof. Kelly spotted other such veins, each dark vessel leading to one of the other hammocks.

With her bandages in hand, she stood as her brother's bloodied wrap was ripped away. Unprepared, still a sister, not a doctor, Kelly grew faint at the sight: the sharp shard of white bone, the rip of shredded muscle, the gelatinous bruise of ruined flesh. A thick flow of dark blood and clots washed from the raw wound and dribbled through the hammock's webbing.

Kelly suddenly found it difficult to breathe. Sounds grew muted and more acute at the same time. Her vision narrowed upon the limp figure in the bed. *It wasn't Frank*, her mind kept trying to convince her. But another part of her knew the truth. Her brother was doomed. Tears filled her eyes, and a moan rose in her throat, choking her.

Kouwe put his arm around her shoulders, reacting to her distress, pulling her to him.

"Oh, God . . . please . . ." Kelly sobbed.

Oblivious to her outburst, the Ban-ali shaman examined the amputated limb with a determined frown. Then he scooped up a handful of the thick red sap, the color of port wine, and slathered it over the stump.

The reaction was immediate—and violent. Frank's leg jerked up and away as if struck by an electric current. He cried out, even through his stupor, an animal sound.

Kelly stumbled toward him, out of the professor's arms. "Frank!"

The shaman glanced toward her. He mumbled something in his native language and backed away, allowing her to come forward.

She reached her brother, grabbing for his arm. But

Frank's outburst had been as short as it was sudden.
He relaxed back into the hammock. Kelly was sure he
was dead. She leaned over him, sobbing openly.

But his lungs heaved up and down, in deep, shud-
dering breaths.

Alive.

She fell to her knees in relief. His limb, exposed,
stood stark and raw before her. She eyed the wound,
expecting the worst, ready with the bandages.

But they proved unnecessary.

Where the sap had touched the macerated flesh, it
had formed a thick seal. Wide-eyed, she reached and
touched the strange substance. It was no longer sticky,
but leathery and tough, like some type of natural bandage. She glanced to the shaman with awe. The bleeding had stopped, sealed tight.

"The Yagga has found him worthy," the shaman
said. "He will heal."

Stunned, Kelly stood as the shaman carried his
bowl toward the other limb and began to repeat the
miracle. "I can't believe it," she finally said, her voice
as small as a mouse.

Kouwe took her under his arm again. "I know
fifteen different plant species with hemostatic properties, but nothing of this caliber."

Frank's body jerked again as the second leg was
treated.

Afterward, the shaman studied his handiwork for
a few moments, then turned to them. "The Yagga
will protect him from here," he said solemnly.

"Thank you," Kelly said.

The small tribesman glanced back to her brother.
"He is now Ban-ali. One of the Chosen."

Kelly frowned.

The shaman continued, "He must now serve the Yagga in all ways, for all times." With these words, he turned away—but not before adding something in his native tongue, something spoken in a dire, threatening tone.

As he left, Kelly turned to Kouwe, her eyes questioning.

The professor shook his head. "I recognized only one word—*ban-yi*."

"What does that mean?"

Kouwe glanced over to Frank. "Slave."

FIFTEEN

Health Care

AUGUST 16, 11:43 A.M.
HOSPITAL WARD OF THE INSTAR INSTITUTE
LANGLEY, VIRGINIA

Lauren had never known such despair. Her granddaughter drifted in a cloud of pillows and sheets, such a tiny thing with lines and monitor wires running to machines and saline bags. Even through Lauren's contamination suit, she could hear the beep and hiss from the various pieces of equipment in the long narrow room. Little Jessie was no longer the only one confined here. Five other children had become sick over the past day.

And how many more in the coming days? Lauren recalled the epidemiologist's computer model and its stain of red spreading over the United States. She had heard cases were already being reported in Canada, too. Even two children in Germany, who had been vacationing in Florida.

Now she was realizing that Dr. Alvisio's grim

model may have been too conservative in its predictions. Just this morning, Lauren had heard rumors about new cases in Brazil, cases now appearing in healthy adults. These patients were not presenting fevers, like the children, but were instead showing outbreaks of ravaging malignancies and cancers, like those seen in Gerald Clark's body. Lauren already had researchers checking into it.

But right now, she had other concerns.

She sat in a chair beside Jessie's bed. Her grandchild was watching some children's program piped into the video monitor in the room. But no smile ever moved her lips, no laugh. The girl watched it like an automaton, her eyes glassy, her hair plastered to her head from fevered sweat.

There was so little comfort Lauren could offer. The touch of the plastic containment suit was cold and impersonal. All she could do was maintain her post beside the girl, let her know she wasn't alone, let her see a familiar face. But she was not Jessie's mother. Every time the door to the ward swished open, Jessie would turn to see who it was, her eyes momentarily hopeful, then fading to disappointment. Just another nurse or a doctor. Never her mother.

Even Lauren found herself frequently glancing to the door, praying for Marshall to return with some word on Kelly and Frank. Down in the Amazon, the Brazilian evacuation helicopter had left from the Wauwai field base hours ago. Surely the rescuers would've reached the stranded team by now. Surely Kelly was already flying back here.

But so far, no word.

The waiting was growing interminable.

In the bed, Jessie scratched at the tape securing her catheter.

"Hon, leave it be," Lauren said, moving the girl's hand away.

Jessie sighed, sinking back into her pillows. "Where's Mommy?" she asked for the thousandth time that day. "I want Mommy."

"She's coming, hon. But South America is a long way away. Why don't you try to take a nap?"

Jessie frowned. "My mouth hurts."

Lauren reached to the table and lifted a cup with a straw toward the girl, juice with an analgesic in it. "Sip this. It'll make the ouchie go away." Already the girl's mouth had begun to erupt with fever blisters, raw ulcerations along the mucocutaneous margins of her lips. Their appearance was one of the distinct symptoms of the disease. There could now be no denying that Jessie had the plague.

The girl sipped at the cup, her face scrunching sourly, then sat back. "It tastes funny. It's not like Mommy makes."

"I know, honey, but it'll make you feel better."

"Tastes funny . . ." Jessie mumbled again, eyes drifting back to the video screen.

The two sat quietly. Somewhere down the row of beds, one of the children began to sob. In the background, the repetitive jingle of the dancing bear sounded tinny through her suit.

How many more? Lauren wondered. *How many more would grow sick? How many more would die?*

The sigh of a broken pressure seal sounded behind her. Lauren turned as the ward door swished open. A bulky figure in a quarantine suit bowed into the room, carrying his oxygen line. He turned, and through the plastic face shield, Lauren recognized her husband.

She was instantly on her feet. "Marshall . . ."

He waved her down and crossed to the wall to snap in his oxygen line to one of the air bibs. Once done, he strode to the girl's bedside.

"Grandpa!" Jessie said, smiling faintly. The girl's love for her grandfather, the only father figure in her life, was special. It was heartening to see her respond to him.

"How's my little pumpkin?" he said, bending over to tousle her hair.

"I'm watching Bobo the Bear."

"Are you? Is he funny?"

She nodded her head vigorously.

"I'll watch it with you. Scoot over."

This delighted Jessie. She shifted, making room for him to sit on the edge of the bed. He put an arm around her. She snuggled up against him, content to watch the screen.

Lauren met her husband's gaze.

He gave his head a tiny shake.

Lauren frowned. *What did that mean?* Anxious to find out, she switched to the suit's radios so they could speak in whispers without Jessie hearing.

"How's Jessie doing?" Marshall asked.

Lauren sat straighter, leaning closer. "Her temperature is down to ninety-nine, but her labs are continuing to slide. White blood cell levels have been dropping, while bilirubin levels are rising."

Marshall's eyes closed with pain. "Stage Two?"

Lauren found her voice cracking. With so many

cases studied across the nation, the disease progression was becoming predictable. Stage II was classified when the disease progressed from its benign febrile state into an anemic stage with bleeding and nausea.

"By tomorrow," Lauren said. "Maybe the day after that at the latest."

They both knew what would happen from there. With good support, Stage II could stretch for three to four days, followed by a single day of Stage III. *Convulsions and brain hemorrhages.* There was no Stage IV.

Lauren stared at the little girl in the bed as she cuddled against her grandfather. *Less than a week.* That's all the time Jessie had left. "What of Kelly? Has she been picked up? Is she on her way back?"

Her suit radio remained silent. Lauren glanced back to Marshall.

He stared at her a moment more, then spoke. "There was no sign of them. The rescue helicopter searched the region where they were supposed to be according to their last GPS signal. But nothing was found."

Lauren felt like a brick had been dropped in her gut. "How could that be?"

"I don't know. We've been trying to raise them on the satellite link all day, but with no luck. Whatever problem they were having with their equipment yesterday must still be going on."

"Are they continuing the air search?"

He shook his head. "The helicopter had to turn back. Limited fuel."

"Marshall . . ." Her voice cracked.

He reached out to her and took her hand. "Once

they've refueled, they're sending it back out for a night flight. To see if they can spot campfires from the air using infrared scopes. Then tomorrow, another three helicopters are joining the search, including our own Comanche." He squeezed her hand, tight. "We'll find them."

Lauren felt numb all over. *All her children . . . all of them . . .*

Jessie spoke up from the bed, pointing an arm that trailed an IV line toward the video. "Bobo's funny!"

1:05 P.M.
AMAZON JUNGLE

Nate climbed down the fifty-foot ladder from the treetop dwelling. The three-story structure rested in the branches of a nightcap oak, a species from the Cretaceous period. Earlier, just after Kelly and the professor had left with Frank, a pair of Ban-ali women had appeared and led the party to the edge of the glade, gesturing and indicating that the dwelling above had been assigned to their group.

Sergeant Kostos had resisted at first, until Private Carrera had made an astute observation. "Up there, it'll be more defensible. We're sitting targets on the ground. If those giant cats should come up during the night—"

Kostos had cut her off, needing no more convincing. "Right, right. Let's move our supplies up there, then set up a defensive perimeter."

Nate thought such caution was unnecessary. Since

arriving, the Indians had remained curious about them but kept a wary distance, peering from the jungle edges and windows. No hostility was shown. Still, Nate had a hard time balancing these quiet people with the murderous savages who had wiped out half their team by unleashing all manner of beasts upon them. But then again, such duality was the way of many indigenous tribes: hostile and brutal by outside appearances, but once you were accepted, they were found to be a peaceful and open people.

Still, so many of their teammates had died horribly at the indirect hands of this tribe. A burning seed of anger smoldered in Nate's chest. And then there were Clark and maybe others of his father's group, held hostage for all these years. At the moment, Nate found it hard to achieve professional detachment. As an anthropologist, he could understand these strange people, but as a son, resentment and fury colored all he saw.

Still, they *were* helping Frank. Professor Kouwe had returned briefly from the white-barked tree to announce that the tribal shaman and Kelly were able to stabilize their teammate. It was a rare bit of good news. Kouwe had not stayed long, anxious to return to the giant tree. The professor's eyes had flicked toward Nate. Despite the tribe's cooperation at the moment, Kouwe was clearly worried. Nate had tried to inquire, but the professor had waved him off as he left. "Later" was all he had said.

Reaching the last rung of the vine ladder, Nate jumped off. Clustered around the base of the tree were the two Rangers and Manny. Tor-tor stood at his master's side. The other members of their dwindling group—Zane, Anna, and Olin—remained secure in their treetop loft, working on their communication equipment.

Manny nodded to Nate as he crossed toward them.

"I'll keep guard here," Kostos instructed Carrera. "You and Manny do a sweep of the immediate area. See what you can discover about the lay of the land."

The private nodded and turned away.

Manny followed at her side. "C'mon, Tor-tor."

Kostos noted Nate's arrival. "What are you doing down here, Rand?"

"Trying to make myself useful." He nodded to the cabin a hundred yards away. "While the sun's still up and the solar cells are still juicing, I'm going to see if I can discover any information in my father's computer records."

Kostos frowned at the cabin but nodded. Nate could read his eyes, weighing and calculating. Right now every bit of intel could be vital. "Be careful," the sergeant said.

Nate hiked his shotgun higher on his shoulder. "Always." He began the walk across the open glade.

In the distance, near the clearing's edge, a handful of children had gathered. Several pointed at him, gesturing to one another. A small group trailed behind Manny and Carrera, keeping a cautious distance from Tor-tor. The curiosity of youth. Among the trees, the timid tribe began to reawaken to their usual activities. Several women carried water from the stream that flowed through the glade and around the giant tree in the center. In the treetop abodes, people began to clamber. Small fires flared atop stone hearths on patios, readying for dinner. In one dwelling, an old woman sat cross-legged, playing a flute made out of a deer bone, a bright but haunting sound. Nearby, a pair of men, armed with hunting bows, wandered past, giving Nate the barest acknowledgment.

The casualness of their manner reminded Nate that, though these folks were isolated, they had lived with white men and women before. The survivors of his father's expedition.

He reached the cabin, seeing again his father's walking stick by the door. As he stared at it, the rest of the world and its mysteries dissolved away. For the moment, only one question remained in Nate's heart: *What truly happened to my father?*

With a final glance to his team's temporary treetop home, Nate ducked through the door flap of the cabin. The musty smell struck him again, like entering a lost tomb. Inside, he found the laptop still open on the workstation, just as he had left it. Its glow was a beacon in the dark.

As he neared the computer, Nate saw the screen saver playing across the monitor, a tiny set of pictures that slowly floated and bounced around the screen. Tears rose in his eyes. They were photos of his mother. Another ghost from his past. He stared at the smiling face. In one, she was kneeling beside a small Indian boy. In another, a capuchin monkey perched on her shoulder. In yet another, she was hugging a short youngster, a white boy dressed in typical Baniwa garb. It was Nate. He had been six years old. He smiled at the memory, his heart close to bursting. Though his father wasn't in any of the pictures, Nate sensed his presence, a ghost standing over his shoulder, watching with him. At this moment, Nate had never felt closer to his lost family.

After a long time, he reached for the mouse pad. The screen saver vanished, replaced with a typical computer screen. Small titled icons lined the screen. Nate read through the files. *Plant Classification, Tribal Customs, Cellular Statistics* . . . so much information. It would take days to sift through them all. But one file caught his eye. The icon was of a small book. Below it was the word *Journal*.

Nate clicked the icon. A file opened:

Amazonian Journal—Dr. Carl Rand

It was his father's diary. He noted the first date. *September 24.* The day the expedition had headed into the jungle. As Nate scrolled down, he saw that each day had a typed entry. Sometimes no more than a sentence or two, but something was noted. His father was meticulous. As he once quoted to Nate, "An unexamined life is not worth living."

Nate skimmed through the entries, searching for one specific date. He found it. December 16. The day his father's team had vanished.

December 16

The storms continued today, bogging us down in camp. But the day was not a total wash. An Arawak Indian, traveling down the river, shared our soggy camp and told us stories of a strange tribe . . . frightening stories.

The Ban-ali, he named them, which translates roughly to "Blood Jaguar." I've heard snatches in the past concerning this ghost tribe, but few Indians were willing to speak openly of them.

Our visitor was not so reluctant! He was quite talkative. Of course, this may have something to do with the new machete and tangle of shiny fishhooks we offered for the information. Eyeing the wealth, he insisted he knew where the Ban-ali tribe hunted.

Now while my first impulse was to scoff at such a claim, I listened. If there was even a slim chance such a lost tribe existed, how could we not investigate? What a boon it would be for our expedition. As we questioned him, the Indian sketched out a rough map. The Ban-ali appeared to be more than a three-day journey from our location.

So tomorrow, weather permitting, we'll strike out and see how truthful our friend has been. Surely it's a fool's errand . . . but who knows what this mighty jungle could be hiding at its heart?

All in all, a most interesting day.

Nate held his breath as he continued reading from there, hunched over the laptop, sweat dripping down his brow. Over the next several hours, he scanned through the file, reading day after day, year after year, opening other files, staring at diagrams and digital photos. Slowly he began piecing together what had happened to the others.

As he did so, he grew numb with the reading. The horror of the past merged with the present. Nate began to understand. The true danger for their team was only beginning.

5:55 P.M.

Manny called over to Private Carrera. "What's that guy doing over there?"

"Where?"

He pointed his arm toward one of the Ban-ali tribesmen who marched along the streambed, a long spear over his shoulder. Impaled upon the weapon were several haunches of raw meat.

"Making dinner?" the Ranger guessed with a shrug.

"But for whom?"

For the entire afternoon, he and Carrera had been making a slow circuit of the village, with Tor-tor at their side. The cat drew many glances, but also kept curious tribesmen at a distance. As they trekked, Carrera was jotting notes and sketching a map of the village and surrounding lands. *Recon*, Manny had been informed, *just in case the hostiles get hostile again.*

Right now, they were circling the giant, white-barked tree, crossing behind it, where the stream brushed the edges of the monstrous arching roots. It appeared as if the flow of water had washed away the topsoil, exposing even more of the roots' lengths. They were a veritable tangle, snaking into the stream, worming over it, burrowing beneath it.

The Indian who had drawn Manny's attention was ducking through the woody tangle, squirming and bending to make progress, clearly aiming for a section of the stream.

"Let's get a closer look," Manny said.

Carrera pocketed her small field notebook and

grabbed up her weapon, the shovel-snouted Bailey. She eyed the massive tree with a frown, plainly not pleased with the idea of getting any closer to it. But she led the way, marching toward the tangle of roots and the gurgling stream.

Manny watched the Indian cross to a huge eddy pool, shrouded by thick roots and rootlets. The water's surface was glassy smooth, with only a slight swirl disturbing it.

The Indian noticed he was being observed and nodded in the universal greeting of hello, then went back to his work. Manny and Carrera watched from several yards away. Tor-tor settled to his haunches.

Crouching, the tribesman stretched his pole and the flanks of bloody meat over the still pool.

Manny squinted. "What is he—?"

Then several small bodies flung themselves out of the water toward the meat. They looked like little silvery eels, twitching up out of the water. The creatures grabbed bites from the meat with little jaws.

"The piranha creatures," Carrera said at Manny's side.

He nodded, recognizing the similarity. "Juveniles, though. They've not developed their hind legs yet. Still in the pollywog stage. All tail and teeth."

The Indian stood straighter and shook the meat from his spear. Each bloody chunk, as it plopped into the water, triggered a fierce roiling of the still pool, boiling its surface into a bloody froth. The tribesman observed his handiwork for a moment, then tromped back toward the pair who stared at him, stunned.

Again he nodded as he passed, eyeing the jaguar at Manny's side with a mix of awe and fear.

"I want to get a closer look," Manny said.

"Are you nuts, man?" Carrera waved him back. "We're out of here."

"No, I just want to check something out." He was already moving toward the nest of tangled roots.

Carrera grumbled behind him, but followed.

The path was narrow, so they proceeded in single file. Tor-tor trailed last, padding cautiously through the tangle, his tail twitching anxiously.

Manny approached the root-ringed pool.

"Don't get too close," Carrera warned.

"They didn't mind the Indian," Manny said. "I think it's safe."

Still, he slowed his steps and stopped a yard from the pool's edge, one hand resting on the hilt of his whip. In the shadow of the roots, the wide pool proved crystal clear—and deep, at least ten feet. He peered into its glassy depths.

Under the surface, schools of the creatures swam. There was no sign of the meat, but littering the bottom of the pool were bleached bones, nibbled spotless. "It's a damn hatchery," Manny said. "A fish hatchery."

From the branches spanning the pool overhead, droplets of sap would occasionally drip into the water, triggering the creatures to race up and investigate, searching for their next meal. Tricked to the surface, the beasts provided Manny with a better look at them. They varied in size from little minnows to larger monsters with leg buds starting to develop. Not one had fully developed legs.

"They're *all* juveniles," Manny observed. "I don't see any of the adults that attacked us."

"We must have killed them all with the poison," Carrera said.

"No wonder there wasn't a second attack. It must take time to rebuild their army."

"For the piranhas, maybe . . ." Carrera stood two yards back, her voice suddenly hushed and sick. ". . . but not everything."

Manny glanced back to her. She pointed her weapon toward the lower trunk of the tree, where the roots rode up into the main body. Up the trunk, the bark of the tree bubbled out into thick galls, each a yard across. There were hundreds of them. From holes in the bark, black insects scuttled. They crawled, fought, and mated atop the bark. A few flexed their wings with little blurring buzzes.

"The locusts," Manny said, edging back himself.

But the insects ignored them, busy with their communal activities.

Manny stared from the pool back to the insects. "The tree . . ." he mumbled.

"What?"

Manny stared as another droplet of sap drew a handful of the piranha creatures to the surface, glistening silver under the glassy waters. He shook his head. "I'm not sure, but it's almost like the tree is nurturing these creatures." His mind began racing along wild tracks. His eyes grew wide as he began to make disturbing connections.

Carrera must have seen his face pale. "What's wrong?"

"Oh, my God . . . we have to get out of here!"

6:30 P.M.

Inside the cabin, Nate sat hunched over the laptop computer, numb and exhausted. He had reread many of his father's journal notes, even cross-referencing to certain scientific files. The conclusions forming in his mind were as disturbing as they were miraculous. He scrolled down to the last entry and read the final lines.

We'll try tonight. May God watch over us all.

Behind Nate, the whispery sweep of the cabin's door flap announced someone's intrusion.

"Nate?" It was Professor Kouwe.

Glancing at his wristwatch, Nate realized how long he had been lost in the laptop's records, lost to the world. His mouth felt like dried burlap. Beyond the flap, the sun was sliding toward the western horizon as the afternoon descended toward dusk.

"How's Frank?" Nate asked, dragging his attention around.

"What's wrong?" Kouwe said, seeing his face.

Nate shook his head. He wasn't ready to talk yet. "Where's Kelly?"

"Outside, speaking with Sergeant Kostos. We came down here to report in and make sure everything was okay. Then we'll head back up again. How are things down here?"

"The Indians are keeping their distance," Nate said, standing. He moved toward the door, staring at the sinking sun. "We've finished setting up the tree-house as our base. Manny and Private Carrera are scouting the area."

Kouwe nodded. "I saw them crossing back this

way just now. What about communications with the States?"

Nate shrugged. "Olin says the whole system is corrupted. But he believes he can at least get the GPS to read true and broadcast a signal. Maybe as soon as tonight."

"That's good news," Kouwe said tightly.

Nate recognized the tension in the other's voice. "What's the matter?"

Kouwe frowned. "Something I can't exactly put my finger on."

"Maybe I can help." Nate glanced to the laptop, then unplugged the device from the solar cells. With night approaching, juice would not be flowing anyway. He checked the laptop's battery and then tucked it under his arm. "I think it's time we all compared notes."

Kouwe nodded. "It's why Kelly and I came down. We have our own news."

Again, Nate saw the worried look on the professor's face. As Nate stood up, he was sure his own expression mirrored Kouwe's. "Let's get everyone together."

The pair ducked out of the cabin and into the late afternoon sunshine. Free of the stifling cabin, they felt almost chilled by the slight breezes. Nate crossed over to where Kelly and Sergeant Kostos were talking. Manny and Carrera had joined them.

A few steps away stood one of the Ban-ali tribesmen. It took Nate a moment to recognize him. It was their guide from earlier. He had washed off the black camouflage paint, revealing brown skin and a crimson tattoo on his bare chest.

Nate nodded to Kelly as he stopped beside them. "I heard that Frank is doing better."

Her face was pale, distracted. "For the moment." She noticed the laptop under his arm. "Were you able to learn anything about your father?"

Nate sighed. "I think everyone should hear this."

"It's time we put a plan together anyway," Sergeant Kostos said. "Night is coming."

Kouwe pointed to the three-story dwelling in the towering nightcap oak. "Let's get everyone up to the dwelling."

No one objected. In short order, the group mounted the long ladder and headed up the tree. Tor-tor remained below, on guard. Nate glanced down as he climbed. The jaguar was not alone down there. The Ban-ali tribesman stayed at the foot of the ladder, plainly assigned to their group.

Reaching the top of the ladder, Nate climbed onto the decking of the abode. The entire party clustered on the deck or stood inside the doorway to the lowermost level, a communal room. Above, the two other levels were a honeycomb of smaller, more private chambers, each with its own tiny deck or patio.

The tree house had clearly been some family's domicile, commandeered for their use. Personal touches abounded: bits of pottery and wooden utensils, decorations done in feathers and flowers, abandoned hammocks, tiny carved animal figurines. Even the smell of the place was not the deserted mustiness of the tiny cabin, but the subtle scent of life. Old cooking spices and oils, a hint of bodily odors.

Anna Fong crossed to him. She had a platter of sliced figs. "One of the Indian women dropped off some supplies. Fruits and cooked yams. Bits of dried meat."

Nate remembered his thirst and took one of the moist fruits, biting deep into it, juice dribbling down his chin. Wiping his lips with the back of his hand, he asked, "How's Olin doing with the GPS signal?"

"Still working on it," she said in a hushed, scared voice. "But from the amount of swearing, it doesn't sound good."

Kostos raised his voice from the doorway. "Everyone gather inside!"

As he stepped aside, the party moved into the common room. Inside, Nate saw the other platters of food. Even a few pails of a dark liquid, smelling of fermentation.

Professor Kouwe examined one pail's contents and turned to Nate in surprise. "It's cassiri!"

"What's that?" Kostos asked from the doorway as he closed the flap.

"Cassava beer," Nate explained. "An alcoholic staple of many native tribes."

"Beer?" the sergeant's eyes brightened. "Really?"

Kouwe scooped up a ladleful of the dark amber liquid and poured it into a mug. Nate saw bits of slimy cassava root floating in the pail. The professor passed the mug to the sergeant.

He sniffed it, nose curling in disgust, but he took a deep swig anyway. "Ugh!" He shook his head.

"It's an acquired taste," Nate said, scooping a mug for himself and sipping it. Manny did the same. "Women make it by chewing up cassava root and spitting it into a pail. The enzymes in their saliva aid in the fermentation process."

Kostos crossed to the pail and dumped the contents of his mug back into the pail. "I'll take a Budweiser any day."

Nate shrugged.

Around the room, the others sampled the fare for a bit, then began to settle to woven mats on the floor. Everyone looked exhausted. They all needed a decent night's sleep.

Nate set up the laptop on an overturned stone pot.

As he opened it and turned it on, Olin looked at it hungrily, his eyes red. "Maybe I can cannibalize some circuitry for the communication array." He shifted nearer.

But Nate held him off. "The computer is five years old. I doubt you'll find much to use, and right now its contents are more important than our own survival."

His words drew everyone's attention. He eyed them all. "I know what happened to the other expedition team. And if we don't want to end up like them, we should pay attention to its lessons."

Kouwe spoke up. "What happened?"

Nate took a deep breath, then began, nodding to the open journal file on the laptop. "It's all here. My father's expedition heard rumors of the Ban-ali and met an Indian who said he could take the research team to their lands. My father could not resist the possibility of encountering a new tribe and took the team off course. Within two days, they were attacked by the same mutated species as we were."

Murmurs arose from the others. Manny raised

his hand as if he were in class. "I found where they incubate those buggers. At least the locusts and piranhas." He described what he and Private Carrera had discovered. "I've got my own theories about the beasts."

Kouwe interrupted. "Before we get into theories and conjectures, let's first hear what we know for sure." The professor nodded to Nate. "Go on. What happened after the attack?"

Nate took another breath. The tale was not an easy one to tell. "Of the party, all were killed except Gerald Clark, my father, and two other researchers. They were captured by the Ban-ali trackers. My father was able to communicate with them and get them to spare their lives. From my father's notes, I guess the Ban-ali native tongue is close enough to Yanomamo."

Kouwe nodded. "It does bear a resemblance. And isolated as the tribe is, the presence of a white man who could speak the tongue of the Ban-ali would surely give them pause. I'm not surprised your father and the survivors were spared."

The little good it did, Nate thought sourly, then continued, "The remaining party were all badly injured, but once here, their wounds were healed. Miraculously, according to my father's notes: gashes sealed without scarring, broken bones mended in less than a week's time, even chronic ailments, like one team member's heart murmur, faded away. But the most amazing transformation was in Gerald Clark."

"His arm," Kelly said, sitting up straighter.

"Exactly. Within a few weeks here, his amputated

stump began to split, bleed, and sprout a raw tumor-ous growth. One of the survivors was a medical doctor. He and my father examined the change. The growth was a mass of undifferentiated stem cells. They were sure it was some malignant growth. There was even talk of trying to surgically remove it, but they had no tools. Over the next weeks, slow changes became apparent. The mass slowly elongated, grow-ing skin on the outside."

Kelly's eyes widened. "The arm was regener-ating."

Nate nodded and turned. He scrolled down the computer journal to the day almost three years ago. He read aloud his father's words. " 'Today it became clear to Dr. Chandler and me that the tumor plagu-ing Clark is in fact a regeneration unlike any seen before. Talk of escape has been put on hold until we see how this ends. It's a miracle that is worth the risk. The Ban-ali continue to remain accommodating cap-tors, allowing us free run of the valley, but banning us from leaving. And with the giant cats prowling the lower chasm, escape seems impossible for the mo-ment anyway.' "

Nate straightened up and tapped open a new file. Crude sketches of an arm and upper torso appeared on the screen. "My father went on to document the transformation. How the undifferentiated stem cells slowly changed into bone, muscle, nerves, blood ves-sels, hair, and skin. It took eight months for the limb to fully grow back."

"What caused it?" Kelly asked.

"According to my father's notes, the sap of the Yagga tree."

Kelly gasped. "The Yagga . . ."

Kouwe's eyes widened. "No wonder the Ban-ali worship the tree."

"What's a Yagga?" Zane asked from a corner, showing the first sign of interest in their discussion.

Kouwe explained what he and Kelly had witnessed up in the healing ward of the giant prehistoric tree. "Frank's wounds almost immediately sealed."

"That's not all," Kelly said. She shifted closer to get a better look at the computer screen. "All afternoon, I've been monitoring his red blood cell levels with a hematocrit tube. The levels are climbing dramatically. It's as if something is massively stimulating his bone marrow to produce new red blood cells for all he lost . . . at a miraculous rate. I've never seen such a reaction."

Nate clicked open another file. "It's something in the sap. My father's group was able to distill the stuff and run it through a paper chromatograph. Similar to the way the sap of copal trees is rich in hydrocarbons, the Yagga's sap is rich in *proteins.*"

Kelly stared at the results. "Proteins?"

Manny scooted next to her, looking over her shoulder. "Wasn't the disease vector a type of a protein?"

Kelly nodded. "A prion. One with strong mutagenic properties." She glanced over her shoulder to Manny. "You were mentioning something about the piranhas and the locusts. A theory."

Manny nodded. "They're tied to this Yagga tree, too. The locusts live in the bark of the tree. Like some type of wasp gall. And the piranhas—their hatchery is in a pond tucked among the roots. There was even sap dripping into it. I think it's the sap that mutates them during early development."

"My father suggested a similar conclusion in his notes," Nate said quietly. In fact, there were numerous files specifically on this matter. Nate had not been able to read through them all.

"And the giant cats and caimans?" Anna asked.

"Established mutations, I'd wager," Manny said. "The two species must've been altered generations ago into these oversized beasts. I imagine by now they're capable of breeding on their own, stable enough genetically to need no further support from the sap."

"Then why don't they leave the area?" Anna asked.

"Perhaps some biological imperative, a genetic territorial thing."

"It sounds like you're suggesting this tree manufactured these creatures purposefully? Consciously?" Zane scoffed.

Manny shrugged. "Who can say? Maybe it wasn't so much will or thought as just evolutionary pressure."

"Impossible." Zane shook his head.

"Not so. We've seen versions of this phenomenon already." Manny turned to Nate. "Like the ant tree."

Nate frowned, picturing the attack on Sergeant Kostos by stinging ants. He remembered how an ant tree's stems and branches were hollow, serving both to house the colony and feed it with a sugary sap. In turn, the ants savagely protected their home against the intrusion of plants and animals. He began to understand what Manny was driving at. There was a distinct similarity.

Manny went on, "What we have here is a symbiosis between plant life and animal, both evolved into a complex shared interrelationship. One serving the other."

Carrera spoke up from her post by a window. The sun was slowly setting behind her shoulder. "Who cares how the beasts came to be? Do we know how to avoid them if we have to fight our way out of the valley?"

Nate answered her question. "The creatures can be controlled."

"How?"

He waved to the laptop. "It took my father years to learn the Ban-ali secrets. It seems that the tribe has developed powders that can both attract and repel the creatures. We ourselves saw this demonstrated with the locusts, but they can do it with the piranhas, too. Through chemicals in the water, they can lure and trigger an aggressive response in the otherwise docile creatures. My father believed it's some type of hormonal compound that stimulates the piranhas' territoriality and makes them attack wildly."

Manny nodded. "Then it's lucky we wiped out a majority of the adult horde so quickly. I imagine it takes time for their hatchery to grow a new supply. Just one of the disadvantages of a biological defense system."

"Perhaps that's why the Ban-ali keep more than one type of creature," Carrera noted astutely. "Backup troops."

Manny frowned. "Of course. I should've thought of that."

Carrera faced Nate. "Then there are those cats and giant caimans to consider."

Nate nodded. "Gatekeepers, like we thought, set up to defend the perimeter. They patrol the entry points to the heart of the territory. But even the jaguars can be made docile by painting a black powder over one's body, allowing the Ban-ali to pass freely back and forth. I imagine the compound must act like caiman dung, a scent repellent to the giant cats."

Manny whistled. "So our guide's body paint wasn't all camouflage."

"Where do we get some of this repellent stuff?" Kostos asked. "Where does it come from?"

Kouwe spoke up. "The Yagga tree." He had not moved, only grown more pale with the telling of the tale.

Nate was surprised by the professor's quick answer. "They're derived from the Yagga's bark and leaf oils. But how did you guess?"

"Everything ties back to that prehistoric tree. I think Manny was quite correct that the specimen behaves like an ant tree. But he's wrong about who the *ants* are here."

"What do you mean?" Manny asked.

"The mutated beasts are just biological tools supplied by the tree for its true workers." Kouwe stared around him. "The Ban-ali."

A stunned silence spread over the group.

Kouwe continued, "The tribesmen here are the soldier ants in this relationship. The Ban-ali name the tree *Yagga*, their word for mother. One who gives birth . . . a caretaker. Countless generations ago, most likely during the first migration of people into South America, the tribe must have stumbled upon the tree's remarkable healing ability and became enthralled by it. Becoming *ban-yin*—slaves. Each serving the other in a complex web of defense and offense."

Nate felt sickened by this comparison. *Humans used like ants.*

"This grove is prehistoric," the professor finished. "It might trace its heritage back to Pangaea, when South America and Africa were joined. Its species may have been around when man first walked upright. Throughout the ages, there are hundreds of myths of such trees, from all corners of the world. *The maternal guardian.* Perhaps this encounter here was not the first."

This thought sank into the others. Nate didn't think even his father had extrapolated the history of the Yagga to this end. It was disturbing.

Sergeant Kostos shifted his M-16 to his other shoulder. "Enough history lessons. I thought we were supposed to be developing an alternate plan. A way to escape if we can't raise someone on the radio."

"The sergeant is right." Kouwe turned. "You never did tell us, Nate. What happened to your father and the others? How did Gerald Clark escape?"

Nate took a deep breath and turned back to the computer. He scrolled down to the last entry and read it aloud.

"**April 18**

We've gathered enough powders to chance an escape tonight. After what we've learned, we must attempt a break for civilization. We dare not wait any longer. We'll dust our bodies black and flee with the setting moon. Illia knows paths that will quickly get us past any trackers and out of these lands, but the trek back to civilization will be hard and not without threat. Still, we have no choice . . . not after the birth. We'll try tonight. May God watch over us all."

Nate straightened from the laptop, turning to the others. "They all attempted to flee, not just Gerald Clark."

Across the many faces, Nate saw the same expression. *Only Gerald Clark made it back to civilization.*

"So they all left," Kelly mumbled.

Nate nodded. "Even a Ban-ali woman, a skilled tracker named Illia. She had fallen in love and married Gerald Clark. He took her with him."

"What happened to them?" Anna said.

Nate shook his head. "That was the last entry. There is no more."

Kelly's expression saddened. "Then they didn't make it . . . only Gerald Clark."

"I could ask Dakii for more details," Kouwe said.

"Dakii?"

Kouwe pointed below. "The tribesman who guided us here. Between what I know of the Ban-ali language and his smattering of English, I might be able to find out what happened to the others, how they died."

Nate nodded, though he wasn't sure he wanted to know the details.

Manny spoke up. "But what made them flee *that*

night? Why the hint at some urgency in that last note?"

Nate took a deep breath. "It's why I wanted everyone to hear this. My father came to some frightening conclusions about the Ban-ali. Something he needed to relay to the outside world."

"What?" Kouwe asked.

Nate wasn't sure where to begin. "It took years of living with the Ban-ali for my father to begin piecing facts together. He noticed that the isolated tribe showed some hints of remarkable advancements over their Indian counterparts in the greater Amazon. The invention of the pulley and wheel. A few of the homes even have crude elevators, using large boulders and counterweights. And other advancements that seemed strange considering the isolated nature of this tribe. He spent much of his time examining the way the Ban-ali think, the way they teach their children. He was fascinated by all this."

"So what happened?" Kelly asked.

"Gerald Clark fell in love with Illia. They married during the second year of the group's incarceration here. During the third, they conceived a baby. During the fourth year, Illia gave birth." He stared hard at the gathered faces. "The child was stillborn, rife with mutations." Nate recalled his father's words. " 'A genetic monster.' "

Kelly cringed.

Nate pointed to the laptop. "There are more details in the files. My father and the medical doctor of the group began to formulate a frightening conclusion. The tree hadn't just mutated the lower species. It had also been changing the Ban-ali over the years, subtly heightening their cognitive abilities, their reflexes, even their eyesight. While outwardly they appeared the same, the tree was improving the species. My father suspected that the Ban-ali were heading genetically away from mankind. One of the definitions that separates different species is an inability to breed together."

"The stillborn child . . ." Manny had paled.

Nate nodded. "My father came to believe that the Ban-ali were near to leaving Homo sapiens behind, becoming their own species."

"Dear God," Kelly gasped.

"It was why their need to escape became urgent. This corruption of mankind in the valley has to be stopped."

No one spoke for a full minute.

Anna's voice, full of horror, whispered, "What are we going to do?"

"We're going to get that damn GPS working," Kostos said harshly. "Then we're gonna bug out of this damn place."

"And in the meantime," Carrera added, "we should gather as much of that repellent powder as possible, just in case."

Kelly cleared her voice and stood up. "We're all forgetting one vital thing. The disease spreading across the Americas. How do we cure it? What did Gerald Clark bring out of this valley?" Kelly turned to Nate. "In your father's notes, is there any mention of a contagious disease here?"

"No, with the inherent healing properties of the Yagga tree, everyone remained incredibly healthy.

The only suggestion is the taboo against one of the Chosen, the Ban-ali, leaving the tribe. A shadowed curse upon he who leaves and all he encounters. My father had dismissed this as a myth to frighten anyone from leaving."

Manny mumbled, "The curse upon he who leaves and all he encounters . . . that sounds like our contagion."

Kelly turned back to Nate. "But if true, where did the disease come from? What triggered Clark's body to suddenly become riddled with tumors? What made him contagious?"

"I wager it has something to do with the Yagga tree's healing sap," Zane said. "Maybe it keeps the disease in check here. When we leave, we need to make sure we collect a generous sample. That's clearly vital."

Kelly ignored Zane, her gaze unfocused. "We're missing something . . . something important," she said, low and quiet. Nate doubted anyone else heard her.

"I can see if Dakii will cooperate," Kouwe said. "See if he has any answers—both to the final fate of the others and about this mysterious disease."

"Good. Then we have a working plan for now," Sergeant Kostos said by the door. He pointed around the room and assigned missions for each of them. "Olin will work on the GPS. At daybreak, Kouwe and Anna, our Indian experts, will act as intel. Gather as much information as possible. Manny, Carrera, and I'll search out where the repellent powder is stored. Zane, Rand, and Kelly will watch over Frank, ready him for a quick evac if necessary. While at the tree, it will be up to you three to collect a sample of the healing sap."

Slowly everyone nodded. If nothing else, it would keep them busy, keep their minds off the biological horrors hidden in the pristine valley.

Kouwe pushed to his feet. "I might as well get started. I'll chat with Dakii while he's alone down below."

"I'll go with you," Nate said.

Kelly moved toward them. "And I'm going to check on Frank one last time before full night falls."

The trio left the common room and crossed the deck to the ladder. The sun was only a sharp glow to the west. Dusk had rolled like a dark cloud over the glade.

In silence, the three descended the ladder in the gloom, each in a cocoon of their own thoughts.

Nate was the first one down and helped Kouwe and Kelly off the ladder. Tor-tor wandered over and nuzzled Nate for attention. He scratched absently at the tender spot behind the jaguar's ear.

A few yards away, the tribesman named Dakii stood.

Kouwe crossed toward him.

Kelly stared up at the Yagga, its upper branches still bathed in sunlight. In her narrowed eyes, Nate saw a wary glint.

"If you'll wait a moment, I'll go with you," he said.

She shook her head. "I'm fine. I've got one of the Rangers' radios. You should get some rest."

"But—"

She glanced over at him, her face tired and sad. "I won't be long. I just need a few minutes alone with my brother."

He nodded. He had no doubt the Ban-ali would leave her unmolested, but he hated to see her alone with such raw grief. *First her daughter, now her brother . . .* so much pain shone in every plane of her face.

She reached to him, squeezed his hand. "Thanks for offering, though," she whispered, and set off across the fields.

Behind Nate, Kouwe already had his pipe lit and was talking with Dakii. Nate patted Tor-tor's side and walked over to join them.

Kouwe glanced back at him. "Do you have a picture of your father?"

"In my wallet."

"Can you show it to Dakii? After four years spent with your father, the tribesmen must be familiar with recorded images."

Nate shrugged and pulled out his leather billfold. He flipped to a photo of his father, standing in a Yanomamo village, surrounded by village children.

Kouwe showed it to Dakii.

The tribesman cocked his head back and forth, eyes wide. "Kerl," he said, tapping at the photo with a finger.

"Carl . . . right," Kouwe said. "What happened to him?" The professor repeated the question in Yanomamo.

Dakii did not understand. It took a few more back-and-forth exchanges to finally communicate the question. Dakii then bobbed his head vigorously, and a complicated exchange followed. Kouwe and Dakii spoke rapidly in a mix of dialects and phonetics that was too quick for Nate to follow.

During a lull, Kouwe turned to Nate. "The others were slain. Gerald escaped the trackers. His background as a Special Forces soldier must have helped him slip away."

"My father?"

Dakii must have understood the word. He leaned in closer to the photograph, then back up at Nate. "Son?" he said. "You son man?"

Nate nodded.

Dakii patted Nate on his arm, a broad smile on his face. "Good. Son of *wishwa*."

Nate glanced to Kouwe, frowning.

"*Wishwa* is their word for shaman. Your father, with his modern wonders, must have been considered a shaman."

"What happened to him?"

Kouwe again spoke rapidly in the mix of pidgin English and a mishmash of Yanomamo. Nate was even beginning to unravel the linguistic knot.

"Kerl . . . ?" Dakii bobbed his head, grinning proudly. "Me brother *teshari-rin* bring Kerl back to shadow of Yagga. It good."

"Brought back?" Nate asked.

Kouwe continued to drag the story from the man. Dakii spoke rapidly. Nate didn't understand. But at last, Kouwe turned back to Nate. The professor's face was grim.

"What did he say?"

"As near as I can translate, your father was indeed brought back here—dead or alive, I couldn't say. But then, because of both his crime and his *wishwa* status, he was granted a rare honor among the tribe."

"What?"

"He was taken to the Yagga, his body fed to the root."

"Fed to the root?"

"I think he means like fertilizer."

Nate stumbled back a step. Though he knew his father was dead, the reality was too horrible to fathom. His father had attempted to stop the corruption of the Ban-ali by the prehistoric tree, risking his own life to do so, but in the end, he had been fed to the damn thing instead, nourishing it.

Past Kouwe's shoulder, Dakii continued to bob his head, grinning like a fool. "It good. Kerl with Yagga. *Nashi nar!*"

Nate was too numb to ask what the last word meant, but Kouwe translated anyway.

"*Nashi nar.* Forever."

8:08 P.M.

In the jungle darkness, Louis lay in wait, infrared goggles fixed to his head. The sun had just set and true night was quickly consuming the valley. He and his men had been in position for hours.

Not much longer.

But he would have to be patient. *Make haste slowly*, he had been taught. One last key was needed before the attack could commence. So he lay on his belly, covered by the fronds of a fern, face smeared in streaks of black.

It had been a long and busy day. This morning, an hour after sunrise, he had been contacted by his mole. *His spy was still alive! What good fortune!* The agent had informed him that the Ban-ali village did indeed lie in a secluded valley, only approachable through the side canyon in the cliffs ahead. What could be more perfect? All his targets trapped in one place.

The only obstacle had been the valley's damned jaguar pack.

But his darling Tshui had managed to handle that nasty problem. Covered by the early morning gloom, she had led a handpicked team of trackers, including the German commando, Brail, into the valley's heart and planted poisoned meat, freshly killed and dripping with blood. Tshui had tainted each piece with a terrible poison, both odorless and tasteless, that killed with only the slightest lick. The pack, its blood lust already up from the attack upon the Rangers, found these treats too hard to resist.

Throughout the early morning, the great beasts dropped into blissful slumbers from which they would never wake. A few of the cats had remained suspicious and had not eaten. But hunting with the infrared goggles, Tshui and the others had finished off these last stubborn cats, using air guns equipped with poisoned darts.

It had been a quiet kill. With the way clear, Louis had moved his men into a guard position near the mouth of the side chasm.

Only one last item was needed, but he would have to be patient.

Make haste slowly.

At last, he spotted movement in the chasm. Through his infrared goggles, the two figures appeared as a pair of blazing torches. They slipped down the crude steps, alone. This morning, Louis had posted guards at the chasm mouth, ready to silence any tribesman who came down to scout for them. But none of the Ban-ali had shown their heads. Most likely the tribe's attention had remained focused on the strangers in their village, confident that the jaguar pack would keep them protected or alert them of any further intruders.

Not this day, *mes amis.* Something more predatory than your little pack has come to your valley.

The figures continued to thread down the chasm. Louis lowered his infrared goggles for a moment. Though he knew the figures were there, the black camouflage was so perfect that Louis could not spot them with his unaided eye. He slipped the goggles back in place and smiled thinly. The figures again blazed forth.

Ah, the wonders of modern science . . .

In a matter of moments, the two figures reached the bottom of the chasm. They seemed to hesitate. Did they sense something was amiss? Were they wary of the jaguars? Louis held his breath. Slowly the pair set out down the escarpment, ready for the night's patrol.

At last.

A new blazing figure stepped forth from the jungle, into their path. A slender torch that burned brighter than the other two. Louis lowered his goggles. It was Tshui. Naked. Ebony hair flowed in a silky waterfall to her shapely buttocks. She sidled toward the pair of scouts, a jungle goddess awoken from a slumber.

The pair of painted tribesmen froze in surprise.

A cough sounded from the bushes nearby. One of the Indians slapped his neck, then slipped to the ground. There was enough poison in each dart to drop a half-ton jaguar. The man was dead before his head hit the rocky ground.

The remaining scout stared for a moment, then fled as quickly as a snake toward the chasm. But Louis's mistress was even faster, her blood hyped on stimulants, her reflexes sharper. Effortlessly, she danced back into his path, blocking him. He opened his mouth to scream a warning, but again Tshui was quicker. She shot out her arm and tossed a handful of powder into his face, into his eyes, into his open mouth.

Reflexively choking, his call was gargled, more a strangled wheeze. He fell to his knees as the drug hit his system.

Tshui remained expressionless. She knelt beside her prey as the man toppled to the ground. She then stared over his body toward Louis's hiding place, a ghost of a smile on her lips.

Louis stood. They now had the final piece of the puzzle, someone to inform them about the tribe's defenses. Everything was now in place for the assault tomorrow.

9:23 P.M.

Kelly sat cross-legged beside her brother's low hammock.

Wrapped in a thick blanket, Frank sipped weakly through a reed straw poking from a cantaloupe-sized hollow nut.

Kelly recognized it as one of the fruits that grew in clusters along the branches of the Yagga. The nut's content was similar to coconut milk. She had tasted it first when one of the tribesmen in the healing ward had brought it over to her brother. It was sweet and creamy with sugars and fats, an energy boost her brother needed.

She waited as Frank finished the contents of his natural energy drink and passed it to her, his hand trembling slightly. Though awake, his eyes were still hazy with a morphine glaze.

"How are you feeling?" she asked.

"Like a million bucks," he said hoarsely. His eyes twitched to the stumps hidden under the blanket.

"How's the pain?"

His brow furrowed. "No pain," he said with half a laugh, strained joviality. "Though I swear I can feel my toes itching."

"Phantom sensations," she said with a nod. "You'll probably feel them for months."

"An itch I can never scratch . . . great."

She smiled up at Frank. The mix of relief, exhaustion, and fear in her own heart was mirrored in her brother's expression. But at least his color had much improved. As horrible as their situation was here, Kelly had to appreciate the healing sap of the Yagga. It had saved her brother's life. His recovery had been remarkable.

Frank suddenly yawned, a true jawbreaker.

"You need to sleep," she said, getting to her feet.

"Miraculous healing or not, your body needs to re-charge its batteries." She glanced around and tucked in her shirt.

Around the cavernous chamber, only a pair of tribesmen remained in the room. One of them was the head shaman, who glared at her with impatience. Kelly had wanted to spend the night at her brother's side, but the shaman had refused. He and his workers, the tribesman had explained in stilted English, would watch over their new brother. "Yagga protects him," the shaman had said, brooking no argument.

Kelly sighed. "I had better go before I get kicked out."

Frank yawned again and nodded. She had already explained to him about tomorrow's plan and would see him at first light. He reached out and squeezed her hand. "Love you, sis."

She bent and kissed his cheek. "Love you, too, Frank."

"I'll be fine . . . so will Jessie."

Straightening, she bit her lip to hold back a sudden sob. She couldn't let go of her feelings, not in front of Frank. She dared not, or she'd never stop crying. Over the past day, she had bottled her grief tightly. It was the O'Brien way. Irish fortitude in the face of adversity. Now was not the time to dissolve into tears.

She busied herself with checking his intravenous catheter, now plugged with a heparin lock. Though he no longer needed fluid support, she kept the catheter in place in case of emergencies.

Across the way, the shaman frowned at her.

Screw you, she thought silently and angrily, *I'll go*

when I'm good and ready. She lifted the blanket from over her brother's legs and made one final check on his wounds. The sap seal on the stumps remained tenaciously intact. In fact, through the semitransparent seal, she saw a decent granulation bed had already formed over the raw wounds, like the healing tissue under a protective scab. The rate of granulation was simply amazing.

Tucking back the blankets, she saw that Frank's eyes were already closed. A slight snore sounded from his open mouth. She very gently leaned over and kissed his other cheek. Again she had to choke back a sob, but couldn't stop the tears. Straightening up, she wiped her eyes and surveyed the room one final time.

The shaman must have seen the wet glisten on her cheeks. His impatient frown softened in sympathy. He nodded to her, his eyes intent, repeating a silent promise that he would watch closely over her brother.

With no choice, she took a deep breath and headed toward the exit. The climb back down the tree seemed interminable. In the dark passage, she was alone with her thoughts. Worries magnified and multiplied. Her fears bounced between her daughter, her brother, and the world at large.

At last, she stumbled out of the tree's trunk and into the open glade. An evening breeze had kicked up, but it was warm. The moon was bright overhead, but already scudding clouds rolled across the spread of stars. Somewhere in the distance, thunder rumbled. They would get rain before the morning.

In the freshening breeze, she hurried across the

wide clearing, heading toward their tree. At its base, she spotted someone standing guard with a flashlight—Private Carrera. The Ranger pegged her with the light, then waved. At her side, Tor-tor lay huddled. The jaguar glanced up at her approach, sniffed the air, then lowered his head back to his curled body.

"How's Frank?" Carrera asked.

Kelly did not feel like talking but could not dismiss the soldier's concern. "He seems to be doing well. Very well."

"That's good." She jabbed a thumb to the ladder. "You should try to get as much sleep as possible. We've a long day ahead of us."

Kelly nodded, though she doubted sleep would come easily. She mounted the ladder.

"There's a private room on the third level of the dwelling left empty for you. It's the one on the right."

Kelly barely heard her. "Good night," she muttered and continued her climb, lost in her own worries.

At the top of the ladder, she found the deck empty, as was the common room. Everyone must have already retired, exhausted by the number of days with so little sleep.

Craning back, she stared at the dark upper stories, then crossed to the longer of the two secondary ladders.

Third level, Private Carrera had said.

Great . . . just what I get for being the last one to claim a room.

The third story was a good deal higher than the

other two. Built on its own level of branches, it was more a separate structure, a two-room guest house.

Her legs aching, she mounted the long ladder. The wind began to kick up a bit as she climbed, whispering the branches, swaying the ladder ever so slightly. The gusts smelled of rain. Overhead, the moon was swallowed by dark clouds. She hurried up as the storm swept toward the village.

From this height, she saw lightning fork across the sky in a dazzling burst. Thunder boomed and echoed like a bass drum. Suddenly, living in a giant tree did not seem like such a wise choice. Especially the uppermost level.

She hurried as the first raindrops began pelting through the leaves. Pulling herself up onto the tiny deck, she rolled to her feet. The wind and rain grew quickly. Storms in the Amazon were usually brief, but they often came swiftly and fiercely. This one was no exception. Standing half crouched, she faced the doors that led to the two rooms on this level.

Which room had Carrera told her was hers?

Lightning crackled overhead in small angry spears, while thunder rattled. Rain swept in a sudden torrent, and breezes became fierce gusts. Under her feet, the planking rolled like the deck of a ship at sea.

Beyond caring if she woke someone, Kelly dove toward the nearest opening, half falling through the flap, seeking immediate shelter.

The room was dark. Lightning burst, shining brightly through a smaller back door to the chamber. The lone hammock in the room was thankfully empty. She stumbled gratefully toward it.

As she crossed toward the hammock, her feet tripped over something in the dark. She fell to her knees with a sharp curse. Her fingers reached back and discovered a pack on the floor.

"Who's there?" a voice asked from beyond the back door. A silhouetted figure stepped into the frame of the doorway.

On her knees, Kelly felt a moment of sheer terror.

Thunder echoed, and a new flicker of lightning revealed the identity of the dark figure. "Nate?" she asked timidly, embarrassed. "It's Kelly."

He crossed quickly to her and helped her to her feet. "What are you doing here?"

She wiped the wet strands of hair from her face, now burning hotly. *What a fool he must think I am.* "I . . . I stumbled into the wrong room. Sorry."

"Are you okay?" Nate's hands still held her arms, his palms warm through her soaked shirt.

"I'm fine. Just feeling especially foolish."

"No reason to be. It's dark."

Lightning crackled, and she found his eyes on hers. They stared at each other in silence.

Finally, Nate spoke. "How's Frank?"

"Fine," she said in a hushed voice. Thunder boomed distantly, rolling over them, making the world seem much larger, them much smaller. Her voice was now a whisper. "I . . . I never said . . . I was sorry to hear about your father."

"Thanks."

His single word, softly spoken, echoed with old pain. She moved a step toward him, unwilled, a moth drawn to a flame, knowing she would be destroyed but having no choice. His sorrow touched something inside her. That hard and fast wall around her heart weakened. Tears again welled in her eyes. Her shoulders began to tremble.

"Hush," he said, though she hadn't said a word. He pulled her closer to him, arms wrapping around her shoulder.

The trembling became sobs. All the grief and terror she had held in her heart released in a blinding torrent. Her knees gave out, but Nate caught her in his grip and lowered her to the floor. He held her tight, his heart beating against hers.

They remained on the floor in the center of the room as the storm raged outside, swaying the trees, booming with the clash of Titans. At last, she glanced up toward Nate.

She reached up to him and pulled his lips to hers. She tasted the salt of his own tears, of hers. At first, it was just survival in the face of the intense sorrow, but as their lips opened, an unspoken hunger awoke. She felt his pulse quicken.

He pulled away for a moment, gasping. His eyes were bright, so very bright in the darkness.

"Kelly . . ."

"*Hush*," she sighed, using his own word. She pulled him back to her.

Wrapped in each other's arms, they lowered themselves to the floor. Palms explored . . . fingers loosened and peeled away damp clothes . . . limbs entwined.

As the storm hammered, their passions grew white hot. Grief faded away, lost somewhere between pain and pleasure, age-old rhythms and silent cries. They found the room too small, falling out onto the back deck.

Lightning rode the clouds, thunder roaring. Rain lashed under the awning, sweeping across their bare skin.

Nate's mouth was hot on her breast, on her throat. She arched into him, eyes closed, lightning flaring red through her lids. His lips moved to hers, hungry, their breath shared. Under the storm, under him, she felt the exquisite tension build inside her, at first slowly, then ever more rapidly, swelling through and out of her as she cried into his lips.

He met her cry with his own, sounding like thunder in her ears.

For an untold time, they held that moment. Lost to the world, lost to the storm, but *not* lost to each other.

ACT FIVE

Root

UNA DE GATO, "CAT'S CLAW"
family: *Rubiaceae*
genus: *Uncaria*
species: *Tomentosa, Guianensis*
common names: *Cat's Claw, Una de Gato, Paraguayo,
Garabato, Garbato Casha, Samento, Toroñ, Tambor Huasca,
Aun Huasca, Una de Gavilan, Hawk's Claw*
part used: *Bark, Root, Leaves*
properties/actions: *Antibacterial, Antioxidant,
Antiinflammatory, Antitumorous, Antiviral, Cytostatic,
Depurative, Diuretic, Hypotensive, Immunostimulant,
Vermifuge, Antimutagenic*

SIXTEEN

Betrayal

AUGUST 17, 7:05 A.M.
AMAZON JUNGLE

Nate woke to find his arms around a naked woman. Her eyes were already open. "Good morning," he said.

Kelly inched closer to him. He could still smell the rain on her skin. She smiled. "It's been morning for some time."

He rose to one elbow, which wasn't easy in a hammock, and stared down into her face. "Why didn't you wake me?"

"I figured you could use at least one full hour of sleep." She rolled out of the hammock, setting it swinging, and artfully drew off the single blanket and wrapped it around her.

With one hand, he grasped for her.

She stepped out of reach. "We have a long day ahead of us."

With a groan, he rolled to his feet and pulled his

boxers from the pile of hastily discarded clothes as Kelly gathered her things. Through the rear door to the room, he stared out at the jungle.

Last night, he and Kelly had talked into the wee hours of the morning, about fathers, brothers, daughters, lives, and losses. There were still more tears. Afterward they had made love again, slower, with less urgency, but with a deeper passion. Sated, they had collapsed into the hammock to catch a few hours of sleep before dawn.

Stepping onto the rear deck, Nate studied the forest. The morning skies were blue and clear, last night's storm long gone, the light sharp and bright. Raindrops still clung to every leaf and blade, glistening like jewels. But that wasn't all. "You should see this," he called back to the room.

Kelly, now dressed in her khakis with her shirt half buttoned, joined him. He glanced to her, stunned again by her beauty. Her eyes widened as she stared beyond the deck's edge. "How marvelous . . ."

She leaned into him, and he instinctively circled her with his arm.

Covering the upper limbs of the tree, drawn by the moisture, were hundreds of butterflies, perched on branches and leaves, fluttering through the bower. Each had wings about a handspan wide, brilliant blue and crystalline green.

"*Morpho* species," Nate said. "But I've never seen this color pattern."

Kelly watched one specimen waft by overhead through a beam of sunlight. It seemed to shine with its own luminescence. "It's like someone shattered a stained-glass window and showered the slivers over the treetops."

He tightened his arm around her, trying to capture this moment forever. They stood in silence and awe for several minutes. Then distant voices intruded, rising up from below.

"I suppose we should go down," Nate finally said. "We have a lot to accomplish."

Kelly nodded and sighed. Nate understood her reluctance. Here, isolated above everything else, it was possible to forget, at least for a while, the heartaches and hardships ahead of them. But they could not escape the world forever.

Slowly, they finished dressing. As they were about to leave, Nate crossed to the rear deck and unhooked the bamboo-and-palm-leaf awning so it fell back across the rear door, returning the room to the way he found it.

Kelly noticed what he did and moved nearer, examining the hinges along the top margin of the door. "Closed, it blocks the doorway . . . pushed open and stilted, it's a shade cover for the deck. Clever."

Nate nodded. Yesterday he had been surprised by the ingenuity, too. "I've never seen anything like it out here. It's like my father mentioned in his notes. An example of the tribe's advancement over other indigenous peoples. Subtle engineering improvements, like their crude tree elevators."

"I could use an elevator right now," Kelly noted, stretching a kink from her back. "It does make you wonder, though," she went on, "about the Yagga—about what it's doing to these people."

Nate grunted in agreement, then turned to reassemble his own pack. There was *much* to wonder about here. Once ready, Nate gave the room a final inspection, then crossed to the door where Kelly crouched.

As Kelly slung her pack to her shoulder, Nate leaned in and kissed her deeply. There was a moment of surprise . . . then she returned the kiss with a matching passion. Neither of them had spoken of where the two would go from here. Both knew much of their urgency last night had come from a pair of wounded hearts. But it was a start. Nate looked forward to seeing where it would lead. And if her kiss was a clue, so did Kelly.

They parted, and without another word, they headed to the ladder leading down to the common areas of the dwelling.

As Nate descended, cooking scents swelled around him. He reached the bottom rung and hopped off. After helping Kelly down, they both walked through the common area to the large front deck. Nate's stomach growled, and he suddenly remembered his hunger.

Around a stone hearth set into the deck, Anna and Kouwe were finishing the final preparations for breakfast. Nate spotted a loaf of cassava bread and a tall stone pitcher of cold water.

Anna swung around with a platter of honest-to-goodness bacon in her arms. She lifted her bounty. "From wild boar," she explained. "A pair of tribeswomen arrived with a feast at daybreak."

Nate's mouth watered. There was also more fruit, some type of egg, even what looked like a pie.

"No wonder your father stayed here for so long," Private Carrera mumbled around a mouthful of bacon and bread.

Even this reminder of his father failed to squelch Nate's appetite. He dug in along with the rest.

As he stuffed himself, Nate realized two of their party were missing. "Where are Zane and Olin?"

"Working on the radio," Kostos said. "Olin got the GPS up and running this morning."

Nate choked on a piece of bread. "He got it working!"

Kostos nodded, then shrugged. "He has it recalibrated, but who knows if anyone's receiving."

Nate let this information sink in. His eyes flicked to Kelly. If the signal was received with the revised coordinates, they could be rescued as soon as this evening. Nate recognized the glimmer of hope in Kelly's eyes, too.

"But without the main radio to confirm," Kostos continued, "we may just be spittin' in the wind. And until I get solid confirmation, we proceed with our backup plan. Your mission today—along with Kelly and Zane—will be to make sure Frank is ready for a quick evac if necessary."

"Plus to gather some of the tree's sap," Kelly said.

Kostos nodded, chewing hard. "While Olin works on the radio, the others of us will split up and see if we can't find out more from the Indians. Get intel on those damned repellent powders."

Nate didn't argue with the sergeant's plan. GPS or not, it was safest to proceed as cautiously and expeditiously as possible. The remainder of the meal was finished in silence.

Afterward, the party vacated the dwelling in the nightcap oak and climbed down to the glade, leaving Olin alone in the dwelling with his satellite equipment. Manny and the two Rangers headed in one direction, Anna and Kouwe in another. The plan was to rendezvous back at the tree at noon.

Nate and Kelly headed toward the Yagga with Richard Zane in tow. Nate hitched his shotgun higher. The sergeant had insisted every member of the party go armed with at least a pistol. Kelly had a 9mm holstered at her waist. Zane, ever suspicious, had his Beretta in hand, eyes darting all around.

In addition to the weapons, each of the three teams had been equipped with one of the Rangers' short-range Saber radios, to keep in contact with one another. "Every fifteen minutes, I want to hear an all-clear from each group," Kostos had said dourly. "No one stays silent."

Prepared as well as they could be, the group split up.

As Nate walked across the glade, he stared up at the giant prehistoric gymnospore. Its white bark glistened with dew, as did its leaves, flickering brightly. Among the tiered branches, the clusters of giant nut pods hung, miniature versions of the man-made huts. Nate was anxious to see more of the giant tree.

They reached the thick, knobbed roots, and Kelly guided them between the woody columns to the open cavity in the trunk. As Nate approached, he could appreciate why the natives called their tree Yagga, or Mother. The symbolism was not lost to him. The two main buttress roots were not unlike open legs, framing the tree's monstrous birth canal. It was from here that the Ban-ali had been born into the world.

"It's big enough to drive a truck through," Zane said, staring up at the arched opening.

Nate could not suppress a small shudder as he entered the shadowy heart of the tree. The musky scent of its oil was thick in the passage. All around the lowermost tunnel, small blue handprints decorated the wood wall, hundreds, some large, others small. Did they represent members of the tribe? Did his own father's palm mark this wall somewhere?

"This way," Kelly said, leading them toward the passage winding up the tree.

As Nate and Zane followed, the blue prints disappeared eventually.

Nate glanced along the plain walls, then back toward the entrance. Something was bothering him, but he couldn't exactly put his finger on it. Something didn't look right. Nate studied the flow channels in the wood, the tubules of xylem and phloem that moved water and nutrients up and down the trunk. The channels ran down in graceful, winding curves around the passage walls. But down below, where the passage bluntly ended, the flow channels were jagged, no longer curving smoothly. Before he could examine this further, the group had passed beyond the tunnel's curve.

"It's a long climb," Kelly said, pointing ahead. "The healing chamber is at the very top, near the crown of the tree."

Nate followed. The tunnel looked like some

monstrous insect bore. In his study of botany, he was well familiar with insect damage to trees: mountain pine beetle, European elm bark beetle, raspberry crown borer. But this tunnel had not been cored out—he would stake his life on it. It had formed naturally, like the tubules found inside the stems and trunk of an ant tree, an evolutionary adaptation. But even this raised a new question. Surely this tree was centuries older than the first arrival of the Ban-ali to this region. So why did the tree grow these hollowed tubules in the first place?

He remembered Kelly's muttered words at the end of last night's group discussion. *We're missing something . . . something important.*

They started passing openings through the tree's trunk to the outside. Some led directly into huts, others led out onto branches with huts beyond. He counted as they climbed. There had to be at least twenty openings.

Behind him, Zane reported in on the Saber radio. All was well with the other teams.

At last, they reached the end of the passage, where it ballooned out into a cavernous space with slits cut high in the walls to allow in the sunlight. Still, the chamber was dim.

Kelly hurried over to her brother.

The small shaman stood across the room, checking on another patient. He glanced up at their approach. He was alone. "Good morning," he said in stiff English.

Nate nodded. It was strange knowing these words were most likely taught to the man by his own father. He knew from reading his father's notes that this shaman was also the Ban-ali's nominal leader. Their class structure here was not highly organized. Each person seemed to know his place and role. But here was the tribe's king, the one who communed closest with the Yagga.

Kelly knelt at Frank's side. He was sitting up and sucking the contents of one of the tree's nuts through a reed straw.

He set his liquid meal aside. "The breakfast of champions," he said with his usual good-natured smirk.

Nate saw he still wore his Red Sox cap—and nothing else. He had a small blanket over his lower half, hiding his stumped legs. But he was bare-chested, revealing plainly what was painted there.

A crimson serpent with a blue handprint in the center.

"I woke up with it," Frank said, noticing Nate's gaze. "They must have painted it on me during the night when I was drugged out."

The mark of the Ban-ali.

The shaman stepped to Nate's side. "You . . . son of *Wishwa* Kerl."

Nate turned and nodded. Apparently their guide, Dakii, had been telling tales. "Yes, Carl was my father."

The shaman king clapped him on the shoulder. "He good man."

Nate did not know how to respond to this. He found himself nodding while really wanting to rip into the shaman. *If he was such a good man, why did you murder him?* But from working and living with indigenous tribes throughout the region, he knew there would never be a satisfactory answer. Among the tribes, even a good man could be killed for breaking a taboo—one could even be honored by being turned into plant fertilizer.

Kelly finished her examination of Frank. "His wounds have entirely sealed. The rate of granulation is amazing."

Her expression must have been clear to the shaman. "Yagga heals him. Grow strong. Grow—" The shaman frowned, clearly struggling to remember a word. Finally, he bent down and slapped his own leg.

Kelly stared at the shaman, then at Nate. "Do you think it's possible? Could Frank's legs really grow back?"

"Gerald Clark's arm regenerated," Nate said. "So we know it's possible."

Kelly crouched. "If we could watch the transformation in a modern medical facility . . ."

Zane interrupted her, lowering his voice and keeping his back toward the shaman. "Remember, we have a mission here."

"What mission?" Frank asked.

Kelly quietly explained.

Frank brightened. "The GPS is working! Then there's hope."

Kelly nodded.

By now, the shaman had wandered off, losing interest in them.

"In the meantime," Zane hissed, "we're supposed to gather a sample of the sap."

"I know where it comes from," Kelly said, nodding toward a channel carved deep into the wall. Shielded by the two men, she picked up the empty nut drained by her brother and pulled out the straw. She crossed to the wall and removed a small wooden plug. A thick red sap began to flow into the channel. She bent the nut's opening into the flow and began collecting the sap. It was slow work.

"Let me," Zane said. "You look after your brother."

Kelly nodded and stepped to Nate. "The stretcher is still here," she said, pointing an arm to the make-shift travois. "When and if we get the signal, we'll have to move fast."

"We should—"

The first explosion shocked them all. Everyone froze as the blast echoed away. Nate stared at the open slits high up the curved walls. It was not thunder. Not from blue skies. Then more and more booms followed. Beyond the roar, sharper cries arose.

Screams.

"We're under attack!" Nate exclaimed.

He turned and found a pistol pointed at him.

"Don't move," Zane said, crouching by the wall, a tight and scared expression on his face. He held the nut, now overflowing with sap, cradled in one arm, and the 9mm Beretta in the other. "No one move."

"What are you—" Kelly began.

Nate interrupted, immediately understanding. "You!" He remembered Kouwe's suspicions: *other trackers on their trail, a spy among them.* "You goddamn bastard. You sold us out!"

Zane slowly stood. "Back away!" The pistol was held rock steady on them.

Beyond the tense room, explosions continued to boom. Grenades.

Nate pulled Kelly away from Zane's threatening gun.

Behind them, the shaman suddenly bolted toward the opening, frightened by the explosions, oblivious to the closer threat. A sound of alarm rose on his lips.

"Stop!" Zane screamed at the tribesman.

The shaman was too panicked to listen or to comprehend the stranger's tongue. He continued to run.

Zane twitched his gun and fired. In the enclosed space, the blast was deafening. But not so deafening as to drown out the cry of surprise from the shaman.

Nate glanced over his shoulder. The shaman fell on his side, clutching his belly, gasping. Blood flowed from around his fingers.

Red with anger, Nate turned on Zane. "You bastard. He couldn't understand you."

The gun again pointed at them. Zane slowly circled around, keeping his weapon aimed. He even kept a safe distance from Frank's hammock, not taking any chances. "You were always the gullible fool," the Tellux man said. "Just like your father. Neither of you understood anything about money and power."

"Who are you working for?" Nate spat.

Zane now had his back to the exit. The shaman had rolled into a moaning ball off to the side. Zane stopped and motioned with his pistol. "Toss your weapons out the window slits. One at a time."

Nate refused to budge, shaking with rage. Zane fired, blasting wood chips from between Nate's toes.

"Do as he says," Frank ordered from the hammock.

Scowling, Kelly obeyed. She freed her pistol from its holster and flung it out one of the windows.

Nate still hesitated.

Zane smiled coldly. "The next bullet goes through your girlfriend's heart."

"Nate . . ." Frank warned from the bed.

Teeth clenched, Nate edged to the wall, weighing his chances of firing at Zane. But the odds weren't good, not with Kelly's life at risk. He unslung his gun and heaved it through one of the slits.

Zane nodded, satisfied, and backed toward the exit. "You'll have to excuse me, but I have a rendez-vous to make. I suggest you three remain here. It's the safest spot in the valley at the moment."

With those snide words, Zane slipped out of the chamber and disappeared down the throat of the tunnel.

8:12 A.M.

Deep in the jungle, Manny ran alongside Private Carrera. Tor-tor raced beside them, ears flattened to his skull. Explosions ripped through the morning, smoke wafted through the trees.

Kostos ran ahead of them, screaming into his radio. "Everyone back to home base! Rally at the dwelling!"

"Could they be our people?" Manny asked. "Responding to the GPS?"

Carrera glanced back at him and frowned. "Not this quick. We've been ambushed."

As if confirming this, a trio of men, dressed in

camouflage gear and armed with AK-47s and grenade launchers, trotted into view.

Kostos hissed and waved them all down.

They dropped to their bellies.

An Indian ran at the group with a raised spear.
He was nearly cut in half by automatic fire.

Tor-tor, spooked by the chattering gunfire, bolted
forward.

"Tor-tor!" Manny hissed, rising to one knee, reaching for the cat.

The jaguar dashed into the open, across the path
of the gunmen.

One of them barked something in Spanish and
pointed. Another grinned and lifted his weapon,
eyeing down the barrel.

Manny raised his pistol. But before he could fire,
Kostos rose up ahead of him, the M-16 at his shoulder, and popped off three shots, three squeezes of
the trigger. *Blam, blam, blam.*

The trio fell backward, heads exploding like
melons.

Manny froze, stunned.

"C'mon. We need to get back to the tree." Kostos
scowled at the jungle. "Why the hell aren't the others responding?"

8:22 A.M.

Kouwe kept Anna behind him as he hid behind a
bushy fern. Dakii, the tribal guide, crouched beside
him. The four mercenaries stood only six yards away,
unaware of the eyes watching them. Though Kouwe

had heard the sergeant's order to regroup at the night-cap oak, with the marauders so near, he dared not signal his acknowledgment. They were pinned down. The group of mercenaries stood between them and the home tree. There was no way to get past them unseen.

Behind him, Dakii crouched as still as a stone, but the tension emanating from him was fierce. While hidden, he had watched more than a dozen of his tribesmen—men, women, children—mowed down by this group.

Further in the wood, explosions continued to boom. They heard screams and the crash of dwellings from the treetops. The marauders were tearing through the village. The only hope for Kouwe's party was to flee to some sheltered corner of the jungled plateau, hope to be overlooked.

One of the soldiers barked into a radio in Spanish. "Tango Team in position. Killzone fourteen secure."

Kouwe felt something brush his knee. He glanced over. Dakii motioned for him to remain in place. Kouwe nodded.

Dakii rolled from his side, moving swiftly and silently. Not a single twig was disturbed. Dakii was *teshari-rin*, one of the tribe's ghost scouts. Even without his paint, the tribesman blended into the deeper shadows. He raced from shelter to shelter, a dark blur. Kouwe knew he was witnessing a demonstration of the Yagga's enhancement of its wards. Dakii circled around the band, then even Kouwe lost track of him.

Anna grabbed his hand and squeezed. *Have we just been abandoned?* she seemed to silently ask.

Kouwe wondered, too, until he spotted Dakii. The tribesman crouched across the way. He was in direct sight of Kouwe and Anna, but still hidden from the four guards.

Dakii rolled to his back in the loam, aiming the small bow he had found high into the air. Kouwe followed where his arrow pointed. Then back down to the mercenaries.

He understood and motioned for Anna to be ready with her own weapon. She nodded, staring up, then back down, understanding.

Kouwe signaled Dakii.

The tribesman pulled taut his bowstring and let fly an arrow. A tiny *twang* was heard, as was the louder rip of arrow through leaf. The mercenaries all turned in Dakii's direction, weapons raised.

Kouwe ignored them, his gaze focused above. High in the branches was the ruin of a dwelling, but left intact among the branches was one of the little ingenious inventions of the Ban-ali, one of their makeshift elevators. Dakii's arrow sliced the support rope that held aloft a cradled counterweight, a large chunk of granite.

The boulder came crashing down, straight at the group of mercenaries.

One was smashed under its weight, his face crushed as he glanced up a moment too late.

Kouwe and Anna were already on their feet. From such close range, they emptied their pistols at the remaining trio, striking chests, arms, and bellies. The group fell. Dakii rushed out, an obsidian dagger in his hand. He ran at the mercenaries and slit the throats of any who still moved. It was quick and bloody work.

With a hand, Kouwe steadied Anna, who had paled at the display. "We have to get back to the others."

9:05 A.M.

From the height of the chasm, Louis had a wide view of the isolated valley. A pair of binoculars hung around his neck, forgotten. Across the jungle, smoke rose from countless fires and signal flares. In just over an hour, his team had encircled the village and was now closing slowly toward the center, toward his goal and prize.

Brail, who had been assigned as his new lieutenant after Jacques disappeared, spoke near his feet. The tracker knelt over a map, marking off small *X*'s as his units reported in. "The net's secure, *Herr Doktor*. Nothing left now but mopping up."

Louis could tell the man was anxious to bag his own limit here.

"And the Rangers? The Americans?"

"Herded toward the center, just as you ordered."

"Excellent." Louis nodded to his mistress at his side. Tshui was naked, armed only with a little blow-gun. Between her breasts rested the shrunken head of Corporal DeMartini, hung around Tshui's neck by the man's own dog tags.

"Then it's time we joined the party." He lifted his twin pair of snub-nosed mini-Uzis. They felt powerful in his hands. "It's high time I made the acquaintance of Nathan Rand."

9:12 A.M.

"You watch over your brother and the shaman," Nathan said, sensing time was running out. "I'm going after Zane."

"You don't have a weapon." Kelly knelt beside the shaman. With Nathan's help, the two had wrangled the tribesman into a hammock. Kelly had shot him full of morphine, quieting his pained thrashing. A belly wound was one of the most agonizing. With no better solution, she was now slathering the entry and exit wounds with Yagga sap. "What are you going to do if you catch him?"

Nate felt a fire in his own belly, just as agonizing as a bullet wound. "First he betrayed my father, now he betrayed us." His voice choked with anger. He wanted only one thing from the man. *Vengeance.*

Frank spoke from his hammock. "What are you going to do?"

Nathan shook his head. "I have to try."

He headed toward the exit. Distantly the explosions had died down, but gunfire spat sporadically. The fewer the shots, the more obvious it became that the village was being wiped out. Nate knew they would fare no better, not unless something was done. But what?

Stalking down the passage, at first cautiously, then faster and faster, around and around, Nate was reminded of the serpentine pattern of the Ban-ali symbol, winding in a spiral. Could this passage be what the symbol represented, or was it what Kelly had conjectured earlier, a crude representation of the twisted protein model, the mutagenic prion? If it represented the Yagga's tunnel, what did the helixes at each end of the spiral mean? Did one depict the healing ward? And if so, what did the other represent? And the blue handprint? Nate recalled the painted handprints decorating the entrance to the passage and shook his head. What did it all mean?

He ran around a corner and stumbled over a dead Indian lying in the tunnel. Nate fell to his hands, skidding on his knees. Once stopped, he rolled around and saw the bullet hole in the man's chest and a second in the back of his head.

Nate looked down and saw another body, just its legs, around the next curve. Another Indian.

Zane.

Nate scrambled to his feet, his blood on fire. The man was picking off the unarmed stragglers here, healers and aides to the shaman, brutally clearing a bloody path to the tunnel's end. *The fucking coward.*

Nate shoved down the tunnel, counting off the openings on his left. When he reached the last one, he ducked out of the passage and through a small, empty dwelling. He found himself on a branch at least five feet thick. Before continuing, he needed some idea of what was happening below. Smoke billowed and wafted through the open glade.

In the clearing around the tree, a few Indians retreated toward the Yagga.

By now, an ominous quiet had settled over the village.

Nate edged along the branch, but he couldn't get a good look across the glade toward the nightcap oak and his team's temporary homestead. The branch pointed the wrong way. He couldn't even spy the entrance to the Yagga. *Damn it.*

Pistol fire sounded from below. Zane! A scream erupted from the field on the tree's far side. The coward must be hiding down at the tunnel's end, killing any Indians who neared. Nate knew the bastard had enough ammo to hold them off for a while.

The Indians in direct sight below fled toward the cover of the thicker wood.

Nate stared across the glade. There was no sign of his friends.

As Nate sidled along the thick limb, his toe nudged a rope coiled atop the branch. He looked closer. Not rope, he realized, but one of the vine ladders.

"A fire escape," he mumbled. An idea flashed into his mind—a plan forming.

Before he lost his nerve, he shoved the piled vine over the edge.

The ladder unrolled with a whispery sound until it snapped to its full length, only three feet from the ground. It was a long climb, but if Zane was down there, perhaps Nate could sneak up on him.

With no more plan than that, Nate mounted the ladder and began a hurried climb earthward. He raced down the rungs. If his group and the remaining Indians could fall back here, they might have a more defensible position. But before that could happen, Zane had to be eliminated.

Nate reached the end of the ladder and hopped off.

Tall roots rose all around him, and it took Nate a moment to orient himself. The stream was behind and off to the left. That meant he was at about the four o'clock position from the tunnel entrance. He began to wind counterclockwise around the trunk.

Three o'clock . . . two o'clock . . .

Somewhere off in the forest, a spatter of automatic gunfire erupted. Another grenade exploded. Clearly the fighting had not entirely ceased in some parts of the village.

Using the cover of the noise, Nate crawled and edged his way around the tree's base. At last, he spotted one of the tall buttress roots that flanked the entrance. *One o'clock.*

Nate leaned against the trunk. Zane was beyond the obstruction . . . but how to proceed from here was the tricky part. Another pistol shot rang out from Zane's bunker. Nate frowned down at his empty hands.

What plan now, hero boy?

9:34 A.M.

Zane knelt on one knee, aiming out with his pistol. Tiring, he supported his weapon arm with his other. But he refused to let down his guard, not when victory was so close. He only had to hold out a little longer, then his role in this mission would be over.

One eye twitched to the nut full of the miraculous

sap. It was a fortune worth billions. Though St. Savin Pharmaceuticals had made a sizable deposit in Zane's Swiss account to buy his cooperation, it was the promised bonus of a quarter percentage point of gross sales that had finally sold him on the betrayal. With the potential in the Yagga's sap, there was no limit to the wealth that could flow his way.

Zane licked his lips. His role here was almost at an end. Days ago, he had successfully slipped the computer virus into the team's communication equipment. Now all that remained was the final endgame.

Late last night, Favre had instructed Zane to obtain a sample of the sap and protect it with his life. "If those damn natives pull some jackass stunt," Louis had warned, "like setting fire to their precious tree to protect their secret, then you're our failsafe."

Zane had, of course, agreed, but unknown to his murderous partner, Zane had his own backup plan in mind, too. Once secure here, Zane had poured a small sample of the sap from the nut, sealed it in a latex condom, tied it off, and swallowed it. An extra bit of insurance on his own part. Any betrayal and a competing pharmaceutical company, like Tellux, would find itself in possession of the miraculous substance instead of St. Savin.

Distant rifle shots sounded from the woods. He spotted flashes of muzzle fire. Favre's men were cinching the noose. It would not be long.

As if confirming this, a grenade exploded at the glade's fringe. A dwelling in one of the huge trees blew apart, casting leaf and branch high into the air.

Zane smiled—then he heard a voice within the echo of the blast. It sounded close.

"Watch out! Grenade!"

Something hit the trunk of the tree just over his head and bounced into the flanking root. *Grenade!* his mind echoed.

With a cry of alarm, he dove away from the entrance and rolled deeper into the shaft, arms shielding his head. He waited several tense seconds, then several more. He panted, ragged from the near escape. The expected explosion never came. Cautiously uncovering his head, he clenched his teeth. Still no blast.

He sat up, crawled slowly back toward the entrance, and peeked around the corner, where he spotted the small coconut-shaped object resting in the dirt. It was just one of the immature nut pods from the damn tree! It must have fallen from an overhead branch.

"Goddamn it!" He felt foolish at his panic.

He straightened, raising his weapon, and stepped back to his guard position. *Getting too damn jumpy . . .*

A blur of motion.

Something solid struck his wrist. The pistol flew from his fingers as his wrist exploded with pain. He started to fall backward—then his arm was grabbed by someone stepping from the blind side of the entrance. He was yanked out of the entrance and thrown bodily forward.

His shoulder hit the dirt. He rolled and stared back around. What he saw was impossible. "Rand? How?"

Nathan Rand towered over him at the entrance to the tunnel, a long, thick section of branch in his hand, which he raised menacingly.

Zane crab-crawled backward.

"How?" Nate asked. "A little lesson from our Indian friends. The power of suggestion." Rand kicked the immature seed pod toward him. "Believe something strongly enough, and others will believe, too."

Zane scrambled to his feet.

Nate swung the branch like a bat, striking him on the shoulder and knocking him back down. "That was for the shaman you shot like a dog!" Nate lifted the branch again. "And this is for—"

Zane glanced over Nate's shoulder. "Kelly! Thank God!"

Nate turned half around.

Using the moment of distraction, Zane shot to his feet and darted away. He cleared the side root in three steps.

He heard the blistering protest behind him and smiled.

What a . . .

. . . fool! Tricked by his own damn ruse! No one stood at the tunnel entrance. Kelly was not there.

Nate watched Zane race around the thick buttress. "No, you don't, you bastard!" With club in hand, he gave chase.

Still ringing with anger, Nate flew around the tree and spotted Zane fleeing along the base of the trunk, toward a tangle of roots. The traitor could easily get lost among them and escape. Nate thought of going back for the abandoned pistol, but he didn't have the time. He dared not lose sight of the bastard.

Ahead, Zane ducked under an arched root and wriggled through agilely. He was one wiry son of a bitch. In this race, Zane's smaller frame and lighter build were advantageous.

Realizing they were matched now fist to fist, Nathan tossed aside his club and pursued Zane. They fought through the snarl, crawling, climbing, leaping, squirming their way through the tangled maze. Zane was making headway on him.

Then the roots opened. They both stumbled onto some path amid the mess. Zane ran, pounding down the trail. Nate swore and went after him.

Ahead, water glistened. As they raced along the snaking trail, Nate saw the path ended at a wide pool, blocking the way. A dead end.

Nate smiled. *End of the line, Zane!*

As they neared the pool, his quarry also realized he had run himself into a blind alley and slowed— but instead of a groan of defeat, Nate heard a snarl of glee.

Zane leaped to the side, diving for the ground.

Nate closed the distance.

Zane swung to face him, a gun in hand. A 9mm Beretta.

It took Nate a startled moment to fathom this miracle. Then he saw his own shotgun, hanging by its shoulder strap from a rootlet a few steps to his right. The pistol was Kelly's! One of the weapons Zane had made them toss out of the treetop.

Nate groaned. The gods were not smiling on

him. He took a step toward his shotgun, but Zane clucked his tongue.

"Move another inch, and you get a third eye!"

9:46 A.M.

Kouwe herded Anna ahead of him. The crack of rifle fire was closing all around them. Dakii led the way, expressionless, in scout mode. He wound with calm assurance through his village forest, guiding them back toward the nightcap oak. They needed to rendezvous with the Rangers. Put together some semblance of a plan.

Kouwe had been able to contact Sergeant Kostos over the radio and inform him of their status. He had also learned that Olin, left up in the dwelling, had been able to report in, too. The Russian was keeping himself well hidden in the tree. But so far no word had come from Nate's party. He prayed they were okay.

At last, Kouwe spotted sunlight ahead. The central glade! His team had been circling around from the south, keeping within the jungle cover. According to the sergeant, the Rangers were angling down from the north side.

Dakii slowed and pointed from a half crouch.

Anna and Kouwe moved up with him. Through a break in the foliage, Kouwe spotted the small log cabin in the clearing. He was able to orient himself. He followed the tribesman's arm. The nightcap oak, their destination, lay only fifty yards ahead. But that was not what Dakii was pointing out. Beyond the giant oak, Kouwe spotted Tor-tor. The jaguar raced along the clearing's edge. Drawn by the motion, Kouwe was able to see figures moving through the deeper shadows.

The Ranger team and Manny! They had made it back!

Dakii led them onward, speeding deftly through the glade's fringe.

In a few minutes, the two parties reunited at the base of the tree. Sergeant Kostos clapped Kouwe on the shoulder. Anna and Manny hugged.

"Any word from Nate?" Kouwe asked.

The sergeant shook his head, then waved to the dwelling. "I've ordered Olin to pack up his GPS and join us."

"Why? I thought the plan was to rendezvous at the tree."

"This is close enough. As near as I can tell, we're boxed in. The tree is no protection."

Kouwe frowned but understood. The marauders were systematically destroying every dwelling. They'd be trapped up there. "What then?"

"We bug out of here. Find a way through their line as silently as possible. Once past them, we'll seek shelter, somewhere where they can't find us."

Manny edged closer to them, glancing at his watch. "The sergeant set one of his napalm bombs back in the woods, timed to explode in another fifteen minutes."

"A distraction," Sergeant Kostos said. He hiked his pack on his shoulder. "And we have more if we need them."

"It's why we can't wait for Nate," Manny said, reading his friend's eyes.

Kouwe gazed at the Yagga. The sound of gunfire was trickling away . . . as was their time. If they were going to have any chance, they would have to take it now. Kouwe reluctantly nodded, conceding.

Overhead, the vine ladder shuddered. He glanced up. Olin was climbing down, his radio pack in place.

Kostos waved his M-16. "Let's get ready to—"

The blast rocked them all to their knees. Kouwe swung around and watched the roof of the cabin sail high into the air. Bits of debris blew outward with tremendous force. A section of log shot by overhead, a flying battering ram, slicing into the jungle and crashing into its depths. Smoke billowed outward.

That was no grenade blast.

Through the smoke, a cadre of soldiers appeared, weapons raised and ready.

Kouwe noticed two things simultaneously. First, walking in the lead was a naked woman, hand in hand with a tall gentleman dressed all in white.

But the second thing Kouwe noted was of more immediate menace, something carried by one of the soldiers. The man dropped to a knee and lifted a long black tube on his shoulder.

Kouwe had seen enough Hollywood movies to recognize the weapon.

"*Rocket launcher!*" Carrera screamed behind him. "Everyone down!"

10:03 A.M.

The first blast had frozen both Nate and Zane in place. Nate kept focused on his adversary's weapon.

From only a few yards away, the pistol was pointing square at his chest. He dared not move. He held his breath.

What was going on out there?

As the second blast sounded, Zane's eyes twitched in the direction of the explosion. Nate knew he wouldn't have another chance. He was dead unless he did something . . . even something stupid.

Nate lunged through the air, not toward Zane, but toward the dangling shotgun. His movement did not go unnoticed. Nate heard the sharp report of Zane's pistol and felt something sting his upper thigh, but he didn't stop.

His body struck the root, his arms scrambling for the shotgun. He didn't have time to unhook the strap. From where it hung, he just blindly swung the barrel in Zane's general direction and yanked the trigger. Recoil tore the weapon from his hand.

Nate ducked and swung around.

He saw Zane flying backward, his belly bloody, arms flung out. Zane landed in the small pond at the end of the blocked trail. He sputtered to the surface—the water was surprisingly deep, even near shore—and cried in alarm and pain.

Zane was now learning the lesson he had taught the unarmed Ban-ali shaman: a belly shot was one of the most agonizing.

Nate pushed up and unhooked his shotgun. He pointed it at the floundering man. He had not seen where the pistol had gone and was taking no chances this time.

Zane, his face a mask of torment, struggled toward the shore. Then his body suddenly jerked, his eyes widened in shock. His moaning turned to fresh screams. "Nate! Help me!"

Responding instinctively, Nate took a step forward.

Zane reached toward him, face pleading, terrified—then all around his body, the waters erupted in a fierce churning.

Nate caught several flashes of silver bodies. *Piranhas.* He backed away, realizing where he was: the birthing pool, the hatchery that Manny had described finding.

Zane thrashed, jerking and twitching, screeching. He began to sink into the froth. His eyes rolled with panic as he fought to keep his mouth above water. He failed. His head sank away. Only one arm remained above the pool—then even this disappeared under the roiling waters.

Nate turned from the pool and crossed down the path, feeling no pity for the man. He briefly checked the stinging burn in his thigh. He found a bullet hole in his pants and a trickle of blood. Just a graze, nothing more. He had been damned lucky.

He clenched the shotgun in his grip and marched down the trail, praying his luck would hold.

10:12 A.M.

Manny shifted under a pile of debris, shoving with his shoulders. Smoke choked him. The explosion of the rocket in the treetop still rang in his head. It hurt to move his jaw. He crawled free amid shouts and yells. All commands.

"Throw down your weapons!"

"Show us your hands!"

"Move now, or I'll shoot you dead where you lie!"

That was incentive enough. Manny groaned and spat out blood. He glanced up into chaos. He saw Anna Fong on her knees, hands on her head. She looked all but unscathed. Professor Kouwe knelt at her side, bearing a scalp gash that dripped blood down his cheek. Dakii was also there, wearing an expression of stunned disbelief.

Turning, Manny saw Tor-tor's spotted face peering out from under a bush. He motioned the jaguar to stay put. Near the same bush, he watched Private Carrera furtively shove her Bailey under a section of the roof thatch from one of the abodes above.

"You!" someone barked. "On your feet!"

Manny didn't know who the man was talking to until he felt the hot barrel of a gun on his temple. He froze.

"On your feet!" the man repeated. His words were heavily accented, German perhaps.

Manny clambered to his knees, then to his feet. He wobbled, but this seemed to satisfy the mercenary.

"Your weapon!" he barked.

Manny glanced around him as if searching for a missing shoe or sock. He saw his pistol lying there and nudged it with a toe. "There."

A second soldier appeared out of nowhere and confiscated it.

"Join the *anderen*!" the man said with a shove toward the others.

As he stumbled toward his kneeling friends,

Manny saw Carrera and Kostos escorted by other guards. Their holsters were empty, packs gone. They were all forced to their knees, hands on their heads. The sergeant's left eye was swollen, his nose crooked and bloodied, broken. Kostos had clearly put up more fight than Manny.

Suddenly a distant section of deeper forest blew up into a ball of fire. The soft explosion echoed out to them, along with the smell of napalm.

So much for Kostos's planned "distraction." Too little, too late.

"Herr Brail, this one's not moving!" one of the mercenaries shouted behind them in a mix of German and Spanish.

Manny glanced back to the base of the nightcap oak. It was Olin. He lay in a crumpled heap. A spear of wood had pierced through his shoulder and blood flowed brightly across his light khaki shirt. Manny saw he was still breathing.

The one named Brail tore his gaze from the burning forest and wandered over to check on the Russian. "Hundefleisch," the German said. *Dog meat.* He lifted his pistol and shot Olin in the back of the head.

Anna jumped at the noise, a sob escaping her.

From near the ruins of the log cabin, the two leaders of the attack force casually wandered toward them. The small Indian woman, though naked, moved casually, as if through a garden party, all curves and smooth legs. She wore a talisman resting between her breasts. Manny had first thought it was a leather satchel, but as she neared, he recognized it as a shrunken head. The hair atop the disgusting trinket was shaved.

The slender man at her side, dressed in white khakis and a rakish Panama hat, noticed his attention. He lifted the necklace for the others' view.

Manny spotted the dog tags.

"May I reintroduce you to Corporal DeMartini." He laughed lightly, as if he had made a joke, a party amusement, and dropped the defiled head of their former teammate back to the woman's chest.

Sergeant Kostos grumbled a threat, but the AK-47 pointed at the nape of his neck kept him on his knees.

Louis smiled at the line of kneeling prisoners. "It's good to see you all together again."

Manny recognized a distinctly French accent. *Who was this man?*

Professor Kouwe answered his silent question. "Louis Favre," the professor mumbled under his breath, his expression sickened.

The Frenchman's gaze swung to Kouwe. "That's *Doctor* Favre, *Professor* Kouwe. Please let's keep this courteous, and we can be done with this unpleasant matter as quickly as possible."

Kouwe simply glowered.

Manny knew the man's name. He was a biologist banned from Brazil for black-market profiteering and for crimes against the indigenous people. The professor, along with Nate's father, had shared an infamous past with this man.

"Now, we've counted heads here and seem to have come up a few short," Favre said. "Where are the last members of your little troupe?"

No one spoke.

"Come now. Let's keep this friendly, shall we? It's

such a pleasant day." Favre marched up and down the row of prisoners. "You don't want this to turn ugly now, do you? It's a simple question."

Still no one moved. Everyone stared blankly forward.

Favre shook his head sadly. "Then ugly it is." He turned to the woman. "Tshui, *ma chérie*, take your pick." He brushed his hands primly as if done with the matter.

The naked woman stalked before them, and hesitated before Private Carrera, cocking her head, then suddenly sprang two places over to kneel before Anna. Her nose was only an inch from the anthropologist's.

Anna recoiled, but the gun behind her held her in place.

"My darling has an eye for beauty."

Moving as quickly as a striking snake, the Indian woman drew a long, slender bone knife from a sheath hidden in her long tresses. Manny had seen knife sheaths like this braided into the hair of warriors in only one Amerindian tribe: the Shuar, the headhunters of Equador.

The bleached-white knife pointed into the tender flesh under Anna's chin. The Asian woman trembled. Red blood dribbled down the white blade. Anna gasped.

Enough, Manny thought, reacting reflexively. His right hand dropped to his waist, settling atop the handle of the short bullwhip. *He* could also move quickly when he wanted, reflexes developed from years of taming a wild cat. With skilled fingers, he snapped out with the whip.

The tip of the leather struck the bone knife, sending it flying, and nicked a cut under the Shuar woman's eye.

Like a cat, she hissed and rolled away, wounded. A second knife appeared in her hand as if by magic. It seemed this cat had many claws.

"Leave Anna be!" Manny yelled. "I'll tell you where the others are!" Before he could say anything else, Manny was clubbed from behind, knocked to his face in the dirt and leaves. A foot kicked his whip away, then stomped on the offending hand, snapping a finger.

"Drag him up!" Favre barked, all traces of his genteel mannerisms falling away.

Manny was hauled up by his hair. He cradled his injured hand to his chest.

Favre stood by the Indian woman and wiped the blood from her cheek. Favre turned to Manny and licked the blood from his fingertip.

"Now was that necessary?" he asked, and reached a hand behind him. One of the gunmen placed a snub-nosed rifle in his palm. Some type of miniature Uzi, from the looks of it.

The fist in Manny's hair twisted hard.

"Release him, Brail," Favre said.

The hand let go of him. Unsupported, Manny almost sagged to his face again.

"Where are they?" Louis asked.

Manny bit past the pain. "In the tree . . . the last time we saw them . . . they've not responded to our radios."

Favre nodded. "So I heard." He reached his free hand and pulled out a matching radio. "Corporal

DeMartini was gracious enough to lend me his Saber and supply me with the proper radio frequencies."

Manny frowned. "If you knew . . . why . . . ?" He glanced over to Anna.

A long sigh followed, exasperated and bored. "Just making sure no one was attempting some deceptive tactic. It seems I've lost contact with my own agent in your party. And that always arouses my suspicious nature."

"Agent?" Manny asked.

"Spy," Kouwe said from the end of the row of prisoners. "Richard Zane."

"Indeed." Favre turned toward the tree and raised the radio to this mouth. "Nate, if you can hear me, stay put. We'll be coming over to join you."

There was no answer.

Manny hoped somehow Nate had fled with Kelly. But in his heart, he knew Kelly would never leave her brother's side. All of them must still be hiding in the ancient tree.

As the Frenchman stared at the white-barked giant, his eyes narrowed. After a moment, he swung back and focused on Manny again. "That leaves me only to address the insult upon my lady here."

The stubby Uzi again was raised in his direction.

"Not very gentlemanly of you, Monsieur Azevedo."

Favre pulled the trigger. Shots rattled and sprayed out.

Manny winced, but not a bullet struck him.

A grunt sounded behind him. The guard at his back collapsed into view, his upper body riddled. He lay on the ground, gasping like a beached fish. Blood poured out from his mouth and nose.

Favre lowered his weapon. Manny stared up at the Frenchman. Favre cocked one eyebrow. "It's not you I blame. Brail should have minded you better. He should never have left that damn whip at your side. Sloppy, sloppy work." Louis shook his head. "Two lieutenants gone in the same number of days."

He turned away and waved his weapon. "Bring the prisoners." He strode toward the Yagga. "I'm done chasing after Carl's boy. Let's see if we can coax the shy fellow to come out and join us."

11:09 A.M.

Nate hid in the shadow of the Yagga's buttress root. Smoke clouded the glade. He heard intermittent gunfire and muffled shouts from the direction of the nightcap oak. *What was going on?*

The only object within sight inside the glade was the cratered husk of his father's log cabin. A mingled sense of dread and despair settled over his body like a shroud. Then, like ghosts from a grave, figures appeared out of the smoke, shadowy and vague.

He slipped deeper into the root's shadow, leveling his shotgun in their direction. Slowly, with each step, the apparitions took form and substance. He recognized Manny and Kouwe in the lead, guarding Anna between them. Kostos and Carrera flanked them, a step behind. Even the tribesman, Dakii, marched with them.

Blood stained all of them and they walked with

their hands behind their backs, stumbling, prodded from behind by shadowy figures. As they approached, the others grew clearer: men in a mix of military and jungle fatigues. They had weapons of every ilk pointed at his friends.

Nate aimed down the barrel of his shotgun. A useless weapon against these odds, these numbers. He needed another plan. But for now, he only had stealth and shadows.

His teammates were drawn to a stop by their guards.

A man dressed all in white lifted a small bullhorn to his lips. "Nathan Rand!" he bellowed, aiming for the Yagga's treetop. "Show yourself! Come out freely or your friends will pay for your absence. I will give you two minutes!"

His teammates and the Indian were forced to their knees.

Nate lowered himself further into hiding. Without a doubt, the man out there was the leader of these mercenaries, a Frenchman judging from his accent. The man glanced at his watch, then back up to the treetop, tapping a toe impatiently. He clearly thought Nate was still in the upper bowers, relying on the last bit of intelligence from his dead spy.

Nate wavered. Show himself or flee? Should he take his chances in the woods? Perhaps try to get around behind the soldiers? Nate mentally shook his head. He was no guerrilla warrior.

"Thirty seconds, Nathan!" the man roared through the bullhorn.

A tiny voice echoed down from above. "Nate's not up here! He left!"

It was Kelly!

The Frenchman lowered his bullhorn. "Lies," he muttered under his breath.

Kouwe spoke up from where he knelt. "Dr. Favre . . . a word with you, please."

Nate found his fingers tightening on his shotgun, instantly recognizing the name. He had heard tales from his father about the atrocities attributed to Louis Favre. He was the bogeyman of the Amazon, a devil whispered about among the tribes, a monster banished from the region by his own father. But now here again.

"What is it, Professor?" Favre asked with irritation.

"That was Kelly O'Brien. She's with her injured brother. If she says Nate's not up there, then he's not."

Favre frowned and checked his watch. "We'll see." He raised his bullhorn. "Ten seconds!" He then held out a palm, and a wicked weapon was handed to him: a curved machete as long as a scythe. Even in the smoky sunshine, it shone brightly—freshly sharpened.

Favre leaned and placed the curve of the blade under Anna Fong's neck, then lifted the bullhorn. "Time is running out, Nathan! I've been generous giving you an initial two minutes. From here on out, every minute will cost a friend's life. Come out now, and all will be spared! This I swear as a gentleman and a Frenchman." Favre counted the last seconds. "*Five . . . four . . .*"

Nathan struggled for some plan . . . anything. He knew Louis Favre's sworn word was worthless.

"*Three . . . two . . .*"

He had seconds to come up with an alternative to submission.

"*One . . .*"

He found none.

"*Zero!*"

Nathan rose out of his hiding place. He stepped out with his shotgun over his head. "You win!" he called back.

Favre straightened from his crouch over Anna, one eyebrow raised. "Oh, *mon petit homme*, how you startled me! What were you doing down here all along?"

Tears flowed down Anna's stricken face.

Nate threw his shotgun away. "You win," he said again. Soldiers trotted around to circle him.

Favre smiled. "So I always do." His lips turned from amused to feral.

Before anyone could react, Favre twisted from the hip and swung the machete with all the force of his arm and back.

Blood flumed upward.

His victim's head was shorn clean off at the neck.

"Manny!" Nate cried out, falling to his knees, then his hands.

His friend's body collapsed backward.

Anna screamed, swooning into Kouwe's side.

With his back to Nate, Favre faced the shock and dismay of the other prisoners. "Please, did any of you truly think I'd let Monsieur Azevedo strike my love without recourse? *Mon Dieu!* Where's your chivalry?"

Beyond the kneeling line, Nate saw the Indian woman touch a gash on her cheek.

Favre then turned back around to face Nate. His white outfit was now decorated with a crimson sash of Manny's blood. The monster tapped his wristwatch and waggled a finger at him. "And, Nathan, the count *did* reach zero. You *were* late. Fair is fair."

Nathan hung his head, sagging toward the ground. "Manny . . ."

Somewhere in the distance, a feline howl pierced the morning, echoing over the valley.

SEVENTEEN

Cure

AUGUST 17, 4:16 P.M.
AMAZON JUNGLE

Louis surveyed the final preparations in the valley. He carried his soiled field jacket over one arm, his shirtsleeves rolled up. The afternoon turned out to be a scorcher—but it would get hotter here, much hotter. He smiled grimly, satisfied, as he stared over the ruins of the village.

A Colombian soldier named Mask snapped to attention at his approach. The fellow, standing well over six feet, was as lethal as he was tall. A former bodyguard for the captain of a drug cartel, the swarthy man had taken a face full of acid protecting his boss. His skin was a boiled mass of scar tissue on one side. He had been fired afterward by his ungrateful ward, too ugly and too awful a reminder of how close death had come. Louis, on the other hand, respected the man's show of stalwart loyalty. He made an excellent replacement for Brail.

"Mask," Louis said, acknowledging the man, "how much longer until all the charges are set in the valley?"

"Half an hour," his new lieutenant answered sharply.

Louis nodded and glanced at his watch. Time was critical, but everything was on schedule. If that Russian hadn't gotten that damned GPS working and a signal transmitted, Louis would have had more time to enjoy his victory here.

Sighing, Louis surveyed the field before him. There were eighteen prisoners in all, on their knees, hog-tied with their hands behind their backs and secured to their crossed ankles behind them. A loop of rope ran from the bindings and encircled their necks. A strangler's wrap. Struggle against your knots and the noose tightened around your neck.

He watched a few of the prisoners already gasping as the ropes dug deep. The others sat sweating and bleeding under the hot sun.

Louis noticed Mask still standing at his side. "And the village has been scoured?" he asked. "There are no more of the Ban-ali?"

"None living, sir."

The village had numbered over a hundred. Now they were just one more lost tribe.

"How about the valley? Has it been thoroughly scouted?"

"Yes, sir. The only way onto or off this plateau is the chasm."

"Very good," Louis said. He had already known this from torturing the Ban-ali scout last night, but he had wanted to be sure. "Do one last sweep through all stations. I want to be out of here no later than five o'clock."

Mask nodded and turned smartly away. He strode swiftly toward the giant central tree.

Louis followed him with his eyes. At the tree, two small steel drums were being rolled out of the trunk's tunnel. After the valley had been secured, men with axes and awls had hiked up inside the tree, set deep taps into the trunk, and drained large quantities of the priceless sap. As the men pushed the drums into the field, Louis studied another team laboring around the base of the giant Yagga tree. His eyes narrowed.

Everything was running with a clockwork precision. Louis would have it no other way.

Satisfied, he strode over to the line of segregated prisoners, the survivors of the Ranger team, baking and burning under the sun. They sat slightly apart from the remaining members of the Ban-ali tribe.

Louis stared at his catch, slightly disappointed that they hadn't offered more of a challenge. The two Rangers glared back at him murderously. The small Asian anthropologist had calmed significantly, eyes closed, lips moving in prayer, resigned. Kouwe sat stoically. Louis stopped in front of the last prisoner in the lineup.

Nathan Rand's gaze was as hard as the Rangers', but there was a glint of something more. A vein of icy determination.

Louis had a hard time maintaining eye contact with the man, but he refused to look away. In Nathan's face, he saw a shadow of the man's father: the sandy hair, the planes of the cheek, the shape of his nose. But this was not *Carl* Rand. And to Louis's surprise, this disappointed him. The satisfaction he had expected to feel at having Carl's son kneeling at his feet was hollow.

In fact, he found himself somewhat respecting the young man. Throughout the journey here, Nathan had demonstrated both ingenuity and a stout heart, even dispatching Louis's spy. And finally, here at the end, he had proven his loyalty, with a willingness to sacrifice his own life for his team. Admirable qualities, even if they were directed at cross purposes to Louis's own.

But finally, it was those eyes, as hard as polished stone. He had clearly known inconsolable grief and somehow survived. Louis remembered his elderly friend from the bar back at his hotel in French Guiana, the survivor of the Devil's Island penal system. Louis pictured the old man sipping his neat bourbons. The chap had the same eyes. These were not *Carl* Rand's eyes, his father's eyes. Here was a different man.

"What are you going to do with us?" Nate said. It was not a plea, but a simple question.

Louis removed a handkerchief from his pocket and wiped his brow. "I swore as a gentleman that I wouldn't kill you or your friends. And I will honor my word."

Nate's eyes narrowed.

"I'll leave your deaths to the U.S. military," he said sadly, the emotion surprisingly unfeigned.

"What do you mean?" Nate asked suspiciously.

Louis shook his head and took two steps to reach Sergeant Kostos. "I think that question should be answered by your companion here."

"I don't know what you're talking about," Kostos said with a glower.

Louis bent down at the waist and stared into the sergeant's face. "Really . . . are you saying Captain Waxman didn't confide in his staff sergeant?"

Kostos glanced away.

"What is he talking about?" Nate asked, directing the question to the sergeant. "We're well past secrets now, Kostos. If you know something . . ."

The sergeant finally spoke, awkward with shame. "The napalm minibombs. We were under orders to find the source of the miraculous compound. Once a sample was secured, we were to destroy the source. Total annihilation."

Louis straightened, enjoying the shocked expressions on the others' faces. Even the female Ranger looked surprised. It seemed the military liked to keep its secrets to only a select few.

Raising an arm, Louis pointed back to the small group of men gathered around the giant tree. They were his own demolitions team. Against the white bark of the trunk, the Rangers' remaining nine minibombs appeared like flat black eyes peering toward them. "Thanks to the U.S. government, there's enough firepower here to wipe out even a giant monster of a tree like this one."

Kostos hung his head, as well he should.

"So you see," Louis said, "our two missions are not so different. Only who benefits—the U.S. military complex or a French pharmaceutical company.

Which in turn raises the question, who would do the greater good with the knowledge?" He shrugged. "Who can say? But conversely, we might ask—who would do the greater harm?" Louis eyed the sergeant. "And I think we can all answer that one."

A distinct quiet settled over the group.

Nate finally spoke. "What about Kelly and Frank?"

Ah, the missing members of the group . . . Louis was not surprised it was Nate who brought up the question. "Don't worry about their health. They'll be coming with my party," Louis explained. "I've been in contact with my financiers. Monsieur O'Brien will prove an ideal guinea pig to investigate this regenerative process. The scientists at St. Savin are itching to get their hands and instruments on him."

"And Kelly?"

"Mademoiselle O'Brien will be coming along to make sure her brother cooperates."

Nathan paled.

During the discourse, Louis had noticed Nate's gaze flick toward the tree. He waved an arm back to the giant. "The timers are set for three hours from now. Eight o'clock, to be precise," Louis said. He knew everyone here had seen the force of a *single* napalm bomb. Multiplied by nine, he watched the hopelessness settle into their faces.

Louis continued, "We've also seeded other incendiary bombs throughout the canyon, including the chasm leading up here, which we'll explode as soon as we vacate the area. We couldn't risk the possibility that we missed an Indian hidden up here who might free you. And I'm afraid, tied up or not, there's no escape. This entire isolated valley will become one mighty firestorm—destroying all remnants of the miracle sap and acting as a bonfire in the night to attract any helicopters winging this way. A fiery diversion to cover our flight."

The utter defeat in their eyes shone dully.

Louis smiled. "As you can see, it's all well planned."

Behind him, Louis's lieutenant approached briskly and stopped at his shoulder. The Colombian ignored the prisoners as if they were mere sheep.

"Yes, Mask?"

"All is in order. We can evacuate at your word."

"You have it." Louis glanced again at the line of men and women. "I'm afraid duty calls. I must bid you all a fond *adieu*."

Turning away, Louis felt a twinge of satisfaction, knowing that it was ultimately the young man's father, Carl Rand, who had truly brought his proud son to his doom. *Following in his father's footsteps . . .*

He hoped the old man was watching from hell.

4:55 P.M.

Nate knelt with the others, beaten and crushed by the news. He watched dully as the camp organized for their departure.

Kouwe spoke at his shoulder. "Favre has placed all this faith in the Yagga's sap."

Nate turned his head, careful of the noose around his neck. "What does it matter now?"

"He expects it to cure the contagion, like it does physical wounds, but we've no proof it can."

Nate shrugged. "What do you want us to do?"

"Tell him," Kouwe said.

"And help him? Why?"

"It's not him I'm trying to help. It's all those out in the world dying of the disease. The cure to the contagion lies here. I feel it. And he's going to destroy it, wiping out any chance to stop the curse of the Ban-ali. We must try to warn him."

Nate frowned. In his mind, he saw Manny's murder . . . his friend's body falling to the dirt. He understood in his mind what Kouwe was suggesting, but he just couldn't get his heart to go along with it.

"He won't listen anyway," Nate said, seeking some compromise between heart and mind, some justification for remaining silent. "Favre's operating under a strict timetable. He has another six to eight hours at the most before a military response is mustered. All he can do is plunder what he can and run."

"We must make him listen," Kouwe insisted.

Raised voices echoed to them from the Yagga. Both men glanced toward the tunnel in the trunk. A pair of mercenaries strode out with a stretcher between them. Nate recognized their own makeshift travois and Frank tied on top. He was bound like a trussed pig, ready for the spit.

Next came Kelly, walking on her own, her hands tied behind her back. She shuffled beside Favre and his naked Indian mistress. They were all trailed by additional gunmen.

"You don't know what you're doing!" Kelly argued loudly. "We don't know if the sap can cure anything!"

Nate heard their own argument from a moment ago.

Louis shrugged. "St. Savin will have paid me long

before it's ever discovered if you're right or not. They'll look at your brother's legs—or what's left of them—and shovel the contracted millions into my account."

"What about all those dying? The children, the elderly."

"What do I care? My grandparents are already dead. And I have no children."

Kelly blustered hotly, then her eyes fell on the group of her friends. Her face crinkled in confusion. She glanced ahead to the trail of thirty or so men marching out of the valley, then back at the group of prisoners.

"What's going on?" she asked.

"Oh, your friends . . . they'll be staying here."

Kelly stared at the ring of explosives set around the tree, then over to them, her eyes settling on Nate. "You . . . You can't just leave them here."

"I can," Louis said. "I certainly can."

She stumbled to a stop, her voice soft with tears. "At least, let me say good-bye."

Louis sighed with dramatic exasperation. "Fine. But make it quick." He took Kelly by the upper arm and guided her out of line, accompanied by his mistress and four armed guards.

Louis shoved her in front of them.

Nate's heart ached at seeing her. It would've been better if she had simply continued past them.

Tears rolled down her face. Kelly shuffled before each of them and said how sorry she was—as if all this were her fault. Nate barely listened, drinking up the sight of her with his eyes, knowing this would be the last time he ever saw her. She bent and placed her cheek against Professor Kouwe's, then moved to Nate at the end of the line.

She stared down at him, then dropped to her knees. "Nate . . ."

"Hush," he said with a sad smile, the word a secret reminder of their night together. "Hush."

Fresh tears flowed. "I heard about Manny," she said. "I'm so sorry."

Nate closed his eyes and bowed his head. "If you get a chance," he said under his breath, "kill that French bastard."

She leaned into him, sliding her cheek next to his. "I promise," she whispered at his ear, like a lover sharing a secret.

He turned his face and met her lips, not caring who saw. He kissed her one last time. She met his kiss, gasping between their joined lips.

Then she was torn away, yanked to her feet by Favre. He had a hand clenched around her arm. "It would seem you two have been sharing more than just a *professional* relationship," he said with a sneer.

Favre whipped Kelly around and kissed her hard on the mouth. She cried out in surprise and shock. Louis released her, throwing her back toward the Indian woman. Blood dripped from his lip.

Kelly had bitten him.

He wiped his chin. "Don't worry, Nathan. I'll take good care of your woman." He glanced back to Kelly and his mistress. "Tshui and I will make sure her stay with us is an enjoyable one. Won't we, Tshui?"

The Indian witch leaned closer to their prisoner and fingered a curl of Kelly's auburn hair, sniffing at it.

"See, Nathan. Tshui is already intrigued."

Nate struggled to lunge at the man, fighting his bonds. "You bastard," he hissed, choking as the strangle noose tightened.

"Calm yourself, my boy." Louis stepped back, putting an arm around Kelly. "She's in good hands."

Tears of frustration rolled down his face. His breath was a ragged gasp as the noose dug into the flesh of his neck. Still he struggled. He would die anyway. What did it matter if he strangled or burned?

Louis glanced down at him sadly, then dragged Kelly away. The man mumbled as he left, "A shame . . . such a nice boy, but so much tragedy in his life."

Nate began to see stars dancing at the edges of his blackening vision.

Kouwe hissed at Nate. "Stop struggling, Nate."

"Why?" he gasped.

"Where there is life, there is hope."

Nate sagged in his bonds, not so much finding significance in the professor's words as simple defeat. His breathing became incrementally easier. He stared after the retreating mercenary band, but his eyes stayed focused on Kelly. She glanced back one time, just before disappearing into the jungle fringe. Then she was gone.

The group remained silent, except for a mumbled prayer from Anna. Behind them, a few of the Indian prisoners had begun to sing a mournful melody, while others simply cried. They continued to sit, with no hope, baking under the sun as it trailed toward the western horizon. With each breath or sob, their deaths drew nearer.

"Why didn't he just shoot us?" Sergeant Kostos mumbled.

"It's not Favre's way," Professor Kouwe answered. "He wants us to appreciate our deaths. A slow torture. It excites the bastard."

Nate closed his eyes, defeated.

After an hour, a huge explosion shattered off to the south. Nate opened his eyes and watched a thick column of smoke and rock dust blast into the sky.

"They blew the chasm," Carrera said at the other end of the line.

Nate turned away. The explosion echoed for a few seconds, then died away. All of them now waited for one last explosion, the one that would take their lives and burn through the valley.

As silence again descended over them, Nate heard a distinctive cough from the forest's edge. A *jaguar's* cough.

Kouwe glanced over to Nate.

"Tor-tor?" Nate asked, experiencing a twinge of hope.

From the jungle's edge, a jaguar pushed into the open glade. But it was not the spotted face of their friend's pet.

The huge black jaguar slunk into the open, sniffing, lips pulled back in a silent and hungry snarl.

5:35 P.M.

Kelly walked beside Frank's stretcher. The two bearers seemed tireless, marching through the jungles of the lower canyon like muscled robots. Kelly, with no burden except for her heavy heart, found her feet stumbling over every root and branch.

Favre had set a hard pace for the group. He wanted to reach the swamp lake and disappear into the forests south of it before the fiery explosion ripped through the upper canyon.

"After that, the military will be flocking there like flies on shit," Favre had warned. "We must be well gone."

Kelly had also eavesdropped on the chatter among the mercenary grunts, spoken in a patois of Portuguese and Spanish. Favre had radioed ahead and arranged for motor boats to meet them at a river only a day's march from here. Once there, they would quickly speed away.

But first they had to get to the rendezvous spot without getting caught—and that meant speed was essential. Favre would brook no laggers, including Kelly. The monster had confiscated Manny's bull-whip, snapping it periodically as he moved through the line, like a slavemaster overseeing his crew. Kelly already had a taste of its stinging touch, when she had fallen to her knees as the chasm had exploded behind them. She had been so wrung with hopelessness, she had not been able to move. Then fire had lit her shoulder. The whip had split her shirt and stung her skin. She knew better than to falter from that point on.

Frank spoke from his stretcher. "Kelly . . ."

She leaned down toward him.

"We'll get out of this," he said, slurring. Despite her brother's earlier protests, she had given him a jolt of Demerol before being transported from the

Yagga's healing ward. She hadn't wanted him to suffer by their manhandling. "We'll make it."

Kelly nodded, wishing her arms were untied so she could hold her brother's hand. But under the blanket, even Frank's limbs were secured by ropes to the stretcher.

Frank continued with his bleary attempt at consoling her. "Nate . . . and the others . . . they'll find a way to break free . . . rescue . . ." His words drifted into a morphine haze.

Kelly glanced behind them. The sky was mostly blocked by the canopy overhead, but she could still spot the smudge of smoke from the explosion, closing off the upper valley from the lower. She hadn't told her brother about the incendiary devices set throughout the primitive forest. They could expect no help from their old teammates.

Kelly eyed Favre's back as he marched ahead.

Her only hope now was for *revenge*.

She intended to keep her promise to Nate.

She would kill Louis Favre . . . or die trying.

5:58 P.M.

Nate watched the giant black jaguar stalk into the open glade. It was alone. Nate recognized it as the leader of the pack, the sly female. She must have somehow survived Louis's mass poisoning and instinctively returned to the valley of her birth.

Sergeant Kostos groaned under his breath, "This day just gets better and better."

The great beast eyed the bound prisoners, ready-packed meals. Without the repellent black powder, even the Ban-ali were at risk. The black feline god, created by the Yagga to protect them, had just turned feral.

The beast crept toward them, low to the ground, tail flicking.

Then a flash of fire drew Nate's attention over the cat's muscled shoulder. Tor-tor loped out of the jungle in its shadow. Showing no sign of fear, Tor-tor raced past the larger cat and rushed at Nate and the others.

Nate was knocked on his side by the cat's show of exuberance. With his master dead, Tor-tor was clearly relieved to rejoin them, seeking consolation, reassurance.

Nate choked on his tightening noose. "Th . . . That's a good boy, Tor-tor."

The large black cat hung back, watching the strange display.

Tor-tor rolled against him, wanting a pet, something to let him know all was okay. Nate, tied up, couldn't comply—but an idea formed.

Nate rolled around, earning a further twist of his noose, and held the ropes out toward the jaguar. Tor-tor sniffed at his bindings. "Bite through them," Nate urged, shaking his bound wrists. "Then I'll pet you, you big furry lug."

Tor-tor licked Nate's hand, then nosed him in the shoulder.

Nate groaned with frustration. Nate glanced over his shoulder. The giant black cat padded over to him and nudged Tor-tor aside with a small growl.

Nate froze.

The monster sniffed at the hand that Tor-tor had licked, then gazed up at Nate with those penetrating black eyes. He was sure it could smell the abject fear in the man curled at its feet.

Nate remembered how it had torn Frank's limbs off in a single swooping attack.

The jaguar lowered its head to Nate's arms and legs. A rumble sounded through it. Nate felt a fierce tug and was lifted off the ground, strangling in the noose. For a momentary flash, Nate wondered if he would be strangled before being eaten. He prayed for the former.

Instead, Nate found himself dropped back to the ground. He cringed a moment, then realized his arms were loose. Taking advantage of the opportunity, Nate rolled away with a kick and a twist. He sat up, glancing to the severed ropes dangling from his wrists. The cat had freed him.

Nate yanked at the constricting noose.

The large black jaguar watched him. Tor-tor brushed the giant cat's flank, a clear display of affection, and crossed to Nate.

After working free the noose, Nate tossed it aside. His ankles were still bound, but before he could free his legs, he had a friend to thank.

Tor-tor shoved into him, bowing his furry head into Nate's chest.

He scratched that special spot behind both ears, earning a rumbled purr of satisfaction. "That's a good boy . . . you did good."

A small sad whine flowed from the cat.

Nate pulled Tor-tor's head up and stared into

those golden eyes. "I loved Manny, too," Nate whispered.

Tor-tor nuzzled his face, snuffling.

Nate endured it, making small soothing sounds to the cat. Eventually Tor-tor backed a step away. Nate was able to free his ankles.

Beyond Tor-tor, the giant black jaguar sat on its haunches. Tor-tor must have run into the female after Manny's death. He must have directed her here. Manny had been proven right a couple nights back. Some bond must have developed between the two young cats. Perhaps the ties had grown even deeper by their shared grief: Tor-tor for his master, the female for her pack.

Nate stood and freed Kouwe. Together they unbound the others. Nate found himself untying the ropes from Dakii's limbs. Here was the Indian scout who had been principally responsible for sending the piranhas and locusts upon their party. But Nate could no longer touch his old anger. The Indian had only been protecting his people—and as it turned out, rightly so. Nate helped Dakii up, staring at the smoky ruins of the village. Who were the true monsters of the jungle?

Dakii hugged Nate tightly.

"Don't thank me yet," Nate said. Around the glade, the other Indians were being untied, but Nate focused on the booby-trapped tree with its nine napalm bombs chained around its trunk.

Sergeant Kostos passed by, rubbing his chafed wrists. "I'm going to see about disarming the charges. Carrera's off to see if she can find the weapon she hid."

Nate nodded. Nearby, the freed Ban-ali gathered around the two jaguars. Both cats were now lounging in the shade, seemingly oblivious to the audience. But Nate noticed the larger female watching everything through slitted eyes. The cat was not letting its guard down.

Anna and Kouwe stepped over to join him. "We're free, but what now?" the professor asked.

Nate shook his head.

Anna crossed her arms.

"What's wrong?" Nate asked, noticing her deeply furrowed brow.

"Richard Zane. If we ever get out of this mess, I'm quitting Tellux."

Nate smiled despite their situation. "I'll be right behind you with my own letter of resignation."

After a bit, Sergeant Kostos strode back to them, wearing his usual scowl. "The bombs are all hard-wired and booby-trapped. I can't stop the detonation sequence or remove the devices."

"There's nothing you can do?" Kouwe asked.

The Ranger shook his head. "I have to give that French bastard's team some credit. They did a great job, damn them."

"How much time?" Anna asked.

"Just under two hours. The digital timers are set to blow at eight o'clock."

Nate frowned at the tree. "Then we'll either have to find another way out of this valley or seek some type of shelter."

"Forget shelter," Kostos said. "We need to be as fucking far from here as possible when those babies blow. Even without the additional incendiaries placed by Favre's men, those nine napalmers are enough to fry this entire plateau."

Nate took him at his word. "Where's Dakii? Maybe he knows another way out of here."

Kouwe pointed to the entrance to the Yagga. "He went to check on the status of his shaman."

Nate nodded, remembering the poor man who had been shot in the gut by Zane. "Let's go see if Dakii knows anything helpful."

Kouwe and Anna followed him.

Sergeant Kostos waved them on. "I'll keep examining the bombs. See if I can come up with anything."

Once inside the tree's entrance, Nate again was struck by the scent, musky and sweet. They followed the blue handprints up the tunnel.

Kouwe marched at Nate's side. "I know escape is foremost on everyone's mind, but what about the contagious disease?"

"If there's a way out," Nate said, "we'll collect as many plant specimens as time allows. That's all we can do. We'll have to hope we stumble on the correct one."

Kouwe looked pensive, not satisfied with Nate's answer, but had no other rebuttal. A cure discovered here would do the world no good if they themselves didn't survive.

As they continued to wend their way up the tree, the sound of footfalls echoed down to them. Nate glanced to Kouwe. Someone was coming.

Dakii suddenly appeared around the corner, winded and wide-eyed. He was startled to find them in front of him. He spoke rapidly in his own tongue. Even Kouwe couldn't entirely follow it.

"Slow down," Nate said.

Dakii grabbed Nate's arm. "Son of *wishwa*, you come." He tugged Nate toward the upper tunnel.

"Is your shaman okay?"

Dakii bobbed his head. "He live. But sick . . . very big sick."

"Take us to him," Nate said.

The Indian was clearly relieved. They hurried up at a half trot. In a short time, the group entered the healing ward at the top.

Nate spotted the shaman in one of the hammocks. He was alive but did not look well. His skin was yellowish and shone with fever sweat. *Very big sick, indeed.*

As they approached, the prone man sat up, though clearly it pained him immensely to do so. The shaman waved to Dakii, ordering him across the room on an errand, then stared at Nate. He was glassy-eyed but lucid.

Nate noticed the ropes lying on the floor under the hammock. Even gravely injured, the man had been bound by Favre.

The shaman pointed at Nate. "You *wishwa* . . . like father."

Nate opened his mouth to say no. He was certainly no shaman. But Kouwe interrupted. "Tell him yes," the professor urged.

Nate slowly nodded, obeying Kouwe's instinct.

The response clearly relieved the suffering man. "Good," the shaman said.

Dakii returned, burdened with a leather satchel and a pair of footlong lengths of reed. He held the gear out to his leader, but the shaman was too weak. He directed Dakii from his hammock.

Obeying, Dakii lifted the pouch.

"A dried jaguar scrotum," Kouwe said, pointing to the pouch.

"All the rage in Paris," Nate grumbled.

Dakii fingered open the pouch. Inside was a crimson powder. The shaman spoke from the bed, instructing.

Kouwe translated, though Nate caught a word here and there. "He describes the powder as *ali ne Yagga.*"

Nate understood. "Blood of the Mother."

Kouwe glanced at Nate as Dakii tamped some of the powder into the tips of the two straws. "You know what's about to happen, don't you?"

Nate could certainly guess. "It's like the Yanomamo drug *epena.*" Over the years, he had worked with various Yanomamo tribes and been invited to participate in *epena* ceremonies. *Epena*, translated as "semen of the sun," was a hallucinogenic drug Yanomamo shamans used to enter the spirit world. It was strong stuff, fabled to bring the *hekura*, or little men of the forest, to teach medicine to a shaman. When Nate had tried the stuff, all he had ever experienced was a severe headache followed by swirls of color. Furthermore, he was not particularly fond of the drug's delivery system. It was snuffed up the nose.

Dakii handed one of the loaded straws to Nate and one to the shaman. The Ban-ali leader waved Nate to kneel beside the hammock.

Nate obeyed.

Kouwe cautioned him, "The shaman knows he's about to die. What he is offering is more than a casual ritual. I think he's passing the mantle of his responsibility to you, for the tribe, for the village, for the tree."

"I can't take that on," Nate said, glancing back at Kouwe.

"You must. Once you're shaman, the tribe's secrets will be open to you. Do you understand what that means?"

Nate took a deep breath and nodded. "The cure."

"Exactly."

Nate stepped to the hammock and knelt.

The shaman showed Nate what to do, but it was similar to the Yanomamos' ritual. The small man positioned the drug-loaded end of his reed straw to his own nose. Then motioned for Nate to bring his lips to the other end. Nate's job was to blow the drug up the other's nose. He, in turn, positioned his own straw to his left nostril. The shaman brought the other end to his mouth. Through the straws, the two men would simultaneously blow the drug into each other's sinuses.

The shaman lifted an arm. They both took a deep breath.

Here we go . . .

The Indian brought his arm down.

Nate exhaled sharply through the reed, while bracing for the jolt to his own sinuses. Before he even finished blowing on his end of the straw, the drug hit him.

Nate fell backward. A burning flame seared into

his skull, followed by a blinding explosion of pain. It felt as if someone had blown the back of his head off. He gasped as the room spun. The sense of vertigo overwhelmed him. A pit opened in his mind, and he was falling. He tumbled, spinning away into a darkness that was somehow bright at the same time.

Distantly he heard his name called, but he couldn't find his mouth to speak.

Suddenly his falling body shattered through something solid in this otherworld. The darkness fragmented around him like broken glass. Midnight shards fell away and disappeared. What was left was a shadow shaped into a stylized tree. It appeared to be rising from a dark hill.

Nate hovered before it. As he stared, details emerged. The tree developed three-dimensional conformations, tiny midnight leaves, tiered branches, clustered nut pods.

The Yagga.

Then, from beyond the hill's edge, small figures marched into view, all in a line, heading up the slope to the tree.

The *hekura*, Nate guessed dreamily.

But like the tree, the figures grew in detail as Nate floated nearby, and he realized he was mistaken. Instead of little men, the line was a mix of animals of every ilk—monkeys, sloths, rats, crocodiles, jaguars, and some Nate couldn't identify. Interspersed among these darkly silhouetted animals were men and women, but Nate knew these weren't the *hekura*. The entire party marched up to the tree—and into it. The shadowy figures merged with the black form of the tree.

Where had they gone? Was he supposed to follow?

Then, from the other side of the tree, the figures reemerged. But they had transformed. They were no longer in shadow, but glowing with a brilliant radiance. The shining troupe spread to circle the tree. Man and beast. Protecting the Mother.

As Nate hovered, he sensed the passage of time accelerate. He watched the men and women occasionally wander back to the tree as their radiance dimmed. They would eat the fruit of the tree and shine anew, refreshed to take their place again in the circle of Yagga's children. The ritual repeated over and over again.

Like a worn record, the image began to fade, repeating still, but growing dimmer and dimmer—until there was only darkness again.

"Nate?" a voice called to him.

Who? Nate sought the speaker. But all he found was darkness.

"Nate, can you hear me?"

Yes, but where are you?

"Squeeze my hand if you can hear me."

Nate drew toward the voice, seeking it out of the darkness.

"Good, Nate. Now open your eyes."

He struggled to obey.

"Don't fight it . . . just open your eyes."

Again the darkness shattered, and Nate was blinded by brilliance and light. He gasped, sucking in huge gulps of air. His head throbbed with pain. Through tears, he saw the face of his friend leaning over him, cradling his head.

"Nate?"

He coughed and nodded.

"How do you feel?"

"How do you think I feel?" Nate wobbled up from the floor.

"What did you experience?" Kouwe asked. "You were mumbling."

"And drooling," Anna added, kneeling beside him.

Nate wiped his mouth. "Hypersalivation . . . an alkaloid hallucinogen."

"What did you see?" Kouwe asked.

Nate shook his head. A mistake. The headache flared worse. "How long have I been out?"

"About ten minutes," the professor said.

"Ten minutes?" *It had felt like hours, if not days.*

"What happened?"

"I think I was just shown the cure to the disease," Nate said.

Kouwe's eyes widened. "What?"

Nate explained what he saw. "From the dream, it's clear that the nuts of this tree are vital to the health of the humans in the tribe. The animals don't need it, but people do."

Kouwe nodded, his eyes narrowed as he digested what was said. "So it's the nut pods." The professor pondered a bit longer, then spoke slowly. "From your father's research, we know the tree's sap is full of mutating proteins—prions with the ability to enhance each species it encounters, making them better protectors of the tree. But such a boon must come with a high cost. The tree doesn't want its children to abandon it, so it built a fail-safe into its enhancements. Animals are probably given some instinct to remain in the area, something to do with territoriality, something that can be manipulated as needed, like the powders used with the locusts and piranhas. But humans, with our intellect, need firmer bonds to bind us to the tree. The humans must eat from the fruit on a regular basis to keep the mutating prions in check. The milk of the nut must contain some form of an *antiprion*, something that suppresses the virulent form of the disease."

Anna looked sick. "So the Ban-ali have not stayed here out of obligation, but enslavement."

Kouwe rubbed his temples. "*Ban-yi*. Slave. The term was not an exaggeration. Once exposed to the prions, you can't leave or you'll die. Without the fruit, the prion reverts to its virulent form and attacks the immune system, triggering deadly fevers or riotous cancers."

"Jekyll and Hyde," Nate mumbled.

Kouwe and Anna glanced to him.

Nate explained, "It's like what Kelly reported about the nature of prions. In one form, they're benign, but they can also bend into a new shape and become virulent, like mad cow disease."

Kouwe nodded. "The nut milk must keep the prion suppressed in the beneficial form . . . but once you stop using the milk, it attacks, killing the host and spreading to everyone the host encounters. This again would serve the tree's end. Clearly the tree wants to keep its privacy. If someone flees, anyone the escapee encounters would sicken and die, leaving a trail of death."

"With no one left to tell the tale," Nate said.

"Exactly."

Nate felt well enough to try to stand. Kouwe helped him up. "But the bigger question is why I dreamed up the answer in the first place. Was it just my own subconscious working out the problem, unfettered by the hallucinogenic drug? Or did the shaman communicate it to me somehow . . . some form of drug-induced telepathy?"

Kouwe's face tightened. "No," he said firmly and pointed to the hammock. "It wasn't the shaman."

The Indian lay in his hammock, staring up at the ceiling. Blood dripped from both his nostrils. He was not breathing. Dakii knelt beside his leader, head bowed.

"He died immediately. A massive stroke from the look of it." Kouwe glanced to Nate. "Whatever you experienced didn't come from the shaman."

Nate found it hard to think. His brain felt two sizes too big for his skull. "Then it must have been my subconscious," he said. "When I first saw the pods, I remember thinking that the nuts looked like the fruiting bodies of *Uncaria tomentosa*. Better known as cat's claw. Indians use it against viruses, bacteria, and sometimes tumors. But I didn't make the correlation until now. Maybe the drug helped my subconscious make the intuitive leap."

"You could be right," Kouwe said.

Nate heard the hesitation in the professor's voice. "What else could it be?"

Kouwe frowned. "I talked with Dakii while you were drugged out. The *ali ne Yagga* powder comes from the root of this tree. Desiccated and powdered root fiber."

"So?"

"So maybe what you dreamed wasn't your sub-conscious. Maybe it was some type of prerecorded message from the tree itself. An instruction manual, so to speak: *Consume the fruit of the tree and you will stay healthy.* A simple message."

"You can't be serious."

"Considering the setup in this valley—mutated species, regenerating limbs, humans enslaved in ser-vice to a plant—I wouldn't put anything beyond this tree's abilities."

Nate shook his head.

Anna frowned. "The professor may have a point. I can't even imagine how this tree is able to produce prions specific to the DNA of so many different spe-cies. That alone is miraculous. How did it learn? Where did the tree even get genetic material to learn from?"

Kouwe waved an arm around the room. "This tree traces its roots back to the Paleozoic era, when the land was just plants. Its ancestors must have been around as land animals first evolved, and rather than competing, it incorporated these new species into its own life cycle, like the Amazon's ant tree does today."

The professor continued with his theories, but Nate found himself tuning him out. He was drawn back to Anna's last question. *Where did the tree even get genetic material to learn from?* It was a good ques-tion, and it nagged at Nate. How *had* the Yagga learned to produce its wide variety of species-specific prions?

Nate remembered his dream: the line of animals and people disappearing inside the tree. Where had they gone? Was it more than just symbolic? Did they go *somewhere*? Nate found his eyes on Dakii, kneeling by the hammock. Maybe it was another intuitive leap, or a residual effect of the drug, but Nate began to get a suspicion where that *somewhere* might be.

Ali ne rah. Blood of the Yagga. From the root of the tree.

Nate's gaze narrowed on Dakii. He recalled the Indian's description of his father's fate, spoken with gladness. *He's gone to feed the root.*

Nate found his feet stepping toward the tribesman. Kouwe stopped his discourse. "Nate . . . ?"

"There's one piece of the puzzle we're still missing." Nate nodded to Dakii. "And I know who has it."

He crossed to the kneeling tribesman. Dakii glanced up, tears running down his face. The loss of the leader had struck the man hard. He hauled to his feet as Nate stopped before him.

"*Wishwa*," he said, bowing his head, acknowledging the passing of power.

"I'm sorry for your loss," Nate said, "but we must speak." Kouwe came over and assisted with the translations, but Nate was now becoming skilled at mixing English and Yanomamo words to get his message across.

Dakii pointed to the bed, wiping an eye. "He named Dakoo." The native touched a palm to the dead man's chest. "He father of me."

Nate bit his lip. He should have guessed. Now that Dakii had mentioned it, he saw the similarities. Nate placed a hand on the man's shoulder. He knew what it was like to lose a father. "I'm truly sorry," he repeated, this time with more feeling.

Dakii nodded. "Thank you."

"Your father was an amazing man. He will be mourned by all of us, but right now we're in grave danger. We need your help."

Dakii bowed his head. "You *wishwa*. You say . . . I do."

"I need you to take me to the root of the tree, to where the tree is fed."

Dakii's head snapped up, his face showing both fear and worry.

"Gently," Kouwe warned him in a whisper. "You are clearly treading on sacred ground."

Nate waved away the professor's caution and placed a palm to his own chest. "I am *wishwa* now. I must see the root."

The tribesman bobbed his head. "I go show you." He glanced to his dead father in the hammock, then turned toward the exit.

They began to wind back down the tunnel. Anna and Kouwe whispered behind Nate, leaving him to his own thoughts. He again remembered his comparison of the Ban-ali symbol to the serpentine tunnel through the Yagga's trunk. But did it represent more? Did it also symbolize the essential molecular shape of the mutating prion, as Kelly had suggested? Was there indeed some communication between plant and human? Some shared memory? After what Nate had experienced under the effect of the drug, he was not so sure he could dismiss this last possibility. Perhaps the symbol did indeed represent both. The true heart of the Yagga.

Nate and the group continued down.

"Someone come," Dakii said, slowing.

Then Nate heard it, too. Footsteps, trotting or running.

From around a corner, a familiar figure appeared.

"Private Carrera," Kouwe said.

She nodded, hardly out of breath from the steep run up the tunnel. Nate noticed she had recovered her weapon. "I was sent to fetch you. To see if you found another way off this plateau. Sergeant Kostos had no luck disarming the explosives."

Nate realized, in all the disturbing revelations, he had failed to ask the most important question. Was there another way out of the valley?

"Dakii," Nate said. "We need to know if there is a secret path to the lower valley. Do you know one?" This communication took much gesturing and Kouwe's help.

While Kouwe translated, Carrera glanced at Nate with an eyebrow raised. "You've not already interrogated the man?" she whispered. "What have you been doing?"

"Doing drugs," Nate said, distracted and concentrating on the conversation with the tribesman.

Dakii finally seemed to understand. "Go away? Why? Stay here." He pointed to his feet.

"We can't," Nate said with exasperation.

Anna spoke at his shoulder, "He doesn't understand about the bombs. He doesn't know the valley is going to be destroyed. Such a concept is beyond him."

"We'll have to make him understand," Nate said. He turned to Carrera. "In the meantime, I need you and the sergeant to gather as many of this tree's nuts as you can into packs."

"Nuts?"

"I'll explain later. Just do it . . . please."

She nodded, turning away. "But remember, guys . . . tick-tock." She glanced significantly at them, then took off.

Nate faced Dakii. *How to tell the man that his entire homeland was about to be wiped out?* It wouldn't be easy. Nate sighed. "Let's keep heading to the root."

As they continued down, Nate and Kouwe flanked the tribesman and slowly communicated the danger here. Dakii's confused expression slowly twisted into horror as he got the message. The scout's feet stumbled as he walked, as if the knowledge were a physical burden.

By now they had reached the tunnel exit, surrounded by a gallery of blue palm prints. Beyond the opening, the light in the glade had taken on a dark honey color, suggesting sunset was at hand. Time was running out.

"Is there another way out of the valley?" Nate asked again.

Dakii pointed to where the tunnel ended at a slightly concave wall covered with the blue prints. "Through the root. We go through the root."

"Yes, I want to see the root, too, but what about the way out?"

Dakii stared at him. "Through the root," he repeated.

Nate nodded, finally understanding. Their two missions had just become one. "Show us."

Dakii crossed to the wall, glancing over the prints, then he reached out to one near the innermost wall. He placed his palm over it and pushed with arm and shoulder. The entire wall pivoted on a central axis, opening a new section of passage, winding deeper underground.

Nate glanced up, recalling that the flow channels here hadn't exactly matched. A secret door. The answer was before him this entire time. Even the palm prints on the walls—they were like the one on the Ban-ali symbol, guarding the double helix that represented the root.

Anna slipped a flashlight from her field jacket. Nate patted his own jacket, but came up empty. He must have lost his. Anna passed him hers, indicating he should go first.

Nate moved to the door. Wafting out was the musk of the tree, humid and thicker, dank like the breath from an open grave. Nate readied himself and pushed through the opening.

EIGHTEEN

The Last Hour

7:01 P.M.
AMAZON JUNGLE

As Louis's band took a rest break, he checked his watch. It was an hour before the explosion would turn the upper valley into a whirling firestorm. He focused his attention on the swamp lake ahead. The setting sun had turned the water a tarnished silver.

They were making good time. Skirting to the south of the swamp, where the jungle was thickest and the river channels many, they would easily slip away through the dense forest. He had no doubt of that.

He sighed contentedly, but with a trace of disappointment. Everything was downhill from here. He always felt this way after a successful mission. Some form of postcoital depression, he imagined. He would return to French Guiana a much richer man, but money didn't buy the excitement of the last couple of days.

"*C'est la vie,*" he said. *There will always be other missions.*

A small ruckus drew his attention back around.

He saw Kelly being shoved to her knees by two men. A third was on the ground a couple of yards away, rolling, cursing, clutching between his legs.

Louis strode over to them, but Mask was already there.

The scarred lieutenant pulled the moaning guard to his feet.

"What happened?" Louis asked.

Mask thumbed at the man. "Pedro reached a hand down her shirt, and she kneed him in the groin."

Louis smiled, impressed. One hand settled to the bullwhip trophy at his waist.

He sauntered over to Kelly, now on her knees. One of her two captors had his fist tight in her hair, pulling her head back to expose her long neck. She snarled as the two men taunted her with the vilest innuendoes.

"Let her up," Louis said.

The men knew better than to disobey. Kelly was yanked to her feet.

Louis took off his hat. "I apologize for the rudeness here. It won't happen again, I assure you."

Other men gathered.

Kelly fumed. "Next time I'll kick the asshole's balls into his belly."

"Indeed." Louis waved off his men. "But punishment is my department." He tapped the bullwhip on his side. Earlier he had struck the woman as a lesson. Now it was time for another.

He turned and struck out with the whip, splitting the twilight with a loud *crack.*

Pedro screamed, covering his left eye. Blood spurted through his fingers.

Louis faced the others. "No one will harm the prisoners. Is that understood?"

There was a general sound of agreement and many nods.

Louis replaced his whip. "Someone see to Pedro's eye."

He turned back around and saw Tshui standing near Kelly, one palm raised to the woman's cheek.

As he watched, he noticed that Tshui had wrapped her fingers around a curl of fiery auburn hair.

Ah, Louis thought, *the red hair. A unique trophy for Tshui's collection.*

7:05 P.M.

In the flashlight's glow, Nate noticed that the passage beyond the handprinted door was similar to the main tunnel, but the woody surfaces were of a coarser grain. As he walked, the musk of the tree flowed thick and fetid.

With Dakii at his side, he led Anna and Kouwe down the tunnel. It narrowed rapidly, twisting tighter and tighter, causing the group to crowd together.

"We must be in the tree's taproot," Nate mumbled.

"Heading underground," Kouwe said.

Nate nodded. Within a few more twisting yards, the tunnel exited the woody root, and stone appeared underfoot, interspersed with patches of loam. The tunnel headed steeply downward. They now ran parallel to the branching root system.

Dakii pointed ahead and continued.

Nate hesitated. Strange lichens grew on the walls, glowing softly. The musk was almost overpowering, now rich with a more fecund odor. Dakii pushed on.

Nate glanced to Kouwe, who shrugged. It was encouragement enough.

As they continued forward, the root branch that ran overhead split and divided, heading out into other passageways. From the ceiling, drapes of root hairs hung, vibrating ever so gently, rhythmically swaying as if a wind blew softly through the passage. But there was no wind.

The top of Nate's head brushed against the ceiling as the tunnel lowered. The tiny root fibrils tangled into his hair, clinging, pulling. Nate wrenched away with a gasp.

He shone his flashlight overhead, wary.

"What is it?" Kouwe asked.

"The root grabbed at me."

Kouwe lifted a palm to the root branch. The smaller hairs wrapped around his fingers in a clinging embrace. With a look of disgust, Kouwe tugged his hand away.

Nate had seen other Amazonian plants demonstrate a response to stimulation: leaves curling if touched, puff pods exploding if brushed, flowers closing if disturbed. But this felt somehow more malignant.

Nate fanned his flashlight across the path. By now,

Dakii was waiting several yards down the passage. Nate urged the others to catch up. Once abreast of Dakii, Nate studied the splitting roots that now turned riotous, dividing and cross-splitting in all directions. Small blind cubbyholes dotted the many passages, each choked and clogged with a tangle of roots and waving hairs. The little cubbies reminded Nate of nitrogen bulbs, seen among root balls of many plants, that served as storage fertilizing sites.

Dakii stood before one such alcove. Nate shone his light into the space. Something was tangled deep inside the mass of twining branches and churning root fibrils. Nate bent closer. A few wiggling hairs curled out toward him, questing, waving like small antennae.

He kept back.

Deep in the root pack, wrapped and entwined like a fly in a spider's webbing, was a large fruit bat. Nate straightened in disgust.

Kouwe leaned in and grimaced. "Is it feeding on the bat?"

Anna spoke behind them. "I don't think so. Come see this."

They both turned to her. She knelt by an even larger cubby, but one similarly entangled. She pointed into its depths.

Nate flashed his light inside. Entombed within was a large brown cat.

"A puma," Kouwe said at his shoulder.

"Watch," Anna said.

They stared, not knowing what to expect. Then suddenly the large cat moved, breathed. Its lungs expanded and collapsed in a sigh. But the movement did not look natural, more mechanical.

Anna glanced back at them. "It's alive."

"I don't understand," Nate said.

Anna held out her hand. "Can I see the flashlight?"

Nate passed it to her. The anthropologist quickly surveyed several of the other alcoves, moving through the neighboring, branching passages. The variety of animals was impressive: ocelot, toucan, marmoset, tamarin, anteater, even snakes and lizards, and oddly enough one jungle trout. And each one of them seemed to be breathing or showing some signs of life, including the fish, its small gill flaps twitching.

"They're each unique," Anna said, eyes bright as she stared down the maze of passages. "And all alive. Like some form of suspended animation."

"What are you getting at?"

Anna turned to them. "We're standing in a biological storehouse. A library of genetic code. I wager this is the source of its prion production."

Nate turned in a slow circle, staring at the maze of passages. The implication was too overwhelming to contemplate. The tree was storing these animals down here, learning from them so it could produce prions to alter and bind the species to it. It was a living, breathing genetics lab.

Kouwe gripped Nate's shoulder. "Your father."

Nate glanced to him in confusion. "What about my—?" Then it hit him like a hammer to the forehead. He gasped. His father had been fed to the root. *Not as fertilizer*, Nate realized, swinging around, aghast, *but to be a part of this malignant laboratory!*

"With his white skin and strange manners, your father was unique," Kouwe said in a low voice. "The Ban-ali or the Yagga would not want to lose his genetic heritage."

Nate turned to Dakii. He could barely speak, too choked with emotion. "My . . . my father. Do you know where he is?"

Dakii nodded and lifted both arms. "He with root."

"Yes, but where?" Nate pointed to the closest cubby, one with an enshrouded black sloth. "Which one?"

Dakii frowned and glanced around the maze of passages.

Nate held his breath. There had to be hundreds of passages, countless alcoves. He didn't have time to search them all, not with the clock running. But how could Nate leave, knowing his father was down here somewhere?

Dakii suddenly strode purposefully down one passage and waved for them to follow.

They hurried, winding deeper and deeper into the subterranean maze. Nate found it increasingly difficult to breathe, not because of the sickening musk, but because of his own mounting anxiety. All along this journey, he had held no real hope his father was still alive. But now . . . he teetered between hope and despair, almost panicked with trepidation. *What would he find?*

Dakii paused at an intersection, then stepped to the left passage. But after two strides, he shook his head and returned to follow the trail to the right.

A scream built up inside Nate's chest.

Dakii continued down this new passage, mumbling under his breath. Finally, he stopped beside a large cubby and pointed. "Father."

Nate grabbed the flashlight back from Anna. He dropped to his knees, shining his light inside, oblivious to the questing root hairs that wrapped around his wrist.

Within the mass of roots lay a shadowy figure. Nate moved his light over its form. Curled in a fetal position on the soft loamy floor was a gaunt naked frame, a pale man. His face was covered by a thick beard, his hair tangled with roots. Nate focused on the face hidden beneath the beard. He was not entirely sure it was his father.

As he stared, the man inhaled sharply, mechanically, and exhaled, wafting root hairs from his lips. Still alive!

Nate turned. "I have to get him out of there."

"Is it your father?" Anna asked.

"I . . . I'm not sure." Nate pointed to the bone knife tucked in Kouwe's belt. The professor passed it over to him.

Nate stood and hacked into the root mass.

Dakii cried out, reaching to stop him, but Kouwe blocked the tribesman. "Dakii, no! Leave Nate be."

Nate fought through the outer cords of woody roots. It was like the husk surrounding some nut. Beneath this layer was a mass of finer webbings and draperies of rootlets and thready hairs.

Once through, Nate saw the roots penetrated the man's body, growing into it as if it were soil. It must be how the Yagga sustained its specimens, feeding them, supporting organ systems, delivering nutrients.

Nate hesitated. Would he harm the man, kill him, if he hacked the root's attachments? If this was indeed some type of suspended animation, would its interruption trigger a massive systems failure?

Shaking his head, Nate slashed through the roots. He would take his chances. Left alone, the man would surely die a fiery death.

Once the body was free of the root hairs, Nate tossed the knife aside, grabbed the man by the shoulders, and hauled him into the passage. The last clinging roots broke away, releasing their prey.

In the tunnel, Nate collapsed beside the man. The naked figure choked and gasped. Many of the tiny rootlets and hairs squiggled from his body, dropping away like leeches. Blood flowed from some spots where larger rootlets had penetrated. Suddenly the man seized, contracting, back arching, head thrown back.

Nate cradled the man in his arms, not knowing what to do. The thrashings continued for a full minute. Kouwe helped to restrain the man and prevent further injury.

The figure jerked into a final convulsion, then collapsed with a mighty gasp.

Nate exhaled with relief when the man's chest continued to rise and fall. Then the eyes fluttered open and stared up at him. Nate knew those eyes. They were his *own* eyes.

"Nate?" the figure asked in a dry husky voice.

Nate fell atop the figure. "Dad!"

"Am . . . am I dreaming?" his father asked coarsely.

Nate was too choked to speak. He helped his father, who was light as a pillow, all skin and bones, to sit. The tree had been sustaining him, but just barely.

Kouwe bent down to help. "Carl, how are you feeling?"

Nate's father squinted at the professor, then a look of recognition spread across his face. "Kouwe? My God, what's going on?"

"It's a long story, old friend." He helped Nate get his father on his feet. Too frail to move on his own, Carl Rand clung to Nate and Kouwe. "Right now, though, we have to get you out of this damn place."

Nate stared at his father, tears streaming down his face. "Dad . . ."

"I know, son," he said hoarsely and coughed.

There was no time for a proper reunion now, but Nate wasn't going to let another moment go by without saying the words he had regretted withholding the day his father left for this expedition. "I love you, Dad."

The arm around his shoulder tightened, a small squeeze of affection and love. A familiar gesture. Family.

"We should fetch the others," Anna said. "And head out of here."

"Nate, why don't you stay with your father here?" Kouwe suggested. "Rest. We can collect you both on the way out."

Dakii shook his head. "No. We not come back this way." He waved his arm. "Other way to go."

Nate frowned. "We should stay together anyway."

"And I can handle myself," Carl argued hoarsely.

He glanced back to the cubbyhole. "Besides, I've been resting here long enough."

Kouwe nodded.

With the matter settled, they began to climb toward the surface. Kouwe gave a thumbnail sketch of their situation. Nate's father only listened, leaning more and more heavily upon them as they walked. The only words his father spoke during the discourse were at the mention of Louis Favre and what he had done. "The goddamn bastard."

Nate smiled, hearing a bit of the old fire in his father's voice.

When they reached the surface, it was obvious the two Rangers had been busy. They had all the Ban-ali gathered. Each bore packs full of nuts and weapons.

Nate and his father remained in the entrance, while Kouwe explained about the addition to their team and what they had found below. "Dakii says there's an escape route through the root's tunnel."

"Then we'd best hurry," Sergeant Kostos said. "We have less than thirty minutes, and we want to be as far away from here as possible."

Carrera joined them, her weapon on her shoulder. "All set at our end. We have a couple dozen of those nut pods and four canteens of the sap."

"Then let's haul ass," Kostos said.

7:32 P.M.

As they wound through the root tunnels, Kouwe stayed with Dakii, periodically glancing back at the trail of Indians and Americans. Watching Sergeant Kostos help Nate with his father, Kouwe wished he had had time to rig up a stretcher, but right now every minute was critical.

Though Sergeant Kostos believed the subterranean tunnels would shield them from the worst of the napalm's fiery blast, he clearly feared the maze's integrity. "The rock here is riddled and weakened by the roots. The explosions could bring the roof down atop our heads or trap us here. We need to be well clear of these tunnels before those bombs go off."

So they hurried. Not only for their own sake, but for the world. Inside their packs, they carried the fate of thousands, if not millions—the nut pods of the Yagga, the suppressant for the virulent human prion. The cure to the plague.

They could not be trapped down here.

Glancing over a shoulder, Kouwe again checked the party. The dark tunnels, the softly glowing lichens, the dreadful cubbies with their captured specimens . . . all made Kouwe nervous. This deep in the system, both walls and ceilings ran wild with roots, zigzagging everywhere, crossing, dividing, fusing. Everywhere were the mounds of ubiquitous root hairs, waving and probing toward any passerby. It made the walls look furry, like a living thing, constantly moving and bristling.

Behind Kouwe, the others looked equally wary, even the Indians. The line of men and women ran out of sight around a curve in the twisting passage. Back at the end, pulling up the rear, was Private Carrera. She kept a watch behind them—where Tor-tor and the giant black jaguar followed. It had taken some coaxing to encourage the two cats inside, but Nate had finally been successful in luring Tor-tor. "I'm not going to leave Manny's cat here to die," Nate had argued. "I owe it to my friend to save him."

Once Tor-tor entered, the large female jaguar had followed.

Carrera remained alert, her weapon ready, in case the wild cat decided it needed a snack while traveling.

Dakii paused at the intersection of trails. Sergeant Kostos grumbled, but they dared not force a faster pace. It would be easy to get lost down here. They depended on Dakii's memory.

The tribesman selected a path and led the others. The tunnel descended steeply. Kouwe stared at the low roof. They must be a hundred yards underground . . . and going deeper still. But oddly, instead of the air growing more dank, it seemed to freshen.

After a few minutes, the tunnel leveled out and made a sharp turn, emptying into a huge cavern. The tunnel opening was halfway up one wall of the chamber. A thin trail continued along the nearest wall, a stony lip high above the bowled floor. Dakii stepped out onto the trail.

Kouwe followed, gaping at the room. The chamber had to be a half mile across. Through the center of the chamber, a massive root stalk, as thick around as a giant redwood, penetrated from the roof and continued down through the floor like a great column.

"It's the Yagga's taproot again," Nate said, coming up beside them. "We must have circled back to it."

From the main root, thousands of branches spread like tree limbs in all directions, toward other passages.

"There must be miles and miles of tunnels," Kouwe said. He studied the taproot. The giant tree above must be but a tiny fraction of the plant's true mass. "Can you imagine the number of species encased down here? Suspended in time?"

"The tree must have been collecting its specimens for centuries," Nate's father mumbled beside his son.

"Maybe even longer," Kouwe warned. "Maybe as far back as when these lands first formed."

"Back to the Paleozoic," Nate murmured. "If so, what might be out there in that vast biological storehouse?"

"And what might still be living?" Anna added.

Kouwe cringed. It was both a wondrous and frightening thought. He waved Dakii onward. The sight was too terrible to stare at any longer, and time was running down for both them and the world.

They wound along the lip as it circled the chamber. Dakii led them to another opening, back into the tunnel maze again. Though they left the chamber behind, Kouwe's mind dwelled on the mystery there. His feet slowed, and he found himself marching near Nate and Carl. Sergeant Kostos was on the other side.

"When I studied anthropology," Kouwe said, "I read many myths of trees. The maternal guardian. A caretaker, a storehouse of all wisdom. It makes me wonder about the Yagga. Has man crossed its path before?"

"What do you mean?" Nate asked.

"Surely this tree wasn't the only one of its kind. There must have been others in the past. Maybe these myths are some collective memory of earlier human encounters with this species."

He recognized the doubt in Nate's eyes and continued, "Take, for example, the Tree of Knowledge from the Garden of Eden. A tree whose fruit has all the knowledge in the world, but whose consumption curses those who eat of it. You could draw a parallel to the Yagga. Even when I saw Carl trussed up among the roots, it reminded me of another biblical tale. Back in the thirteenth century, a monk who had starved himself seeking visions from God told a tale of seeing Seth, the son of Adam, returning to Eden. There, the young man saw the Tree of Knowledge, now turned white. It clutched Cain in its roots, some penetrating into his brother's flesh."

Nate frowned.

"The parallels here seem particularly apt," Kouwe finished.

Noticeably quiet for several yards, Nate was clearly digesting his words. Finally he spoke. "You could be on to something. The tunnel through the Yagga's trunk is not manmade, but a natural construct. The tunnels had to have formed as the tree grew. But why would the tree do so unless its ancestors had encountered man before and had evolved these features in kind?"

"Like an ant tree has adapted for its six-legged soldiers," Kouwe added.

Nate's father roused. "And the evolution of the Ban-ali here, their genetic enhancements," Carl rasped. "Have such improvements of the species happened before? Could the tree have played a critical role in human evolution? Is that why we remember it in our myths?"

Kouwe's brow crinkled. He had not extrapolated that far. He stared behind the others to where the giant cat stalked. If the Yagga were capable of enhancing the jaguar's intelligence, could it have done the same to us in the distant past? Could humans owe their own intellect to an ancestor of this tree? A chilling thought.

A silence fell over the others.

In his head, Kouwe reviewed the history of this valley. The Yagga must have grown here, collecting specimens in its hollow root system for centuries: luring them in with its musk, offering shelter, then capturing them and storing them in its cubbies. Eventually man entered the valley—a wandering clan of Yanomamo—and discovered the tree's tunnels and the wonders of its healing sap. Lured in, they were captured as surely as any other species and slowly changed into the Ban-ali, the Yagga's human servants. Since that time, the Ban-ali must have brought other species to the tree—feeding the root to further expand its biological database.

And left unchecked, where would it have led? A new species of man, as Carl had feared after the stillborn birth of Gerald Clark's baby? Or maybe something worse—a hybrid like the piranhas and locusts?

Kouwe squinted at the twisting passages, suddenly glad it was all going to burn.

Dakii called from up ahead. The tribesman pointed

to a side tunnel. From the passage, a slight glow shone. A dull roar echoed back to them.

"The way out," Kouwe said.

7:49 P.M.

Nate hurried as best he could with his father.

Sergeant Kostos growled constantly under his breath on the other side, counting off the minutes until the bombs blew.

It would be a close call.

The group sped toward the sheen of moonlight flowing from ahead. The roaring grew in volume, soon thundering. Around a corner, the end of the tunnel appeared, and the source of the noise grew clear.

A waterfall tumbled past the entrance, the rush of water aglow with moonlight and star shine.

"The tunnel must open into the cliff face that leads to the lower valley," Kouwe said.

They followed Dakii to the tunnel's damp exit. The rushing water rumbled past the threshold. The tribesman pointed down. *Steps.* In the narrow space between the waterfall and the cliff, a steep, wet staircase had been carved into the stone, winding back and forth in narrow switchbacks, down to the lower valley.

"Everyone head down!" the sergeant yelled. "Move quickly, but when I holler, everyone drop and hold on tight."

Dakii remained with Sergeant Kostos to guide his own people.

Kouwe helped Nate with his father. They scrambled as well as they could down the stairs, balancing between haste and caution. They hurried as the others followed.

Nate saw Kostos wave Carrera down the stairs, then followed.

Behind them emerged the two cats. The jaguars hurried out of the opening and onto the stair, clearly glad to be free of the confining tunnels. Nate wished he had their claws.

"One minute," Kouwe said, hobbling under Carl's weight.

They hurried. The bottom was still a good four stories down. A deadly fall.

Then a sharp call broke through the water's rush. "Now! Down! Down!"

Nate helped his father to the steps, then dropped himself. He glanced up and saw the entire group flattened to the stone. He lowered his face and prayed.

The explosion, when it came, was as if hell had come to earth. The noise was minimal—no worse than the dramatic end of a Fourth of July fireworks show—but the effect was anything but insignificant.

Over the top of the cliff's edge, a wall of flame shot half a mile out, and flumed three times that distance into the sky. Currents of rising air buffeted them, swirling eddies of fire moving with them. If it wasn't for the waterfall's insulation, they would've been fried on the stairs. But the waterfall was a mixed blessing. Its flow, shaken by the blast, cast vast amounts of water over them. But everyone held tight.

Soon bits of flaming debris began to tumble over the edge and down the fall. Luckily the swift current cast most of the large pieces of trunk and branch beyond their perch. But it was still terrifying to see entire trees, cracked and blown into the stream, tumble past, on fire.

As the heat welled up and away from them, Kostos yelled down. "Keep moving, but watch for falling debris."

Nate crouched up. Everyone began to climb to their feet, dazed.

They had made it!

As the others started down, he reached for his father. "C'mon, Dad. Let's get out of here."

With his father's hand held in his own, Nate felt the ground vibrate, a tremoring rumble. He instinctively knew this was bad. *Oh, shit . . .*

He dove atop his father, a scream on his lips. "Down! Everyone back down!"

The second explosion deafened them. Nate screamed from the pain. It blew with such force that he was sure the cliff would fall atop them.

From the mouth of the tunnel above, a jet of fire belched out, blasting into the fall of water. Scalding steam rolled down over them.

Nate craned upward and watched a second belch of fire blow from the tunnel, then a third. Smaller flames shot out of tinier crevices in the cliff face all around, like a hundred flickering fiery tongues. All of them an eerie blue.

All the while, the ground continued to shake and rumble.

Nate kept his father pinned under him.

Rocks and dirt shattered outward. Entire up-rooted trees shot like flaming missiles through the sky to crash down into the lower valley.

Then this too died down.

No one moved as smaller rocks tumbled past. Again the waterfall protected them, deflecting most of the debris, or reducing their speed to bruising rather than deadly velocities.

After several minutes, Nate raised his head enough to view the damage.

He spotted Kouwe a step above his father. The professor looked dazed and sickened. He stared back at Nate, face pale with shock. "Anna . . . when you yelled . . . I was too slow . . . the explosion . . . I couldn't catch her in time." His eyes flicked to the long tumble below. "She fell."

Nate closed his eyes. "Oh, God."

He heard mournful cries flow up around them. Anna had not been alone in falling to her death. Nate pushed to his knees. His father coughed and rolled onto his side, looking ashen.

After a time, the group crawled down the stairs, beaten, bloody, and in shock.

They gathered at the foot of the falls, bathed in cool spray. Three Ban-ali tribesmen had also met their deaths on the stair.

"What was that second explosion?" Sergeant Kostos asked.

Nate remembered the strange blue flame. He asked for one of the canteens with the Yagga sap. He poured out a grape-sized drop and used Carrera's lighter to ignite it. A tall blue flame flared up from the dollop of sap. "Like copal," Nate said. "Combustible. The entire tree went up like a roman candle. Roots and all, I imagine, from the way the ground shook."

A deep mournful silence spread over the smaller camp.

Finally Carrera spoke. "What now?"

Nate answered, his voice fierce. "We make that bastard pay. For Manny, for Olin, for Anna, for all the Ban-ali tribespeople."

"They have guns," Sergeant Kostos said. "We have one Bailey. They outnumber us more than two to one."

"To hell with that." Nate kept his voice cold. "We have a card that trumps all that."

"What's that?" Kostos asked.

"They think we're dead."

NINETEEN

Midnight Raid

11:48 P.M.
AMAZON JUNGLE

Kelly's eyes still stung with tears. With her hands bound behind her back, she couldn't even wipe them away. She was secured to a stake under a lean-to of woven palm leaves that deflected the gentle rain that now fell. The clouds had rolled in as full night had set, which had suited her kidnappers just fine. "The darker the better," Favre had exulted. They made good time and were now enveloped in thick jungle cover well south of the swamp.

But despite the darkness and the distance, the northern skies glowed a fiery red, as if the sun were trying to rise from that direction. The explosions that had lit up the night had been spectacular, shooting a fireball high into the sky, followed by a scattering of flaming debris.

The sight had burned all hope from her. The others were dead.

Favre had set a hard pace after that, sure that the government's helicopters would be winging to the fires posthaste. But so far the skies had remained clear. There was no whump-whumping of military air vehicles. Favre kept a constant watch on the skies. *Nothing.*

Maybe Olin's signal had never made it out. Or maybe the helicopters were still en route.

Either way, Favre was taking no chances. No lights, just night-vision glasses. Kelly, of course, was not given a pair. Her shins were bruised and thorn-scraped from falls and missteps in the dark. Her stumblings had amused the guards. Without her hands to break her fall, each trip bloodied her knees. Her legs ached. Mosquitoes and gnats were attracted to the wounds, crawling and buzzing around her. She couldn't even swat them away.

The rain was a relief. As was the short break—a full hour. Kelly stared over at the glowing northern skies, praying her friends hadn't suffered.

Closer at hand, the mercenary band celebrated its victory. Flasks of alcohol passed from hand to hand. Toasts were made, and boasts declared amid jovial whispers of how their money would be spent—much of it involving whores. Favre circulated through the group, allowing his men this celebration but making sure it didn't get out of hand. They were still miles from the rendezvous point where the motorboats were waiting.

So for the moment, Kelly had a bit of relative privacy. Frank was under another makeshift lean-to in the middle of the camp. Her only company here was the single guard: Favre's disfigured lieutenant, the man named Mask. He stood talking with another mercenary, sharing a flask.

A figure approached through the drizzle. It was Favre's Indian woman, Tshui. She seemed oblivious of the rain, still naked, but at least she no longer wore the head of Corporal DeMartini around her neck.

Probably didn't want to get the foul thing wet, Kelly thought sourly.

Mask's companion slid away at the approach of the woman. She had that effect on most of the mercenaries. They were clearly frightened of her. Even Mask took a few steps from the lean-to and sheltered under a neighboring palm.

The Indian woman bent out of the rain and knelt beside Kelly. She carried a rucksack in one hand. She settled it to the dirt and began to rummage silently through it, finally pulling out a tiny clay pot and freeing the lid.

Filling the container was a thick waxy unguent. The witch-woman scooped a dab on a finger, then reached to Kelly.

She flinched away.

The Indian woman grabbed her ankle. Her grip was iron. She slathered the material on Kelly's abraded knees. Instantly the sting and burn faded. Kelly stopped fighting and allowed the woman to treat her.

"Thank you," Kelly said, though she was not sure the treatment was solely for her comfort as much as to make sure she could continue to march. Either way, it felt good.

The Indian woman reached again to her pack and

removed a rolled length of woven linen. She carefully spread it open on the soggy ground. Meticulously lined in tiny pouches of cloth were stainless steel tools and others made of yellowed bone. Tshui removed a long sickle-shaped knife, one of a set of five similar tools. She leaned toward Kelly with the knife.

Kelly again flinched, but the woman grabbed the hair at the nape of her neck and held her still, pulling her head back. The Indian was damn strong.

"What are you doing?"

Tshui never spoke. She brought the knife's curved edge to Kelly's forehead, at the edge of her scalp. Then returned the tool to its place and took another of the curved knives and positioned it at the crown of her scalp.

With horror, the realization hit Kelly. *She's measuring me!* Tshui was determining which tools would be best to scrape the skin off her skull. The Indian woman continued her measuring, fingering different sharp instruments and testing them against chin, cheek, and nose.

She began to line up the proper instruments on the ground beside her knee. The row of tools grew: long knives, sharp picks, corkscrewing pieces of bone.

A noise, a throat being cleared, drew both women's attention outside the lean-to.

Kelly's head was released. Free, Kelly twisted around, kicking, trying to get as far away as possible from the witch. Her feet sent the line of cruel instruments scattering in the dirt.

Favre stood outside the door. "I see Tshui has been entertaining you, Mademoiselle O'Brien."

He entered the lean-to. "I've been trying to gather

some information on the CIA from your brother. Information to assist us in escaping now and planning future missions. A valuable commodity that I don't think St. Savin will mind me gleaning from their patient. But I can't have Frank coming to harm. That my benefactors wouldn't appreciate. They're paying well for the delivery of a *healthy* little guinea pig."

Favre knelt next to her. "But you, my dear, are a different story. I'm afraid I'm going to have to give your brother a little demonstration of Tshui's handiwork. And don't be shy. Let Frank hear your screams— please don't hold back. When Tshui comes over afterward and hands him your ear, I'm sure he'll be more cooperative with his answers." He stood. "But you'll have to excuse me. I don't care to watch myself."

Favre made a half bow and departed into the rainy night.

Kelly's blood iced with terror. She didn't have much time. In her fingers, Kelly clutched a tiny knife. She had grabbed it a moment ago from among the tools she had scattered. Kelly now worked to cut through the ropes behind her back.

Nearby, Tshui picked through her pack and gathered bandage material—to wrap the stump of Kelly's amputated ear. Without a doubt, they would torture her until they had drained every bit of information from her brother. Afterward, she would be tossed aside as unnecessary baggage.

Kelly would not let that happen. A quick death would be better than a tortured one. And if she could believe Favre, no harm would come to Frank—at least not until after he was delivered safely to the scientists at St. Savin.

Kelly sliced savagely at her bonds, covering her motions with jerky thrashings and moans that were only half faked.

Tshui turned back to her, a hooked knife in hand.

The ropes still held Kelly.

The witch leaned over her and grabbed her hair again, yanking her head back. She lifted her knife.

Kelly struggled with her own blade, tears flowing.

A chilling wail split the night, high and feline, full of fury.

Tshui froze with the knife poised at Kelly's ear. The witch cocked her head and glanced to the dark forest.

Kelly could not pass up this opportunity. She bunched her shoulders and ripped free the last fibers of the rope that bound her.

As Tshui turned back to her, Kelly swung around with her knife and planted it into the witch woman's shoulder. Tshui screamed and fell back in surprise.

Adrenaline racing, Kelly burst to her feet and leaped toward the forest. She ran with all the speed in her legs but slammed into a figure who stepped around a tree.

Arms grabbed her. She stared up into the leering and twisted face of Mask. She had forgotten in her panic about the guard. She struggled but had no weapon. He yanked her around, lifting her off her feet, an arm around her throat. She was carried, kicking, back into the open.

Tshui knelt in the dirt, wrapping her wounded shoulder with the bandages meant for Kelly's ear. The glower the woman shot at Kelly burned with intensity.

Kelly stopped kicking.

Then the oddest thing happened—Mask jerked and let her go. Kelly dropped to her knees in the dirt at the sudden release. She turned as the muscled guard fell face forward to the ground.

Something glittered at the back of his skull, embedded deep into it.

A shiny silver disk.

Kelly instantly recognized it. She stared off into the woods as screams began to erupt from all around the camp. She saw men drop where they stood or tumble where they sat. Feathered arrows protruded from necks and chests. Several of the bodies convulsed. *Poisoned.*

Kelly stared again at the limp form of Favre's former lieutenant . . . and the silver disk.

Hope surged.

Dear God, the others must still be alive!

Kelly turned and found Tshui gone, likely fleeing toward the center of camp, toward Favre, toward where her brother was still held prisoner. By now, the camp was in chaos. Shots began to ring out, orders were yelled, but so far not a single attacker appeared.

It was as if they were being attacked by ghosts.

Men continued to drop.

Kelly grabbed the pistol from Mask's dead body. She could not gamble that the others would reach her brother in time. She darted toward the roiling center of camp.

Nate saw Kelly lunge with a gun in hand. *Going after her brother,* he knew with certainty. They could wait no longer. He signaled to Private Carrera. A sharp whistle blew and an ululating wail arose from the score of Indian throats all around the camp. It was a chilling sound.

Nate was already on his feet.

They had painted themselves all in black.

As a group, they lunged into the jungle camp, armed only with arrows, blowguns, and bone knives. Those who knew how to use modern weapons confiscated them from the dead.

Kostos opened fire with an AK-47 on the left. Off to the right, Carrera switched her Bailey to automatic fire and laid down a swath of death. She emptied her weapon, tossed it aside, then grabbed up a discarded M-16, probably one originally taken from the Rangers.

Nate grabbed up a pistol from dead fingers and ran headlong into the main camp. The mercenaries were still in disarray, only now beginning to fall back into a defensive line. Nate raced through the wet shadows, meaning to get behind their lines before they tightened.

As Nate ran, he was spotted by one frightened man, hiding under a bush, clearly unarmed. The man dropped to his knees at the sight of Nate's gun, hands on his head, in a clearly submissive posture.

Nate ran right past him. He had only one goal in mind: to find Kelly and her brother before they came to harm.

On the other side of camp, Kouwe ran with Dakii, flanked by other Indians. He paused to collect a machete from a dead body and toss it to the tribesman. Kouwe confiscated the rifle for himself.

They hurried forward. The line of fighting had fallen toward the camp's center.

But Kouwe suddenly slowed, an instinctual warning tingling through him. He twisted around and spotted an Indian woman slinking from behind a bush. Her skin was dabbed in black like theirs.

Kouwe, having been raised among the tribes of the Amazon, was not so easily fooled. Though she might paint herself to look like them, her Shuar features were distinctive to the educated eye.

He lifted his rifle and pointed it at the woman. "Don't move, witch!" Favre's woman had been trying to slip past their lines and escape into the woods. Kouwe would not let that happen. He remembered the fate of Corporal DeMartini.

The woman froze, turning slowly in his direction. Dakii held back, but Kouwe waved him forward. There was fighting still to be done.

Dakii took off with his men.

Kouwe was now alone with the woman, surrounded by the dead. He stepped toward her with caution. He knew he should shoot her where she stood—the witch was surely as deadly as she was beautiful. But Kouwe balked.

"On your knees," he ordered in Spanish instead. "Hands high!"

She obeyed, lowering herself with subtle grace, slow and fluid like a snake. She stared up at him from under heavily lidded eyes. Smoldering, seductive . . .

When she attacked, Kouwe was a moment too slow in reacting. He pulled the trigger, but the gun just clicked. The magazine was empty.

The woman leaped at him, knives in both hands, poisoned for sure.

Kelly stared at the two mini-Uzis held by Favre. One was pointed at her brother's head, one at her chest. "Drop the pistol, mademoiselle. Or you both die now!"

Frank mouthed to her. "Run, Kelly."

Favre crouched under the lean-to, using her brother's body as a shield.

She had no choice. She would not leave her brother with the madman. She lowered her pistol and tossed it aside.

Favre quickly crossed to her. He dropped one of the Uzis and pressed the other against Kelly's back. "We're going to get out of here," he hissed at her. He snatched up a pack. "I've got a backup supply of tree sap, prepared for just such an emergency."

He shouldered the pack, then grabbed Kelly by the back of her shirt.

A shout barked behind them. *"Let her go!"*

They both turned. Favre twisted around behind her.

Nate stood, bare-chested, in his boxers, painted all in black.

"Gone native, have we, Monsieur Rand?"

Nate pointed a pistol at them. "You can't escape. Drop your weapon and you'll live."

Kelly stared at Nate. His eyes were hard.

Gunfire sounded all around them. Shouts and screams echoed.

"You'll let me live?" Favre scoffed. "What? In

prison? I don't like that proposition. I like freedom better."

The single gunshot, at close range, startled her—more the *crack* than the pain. She saw Nate fly backward, hit in the hip, his weapon spinning away. Then she felt herself fall to the ground, to her knees, pain registering more as shock. She stared at her stomach. Blood soaked her shirt, welling through the smoking hole.

Favre had shot her through her belly, striking Nate.

The pure brutality of the act horrified her more than being shot, more than the blood.

Kelly looked at Nate. Their eyes met for a brief instant. Neither had the strength to speak. Then she was falling—slumping toward the ground as darkness stole the world away.

Kouwe butted the first knife away with his rifle, but the witch was fast. He fell backward under her weight as she leaped on him.

He hit the ground hard, slamming his head, but managing to catch her other wrist. The second knife jabbed at his face. He tried to throw her off, but she clung to him, legs wrapped around him like a passionate lover.

Her free hand scratched gouges in his cheek, going for his eyes. He twisted his face to the side. The knife lowered toward his throat as she leaned her shoulder into its plunge. She was strong, young.

But Kouwe knew the Shuar. He knew about their secret arsenal of weapons: braided in the hair, hidden in loincloths, worn as decoration. He also knew women warriors of the tribe carried an extra sheath as a defense against rape—a common attack between the Shuar tribes during their wars.

Kouwe used his free hand to snatch between her legs as she straddled him. His fingers reached and found the tiny knobbed hilt hidden there, warm from her body heat. He pulled the blade free of its secret leather scabbard.

A scream rose from her lips as she realized this most private theft. Teeth were bared.

She tried to roll away, but Kouwe still had her wrist in his grasp. As she spun, he followed, holding her tight and using her strength to pull himself to his feet.

They crouched at arms' length, Kouwe keeping an iron grip on her wrist.

She met his eyes. He saw the fear. "Mercy," she whispered. "Please."

Kouwe imagined the number of victims who had pleaded with her—but he was no monster. "I'll grant you mercy."

She relaxed ever so slightly.

Using this moment, he yanked her to him and plunged the knife to its hilt between her breasts.

She gasped in pain and surprise.

"The mercy of a quick death," he hissed at her.

The poison struck her immediately. She shuddered and stiffened as if an electric shock had passed through her from head to toe. He pushed her away as a strangled scream flowed from her lips. She was dead before she hit the ground.

Kouwe turned away, tossing aside the poisoned blade. "And that's more than you deserve."

* * *

The gunfire had already died around the camp to sporadic shots, and Louis needed to be gone with his treasure before his defenses completely fell.

Gathering up the second Uzi from the ground, he watched Nate struggle to his elbows, a fierce grimace on his face.

Louis saluted him and swung around—then froze in midstep.

Standing a few yards away was a sight that made no sense. A pale, frail figure leaned against a tree. "Louis . . ."

He stumbled back in fright. *A ghost . . .*

"Dad, get back!" Nate called in a pained voice.

Louis collected himself with a shudder of surprise. Of course it wasn't a ghost. *Carl Rand! Alive! What miracle was this? And what luck?*

He pointed an Uzi at the wraith.

The weak figure lifted an arm and pointed to the left.

Louis's gaze flicked to the side.

Hiding under a bush, a jaguar crouched, spotted and golden, muscles bunched. It leaped at him.

He swung his weapon up, firing, chewing up dirt and leaves as he slashed toward the flying cat.

Then he was struck from the other side, blindsided, sacked, carried several yards, and slammed into the ground, facefirst. With the wind knocked out of him, he snorted and choked dirt. A large weight pinned him.

Who . . . what . . . ? He twisted his neck around.

A black feline face snarled down at him. Claws dug into his back, spears of agony.

Oh, God!

The first jaguar stepped into view, padding with menace. Louis struggled to bring his Uzi around, lifting his arm. Before he could fire, his limb exploded with agony. Teeth clamped to bone and ripped backward, tearing off his arm at the shoulder with a crunch of bone.

Louis screamed.

"Bon appétit," Nate mumbled to the two cats.

He ignored the rest of the attack. He had once watched a documentary of killer whales playing with a seal pup before eating it: tossing it through the air, catching it, ripping it, and tossing it again. Savage and heartless. Pure nature. The same happened here. The two cats showed a pure feline pleasure in killing Louis Favre, not just feeding, but enacting revenge upon the man.

Nate turned his attention to more pressing concerns. He dragged himself toward Kelly, crawling with his hands, pushing with his one good leg. His hip flared with agony. His vision blurred. But he had to reach her.

Kelly lay crumpled on the ground, blood pooling.

At last, he fell beside her. "Kelly . . ."

She shifted at the sound of his voice.

He moved closer, cradling against her.

"We did it . . . right?" Her voice was a whisper. "The cure?"

"We'll get it to the world . . . to Jessie."

His father stumbled over to them and knelt beside the pair. "Help's coming. Hang on . . . both of you."

Nate was surprised to see Private Carrera standing behind his father. "Sergeant Kostos found the mercenary camp's radio," she said. "The helicopters are a half hour out."

Nate nodded, holding Kelly to him. Her eyes had closed. His own vision darkened as he held her. Somewhere in the distance, he heard Frank call. "Kelly! Is Kelly all right?"

TWENTY

Eight Months Later

4:45 P.M.
LANGLEY, VIRGINIA

Nate knocked on the door to the O'Brien residence. Frank was due back from the hospital today. Nate carried a present under his arm. A new Boston Red Sox cap, signed by the entire team. He waited on the stoop, staring across the manicured lawn.

Dark clouds stacked the southern skies, promising a storm to come.

Nate knocked again. He had visited Frank last week at the Instar Institute. His new legs were pale and weak, but he had been up on crutches, managing pretty well. "Physical therapy's a bitch," Frank had complained. "Plus I'm a goddamn pincushion to these white-smocked vampires."

Nate had smiled. Over the past months, the researchers and doctors had been carefully monitoring the regeneration. Frank's mother, Lauren, had said that so far the exact mechanism for her son's prion-induced regeneration remained a mystery. What *was* known was that while the prions triggered a fatal hemorrhagic fever in children and the elderly—those individuals with immature or compromised immune systems—the opposite was seen in healthy adults. Here, the prions seemed capable of temporarily altering the human immune system, allowing for the proliferative growth necessary for regeneration and rapid healing.

This miraculous effect was observed in Frank, but not without danger to the man. He had to be maintained on a diluted mix of nut milk to keep the process from running rampant and triggering the devastating cancers that had struck Agent Clark. And now that the regeneration was complete, Frank was under a more concentrated treatment with the milk to rid his body of the prions and return his immune system to normal. Still, despite Frank's status as guinea pig, much about the prions and their method of action remained a mystery.

"We're a long way from an answer and even longer from replicating the tree's abilities," Lauren had said sadly. "If the tree's history dates back to the Paleozoic era, then it's had a hundred million years' head start on us. One day we might understand, but not today. As much as we might vaunt our scientific skills, we're just children playing in one of the most advanced biological experiments."

"Children who came damn close to burning down their own house this time," Nate had added.

Luckily, the nut pods had indeed proved to be the cure to the contagion. The "antiprion" compound in the fruit, a type of alkaloid, was found to be easy to replicate and manufacture. The cure was quickly dispatched via a multinational effort throughout the Americas and the world. It was discovered that a month's treatment with the alkaloid *totally* eradicated the disease from the body, leaving no trace of the infectious prion. This simple fact, unknown to the Ban-ali, had left them enslaved for generations. But luckily, the manufactured nut milk was the immediate cure the world had needed. The plague was all but over.

Contrarily, the prion itself had proved beyond current scientific capability to cultivate or duplicate. All samples of the prion-rich sap were considered a Level 4 biohazard and confined to a few select labs. Out in the field, the original source of the sap, the Ban-ali valley, was found to be a blasted ruin. All that was left of the great Yagga were ashes and entombed skeletons.

And that's just fine with me, Nate thought as he waited on the stoop and stared at the setting March sun and the brewing storm.

Back in South America, Kouwe and Dakii were still helping the remaining dozen Ban-ali tribesmen acclimate to their new lives. They were the richest Indians in the Amazon. Nate's father had successfully sued St. Savin Pharmaceuticals for the destruction of the tribe's homelands and the slaughter of its people. It seemed Louis Favre had left a clear paper trail back to the French drug company. Though appeals would surely drag on for several more years, the company was all but bankrupt. In addition, its entire executive board faced criminal charges.

Meanwhile, his father remained in South America,

helping resettle the Ban-ali tribe. Nate would be rejoining his father in a few more weeks, but he was not the only one heading south. In addition, geneticists were flocking to study the tribe, to investigate the alterations to their DNA, both to understand how it had been achieved and perhaps to discover a way to reverse the species-altering effects of the Yagga. Nate imagined that if any answers ever came, they would be generations away.

His father was also assisted by the two Rangers, Kostos and Carrera, newly promoted and decorated. The pair of soldiers had also overseen the recovery of the bodies. Difficult and heartbreaking work.

Nate sighed. So many lives lost . . . but so many others saved by the cure their blood had bought. Still, the price was too high.

The sound of approaching footsteps drew Nate's attention back around. The door opened.

Nate found his smile. "What took you so long? I've been waiting here like five minutes."

Kelly frowned at him, holding a palm to her lower back. "You try lugging this belly around."

Nate placed a palm on his fiancée's bulging stomach. She was due in another couple of weeks with their child. The pregnancy had been discovered while Kelly recuperated from the gunshot wound. It seemed Kelly had been infected with the prions during her examination of Gerald Clark's body back in Manaus. Over the two-week Amazon journey—unbeknownst to her—the prions had healed Kelly's postparturient infertility, regenerating what had been damaged. It was a timely discovery. If the prions had been left unchecked for even a couple more weeks, the ravaging cancers would have started, but as with her brother, the nut milk was administered in time, and the prions were eradicated before they could do harm.

As a result of this joyous gift, Nate and Kelly had been blessed. During their treetop lovemaking on the eve of Louis's attack, Nate and Kelly had unwittingly conceived a baby—a brother for Jessie.

They had already chosen a name: *Manny*.

Nate leaned over and kissed his fiancée.

Distant thunder rolled from the skies.

"The others are waiting," she mumbled between his lips.

"Let 'em wait," he whispered, lingering.

Thick raindrops began to fall, tapping at the pavement and rooftop. Thunder rumbled again, and the sprinkle blew into a downpour.

"But shouldn't we—"

Nate pulled her closer, bringing her lips back to his. "Hush."

Epilogue

Deep in the Amazon rain forest, nature takes its own course, unseen and undisturbed.

The spotted jaguar nudges its litter of cubs, mewling and whining in the den. His black-coated mate has been gone a long time. He sniffs the air. A whiff of musk. He paces anxiously.

From the jungle shadows, a silhouette breaks free and pads over to him. He huffs his greeting to his larger mate. They busily rub and brush against each other. He smells the bad scent on her. *Flames, burning, screaming.* It triggers warnings along his spine, bristling his nape. He growls.

His mate crosses to the far side of the glade and digs deep into the soft loam. She drops a knobby seed into the pit, then kicks dirt back over it with her hind legs.

Once done, she crosses to the litter of cubs—some black, some spotted. She sniffs at them. The cubs cry for milk, rolling over one another.

She rubs her mate again and turns her back on the

freshly dug hole, the planted seed already forgotten. It is no longer her concern. It is time to move on. She gathers her litter and her mate, and the group heads deeper into the trackless depths of the forest.

Behind, freshly turned soil dries in the afternoon sun.

Unseen and undisturbed.

Forgotten.

From *New York Times* bestselling author
James Rollins comes a stand-alone thriller
in which a secret from the
dawn of time threatens humankind

ALTAR OF EDEN

Now available in hardcover
from William Morrow
An Imprint of HarperCollins Publishers

During the battle for Baghdad, Republican Guards
and the U.S. 3rd Infantry Division fight over the ruins
of the Baghdad Zoo, opening the floodgates for the
smuggling of hundreds of exotic birds, mammals, and
reptiles to Western nations.

Seven years later, Louisiana state veterinarian Lorna
Polk uncovers a ring of black market smugglers at the
U.S. border carrying puzzling cargo—conjoined twin
monkeys, a lion cub with saber teeth, a featherless
Amazon parrot—all sharing one uncanny trait: a strange
heightened intelligence.

With U.S. Marshall Jack Menard on her side, Lorna
will uncover mysteries of fractal science, genetic engineering, and a secret history tied to the Book of Gen-
esis to expose a horrifying secret that traces back to
humankind's earliest roots.

James Rollins—for the thrill of it!

And Babylon shall become heaps, a dwelling place for dragons, an astonishment, and a hissing, without an inhabitant.

JEREMIAH 51:37

And what rough beast, its hour come round at last, Slouches towards Bethlehem to be born?

W.B. YEATS

The study of Nature makes a man at last as remorseless as Nature.

H.G. WELLS

APRIL 2003
BAGHDAD, IRAQ

The two boys stood outside the lion's cage.

"I don't want to go inside," the smaller one said. He kept close to his older brother and clasped tightly to his hand.

The two were bundled in jackets too large for their small forms, faces swathed in scarves, heads warmed by woolen caps. At this early hour, with the sun not yet up, the pre-dawn chill had crept down to their bones.

They had to keep moving.

"Bari, the cage is empty. Stop being a *shakheef*. Look." Makeen, the older of the two, pushed the black iron gate wider and revealed the bare concrete walls inside. A few old gnawed bones lay piled in a dark corner. They would make a nice soup.

Makeen stared out at the ruins of the zoo. He remembered how it had once looked. Half a year ago, for his twelfth birthday, they had come here to picnic at the Al Zawraa Gardens with its amusement rides and zoo. The family had spent a long warm afternoon wandering among the cages of monkeys, parrots, camels, wolves, and bears. Makeen had even fed one of the camels an apple. He still remembered the rubbery lips on his palm.

Standing here now, he stared across the same park with older eyes, far older than half a year ago. The park sprawled outward in a ruin of rubble and refuse. It was a haunted wasteland of fire-blackened walls, fetid pools of oily water, and blasted buildings.

A month ago, Makeen had watched from their apartment near the park as a firefight blazed across the lush gardens, waged by American forces and the Republican Guard. The fierce battle had begun at dusk, with the rattle of gunfire and the shriek of rockets continuing throughout the night.

But by the next morning, all had gone quiet. Smoke hung thickly and hid the sun for the entire day. From the balcony of their small apartment, Makeen had spotted a lion as it loped out of the park and into the city. It moved like a dusky shadow, then vanished into the streets. Other animals also escaped, but over the next two days, hordes of people had swarmed back into the park.

Looters, his father had named them and spat on the floor, cursing them in more foul language.

Cages were ripped open. Animals were stolen, some for food, some to be sold at the black market across the river. Makeen's father had gone with a few other men to get help to protect their section of the city from the roving bands.

He had never returned. None of them had.

Over the next weeks, the burden had fallen upon Makeen to keep his family fed. His mother had taken to her bed, her forehead burning with fever, lost somewhere between terror and grief. All Makeen could get her to do was drink a few sips of water.

If he could make a nice soup for her, get her to eat something more . . .

He eyed the bones in the cage again. Each morning, he and his brother spent the hour before dawn searching the bombed-out park and zoo for anything they could scrounge to eat. He carried a burlap sack over his shoulder. All it held was a moldy orange and a handful of cracked seed swept up off the floor of a birdcage. Little Bari had also found a dented can of beans in a rubbish bin. The discovery had brought tears to Makeen's eyes. He kept the treasure rolled up inside his little brother's thick sweater.

Yesterday, a larger boy with a long knife had stolen his sack, leaving Makeen empty-handed when he returned. They'd had nothing to eat that day.

But today they would eat well.

Even Mother *inshallah*, he prayed.

Makeen entered the cage and dragged Bari with him. Distant gunfire crackled in short spurts, like the scolding claps of angry hands trying to warn them off.

Makeen took heed. He knew they had to hurry. He didn't want to be out when the sun was up. It would grow too dangerous. He hurried to the pile of bones, dropped his sack, and began shoving the gnawed knuckles and broken shafts inside.

Once finished, he tugged the sack closed and stood.

Before he could take a step, a voice called in Arabic from nearby.

"*Yalla!* This way! Over here!"

Makeen ducked and pulled Bari down with him. They hid behind the knee-high cinderblock wall that fronted the lion's cage. He hugged his brother, urging him to remain silent, as two large shadows passed in front of the lion's cage.

Risking a peek, Makeen caught a glimpse of two men. One was tall in a khaki military uniform. The other was squat with a round belly, dressed in a dark suit.

"The entrance is hidden behind the zoo clinic," the fat man said as he passed the cage. He huffed and wheezed to keep up with the longer strides of the man in military fatigues. "I can only pray we are not too late."

Makeen spotted the holstered pistol on the taller man's belt and knew it would mean death to be found eavesdropping.

Bari shivered in his embrace, sensing the danger too.

Unfortunately, the men did not go far. The clinic was directly across from their hiding spot. The fat man ignored the twisted main door. Days ago, crowbars had forced the way open. The facility had been cleaned out of drugs and medical supplies.

Instead, the heavy figure stepped to a blank wall framed by two columns. Makeen could not make out what the man did as he slipped his hand behind one of the columns, but a moment later, a section of the wall swung open. It was a secret door.

Makeen shifted closer to the bars. Father had read

them stories of Ali Baba, tales of secret caverns and vast stolen treasures hidden in the desert. All he and his brother had found at the zoo were bones and beans. Makeen's stomach churned as he imagined a feast fit for the Prince of Thieves that might wait below.

"Stay here," the fat man said, ducking through the entrance and down a dark set of stairs.

The military man took up a post by the doorway. His palm rested on his pistol. His gaze swung toward their hiding spot. Makeen ducked out of sight and held his breath. His heart pounded against his ribs.

Had he been spotted?

Footsteps approached the cage. Makeen clung tightly to his brother. But a moment later, he heard a match strike and smelled cigarette smoke. The man paced the front of the cage as if he were the one behind the bars, stalking back and forth like a bored tiger.

Bari shook within Makeen's embrace. His brother's fingers were clamped hard in his. What if the man should wander into the cage and find them huddled there?

It seemed an eternity when a familiar wheezing voice echoed out of the doorway. "I have them!"

The cigarette was dropped and ground out onto the cement just outside the cage door. The military man crossed back to join his companion.

The fat man gasped as he spoke. He must have run all the way back up. "The incubators were offline," he said. "I don't know how long the generators lasted after the power went out."

Makeen risked a peek through the bars of the cage door. The fat man carried a large metal briefcase in his hand.

"Are they secure?" the military man asked. He also spoke in Arabic, but his accent was not Iraqi.

The fat man dropped to one knee, balanced the case on his thick thigh, and thumbed open the lock. Makeen expected gold and diamonds, but instead the case held nothing but white eggs packed in molded black foam. They appeared no different than the chicken eggs his mother bought at the market.

Despite his terror, the sight of the eggs stirred Makeen's hunger.

The fat man counted them, inspecting them. "They're all intact," he said and let out a long rattling sigh of relief. "God willing, the embryos inside are still viable."

"And the rest of the lab?"

The fat man closed the case and stood up. "I'll leave it to your team to incinerate what lies below. No one must ever suspect what we've discovered. There can be no trace."

"I know my orders."

As the fat man stood, the military man raised his pistol and shot his companion in the face. The blast was a thunderclap. The back of the man's skull blew away in a cloud of bone and blood. The dead man stood for a moment longer, then flopped to the ground.

Makeen covered his mouth to stifle any sound.

"No trace," the murderer repeated and collected the case from the ground. He touched a radio on his shoulder. He switched to English.

"Bring in the trucks and prime the incendiary charges. Time to get out of this sandbox before any locals turn up."

Makeen had learned to speak a smattering of the American language. He couldn't pick out every word the man spoke, but he understood the message well enough.

More men were coming. More guns.

Makeen sought some means of escape, but they were trapped in the lion's cage. Perhaps his younger brother also recognized the growing danger. Bari's shaking had grown worse since the gunshot. Finally, his little brother's terror could no longer be held inside, and a quiet sob rattled out of his thin form.

Makeen squeezed his brother and prayed that the cry had not been heard.

Footsteps again approached. A sharp call barked toward them in Arabic. "Who's there? Show yourself! *Ta'aal hnaa!*"

Makeen pressed his lips to his brother's ear. "Stay hidden. Don't come out."

Makeen shoved Bari tighter into the corner, then stood up with his hands in the air. He backed a step. "I was just looking for food!" Makeen said, stuttering, speaking fast.

The pistol stayed leveled at him. "Get out here, *walad!*"

Makeen obeyed. He moved to the cage door and slipped out. He kept his hands in the air. "Please, *ahki. Laa termi!*" He tried switching to English to show he was on the man's side. "No shoot. I not see . . . I not know ..."

He fought to find some argument, some words to

save him. He read the expression on the other man's face—a mixture of sorrow and regret.

The pistol lifted higher with merciless intent.

Makeen felt hot tears flow down his cheeks.

Through the blur of his vision, he noted a shift of shadows. Behind the man, the secret door cracked open wider, pushed from inside. A large, dark shape slipped out and flowed toward the man's back. It ran low and stuck to the deeper shadows, as if fearing the light.

Makeen caught the barest glimpse of its oily form: muscular, lean, hairless, with eyes glinting with fury. His mind struggled to comprehend what he was seeing—but failed.

A scream of horror built inside his chest.

Though the beast made no noise, the man must have felt a prickling of warning. He swung around as the creature leaped with a sharp cry. Gunshots blasted, eclipsed by a savage wail that raised the hairs on Makeen's body.

Makeen swung away and rushed back to the cage. "Bari!"

He grabbed his brother's arm and dragged him out of the lion's cage. He pushed Bari ahead of him. "*Yalla!* Run!"

Off to the side, man and beast fought on the ground.

More pistol shots fired.

Makeen heard the heavy tread of boots on pavement behind him. More men came running from the other side of the park. Shouts were punctuated by rifle blasts.

Ignoring them all, Makeen fled in raw terror

across the bombed-out gardens, careless of who might see him. He kept running and running, chased by screams that would forever haunt his nightmares.

He understood nothing about what had happened. He knew only one thing for certain. He remembered the beast's ravenous eyes, shining with a cunning intelligence, aglow with a smokeless fire.

Makeen knew what he had seen.

The beast known as *Shaitan* in the Koran—he who was born of God's fire and cursed for not bowing down to Adam.

Makeen knew the truth.

At long last, the devil had come to Baghdad.

Painter Crowe knew that the symbol tattooed
on the back of the dead man's skull
represented the Freemasons. But what did it have
to do with Native American mythology,
the signing of the Declaration of Independence,
and the very founding of America?

Find out in the next Sigma Force adventure by
New York Times bestselling author James Rollins

THE DEVIL COLONY

Coming July 2010 in hardcover
from William Morrow
An Imprint of HarperCollins Publishers

James Rollins—for the thrill of it!

